Small Magic

SMALL MAGIC

Short Fiction, 1977–2020

TERRY BROOKS

DEL
REY

New York

Published in the United States by Del Rey, an imprint of Random House, a division of Penguin Random House LLC, New York.

DEL REY is a registered trademark and the CIRCLE colophon is a trademark of Penguin Random House LLC.

The following stories have been previously published:
"Imaginary Friends" in *Once Upon a Time: A Treasury of Modern Fairy Tales* edited by Lester Del Rey and Rita Kessler (New York: Del Rey, 1991)
"Indomitable" in *Legends II: New Short Novels by the Masters of Modern Fantasy* edited by Roger Silverberg (New York: Del Rey, 2003)
"Allanon's Quest," "The Black Irix," and "The Weapons Master's Choice" in the ebook edition of *Paladins of Shannara* (New York: Del Rey, 2013)
"The Fey of Cloudmoor" in *Multiverse: Exploring Poul Anderson's Worlds* edited by Greg Bear and Gardner Dozois (Burton, MI: Subterranean Press, 2014)
"An Unfortunate Influx of Filipians" in *Unbound: Tales by Masters of Fantasy* (Auburn, WA: Grim Oak Press, 2015)
Warrior (Auburn, WA: Grim Oak Press, 2018)

Hardback ISBN 978-0-525-61996-3
Ebook ISBN 978-0-525-61997-0

Printed in the United States of America on acid-free paper

randomhousebooks.com

2 4 6 8 9 7 5 1

First Edition

Book design by Fritz Metsch

This one is for everyone

who hung in there with me

on my author journey

Contents

Small Magic

Introduction to

"The Fey of Cloudmoor"

I BEGAN READING science fiction and fantasy in middle school—right about 1956—although there was little enough of the latter being written at that time and most of the kids I knew were reading the former. It was the beginning of the age of space travel and Sputnik and travels to the moon, and that was what every kid I knew was reading about. I shouldn't say *kids* but rather *boys*, because very few girls I knew had found their way to that sort of fiction yet.

Anyway, among those writers whose works I read and admired—while still in my burgeoning wannabe professional writer mode—was Poul Anderson. In those days, I wasn't reading or particularly interested in fantasy. I was strictly a science-fiction kid, with peripheral leanings toward adventure stories (*Boys' Life* and the like), so my favorite stories by Poul tended to fall along those lines.

But I remember one that didn't. I read "The Queen of Air and Darkness" right after it came out in one of the science-fiction magazines, and I was captivated by it. When I was asked to contribute to the Poul Anderson anthology *Multiverse* in 2014, it was the first story I thought of. It always felt to me as if there was more to the story, as if the telling of it wasn't finished. What happened afterward to the Queen and the Old Folk of Cloudmoor and Carheddin? Was that really the end of them when Sherrinford took back Jimmy Cullen? Could they really have been so easily dispatched?

I felt a certain trepidation in trying to make those determinations for Poul. "The Queen of Air and Darkness" had won both the Hugo and Nebula, and has enthralled Poul Anderson readers for decades. Who was I to mess with an icon and his art? But my marching orders were clear: I was to take something from Poul's astounding body of work and build on it. So that was what I tried to do.

I met Poul Anderson once, years ago now, at a family gathering at his daughter's home. I can no longer remember the occasion. He was quiet and unassuming and had about him the grandfatherly look I see in myself these days when I look in the mirror. I said hello and told him how much I admired his work. I have no idea if he knew who I was or what I did. He didn't say, and I didn't ask. It didn't matter. What mattered was how it made me feel. Writers form links in an endless chain, one influencing another in a crucial, necessary rite of interaction and succession, ultimately so we may be inspired and our craft may evolve.

Poul Anderson was one who did that for me.

THE FEY OF
CLOUDMOOR

HE CAME OUT of the world of Men and their cities of steel and
concrete in tatters, all scratched up and dirtied on the surface
and broken and ripped apart inside. He carried what was left of
his life in a blanket clutched to his breast, carefully shielding its
contents from the sights and sounds and smells of the civilization that had ruined him and destroyed her. He thought of her
all the time, but he couldn't make himself remember what she
looked like anymore. He knew only how hard they had tried to
find a way through the morass of their lives, choosing to share
their misery but always searching to break free of their bonds.

Hard to do when nothing in your life is real and every day is
a slog through dark and painful places that strip the skin from
your soul.

When she died, they had been huddled in an alleyway in the
darkest part of Christmas Landing, sheltered poorly in card-
board from a steady downpour that formed a small river only
four feet away. They had scored early and resold what they had
to get money for food and milk for Barraboo. They had made a
good choice for once, but had come to regret it with night's hard
descent and no means to soften the blow. She had been coughing badly for days and her breathing had worsened, and all he
knew how to do was to stay with her. There were medical centers they could go to, but once they entered one of those places

they might as well say goodbye to their baby. She might have gone alone, of course, but she was afraid to do that, as if making that choice would cost her the baby anyway.

As if, in his desperation, he might choose to sell it.

As if, in hers, she might approve.

He stole some medicine off the shelves of a pharmacy, but it didn't seem to help her. Nothing did. She just kept coughing and wheezing, getting worse by the day. He found her an old blanket in a garbage bin and wrapped her in that, then held her close against him to share his body heat. She was so cold, and she didn't look right. But she still held Barraboo and wouldn't let her go, and so he ended up holding them both.

But finally he fell asleep, even though he had told himself he wouldn't do so, and when he woke she was dead.

He never knew her real name. She never gave it to him. He called her Pearl because she was precious to him, and she seemed content enough with that. He told her his own name, though. "I'm Jimmy," he said. "Once upon a time, I was kidnapped by the Old Folk."

He had told that to only a very few before her and then quit doing so because no one believed him. She probably didn't believe him, either, but she came closer to looking as if she did than anyone else. She was like that. Even at her worst, when she was so strung out she could barely put a sentence together and started seeing things that weren't there, she could find a way to listen to him. She was tough, but she was vulnerable, too. She trusted people when she shouldn't have. She had faith in people who didn't deserve it. He was one of those people, he supposed. Mostly, he was good to her and took care of her and the baby and did little things to make her life more bearable when really it was Hell-on-Earth.

He thought all this and more as he rode the hovercraft out of Christmas Landing to Portolondon and his future. His and Barraboo's. For he was determined his daughter would have a future, even if Pearl didn't. He had fought against himself and his habit and his wasteful, reckless existence for too long. He had denied what he had known was true for too many years, persuaded by his mother and the rescuer she had hired to find him, made to believe when in his heart he knew he shouldn't.

Memories surfaced like half-remembered dreams of his time among the Old Folk, the Outlings. He had been only a boy, little more than a baby, and so young he barely realized what was happening to him. Taken from his mother's camp by a pooka, carried to the realm of the Old Folk beyond Troll Scarp, seduced and made happy beyond anything he could have imagined possible, his mother all but forgotten, his world made over—there he had remained until his mother had come for him, finding him with a mother's persistence in the face of formidable odds, taking him back to his old life, telling him he would forget all this one day, it would seem a dream to him, he would become the man he was meant to be and not a pawn in the hands of creatures who could not know and would never care what it was he needed.

"The choices you make in this world should be your own and never another's," she had told him. "You should never be another's pawn."

He disembarked with his precious cargo still asleep and stood looking from the loading platform at the dingy buildings of the town. There was nothing here for him and never would be—not in this hardscrabble collection of housings and shelters, not in this scooped-up mélange of humanity and waste. He wrinkled his nose at it—a measure of its ugliness, given his own sad state. All of Roland was a backwater, light-years away from the civilized universe—the back of beyond. It allowed for habitation—breathable air, drinkable water, sustainable crops—but not for much in the way of sunlight. He shivered in the cold, empty light of the season's perpetual night. Winterbirth, the pooka had called it. It gave him pause that he should remember this, but memory chose to keep what it wanted and discarded the rest. What mattered was how much attention you paid to memory and what you did with it as a consequence. For example, if you knew it was dangerous to go somewhere, you tried hard to remember not to go there again.

Conversely, if you remembered a place where you were happy—even if you were told you weren't and tried very hard to forget it and pretend that what you believed then to be happiness was in fact nothing of the sort—maybe you needed to make sure.

Especially when all other options had been exhausted and nothing in your life was good. Especially when you had more than yourself to worry about, and even in your drug-addicted rootless life you knew babies were pure and innocent and deserved better than what you could give them.

Especially when hope was all you had left to give.

He looked out across the buildings to the far north of Arctica, to the shimmer of the aurora and the green of mountains and valleys and mysteries that everyone knew were waiting there and no one wanted to discover.

No one except him.

"Hoah," a voice greeted. He looked down. A dwarf was standing right beside him, looking up from waist-high, bearded and twinkly-eyed, browned by weather and sun, wrinkled by age. "Need transport?"

He shook his head. "Got no money."

"You don't say? But there's other means to get to where you want to go, youngling. Have you a destination?"

He shrugged. "Out there, somewhere. A place I lived once a long time ago, when I was a boy. Beyond Troll Scarp."

"Scallywags! Flywinds! Danceabouts!" The old one shook his head. "Don't no one wants to go there. They who is not to be named in places like this one live in places like that one, and they keep to themselves. Everyone knows. No one says."

"Old Folk. Outlings. The Fey. The Faerie Kind. There, I've said it for all those who won't. I don't fear them. I lived with them."

The old man cocked his head. "Yet came back to live among the humans who birthed you? That right? But from the look of you, it didn't work out so well."

"Not so well."

"A baby and no mother?"

He looked at the old man sharply. The baby hadn't moved or cried out. He might have been carrying old clothes for all anyone could tell. But this old man knew better.

"The mother died. Pearl. She was like me, an addict. But not strong enough to survive it. The baby is all I have left."

"Ayah. Would you take her with you, then?" Jimmy didn't miss that he hadn't told the old man it was a girl. "Would you give her over to them for a drug that only they could give you?" the old man persisted. "Would you make a trade if it were offered?"

He shook his head. "Not for anything. Not though I were the most desperate of men, and I am very much that. I am the lowest and saddest of all humans, and I would sell anything I could get my hands on to satisfy my need for even five minutes. But not Barraboo. Not my Pearl's child. I have not yet come to that."

The old man studied him as if to ascertain the truth of such a statement. Then he shrugged. "What then?"

Jimmy Cullen, he that was taken by a pooka once upon a time, smiled crookedly. "I have come to take her home."

The old man regarded him quizzically, all knitted brow and scrunched-up mouth, before saying, "Well, then, perhaps I can help you."

THE OLD MAN led him through the city, down its teeming streets and byways, along its alleys and footpaths, past shops and offices, homes and apartments, flowers and filth, way out to the ends of the northside and there to a stable. Inside the stable was a wagon and what appeared to be a reindeer—and soon enough, on closer inspection, proved to be. The old man hauled the wagon out of the stable by himself, grunting with the effort but refusing Jimmy's help, harnessed the reindeer, and got them aboard and settled.

"Bit of a ride ahead. If you need to sleep, put the small one in the necessaries box behind you—there, you see it, don't you? There's blankets to make her snug. What's your name again?"

"Jimmy Cullen," he said.

"I don't think so. But it will do until we reach Cloudmoor."

"What's yours?" Jimmy asked.

The old man shrugged. "Oh, I have all sorts of names. Widdershanks and Skitterfoot and Trundlestump, among others. But you can call me Ben."

They set out, the reindeer pulling the wagon and its load, leaving Portolondon and humankind, making for the Outway and Troll Scarp, solitary and far distant against the always-darkening horizon. No sun this time of year; no daylight, no day. It was night all the time or maybe twilight for a little while each day, and the people who lived in Arctica soon got used to the idea. Behind them, the Gulf of Polaris glimmered green-gray under skies brightened marginally by two small moons brought close together in their present orbits, both dwarfed by the dazzle of Charlemagne. Lights from the city lent their smudged and diffuse glow, but it did not penetrate the darkness far beyond the city. The Outway was its own space and kept its own presence, and did not suffer intrusions from men or the consequences of their inventions.

"Better wrap up in this, Jimmy Cullen," the little man said after a time. He held a long switch in one hand for urging on their wagon's furry engine. He held the reins in the other, but he lay down the switch long enough to hand Jimmy a blanket. "It gets cold out here for those not born of the Outway, especially those come to us as you have, desperate and soul-bereft. Go on, now. Take it."

He did so, pulling it about him, altering it to give further warmth to Barraboo. She was beginning to stir and soon would cry, but he had nothing with which to feed her, neither food nor milk. He had love, but he knew you could not live on that alone or even survive on it. Ask Pearl. Tears flooded his eyes as he thought the name and the memories surfaced.

"How do you know the way?" he asked Ben, anxious to deflect the consequences of his awakened feelings.

"I just do," the other answered, and said nothing more.

"Are you one of them?" Jimmy asked, glancing over for a close look.

Ben shook his head. "Not I. But I know of them, and I do what I can for them. I am a link in what has become a very long chain."

"Were you looking for me back at the station? You seemed quick enough to find me. I don't look the sort that many would want to help. Only avoid. Yet you asked me right out. Do you know me? Have we met before and I've forgotten?"

The old man laughed softly, not in a mean-spirited way, but gentle and kind. "I know you well. Not by name, but by look."

"An addict, you mean?"

"A type, I mean."

"At the end of a rope. Lost to everything, including themselves. Wanderers in a world that wants nothing to do with them—only for them to go away and not come back. Rejects. Embarrassments."

Ben seemed to consider. "I would not use those words, Jimmy Cullen, although they are true enough in the world of humans. In your world, so many have no place. They are discarded and ignored and have no value, as you say. But how did they come to be that way? Have you asked yourself?"

He could not answer right away because he wasn't sure, couldn't remember, so he said nothing. Under him, the wagon rocked about and rolled along, and the night was sweet smelling and deep. He was already in a different place, away from the things that had ground him under their collective boot and left him shattered. The urge to take something to ease the hurt of it had diminished, and he wondered suddenly why that was. By now, he should have been screaming for his drug. By now, he should have been sweating and shaking and clawing at his skin. Barraboo would be howling, and he would be unable to stop her from doing so because his all-encompassing need blinded him to hers.

Something slid along the side of the wagon, a sheeting of dark mist, a skein of dust and shadows. He caught a glimpse of it and then it was gone, disappeared as quickly as water in dry earth. He blinked and looked out among the patches of fire-thorns and steelflowers, watched the shimmer of flitteries as they caught the light in small snatches of iridescence, smelled the brok and thought of how long it had been.

"I was just a boy when they took me," he said suddenly, keeping his voice low so that maybe only Ben could hear. "I was snatched away from my sleep out of an armed camp, right out of my mother's tent where she slept close beside me, and not a single soul knew until the morrow. Dogs were drugged, robot guards blinded, and alarms bypassed. I might have been left to my fate and forgotten if not for my mother. My Barbro. She would not give me up to Old Folk or anything of flesh and blood. She came for me, all steel and fire and determination, carried in a war machine piloted by a detective from Christmas Landing who believed in the Old Folk but wanted to better understand what they were."

He inhaled and exhaled slowly. "They took me back, but I never really returned, never came all the way back. My body was theirs to mold, to shape as they felt they should, but my mind was lost. I heard the stories. You were never the same once the Fey had taken you. You could never be again what you were before. Maybe so. I tried to find my way in my mother's world, but couldn't. I was an outcast even to myself. Sweet Barbro tried to help me, but she never understood. She still doesn't. Drugs are an experience not so different from dreams. They take you somewhere you cannot otherwise be. They reshape your reality.

When you need that to happen, when it's all you can think about, sometimes drugs are the best you can do."

The old man said nothing.

"She was Queen, then," Jimmy Cullen said quietly. "I remember her."

"Was?" Ben asked sharply. "Is that what you think?"

"I think I have to find out. I think I have to know if what was hers once still is." He shook his head, clearing away a few more of the cobwebs that filled it. "I think I have to see if any of it can still be mine. And Barraboo's."

"Hmmm," the old man hummed, as if considering the possibility.

The long switch touched the reindeer's flank softly, and their speed increased.

BARBRO ENGDAHL CULLEN pushed through the door to Chief Constable Dawson's office, ignoring the commands of the deputy at the front desk who ordered her to stop and was attempting futilely to reinforce his words with gestures of displeasure. She was decided on this meeting and no one was going to stop it from happening, least of all a mere functionary. If Sherrinford had been there, he would have been readily admitted. But she was held in less esteem, and Eric was beyond coming through himself.

"Mrs. Cullen," the Chief Constable greeted her, rising from behind the inadequate protection of his desk. "I thought we settled all this in our phone conversation. Apparently, I was mistaken. You will not take no for an answer, will you?"

"I didn't back then, and I certainly won't now. Why don't you just resign yourself to this meeting and we can get this business over with?"

He had grown older, as had she, put on weight and added wrinkles, as she had not, but she would have known him even out of uniform. She was no stranger to him, either; the years had not diminished his memory of when she had come to him for help when Jimmy was stolen and he had rejected her. That led her to Eric and the search and recovery of Jimmy and ultimately to the beginnings of what would become the second true love of her life. Dawson must have thought himself shook of her for good after that, yet here she was again.

"Back looking for your boy, you said." He shook his head at her. "I thought we were done with all that. He's grown now. I don't have any authority to go out looking for him just because he's wandered off again—even if it's back up there in that wilderness where you and Sherrinford found him before. Why isn't your husband out looking if you want him back?"

"Eric is dead, Chief Constable. He died last year. Otherwise, I wouldn't be here, asking you."

Dawson mopped his brow with his hand, then slid the hand down his face and let it drop to his lap. "I'm sorry about that, Mrs. Cullen. I didn't know. I liked your husband. I admired his skill and his dedication to his work. But that doesn't change things. I still can't help you."

"You can't or you won't? He took my granddaughter. Little Barraboo. Not a year old. He left me a note so I wouldn't worry. I can't imagine what he was thinking. I want her back."

Dawson stared at her. "Where's her mother?"

"Dead. She was an addict, like my son. Both of them strung out all the time, five years of it. Maybe more. I can't be certain. It caught up with her just like it's going to catch up with him. Jimmy moved out and didn't stay in touch. Eric tracked him down several times, but he refused to come home. He said he wanted to go back to the Fey. He said that was his real home, those were his real people. Eric tried to tell him why he was wrong, but Jimmy wouldn't listen."

"Mrs. Cullen . . ."

"Let me finish." She was a big woman, and she leaned forward to lend emphasis to her size and the strength of her determination. "My son was never the same after we brought him back. Oh, maybe for a short time, but not after that. The Fey changed him. They seduced him with their magic and they changed him. Once I thought he would be all right after I found him and took him home again. Now I don't think so. I don't think I can ever get him back. But I will not let the Old Folk have my granddaughter, too! I will not stand for that!"

The Chief Constable shook his head. He was sweating, and he couldn't seem to look at her. "The Old Folk are just legend. You know this. In spite of Jimmy and what happened back—"

"Stop talking like that," she interrupted, waving him off. "You don't believe a word of it."

He stopped and looked up again. "What did the note say, Mrs. Cullen?"

"That Barraboo's mother was dead. No surprise in that. She was headed down that road long ago. They found her body two days after I made enough of a fuss about it that they had to go looking. Jimmy's note said he was going home and he was taking Barraboo with him."

"Well, then, couldn't he have meant somewhere in Christmas Landing? Couldn't he have been talking about somewhere other than out here? How would he even get this far if he was an addict? Where would he get the money? Mrs. Cullen, don't you think it would be better just to wait awhile and see if he doesn't come back on his own? Going over Troll Scarp and into the Outway isn't something anyone wants to do."

She drew back from him, straightening herself. "This is twice you have refused to help me, Chief Constable. I don't know why I bother asking."

Dawson held her gaze. "I don't know why, either, Mrs. Cullen."

She nodded. "Perhaps you know of someone I might hire? Not of Eric's caliber, but with a need for money and a bit less concern about trespassing in the lands of the Old Folk?"

He started to say he didn't, but she could tell when he hesitated that he was thinking better of it.

"I might know someone," he said finally.

When she left his office, she found a taxi and rode to the machine shop address he had given her, thinking through what she would say to Stip Quince. She could tell from the way Dawson gave out the information that this wasn't someone you would go to unless you wanted results and didn't care how you got them. Which was fine with her. She wasn't going back into Outway country a young woman searching for her missing baby boy. She was going back a full-grown woman and a grandmother, no longer frightened by much of anything and determined she would not be tricked or intimidated by the Fey.

She found herself humming the old song of Arvid the Ranger, recalling how she had sung it once for Sherrinford. It had a hold on her then, a grip that kept her wondering and doubting, a spell cast by words and music and her own superstitious nature. But that was all gone. The Fey were just an obstacle to be overcome. She had done it once with Eric; she could do it again with this man she was being sent to find.

Even though the Queen of Air and Darkness herself is waiting.

She regretted the thought the instant it was made. She wished she could take it back. She couldn't explain it; it just felt instantly wrong that she had permitted it to surface, even in the privacy of her thoughts.

Eric had once told her that the Old Folk had developed aspects of science different from those of humans, most particularly a command of telepathy born of a deeper understanding of their very different biological makeup. They might not have developed talents in chemistry and physics and mathematics as humans had, but what they had learned to do with telepathy far surpassed anything humans had achieved. Manipulation of human minds had allowed them to create a set of beliefs and superstitions that had helped keep the Old Folk safely isolated in the wilderness of their ancestral lands for centuries. It was only of late, and in part because of her deliberate intrusion, that this had changed and questions about their presence in the Out-way had surfaced.

Sherrinford had always believed those questions would be thoroughly examined once they returned with Jimmy and made their report. What he had missed seeing was the stubborn refusal by the larger part of Arctica's inhabitants to want to challenge the old beliefs and superstitions. By now, with centuries gone, those beliefs and superstitions formed an integral part of their human makeup. It wasn't necessarily true that men wanted to discard them in favor of rational thought. There is in all humans a need to believe in things that cannot be seen or understood, a need to embrace the possibility there are things larger and more powerful than they are so they can find a way to accept that when these things happen, they do not need to make sense of them or explain them away.

So it was that a general reluctance to look too closely into the possibility that the Old Folk might be something other than what the legends said they were prevailed. Dawson sided with the majority; she could tell by his unwillingness to involve himself in her search for Jimmy and Barraboo. Sherrinford had once said that if she had looked closely at Dawson on the monitor during the long conversation the first time Jimmy went missing, she would have seen how afraid he was. Not much had changed. He believed in the Old Folk, Eric had insisted. You could see it in his eyes.

If Sherrinford had been with her this time, as well, he would have seen it in Dawson's eyes again.

Other inhabitants of Arctica, particularly those in Portolon-don and even more so those in the Outway, would have experienced that same fear. Leave well enough alone, they would insist. Let the Old Folk be.

Well, she wasn't going to do any such thing. She wasn't afraid. She was angry.

Stip Quince turned out to be big and burly and curt, disinterested in anything but the money she was offering and the time he would have to expend to accomplish what she was asking. His price was dear, but he was willing enough to trespass into the Outway.

"I've heard the stories, Mrs. Cullen," he told her as they finalized their arrangements. "Bunch of nonsense. Tales of things that go bump in the night fabricated by the locals—people who've been swallowing that nonsense whole since they were babes. Stories get passed down from one generation to the next. Gives people something to do at night when there's no video, no technology, nothing but blank walls and shadow shows to provide entertainment."

She pursed her lips. "I've seen them," she said quietly. "They're real enough."

He nodded. "So you've said. Didn't scare you off, did they? Here you are, ready to stand up to them once more. Nothing to it. When we go into Troll Scarp, we'll be going with armed men carrying weapons and riding in war machines. Whatever we come up against, we can disperse or eradicate. Same as you did before."

Folding his big hands on the top of the desk he had moved behind to write down her story, he leaned forward. "These are illiterate, uneducated, wild-eyed aborigines with a few cheap tricks at their disposal. Sure, it's their land and they know it better than we do. But they can't fight us and expect to win. They can't rely on the sorts of sophisticated arms and varied skills we can bring to bear. In the end, they'll turn and run and go back into hiding."

She believed him. The Old Folk were hopelessly outmatched against civilization, no matter what they really were or how long they had occupied the Outway. They were Old Folk or Fey or Faerie Kind, but ultimately they were barbarians unequipped to deal with civilization and the terrible strength its sciences would use against them. They were a remnant of a different time, and that time was gone.

She would have Barraboo and Jimmy back home within a week, and that would be the end of it.

JIMMY CULLEN LURCHED awake as the wagon bounced through a deep rut and juddered to a stop. He blinked and glanced over at Ben. The little man still held the reins to the hauling beast, but had put down the switch and from somewhere produced a bottle filled with milk.

"Give her this. She needs to eat."

Jimmy looked down at the blanket on his lap. Barraboo was gone.

"Back there in the necessaries box," the old man said. "I was worried you'd let her roll right off your lap after you fell asleep."

Jimmy reached back, found his daughter tucked away and squirming, and brought her back into his lap, rewrapping her in the blanket. She was starting to fuss, but when he placed the bottle to her lips, the nipple sliding into its accustomed place, she went quiet again.

"Why are we stopped?" he asked.

The old man pointed ahead. "Him."

The pooka flew out of the darkness in a rush of air and brightly colored feathers, gliding on widespread wings. Landing in front of the cart, he bounded swiftly to Jimmy's side on claw-footed legs that were muscular and strong.

"Ohoi, the boy who was a baby firstly returns anew!" he whistled. "Remember you Ayoch?"

Jimmy nodded. "I do. Even now."

"'Twas a long time gone. But time can be caught up and made over. I see you brought a present for me?"

He shook his head. "No, not for you. Not for anyone. I brought her to find a better life. Perhaps it will be your present to her."

Ayoch exchanged a glance with the driver. "Bold talk from a newly-come-back penitent. Are you intending to ask forgiveness of the Star Mother for bringing the wrath of your humankind upon the Fey? Or will you simply make your demands and hope we will forget about the before?"

The dwarf shook his head. "Leave him be. He has much to work through and don't need a pooka reminding him."

"How then of Mistherd and Shadow-of-a-Dream who were stripped of their lives and driven back into the unwelcoming arms of humankind? What of them whose lives you ruined, Blackhearted Starling Boy?"

The pooka was hopping back and forth from one clawed foot to the other, his short forearms gesturing in anger and frustration. Jimmy looked at him and did not know what to say. He had done nothing to banish the lovers; they had left on their own, persuaded by Sherrinford they were living a lie and needed to go.

"What happened to them?" he asked tentatively.

Ayoch made a trilling sound and went still as stone. "The cities swallowed them."

"I did not knowingly cause this."

"But caused it nevertheless, I think."

"Who was it who stole me from my mother? Who was it who brought me to Cloudmoor?"

Ayoch started to make response, but then cocked his head and wheeled away. "Enow, this! She comes. Lady Sky walks the night. Bow you down, Witling."

Jimmy took the bottle from Barraboo's lips and handed it back to Ben, instinctively cradling his daughter closer as the air before him assumed fresh darkness. He was not afraid. He was clearheaded and steady. The drugs had left his body, and the need for finding what he had come to find had taken their place.

Ayoch knelt, wings folded against his body, half-human face lowered in deference to her approach. Ben had wrapped the reins about the handle of the wagon brake and now his head was inclined, as well. Jimmy did not hesitate to do the same, feeling the presence of her coming envelop him with perfume of night lilies and cool whispers. His head dipped in recognition of Fey royalty, his strength of will surrendered.

"Welcome home, Shadow Walker," she whispered.

She was very tall and wrapped in starlight and flower shadow, her hair long and flowing and her face aglow with an inner light. She moved out of the darkness as if afloat, her feet not touching the earth, her robes trailing behind her in rippling folds, the Queen of Air and Darkness become. All around her, the world seemed to find fresh light, newly woken and wafting on the winterbirth breeze.

"Do you remember the name I gave you?" she asked.

Jimmy could not reply. He could not speak. He had so much to say, but in her presence he was struck dumb and left helpless and fragile. He knew she spoke to him, knew the name by which she called him, knew indeed it had been given him long ago and knew also he had forgotten it until now. Shadow Walker. He took a deep breath of the sweet night air and exhaled his relief and joy. She had come to collect him, to give him what he so desperately sought; she had come to take him home with her.

In response, he opened the blanket that swaddled Barraboo and held the baby forth. The Queen stood silently and looked upon the child for a long time before she turned to him again.

"You were that baby once, and just by being so and nothing more brought upon the Dwellers such misery."

"I am sorry. But I did not intend any of it. I was a child." He was crying suddenly, unable to help himself, overwhelmed by memories and emotions. "I would take it all back, if I could."

"Sometimes being a child is enough to stir up madness."

He felt his insides collapsing under the weight of failure's dark promise. "Please. If you would take me back, I wish you to take her, too. I wish her to have a home here with me. I have nowhere else for her to go. I am so afraid for her."

"A changeling child to become," the Queen replied. She went silent again, lost in thought, her perfect features still and composed. "Be it so, then. All must come to Worund's Barrow. All of the Dwellers of Carheddin and beyond. Bring them, Ayoch. Gather them together. We will sing and dance and celebrate winterbirth's gifts."

Ayoch bowed lower still, eyes averted.

She turned away, fading back into the darkness. "And there, Shadow Walker, we will wait for those who are certain to follow. But not as before, not as once we might have. See to it, Ayoch."

Her voice died away into the wind's gentle whisper and the night's soft folding.

"Yes, Moon Mistress," the pooka answered, never lifting his feathered head. But when she was well and truly gone, he stood erect and did a little dance.

"I LEAVE YOU here," Ben announced abruptly, taking up the reins and switch again. "Climb down and go with the pooka, Jimmy Cullen that once you were."

"You won't come with us?" Jimmy asked, suddenly troubled by the idea. "After coming so far already?"

"Where you go is not meant for me. I've limits to what I can do for the Fey and limits to what they want me to do. I am done with you now and have others that need me. Ask about it, Shadow Walker. Ask her how her rule goes these days. You should know your address before you settle in for the duration."

He waited patiently until Jimmy had descended the swayspring wagon seat for the solidity of the ground, Barraboo in his arms, and then he jiggled the lines, clucked at the reindeer, and turned the wagon about. In moments, he had disappeared into the darkness.

"Now we must skitter on, Shadow Walker." Ayoch was already looking off in the direction the Queen had gone.

"I'm ready," he answered, arms cradling Barraboo, soft and warm, against him.

"I wonder about that," the pooka said.

They set out on foot, crossing the countryside through the darkness and shimmering white starlight, the twin moons already down or new—he could no longer remember which. Yet the air was not cold, and he found his travel comforting and pleasant. Barraboo had fallen back asleep, sated from her feeding. She was so light she was almost not there. Now and again, he had to look down to make sure he still held her.

Flitteries darted through the brok in small flashes, and kissme-never glimmered whitely in the starglow. Once he saw a crownbuck, majestic as it stood statue-still and watched him from a rise. He was surprised and pleased that he could remember names of things he hadn't seen in more than thirty years, things he had forgotten existed. Those names had all come back to him this night as he traveled into the Outway, and he could not help but think that it was a favorable sign. He was meant to be here. Coming with Barraboo, returning to where he had been happiest, finding his way toward a measure of sanity and health.

The sheeting of dark mist he had seen earlier while riding with the old man (what was his name again?) reappeared suddenly beside him. It floated there for a moment, and then the particles of darkness took form and Pearl was standing beside him, reborn into the world, clean and fresh and young.

He caught his breath and sobbed. "But you're dead, Pearl. You're not really here."

She laughed—a laugh he had so seldom heard her give when they were in the cities—and touched his arm. "Do you feel my fingers? Do you see how they hold you? I am real enough, Jimmy."

"But is it Fey magic . . ."

She leaned over and kissed him quickly on his cheek, and all doubts and fears vanished. "Let me see little Barraboo," she begged, taking a corner of the blanket in which the baby was wrapped and pulling it back. "Oh, such a wee thing. Look at her smile! You've taken such good care of her, Jimmy."

"I've missed you so much." He could barely see her for his tears. "Can you stay with me?"

"For a while, but not forever. I can come back to you, though. I can visit you now and then."

"That would be enough," he managed. "Even if I know, even if I remember you aren't really . . ."

But she was already gone back into the ether, a skein of darkness dissipating in the wind.

A word came to him, unbidden. *Wraith.*

"There is nothing for you in the cities of men," Ayoch declared suddenly. He was bounding along, hopping and skipping, a very energetic pooka. "You've found that out for yourself, haven't you? Better the dreams of our world than the nightmares of your own."

"Better," he echoed.

"Though I have never gone to your world. Not for me the dreariness of such places. I know what it does from what I see in the eyes of those who live there when they happen out our way. They come to us, you know. So many, too. More all the time. Like you, they seek escape from what kills them. Slow or fast, it kills them all the same."

"It killed Pearl," he said.

The pooka shrugged. "All in the past now for her."

They passed through Cloudmoor's rolling hills and leafy forests until all at once the pooka crowed loudly and said, "Hoah, I forget me! I must do as Lady Sky has bidden and gather the others for the celebration." He wheeled away, spread his wings wide, and took to the air. "Farewell now, Shadow Walker!"

Jimmy blanched in terror. "Wait! How am I to find where I . . . ?"

"By walking!" Ayoch chirped, and then he was gone.

Jimmy stood bereft. He had never known where to go before coming here. Not ever. But since he had gotten this far and had no choice in the matter, he began to walk. The feel of the wind freshened him and the glow of the moons comforted him, and so he put one foot in front of the other, eager to reach his destination.

THE WAR MACHINES rumbled over Troll Scarp and into Cloudmoor on the midday, the night still enveloping and pervasive, the land of the Old Folk shadowed and striped with layers of roiling haze. Barbro sat in the first of the pair, next to Stip Quince and right behind the driver. She gave information when she could but for the most part kept quiet. She remembered so little of this land after thirty years, and what she remembered was uncertain. Flashes of events recalled themselves, but mostly out of context and vague enough that she couldn't trust them. What was hard and certain was the emotional weight of first losing and then finding little Jimmy, coupled with her desperate, driving need to find him anew and little Barraboo with him. She was driven by her emotions, ruled by them, and she had set her mind on doing what was needed to regain control.

But there was room in her feelings for distaste, too. She didn't like Quince or his men and had to work hard to mask it. She disliked his bluster and arrogance. She disliked his aura of disdain and contempt. He was a hard and bitter veteran of personal and professional wars, and he had no use for people beyond making use of the opportunities they provided him. He was dismissive of her and Jimmy and their sad lives. He sneered openly at the idea of the Old Folk, his faith placed not in myths and shadows but in steel and explosives. He talked little, but when he said anything it was couched in terms of destruction and self-empowerment.

She regretted she had asked him for transport, and if she could have done so she would have turned him back around. But she could not abandon her search now. To do that would mean giving up on her son and granddaughter.

But how will we find them, in any case? There are no signposts or road markers. There are not even roads. And I have no memory of the land. It is a mystery to me.

Yet Quince seemed undeterred, forging ahead, his machines rolling over firethorn and brok, crushing grasses and flowers, and scaring off birds and animals alike, intruders not equipped to apologize. His confidence in himself and his men and machines was daunting, so she held her tongue and waited to see what would happen.

When they stopped finally to rest and eat, the darkness enfolding and unbroken by either Roland's moons or the distant stars, she felt the weight of her life press down on her and wished she had done so many things differently. She ate and drank and then walked away from the men to look out into the forested hills and be alone. She breathed the air and was reminded suddenly of a moment out of the past.

For there was Jimmy, standing at the edge of the trees, not far away from her, holding his daughter in his arms, smiling. He put a finger to his lips and beckoned her over to him. She glanced back, saw no one paying attention to her, and without further thought went to him.

"Mrs. Cullen!" she heard Quince call to her as she followed her son into the trees. "Get back here!"

But she was already gone.

STIP QUINCE WASTED little time calling his men back to their war machines, closing down the hatches, and firing up the engines. Seconds was all it took. The armored ATVs surged forward, giving chase. Quince could not understand what that woman thought she was doing, but it would be the last time she would be allowed more than an arm's length away. Had she seen something? Had she been summoned and he'd not heard?

The war machines pushed into the woods, finding their way between sparse clumps of trees, rocking over ridges and down gullies, pushing ahead. There was no sign of Mrs. Cullen, but Quince had seen where she went and knew they would catch up to her quickly enough.

Ahead, atop a rise, something moved in the gloom. Figures,

all of different sizes and shapes—some huge and lumbering, some ethereal, and others winged and crouched over. The ones he was looking for. He smiled and, using the intercom, directed the attack. The war machines closed on their targets, weapons loaded and ready. Quince had decided to see how the enemy reacted before opening fire on them. He wanted to scare them off first, hopefully back to wherever they had the woman's son and granddaughter. In case that failed, he would use the nets to trap one or two and make his prisoners take him to their lair. It wouldn't be hard once he used the drugs and prods on them.

When he had Mrs. Cullen and the son and granddaughter safely in hand, he would decide whether to eradicate these troublesome creatures or simply frighten them badly enough that they would flee the country and all this Old Folk nonsense would be ended.

As the war machines crested the rise, the creatures they pursued had already fled into the trees. Quince saw the yawning black chasm directly ahead of them, only yards away, invisible until you were right on top of it. He shouted into the intercom in warning, screaming, "Stop, stop!" But it was too late. The momentum of the vehicles carried both over the edge and into the void.

The war machines tumbled away and the occupants were consumed by their own dark fears.

BARBRO TURNED FROM Jimmy and the baby when she heard the screams, wondering at their source. When she turned back again, they were gone. She looked around wildly, frantic to find them, and saw a tall ethereal figure emerge from the trees. The Queen of Air and Darkness was luminous in her robes of northlights and garlands of snowy kiss-me-never, and a wondrous glow that mimicked the aurora and the rainbows after storms and the dreams of men unrealized and lost, shone about her head.

"Welcome home, Wanderfoot," she greeted, her voice as soft as kitten fur and a child's wishes on a star.

Without knowing why, Barbro inclined her head slightly in recognition that she was in the presence of royalty. "I had forgotten you called me that."

"Once I did, when you were asked to stay and fled."

She shook her head in despair. "I was frightened. I wanted my child back."

The Queen looked off into the distance. "So you took him. But now he is here again."

"With Barraboo. My grandchild. I have come for them."

"With war machines and weapons and the men who use them. Very like another time."

Barbro was crying. "A terrible mistake. I am sorry."

Ayoch appeared, knelt, and bowed to the Queen. "All finished, Lady Moon. Gone into the void, men and machines and their dark intent." He glanced at Barbro. "We were not ready for such wickedness last time. But we can learn and we can adapt and we can be what we need to be. Cockatoo!"

His crowing rattled her further. "I want to see my son and granddaughter. Please let me."

"So you can take them away again? So you can return them to lives you believe will be so much better than ours? To drugs that will numb their minds and steal their wits away? To drinks and potions and pills that will give them no relief? To soul-stealing machines that will offer alternative realities both sterile and empty? To links to millions of words spoken by faceless voices in meaningless interactions that will never allow for the touch of flesh and offer only the pretense of true caring? Why, Wanderfoot? So they can be lost in your cities and your teeming numbers and never know loving and never live unfettered or experience the bliss of wildflowers and close companionships or escape the futility in everything they do? You would give them air filled with ashes and dust and tar and poison to breathe? You would give them concrete roads and stone-block walls that rise up and crush their spirit and steal their hopes? You would see them rot from within and without; you would witness them suffer crushing defeats of rejection and indifference? All that would you give them, even knowing they would never be made happy and fulfilled in the way they would if they remained here with me?"

The Queen's words floated on the air, spoken in a voice absent of disdain and filled only with sadness. "Come hither with me, Wanderfoot," she whispered. "Come see what you ask your child and grandchild to forgo."

She stepped away and Barbro followed obediently, even though aware that what she would be shown was false trickery of the sort that Sherrinford had warned so strongly against.

Ayoch bounded along beside her, his half-human face wreathed in a smile. "You are so sure in your wrongness. Listen to her!"

In an emerald glade washed with the glow of firethorn and starlight, she found Jimmy and Barraboo. Jimmy had the baby lying on a blanket spread wide, her chubby legs kicking and her curious arms reaching for the kiss-me-never vine he dangled over her. There seemed no pretenses about what she was seeing, no false coloring of the landscape or dressing up of father and daughter, no attempt at re-creating fiction to approximate truth. Barbro understood. What she was seeing was real and present. The Queen had learned a few things since last they met.

"This is what you would take from them," the Queen declared. "This is what you would steal away."

"No," Barbro whispered. "This is what I would give them back again. This is what I would help them find. You would let them see this, but I would let them live it. You would give them this only in their minds, and I would give them this for real. Or at least I would try. Not all would be good and kind, but much of it would. Better they see life for what it is than for what pretense would make it seem. Here, there is only the latter."

She was astonished she had spoken so boldly, but the Queen simply gave a small wave of her hand. "You cannot give them what they need, Wanderfoot. You cannot even help them find it.

Not in your world of decay and disintegration. Your failure is already written in the books of your history. Your race is doomed. The Fey are the future as they have been the past."

Barbro straightened and faced her squarely. "Please let me have them," she said. "They belong with me."

The Queen regarded her, tall and regal and distant, her eyes depthless pools of far-seeing and secrets untold. "You will sleep with us tonight and on the morrow I will decide."

Then she was gone, faded back into the night. Ayoch was beside her at once. "Your bed is here, mother love," he said, gesturing vaguely.

She glanced back to where she had seen Jimmy and Barraboo, but they were gone. She felt a sudden, intense weariness steal over her. She could not seem to help herself; she had to sleep.

"Lead me," she told the pooka, and so he did.

WHEN SHE WOKE again, Jimmy was sitting next to her. He had a worn and world-weary look, but there was intensity in his blue eyes that suggested the strength of his resolve. She could tell at once that he had decided on his course of action. She sat up quickly. "Will you come away with me?" she asked.

He shook his head. "I will remain here. I came to find a new life. I need to leave behind the old one. It stole so much away from me that I cannot go back to it. Here, I have a chance to find peace and contentment of the sort I knew as a child."

"It is not real," she insisted.

"It is real enough for me, and more real than the life I was living. I do not believe in that world anymore. I hope I can come to believe in this one."

"And Barraboo? Will you keep her with you or give her to me?"

She had missed seeing the bundle lying by his side. He reached down and picked up the baby and handed it to her.

"Give her what you think she needs and, if that fails, bring her back to me. I will be waiting."

She was in tears as she took the baby and held it to her. Its dark little face peeked out at her with eyes that at once seemed both young and innocent and old and wise. "Oh, Jimmy," she whispered.

He leaned over and kissed her cheek. "Think of me now and then, Mother. Remember how happy I am."

He led her down to where a wagon hitched to a reindeer and driven by an old man barely taller than her waist and wrinkled with age waited. Jimmy helped her climb aboard, taking care to wrap her and Barraboo in a blanket. He smiled a knowing smile at the driver, who gave back a small nod, and then the little man clucked at the reindeer and lightly touched one flank with the switch and the wagon and its occupants rumbled off into the haze.

MORGAREL THE WRAITH waited until they were gone too far for the woman to look back and see him changing back and then walked over to Ayoch. The pooka was staring off into the distance, watching after Wanderfoot and her new baby with sharp, far-seeing eyes.

"Hoah," the pooka said softly. "How long do you give her?"

"Before she comes again? I have no sense of that. Years, I hope. The changeling needs time to adapt and learn."

"Which she will do. She is clever, that one. And how clever our Mistress, too." He looked behind the wraith. "And what of them?"

Jimmy Cullen sat rocking Barraboo as he fed her milk from a goatskin and sang softly to her. Other creatures hovered at the edges of shadows that didn't quite reach to where father and daughter shared a life and watched intently.

"He will live awhile longer and then pass. She will become one of us. The Queen ordains."

"Mother Sky sees our future thusly. We will be them and so make them us, and in the end ours shall be the way." Ayoch cocked his head and hopped once in a sort of minor celebration. "Cockatoo!" he crowed.

The cry echoed over Cloudmoor and into the future.

Introduction to
"Aftermath"

READERS FREQUENTLY ATTACH themselves to favorite characters in my books, and what is interesting is that they seldom seem to settle on the same ones. But there are some so iconic that almost everyone gets on board and stays there. Both Garet Jax, the Weapons Master in *The Wishsong of Shannara*, and Stee Jans, the commander of the Legion Free Corps in *The Elfstones of Shannara*, fall into this category. Both stand out as incredibly durable men whose lives reflect the mutual characteristics of loyalty, bravery, deep commitment to others, and a willingness to sacrifice.

They were main characters in succeeding books with a short time line between them, so readers have wondered repeatedly if they might have met at some point. Was it possible they were related—perhaps father and son? Was there a story waiting to be told, and would I be willing to tell it?

Well, I knew there probably was a story waiting to be told, but I didn't know what it was until recently. Nor did I have the time to write it anyway, because I was swamped with other writing projects that were eating up all my time. It was also difficult for me to persuade myself it needed doing, given the harsh fact of my dislike of writing short fiction. But if there were a story waiting to be told, it didn't need its own book—just a short rendering. So all this gave me time to figure out what that story was.

As you will agree, I think, after you finish, it wasn't at all the story any of us thought it would be.

AFTERMATH

STEE JANS STOOD front and center, looking them over. Twenty in all, mostly still in their teens, with two or three in their early twenties. Young men searching for an identity, for a way in the world, for a life that mattered. He had been one of them once, and he remembered what it felt like. All the uncertainty, masked by a brashness that substituted for confidence. All the excitement and expectation.

It made him feel old and used up.

He was only two years past the terrible battle for Arborlon and the Westland, fought against the demons of the Forbidding by the Elves and his own small command. Sent by the Council of Cities in response to an Elven plea for help—more as a sop than an actual commitment—the Free Corps under his command had been almost completely wiped out. Six hundred had ridden to Arborlon and only twelve had returned. A few of those dozen had died within the following year, and another few had never picked up a weapon again.

Not long after, he had been tasked with training recruits who had signed on to join a new Free Corps—a selection of miscreants and castoffs, a mix of hard men and oversized boys on their way to a quick, unpleasant end if nothing changed. Too many had transgressed in all the wrong ways. Too many had forfeited the right to any kind of respect or expectation of accomplishment. And so they had landed here. They were his to measure and sort as they sought admittance to the corps. They were his to train and fortify, to make over into soldiers. Students who were undisciplined and, in some cases, close to unteachable.

It was not what he had envisioned for himself on his return home. He had hoped to be restored to active duty and sent back into the field. After all, who was better fit than someone who had survived the bloodbath of the Elfitch? And who more deserved to be given a chance to help secure and protect the Borderlands than the one who had fought so hard to save it before? But they had judged him and found him wanting. Too old. Too used up. Too tainted by the loss of too many soldiers.

Damaged goods.

He was devastated at first, unable to believe he could be cast aside so easily. He thought to leave the Border Legion once and for all, to make his way in the world as a mercenary or soldier of fortune. But his roots and his loyalties ran deep. His whole adult life had been spent with the Legion and it was not so easy to walk away. Besides, things could change, he told himself. He could find favor again. He could still be redeemed. He was young enough yet that there was time and opportunity for change.

So, in the end, he stayed. It was true that he possessed the skills and the experience to train these recruits, and a small part of him fancied the idea of shaping their lives and their futures. Of sharing his expertise, giving them the benefits he himself had never enjoyed. In his youth, you were thrown into the fray from the moment you joined up, but he had always been big and strong and durable. He possessed that perfect combination of characteristics that all soldiers needed: a toughness that would not allow him to quit and instincts that enabled him to stay alive.

He would try to provide some sense of how to achieve that to these men and boys. He would accept his lot and give them what help he could, so they could serve long and well and depart in one piece. He would not succeed with all of them, but a handful would be enough. It was a soldier's life each one was seeking, after all, and the best you could do was help them survive.

"You know who I am," he said when he first addressed them. "You likely know all about me—or at least enough to understand why I am the one to be training you. From today forward, you will not speak again of my past—real or imagined. You will simply listen to me and do what I ask you. Who you were matters nothing to me. It is who you will be that counts."

He paused, letting his words sink in and giving them a good look at him. He was well over six feet and two hundred pounds, with long red hair and a beard just beginning to show flecks of gray. He was marked by scars from battles mostly won, and he wore them with pride. He was a soldier through and through. True, the best years of his life were behind him, but a few good ones were left nevertheless. He owed nothing of who or what he was to anyone but himself, and—whatever befell him during the remainder of his life—he would always be his own man.

He looked up and down the line as the twenty new recruits stood facing him until he found the one he was looking for. The enlistment soldier had described him well enough. A slight, almost scrawny boy, well under the age required for all recruits. The boy's eyes met his and did not falter. Something there, maybe.

"You will have no names during the six weeks of your training. You will only have numbers. I will address you by those numbers and you will address yourselves by those numbers. You will each be given a patch with your number on it, and you will wear it at all times on your uniforms. Listen while I count you off, and remember who you are."

He counted from one to twenty, going down the line in order, making sure each recruit was listening to him. And indeed, they each had their eyes fixed on him. When he had finished, he dismissed them back to supply to pick up their uniforms and patches with the number that corresponded to their new identity. All but one.

"Twelve!" he barked as they started to turn away. "Come over here."

The boy came, unawed and steady. There was no slouching, no trudging, and no sign of fear. He stopped three feet away and stood waiting.

Stee Jans moved closer. "They told me you were my sister's child. My nephew. Is this so?"

The boy nodded.

"My sister Sara?"

The boy hesitated, then nodded again.

"Does she know you are here?"

Another nod.

"With the Free Corps? She sent you to me? Address me properly this time. Address me by my title."

"Yes, Commander." No sign of a smirk or irony.

Jans nodded slowly. "I don't have a sister named Sara. I don't have a sister at all." He let it sink in. "What game are you playing?"

Immediately the boy said, "Don't send me back."

"Send you back where?"

"To those people. They're not my parents. They would have kept me a slave until I died. They were monsters! I ran away."

Of course he did. Jans shook his head. "How old are you?"

"Eighteen."

"No, you're not. Stop lying to me. How old?"

The boy hesitated once more. "Fifteen. Please let me stay."

"You're too young. Regulations say you have to be eighteen."

"You weren't eighteen when you joined."

Now it was Stee Jans who hesitated. How did the boy know this? In fact, he had been sixteen. But he had looked eighteen—more than eighteen!—and this boy looked to be about thirteen.

"You have to let me stay. This is all I've wanted. For two years I've waited to come. Yes, I ran away. Yes, I'm too young.

But I am more capable than I look, and I am not afraid to do anything you ask of me. I just need a chance. If you send me back, they'll lock me away again. Please."

Yet the plea was not delivered out of apparent desperation or emotional fragility. The boy's voice never broke or quavered. He spoke the words calmly and with conviction.

Jans nodded. "Very well, Twelve, I'll give you a week. We'll see how you do."

STEE JANS KNEW well enough that he was responsible for turning twenty young men into soldiers, and that each of them deserved an equal amount of his time during their training. Yet he found himself paying special attention to Twelve, drawn to him by how well he had conducted himself during their private talk and by what he had discovered during the week following. What he had seen in the boy's eyes during their talk was determination and a measure of confidence that transcended his own doubts. And what he saw in the following week only cemented that impression.

The boy was small and slight and not very strong. But he was also very quick and agile—and when Jans put his recruits through any exercises that included running or climbing or vaulting over obstacles, Twelve was almost always the first to finish. When he had them spar with one another using quarter-length staffs and blunted lightweight replicas of bladed weapons, Twelve was frequently able to overcome his larger opponents simply by using his superior speed and agility. He was fearless against the larger recruits, and on the rare occasions when he was beaten, he simply accepted it without complaint and prepared to try again. And, in every instance, learned enough from his mistakes that he never repeated them.

But there were a few problems he could not overcome—failings that, try as he might, proved troublesome.

With heavy weapons, he was hopeless. He was neither big nor strong enough to wield them effectively. Nor was he successful in close-quarters combat, hand-to-hand fighting, or anything that involved bulling his way past the others. In time, perhaps, he would grow bigger and stronger, but for now he remained at a decided disadvantage. And because he was only fifteen and life in the Legion Free Corps was hard and demanding—and combat was frequent and rigorous—he might not be given the time he needed to mature. In fact, Jans judged it depressingly likely that he would not live long enough to gain the weight and strength such combat demanded. So although the boy struggled relentlessly to overcome his deficiencies, nothing he tried was quite enough.

Eventually, as the week wore on, his fellows discovered his vulnerabilities and simply used their superior strength and size to bull through his defenses and overpower him in virtually every exercise that would allow for it. He was still faster than they were, but speed alone would suffice only if he were fleeing the battles into which he would be cast.

Still, Jans gave him space and time that first week, allowed him to experience and learn, and watched to see how he handled what he had discovered. It was enlightening. Twelve did not falter and did not quit. He fought back at every turn, and when he was knocked down or overpowered, he simply got back up again. He never once came to his commander for help and never once complained. He seldom showed any emotion at all save for an occasional outburst of frustration. The essential determination of his character would not allow for anything more.

That was when Stee Jans decided that he would help him.

Well, that and his unfortunate fight with One.

The training camp used by the Free Corps and several other Legion units covered almost fifty acres, composed of fields, hills, and forests, with a small river running through the center. A portion was dedicated to housing, supply and weapons storage, and administration buildings. But most of it was dedicated to a series of imitation battlefields and sparring sites. The variety of terrains was important to simulate both technique and combat challenges, and Stee Jans made full use of every square foot for teaching his inexperienced charges.

The fight between One and Twelve happened toward the end of the first week. It had been apparent from the first what sort of man One was. He was older, bigger, and stronger than the others by a considerable margin, and determined to emphasize that superiority. When he wanted something, there was no one big enough to stop him. When he was irritated or disgruntled or simply bored, he took it out on one or more of his fellow recruits. On the first day of training, when Jans gathered them together to introduce himself, One shoved his way to the front of the line and dared the others to do something about it. No one did, so in the days following things got only worse. One bragged openly about his physical prowess. When the recruits exercised, simply completing the skill set was never enough for One; he had to exceed it. In combat, he didn't just overcome his opponent but also put in a few extra blows to emphasize how badly the other was beaten.

Jans knew that what was happening was not unusual. There would always be someone like One to deal with. It was better to let things proceed naturally and see what happened. One's behavior was just another lesson the others would need to learn. Sooner or later, someone would stand up to him. Or maybe it would be all of them at once.

But he had never expected it would be Twelve.

He was not there when the fight started. He was working with a smaller group on various disabling holds and how to break them. Twelve and One were sparring with staffs, and the bigger youth had just flattened the smaller once again. Then something had persuaded One that it was a good idea to deliver a few extra strikes while he had the boy pinned to the ground and disarmed. Twelve had wriggled free, scrambled to his feet, and come at One with fists flying. He had used his quickness to get past the bigger youth's guard, knocking aside his staff, and had gotten in a few good blows to his face before the other bore him to the ground and really went to work on him.

By the time Jans realized what was happening and had reached the combatants, Twelve was bloodied from head to foot. But the fiery look in his eyes and the set of his face told his commander all he needed to know about his state of mind. Even as beaten as he was, he had not given up.

"Stand over there," Jans ordered One as he broke up the fight, bending down to examine Twelve where he lay on the ground. The boy was struggling to rise, but Jans held him down while he felt for broken bones and severe damage to muscles and ligaments. When he found none, he pulled the boy to his feet. "You're all right. Go clean up."

He watched the boy walk back toward the barracks, then ordered the others—One included—to gather close. He addressed the latter first.

"You have all the tools required to be a fine soldier, but you need to remember who to use those tools against. Twelve is your comrade-in-arms. At some point, he might be in a position to save your life. It serves no purpose to make an enemy of him. When you are engaged in actual combat, you will need the support of your fellows. If you can't count on that, your life will be a short one."

He paused, then turned his attention to the others. "As for the rest of you, you let this happen by not intervening. You are a unit, and you need to stand up for one another. Shouting and cheering while one fellow soldier beats on another is not acceptable. So I'd better never see anything like this happen again, because the next time it does, there will be consequences."

He looked each of them in the eye, then made a gesture of dismissal. "Back to work, all of you. Except for you, One. You wait."

When the others had moved away, he drew One closer. "What happened between you and Twelve?"

One shrugged.

"Use your words, soldier. What happened?"

"He wouldn't quit. I had him on the ground, he was beaten, but he kept struggling. He got up and hit me. I felt like he needed a lesson."

"Are you the instructor of this unit, One? Or am I?"

A long hesitation. "You are."

"That's right. So I provide the lessons, not you. Remember that. Now go back to your comrades."

He supervised the remainder of the day's training without further incident. And he was not surprised when Twelve reappeared shortly after and resumed training with the others. Nor was he surprised when Twelve made no mention of his injuries, or let them slow him down. It was not in Twelve's character to complain. Ever.

That night, after dinner, he summoned Twelve to his tent. The boy's damaged face was expressionless as he faced his commander. "Am I being sent back?"

Stee Jans shook his head. "No, but you need to improve. You're quick and you're agile, but you're getting shoved around too much."

The boy said nothing. He just stood there.

"You lack the necessary tools to compensate for your size. There are ways to make up for being small, you know."

Still the boy said nothing.

"Would you like to learn what they are?"

For the first time, a look of interest appeared on the boy's face. "Yes."

"Very well. Every day after regular training is over, you will spend two more hours before dinner with me, just the two of us. I will give you two weeks to master the techniques I teach you. If you haven't managed to do so by then, I will send you back to wherever you came from. Understood?"

The boy nodded. "Thank you."

Jans shook his head in mild admonishment. "You might

want to hold off on thanking me just yet. Better wait and see what I have planned for you. Now get out of here."

STEE JANS KNEW that he shouldn't be giving private lessons to any one recruit; his assignment was to teach them all. And implicit in that charge was the promise that he would offer the benefit of his experience to them equally, giving each the same amount of time and attention. Yet each of his recruits possessed a different level of ability, and he believed that those who needed additional help were entitled to get it.

But particularly in the case of Twelve. His skill set was better than most, but severely lacking in several areas. Still, his promise as a future soldier of the Free Corps was unmistakable. Most soldiers Jans had encountered were adequate to the task, but every now and then there was one who possessed the temperament, tenacity, and dedication to be truly special. Who could exceed expectations and excel at whatever was asked of him. And Twelve was one of these.

They met for their first lesson on the following day, after the regular training session had ended. Jans had arranged for them to meet in training area seven—a heavily wooded area west of the barracks that offered both concealment from the curious and several clearings where exercises could be conducted. All fourteen sessions would take place here, and all fourteen would involve pretty much the same thing—learning how to defend against and overcome someone bigger and stronger.

For their first exercise, Stee Jans handed Twelve a quarter staff and told the boy to hit him with it. When Twelve hesitated, Jans ordered him to do as he was told. So the boy took a wicked sideways swing at his commander and found himself disarmed so quickly he was left wide-eyed in disbelief.

"What just happened?" Jans asked calmly.

Twelve shook his head. "I don't know!"

"Then I'll tell you. Your body language told me exactly what you were going to do before you did it. By the time you acted, I was already in a position to block your swing and twist your staff out of your hands. This is what you have to learn to do."

They progressed from there to how the boy could block other types of attacks where the strength and size of an opponent were an issue. Jans demonstrated each one, then walked Twelve through it in slow motion.

"Everything begins with anticipating and understanding what is required when facing a larger opponent. Remember that a larger man will almost always be depending on his physical advantages to overcome you, so you have to use that against him. You have to make those advantages the key to defeating him. Not many can do this, even *with* the training I am giving you. Most are not quick or smart enough, but I think you might be. So that's what we're going to find out."

They spent every day of the next fourteen doing so. Jans taught Twelve dozens of blocking moves and retaliatory strikes that most would not think to employ. He taught the boy how to turn what appeared to be a disparity of size and weight to his own advantage. They worked with hands and feet and then with weapons. He drilled the boy with constant repetition and an insistence on perfection. He made him practice each defensive move until they came automatically. As he had hoped, Twelve never complained and never asked to rest. He showed he could understand complicated explanations of size and weight ratios, and of the reasoning behind various combinations.

It was a hard, relentless training, but Jans could see Twelve's progress in very measurable ways. And what impressed him most was the obvious facility Twelve had for hand-to-hand combat—how quickly he picked up on techniques and not only implemented them, but expanded on them with new variations. Twelve was a natural fighter—eager to learn, relentless in his determination to master the knowledge underlying each new technique, and committed to being the very best he could.

As they neared the end of the two-week period, Stee Jans could see the effects of the boy's understanding spill over into the regular training sessions as well. Twelve was no longer so easily overpowered by the older, bigger boys, and they were no longer able to defeat him using strength alone. He could see the surprise on their faces when Twelve applied the lessons Jans had taught him. His instincts were becoming much sharper, as was his awareness of how to win in single-handed combat. However, he showed no real interest in defensive teamwork. Some of this was due to his isolation from his unit, and some was just a consequence of how he viewed himself—as someone who would always depend mostly on himself. His skills were all in the area of hand-to-hand fighting, and forms of combined unit combat seemed not to interest him at all.

Because of who he was, there was nothing to be gained by bemoaning the boy's lack of progress in this particular area. Some were born to be soldiers who fought best in a unit, while others would always excel when left to their own devices and abilities. And it was always better to accept the direction chosen by the student rather than to try to change him. Success depended more on the willingness of the student to embrace what he was taught than on an instructor's force of will to alter his thinking.

It was so here—and in Twelve's case, Stee Jans believed it was more than sufficient.

At the end of the two weeks—now three weeks into the six-week training session—the commander concluded their private sessions and dismissed his young student from further instruction.

"I've given you more than enough to work with, and you've shown both a comprehensive understanding of the lessons and the ability to apply yourself," he advised. "You've convinced me you have what it takes to be a good soldier. Much of what you learn from here on you will learn on your own and from experience. What matters is that you have earned your place in this unit. You will be allowed to finish your training; you won't be sent away."

He paused. "Congratulations, soldier."

The boy, as was his way, only smiled and said nothing.

THE REMAINDER OF the six-week training course proceeded without incident, and progress in all the recruits was notable. By the end, a new batch of recruits was waiting for instruction, already designated for admission into the new Free Corps unit. It was a larger group, but Jans was already looking forward to the challenge. By now he had developed a feel for the training process and found that he enjoyed it far more than he had expected. He had not yet given up his dream of leading a new command, but he had embraced the task he had been given and found an unexpected satisfaction in carrying it out.

But one more challenge remained for the initial group.

Stee Jans considered war the ultimate form of competition— one where lives and futures were at stake. So for the final day of his instruction, he paired off his twenty recruits in hand-to-hand combat. Admittedly, he was curious to see what Twelve would do against his fellows—and how well he could apply the lessons Jans had taught him. But this final test was something he had decided on even before he had set eyes on those who were assigned to him. It was to be a measure of their progress and an opportunity for each of them to decide for themselves how far they had come.

He paired them off by size, the two largest against each other and continuing down to the two smallest. They were given a span of five minutes to subdue their opponent; then the loser was eliminated from the competition. There were to be breaks between each match to allow for rest and reflection, but the competition would continue until only one combatant remained. Weapons were forbidden. Hand-to-hand fighting was all that was allowed, and Jans would be watching closely for low blows or sneak attacks. Violations would get you disqualified. And each match would end when a combatant called "Yield."

He probably should have known how it would end, but there

was enough uncertainty in his mind that he was curious to see how it all played out. Yet indeed, when all the matches but the last had been fought, only Twelve and One were still standing. It felt inevitable, but it also felt right. In each one, there was an unmistakable combination of strength and resilience, and a willingness to go beyond what seemed possible. Each had found a path to this final confrontation, although their paths had been noticeably different. One had overpowered his opponents while Twelve had outsmarted them.

And now they would pit these very different skills against each other to see which would prevail.

Jans had faith that Twelve would be a match for One, now that he had received those two weeks of extra training. He had demonstrated to the boy how size and strength alone could be negated. But One had progressed as well. He was an apt student and had applied himself diligently. He had grown stronger and more agile as the six weeks progressed. He had learned the lessons of hand-to-hand combat better than any of them. A nagging feeling persisted that, for all Twelve's progress, it would still not be enough to defeat One.

The remaining students formed a circle around the two, and Stee Jans brought them face-to-face in the center of the ring. "Five minutes," he reminded them. "When one of you calls 'Yield,' the match ends. This match is as much about intelligence as it is about skill, and that will be true in every fight you are engaged in. Do your best."

He stepped back. "Begin!"

There was a brief round of cheers and shouts of encouragement from the spectators as the two combatants took fighting stances and began to circle each other. Jans had expected One to go right at Twelve in an effort to overpower him, but apparently One had been paying attention to Twelve's progress over the last few weeks. He kept his guard up and seemed content to wait for the boy to make the first move.

Which was the last thing Twelve should do.

It was, nevertheless, exactly what he did.

Twelve gave it maybe thirty seconds, then he went in low and hard. One was ready for him and blocked his rush, then brought his elbow down toward his attacker's exposed head to put an end to the fight. But Twelve was too quick, already rolling under the blow and taking One's legs out from under him. They went down in a tangle, and the older managed to get a hand lock on the younger's leg as he tried to roll away, dragging him back again.

Once more, the boy was able to free himself with a counter-twist of his body that loosened the other's grip, which enabled him to spring back to his feet.

They resumed circling. Slowly, deliberately, they feinted without advancing, each waiting on the other. Then again Twelve attacked, coming in low once more. And again, One tried to block him. But Twelve had different plans this time, launching himself off the ground and sending a roundhouse kick into One's exposed head. It was a risky maneuver, but well executed. The kick caught One by surprise and sent him reeling backward, and Twelve was on top of him at once, raining down blows that seemed to come from everywhere.

Jans understood Twelve's attack plan by now. Strike early and often. Strike when it was not expected. Keep One off guard. Avoid close contact once the strike was executed. It was a sound plan, and Twelve had executed it perfectly. But One was starting to look frustrated and angry, and that was when he was most dangerous. That was when Twelve had to watch him most carefully.

Twelve was dancing about, moving fast enough that he was able to get fresh blows through One's defenses, but One didn't seem to care anymore. He was shrugging everything off and watching his opponent with stoic determination. Jans realized what he was about to do, but could not do anything about it save hope that Twelve was paying attention. The boy was, but it didn't matter. When One abruptly charged, he did so with no intention of stopping. Twelve hit him with two blistering head shots and a hard kick to one knee, but One bulled his way through and slammed into Twelve, bearing him to the ground. Holding him in place by his weight alone, he pinned the boy's arms and legs and rose to a sitting position to look down at him.

"You're done, rodent," he sneered through blood and sweat, his big hands fastened around the boy's wrists, his legs pinning down everything else. "Give it up. Say the word, and I'll let you go."

Twelve was staring up at him, struggling without success to get any part of his body free so he might have a chance to escape. He hesitated a moment and then muttered something.

"What was that?" His captor shook his head angrily. "Take the crap out of your mouth and speak up!"

Twelve muttered something else, likewise unintelligible. He had stopped struggling by now, but was still looking up with what appeared to be exhaustion and fury.

One bent close, head lowered to within inches of the other's face and spit on it. "I said, speak . . ."

Twelve threw his head forward and slammed it into One's face, breaking his nose. One had gotten too close—close enough that he had made himself vulnerable. He jerked back in shock, his hands going automatically to his face, and Twelve's hands were free.

Instantly, Twelve hit him twice, so hard you could hear the sound of the blows—once in the stomach and once in the face. One went over backward and lay gasping, all but incapacitated.

Stee Jans stepped in at that point, pulling them apart and hauling Twelve to his feet. "Your winner," he announced to the others, and was greeted with a smattering of cheers and shouts.

But when he turned to One to reset his nose, he was not at all sure he was satisfied with the way things had turned out.

THE FOLLOWING DAY, a small ceremony was held to celebrate the recruits who had completed their training and were now officially members of the newly re-formed Free Corps. Over the next few months, dozens of additional recruits would be conscripted, trained, and incorporated into the still woefully inadequate command, and then dispatched to various trouble spots throughout the Borderlands and beyond. The ceremony to honor this very first group was brief and rather sparsely attended, but it served its purpose. Suitable recognition had been provided to the reassembling of the Free Corps, heralding the start of a growth that would continue until the command was back to its original complement of six hundred soldiers.

Of the twenty who had entered the program and completed its requirements, nineteen attended.

Only one had failed to appear.

On his way back to his quarters afterward, Stee Jans found himself wondering why Twelve had chosen to stay away. He had said nothing to anyone about not attending; nothing about his decision not to become a member of the Free Corps. Nothing about where he would go from here. His silence was not entirely unexpected; the boy had never been much of a talker the entire time he was in training. But Jans found himself wondering, nevertheless, what the reasons were for Twelve's abrupt departure.

If he knew the boy's name, he could inquire after him. But he had asked not to be told any of their names, and he did not think it necessary to alter that now. When he had lost his command, he had lost almost six hundred men he could call by name. He did not think he wanted to have anything even remotely approaching that experience again.

But it didn't matter. Twelve was waiting for him inside the tent, sitting at the desk Jans used for writing up his daily schedules and unit orders. He was busy writing, but he looked up at once when the Borderman entered, then turned to face him.

"You missed the ceremony," Jans observed drily.

The boy nodded. "The Free Corps is not for me. But it taught me a lot. *You* taught me a lot. I'll never forget that."

Jans walked to his cot and sat down on it, looking pensive. "I think maybe you've decided you prefer working by yourself to working with others. I'm not sure I agree with this, but the choice is yours to make. So, will you be a soldier of fortune? A blade for hire?"

A long pause. "I'm not sure yet. Something of the sort, probably. But I need to learn more first. I want to get even better."

"You're pretty good, as it is."

"No, I'm not. Right now, I'm just adequate. But I want to be more than that." Twelve paused, looked down at the paper he had been writing on, and crumpled it up. "I wanted to write all this down because I didn't think I would see you again. But it's better, having you here."

He rose, walked over to Jans, and extended his hand. Jans took it wordlessly and smiled. He was perplexed by the boy's decision, even as he accepted it as somehow inevitable. It troubled him that he had known nothing of Twelve when they first met and now that he was leaving he still knew almost nothing.

Save that he had grown up in ways you couldn't see and couldn't measure on the surface.

"Commander," the boy said quietly. "I've set a goal for myself. I want to master not only your fighting skills, but your ability to project both self-confidence and humility in equal measure. And I want to know about myself what I think you know about *your*self—that I can overcome all doubts and fears that confront me."

Jans stared. It was perhaps the most impossible task that anyone he knew had ever undertaken. It was at once the most intimate confidence the boy had ever revealed to him and at the same time the most disturbing. "I'm not that man. No one is."

"I disagree. You are skilled at all forms of fighting—both with weapons and without. I want to be like that. I want to learn how to be prepared for any situation. I want to be as good as you are."

Stee Jans smiled and stood. He put his hands on the boy's

shoulders and rested them there. "Do this instead. Don't just be as good as I am. Be better."

The boy shook his head. "I don't think I can do that. But I will try."

As he turned and started for the door, Jans made a snap decision. "Tell me your name, Twelve."

The boy turned back. "Garet Jax," he said.

And then he was gone.

Introduction to
"Imaginary Friends"

BEFORE I WROTE the definitive version of *Running with the Demon*, the first book in the Word and the Void series, way back in 1991, I wrote "Imaginary Friends." It was a short story written for a Del Rey Books collection of ten short stories by ten fantasy and science-fiction authors that apparently Lester had something on—making them unable to refuse his offer. I was among these unfortunates, although I refuse to divulge what sort of hold he had over me. I wasn't looking to write a short story for reasons set forth in the introduction to "Aftermath," which presumably you have just finished. But once I realized I was signed up, like it or not, I decided I would write something different. Up until then, I was almost strictly a Shannara and Magic Kingdom writer, with no other fantasy story to my name.

Well, not counting my college applications.

So, what to write? The title to the collection was *Once Upon a Time: A Treasury of Modern Fairy Tales*. Practically screams out *Imaginary*, doesn't it? I didn't want to riff on old fairy tales, only suggest something like them with a story that might take place in the present. I went right back to when I was a boy growing up in Sterling, Illinois, and spending hours in my very early years with role-playing and reimagining. Back then, the appearance of magic was a real possibility and sometimes a real event. So I decided I would write a story about a boy and an Elf (sort of) and a very real monster living in the park they lived next to—as I once did. I used the setting of my hometown and my memories of that period of time to make it come alive.

At the heart of the story was Jack McCall, a thirteen-year-old boy who was living with the very real possibility that he was dying from cancer. He would be facing an evil much larger and more dangerous than any he had ever faced, and he was coming to terms with a harsh truth: This might be something he could not defeat.

I wrote this story thirty years ago, and at the time I'd had no personal encounters with this insidious disease. Since then, I've watched it attack Judine twice, take my daughter, Lisa, and many friends and acquaintances, and make itself a presence in my life in a way I had not expected. At thirteen, your approach to being told you have cancer is a bit different than when you are older. And your faith in yourself at a young age is grounded in things that tend to fall away as you grow older.

When you are thirteen, magic is sometimes still more real than not.

IMAGINARY

FRIENDS

JACK MCCALL WAS ten days shy of his thirteenth birthday when he decided that he was dying. He had been having headaches for about six months without telling anyone, and the headaches were accompanied by a partial loss of vision that lasted anywhere from ten to twenty minutes. He hadn't thought much about it since it happened only once in a while, believing that it was simply the result of eyestrain. After all, there was a lot of homework assigned in the seventh grade.

But ten days before his birthday he had an attack as he was about to go out the door to school, and since he couldn't very well ride his bike in that condition or stand around pretending that nothing was wrong, he was forced to admit the problem to his mother. His mother made an immediate appointment with Dr. Muller, the family pediatrician, for that afternoon, sat Jack down until his vision cleared, then drove him to school, asking him all the way there if he was all right and calling him "Jackie" until he thought he would scream.

She returned promptly when school let out to take him to his appointment. Dr. Muller was uncharacteristically cheerful as he checked Jack over, even going so far as to ruffle his hair and remark on how quickly he was growing. This was the same Dr. Muller who normally didn't have two words for him. Jack began to worry.

When the doctor was finished, he sent Jack and his mother over to the hospital for further tests. The tests included X-rays, blood workups, an EKG, and a barrage of other examinations— all of which were administered by an uncomfortably youthful collection of nurses. Jack endured the application of cold metal implements to his body, let himself be stuck repeatedly with needles, breathed in and out, lay very still, jumped up and down, and mostly waited around in empty, sterile examination rooms. When the tests were all done, he was sent home knowing nothing more than he had when he arrived beyond the fact that he did not care ever to go through such an ordeal again.

That night, while Jack was upstairs in his room fiddling with his homework and listening to his stereo, Dr. Muller paid a visit to his house. His parents didn't call for him, but that didn't stop him from being curious. He slipped down the stairway to the landing and sat there in the dark on the other side of the half wall above the living room while Dr. Muller and his parents spoke in hushed tones. Dr. Muller did most of the talking. He said that the preliminary test results were back. He talked about the body and its cells and a bunch of other stuff, throwing in multisyllabic medical terms that Jack couldn't begin to understand.

Then he used the words *blood disorder* and *leukemia* and *cancer.* Jack understood that part. He might only be in seventh grade, but he wasn't stupid.

He stayed on the stairway until he heard his mother start to cry, then crept back up to his room without waiting to hear any more. He sat there staring at his unfinished homework, trying to decide what he should be feeling. He couldn't seem to feel anything. He heard Dr. Muller leave, and then his parents came up to see him. Usually they visited him individually; when they both appeared it was serious business. They knocked on the door, came inside when invited, and stood there looking decidedly uncomfortable. Then his father told him that he was sick and would have to take it easy for a while, his mother started crying and calling him "Jackie" and hugging him, and all of a sudden he was scared out of his socks.

He didn't sleep much that night, letting the weight of what he had discovered sink in, trying to comprehend what his dying meant, trying to decide if he believed it was possible. Mostly, he thought about Uncle Frank. Uncle Frank had been his favorite uncle, a big man with strong hands and red hair who taught him how to throw a baseball. Uncle Frank used to take him to ball games on Sunday afternoons. Then he got sick. It happened all at once. He went into the hospital and never came out. Jack's parents took him to see Uncle Frank a couple of times. There was not much left of Uncle Frank by then. His once-strong hands were so frail, he could barely lift them. All his hair had fallen out. He looked like an old man.

Then he died. No one came right out and said it, but Jack knew what had killed him. And he had always suspected, deep down inside where you hid things like that, that it might some-day kill him, too.

The next morning Jack dressed, wolfed down his breakfast as quickly as he could, and got out of there. His parents were behaving like zombies. It was Friday, always a slow-moving day at Roosevelt Junior High, but never more so than on this occasion. The morning seemed endless, and Jack didn't remember any of it when it was finally over. He trudged to the lunchroom, found a seat off in a corner where he could talk privately, and told his best friend, Waddy Wadsworth, what he had discovered. Reynolds Lucius Wadsworth III was Waddy's real name—the result of a three-generation tradition of unparalleled cruelty in the naming of firstborn boys. No one called Waddy by his real name, of course, but they didn't call him anything sensible, either. It was discovered early on that Waddy lacked any semblance of athletic ability. He was the kid who couldn't climb the knotted rope or do chin-ups or high-jump when the bar was only two feet off the ground. Someone started calling him Waddy and the name stuck. It wasn't that Waddy was fat or anything; he was just earthbound.

He was also a good guy. Jack liked him because he never said anything about the fact that Jack was only a little taller than most fire hydrants and a lot shorter than most girls.

"You look okay to me," Waddy said after Jack had finished telling him he was supposed to be dying.

"I know I look okay." Jack frowned at his friend impatiently. "This isn't the kind of thing you can see, you know."

"You sound okay, too." Waddy took a bite of his jelly sandwich. "Does anything hurt?"

Jack shrugged. "Just when I have the headaches."

"Well, you don't have them more often now than you did six months ago, do you?"

"No."

"And they don't last any longer now than they did then, do they?"

"No."

Waddy shoved the rest of the sandwich into his mouth and chewed thoughtfully. "Well, then, who's to say you're really dying? This could be one of those conditions that just goes on indefinitely. Meantime, they might find a cure for it; they're always finding cures for this kind of stuff." He chewed some more. "Anyway, maybe the doctor made a mistake. That's possible, isn't it?"

Jack nodded doubtfully.

"The point is, you don't know for sure. Not for sure." Waddy cocked his head. "Here's something else to think about. They're always telling someone or other that they're going to die and then they don't. People get well all the time just because they believe they can do it. Sometimes believing is all it takes." He gave Jack a lopsided grin. "Besides, no one dies in the seventh grade."

Jack wanted to believe that. He spent the afternoon trying to convince himself. After all, he didn't personally know anyone his age who had died. The only people he knew who had died were much older—even Uncle Frank. He was just a kid. How could he die when he still didn't know anything about girls? How could he die without ever having driven a car? It just didn't seem possible.

Nevertheless, the feeling persisted that he was only fooling himself. It didn't make any difference what he believed. It didn't change the facts. If he really had cancer, believing he didn't wouldn't make it go away. He sat through his afternoon classes growing steadily more despondent, feeling helpless and wishing he could do something about it.

It wasn't until he was biking home that he suddenly found himself thinking about Pick.

THE MCCALL HOUSE was a large white shake-shingle rambler that occupied almost an acre of timber bordering the north edge of Sinnissippi Park. The Sinnissippi Indians were native to the area, and several of their burial mounds occupied a fenced-off area situated in the southwest corner of the park under a cluster of giant maples. The park was more than forty acres end-to-end, most of it woods, the rest consisting of baseball diamonds and playgrounds. The park was bordered on the south by the Rock River, on the west by Riverside Cemetery, and on the north and east by the private residences of Woodlawn. It was a sprawling preserve, filled with narrow, serpentine trails; thick stands of scrub-choked pine; and shady groves of maple, elm, and white oak. A massive bluff ran along the better part of its southern edge and overlooked the Rock River.

Jack was not allowed to go into the park alone until he was out of fourth grade, not even beyond the low maintenance bushes that grew where his backyard ended at the edge of the park. His father took him for walks sometimes, a bike ride now and then, and once in a while his mother even came along. She didn't come often, though, because she was frequently busy vol-

unteering for various charitable causes, and his father worked at
the printing company and was usually not home until after
dark. So for a long time the park remained a vast, unexplored
country that lay just out of reach and whispered enticingly in
Jack's youthful mind of adventure and mystery.

Sometimes, when the lure was too strong, he would beg to be
allowed to go into the park by himself, just for a little ways, just
for a few tiny minutes. He would pinch his thumb and index
finger close together to emphasize the smallness of his request.
But his mother's reply was always the same—his own backyard
was park enough for him.

Things have a way of working out, though, and the summer
before he entered second grade he ended up going into the park
alone in spite of his parents. It all came about because of Pick.
Jack was playing in the sandbox with his toy trucks on a hot
July afternoon when he heard Sam whining and barking at
something just beyond the bushes. Sam was the family dog, a
sort of mongrel terrier with a barrel body. He was carrying on
as if he had unearthed a mountain lion, and finally Jack lifted
himself out of the maze of crisscrossing paths he was construct-
ing and wandered down to the end of the yard to see what was
happening. When he got there, he found that he still couldn't
see anything because Sam was behind a pine tree on the other
side of the bushes. Jack called, but the dog wouldn't come. After
standing there for a few minutes, Jack glanced restlessly over
his shoulder at the windows of his house. There was no sign of
his mother. Biting his lower lip with stubborn determination,
he stepped cautiously onto forbidden ground.

He was concentrating too hard on what lay behind him. As
he passed through the bushes, he stumbled and struck his head
sharply on a heavy limb. The blow stung, but Jack climbed back
to his feet almost immediately and went on.

Sam was jumping around at the base of the pine, darting in
and out playfully. There was a gathering of brambles growing
there and a bit of cloth caught in them. When Jack got closer, he

saw that the bit of cloth was actually a doll. When he got closer still, he saw that the doll was moving.

"Don't just stand there!" the doll yelled at him in a very tiny but angry voice. "Call him off!"

Jack caught hold of Sam's collar. Sam struggled, twisting about in Jack's grip, trying to get back to his newfound discovery. Finally Jack gave the dog a sharp slap on its hind end and sent it scurrying away through the bushes. Then he crouched down beneath the pine, staring at the talking doll. It was a little man with a reddish beard, green shirt and pants, black boots and belt, and a cap made out of fresh pine needles woven together.

Jack giggled. "Why are you so little?" he asked.

"Why am I so little?" the other echoed. He was struggling mightily to free himself. "Why are you so big? Don't you know anything?"

"Are you real?" Jack pressed.

"Of course I'm real! I'm an Elf!"

Jack cocked his head. "Like in the fairy tales?"

The Elf was flushed redder than his beard. "No, not like in the fairy tales! Since when do fairy tales tell the truth about Elves? I suppose you think Elves are just cute little woodfolk who spend their lives prancing about in the moonlight? Well, we don't! We work!"

Jack bent close so he could see better. "What do you work at?"

The Elf was apoplectic. "Everything!"

"You're funny," Jack said, rocking back on his heels. "What's your name?"

"Pick. My name is Pick," muttered the Elf. He twisted some more and finally gave up. "What's yours?"

"Jack. Jack Andrew McCall."

"Well, look, Jack Andrew McCall. Do you think you could help me get out of these brambles? It's your fault, after all, that I'm in them in the first place. That is your dog, isn't it? Well, your dog was sneaking around where I was working and I didn't hear him. He barked and frightened me so badly, I got myself caught. Then he began sniffing and drooling all over me, and I got tangled up even worse!" He took a deep breath, calming himself. "So how about it? Will you help me?"

"Sure," Jack agreed at once.

He started to reach down, and Pick cried out, "Be careful with those big fingers of yours! You could crush me! You're not a clumsy boy, are you? You're not one of those boys that goes around stepping on ants?"

Jack was always pretty good with his hands, and he managed to free the Elf in a matter of seconds with little or no damage to either from the brambles. He put Pick on the ground in front of him and sat back. Pick brushed at his clothes, muttering inaudibly.

"Do you live in the park?" Jack asked.

Pick glanced up, sour-faced once more. His pine-needle cap was askew. "Of course I live in the park! How else could I do my work if I didn't?" He jabbed out with one finger. "Do you know what I do, Jack Andrew? I look after this park! This whole park, all by myself! That is a terrible responsibility for a single Elf!"

Jack was impressed. "How do you look after it?"

Pick shoved the cap back into place. "Do you know what magic is?"

Jack scratched at a mosquito bite on his wrist. "It turned Cinderella into a fairy princess," he answered doubtfully.

"Good gosh golly, are they still telling that old saw? When are they ever going to get this fairy-tale business right? They keep sticking to those ridiculous stories about wicked stepmothers, would-be princesses, and glass slippers at a royal ball—as if a glass slipper would last five minutes on a dance floor!" He jumped up and down so hard that Jack started. "I could tell them a thing or two about real fairy tales!" Pick exploded. "I could tell them some stories that would raise the hair on the backs of their necks!"

He stopped, suddenly aware of Jack's consternation. "Oh,

never mind!" he huffed. "This business of fairy tales just happens to be a sore subject with me. Now about what I do, Jack Andrew. I keep the magic in balance, is what I do. There's magic in everything, you know—from the biggest old oak to the smallest blade of grass, from ants to elephants. And it all has to be kept in balance or there's big trouble. That's what Elves really do. But there're not enough of us to be everywhere, so we concentrate on the places where the magic is strongest and most likely to cause trouble—like this park." He swept the air with his hand. "There's lots of troublesome magic in this park."

Jack followed the motion of his hand and then nodded. "It's a big place."

"Too big for most Elves, I'll have you know!" Pick announced. "Want to see how big?"

Jack nodded yes and shook his head no all in the same motion. He glanced hurriedly over his shoulder, remembering anew his mother. "I'm not supposed to go into the park," he explained. "I'm not even supposed to go out of the yard."

"Oh," said Pick quietly. He rubbed his red-bearded chin momentarily, then clapped his hands. "Well, a touch of magic will get the job done and keep you out of trouble at the same time. Here, pick me up, put me in your hand. Gently, Boy! There! Now let me settle myself. Keep your hand open, palm up. Don't move. Now close your eyes. Go on, close them. This won't hurt. Close your eyes and think about the park. Can you see it? Now watch . . ."

Something warm and syrupy drifted through Jack's body, starting at his eyes and working its way downward to his feet. He felt Pick stir.

And suddenly Jack was flying, soaring high above the trees and telephone poles across the broad green expanse of Sinnissippi Park. He sat astride an owl, a great brown-and-white feathered bird with wings that seemed to stretch on forever. Pick sat behind him, and amazingly they were the same size. Jack blinked in disbelief, then yelled in delight. The owl swooped lazily earthward, banking this way and that to catch the wind, but the motion did not disturb Jack. Indeed, he felt as if nothing could dislodge him from his perch.

"This is how I get from place to place," he heard Pick say, the tiny voice unruffled by the wind. "Daniel takes me. He's a barn owl—a good one. We met some time back. If I had to walk the park, it would take me weeks to get from one end to the other and I'd never get anything done."

"I like this!" Jack cried out joyously, laughing, and Pick laughed with him.

They rode the wind on Daniel's back for what seemed like hours, passing from Riverside Cemetery along the bluff face east to the houses of Woodlawn and back again. Jack saw everything with eyes that were wide with wonder and delight. There were gray and brown squirrels, birds of all kinds and colors, tiny mice and voles, opossums, and even a badger. There was a pair of deer in a thicket down along the riverbank, a fawn and its mother, slender and delicate, their stirrings barely visible against the trees. There were hoary old pines with their needled boughs interlaced like armor over secretive earthen floors, towering oaks and elms sticking out of the ground like massive spears, deep hollows and ravines that collected dried leaves and shadows, and inlets and streams filled with lily pads, frogs, and darting tiny fish.

But there was more than that for a boy who could imagine. There were castles and forts behind every old log. There were railroads with steam engines racing over ancient wooden bridges where the streams grew too wide to ford. There were pirate dens and caves of treasures. There were wild ponies that ran faster than the wind, and mountain cats as sleek as silk. Everywhere there was a new story, a different tale, a dream of an adventure longing to be embraced.

And there were things of magic.

"Down there, Jack Andrew—do you see it?" Pick called as they swung left across the stone bridge that spanned a split in the bluff where it dropped sharply downward to the Rock. "Look closely, Boy!"

Jack looked, seeing the crablike shadow that clung to the underside of the bridge, flattened almost out of sight against the stone.

"That's Wartag the Troll!" Pick announced. "Every bridge seems to have at least one Troll in these parts, but Wartag is more trouble than most. If there's a way to unbalance the magic, Wartag will find it. Much of my own work is spent in undoing his!"

Daniel took them down close to the bridgehead, and Jack saw Wartag inch farther back into the shadows in an effort to hide. He was not entirely successful. Jack could still see the crooked body covered with patches of black hair and the mean-looking red eyes that glittered like bicycle reflectors.

Daniel screamed and Wartag shrank away.

"Wartag doesn't care much for owls!" Pick said to Jack, then shouted something spiteful at the Troll before Daniel wheeled them away.

They flew on to a part of the park they had not visited yet, a deep woods far back in the east-central section where the sunlight seemed unable to penetrate and all was cloaked in shadow. Daniel took them down into the darkness, a sort of gray mistiness that was filled with silence and the smell of rotting wood. Pick pointed ahead, and Jack followed the line of his finger warily. There stood the biggest, shaggiest tree that he had ever seen—a monster with crooked limbs, splitting bark, and craggy bolls that seemed waiting to snare whatever came into its path. Nothing grew about it. All the other trees, all the brush and grasses were cleared away.

"What is it?" he asked Pick.

Pick gave him a secretive look. "That, young Jack Andrew, is the prison, now and forevermore, of the Dragon Desperado. What do you think of it?"

Jack stared. "A real Dragon?"

"As real as you and I. And very dangerous, I might add. Too dangerous to be let loose, but at the same time too powerful to destroy. Can't be rid of everything that frightens or troubles us in this world. Some things we simply have to put up with—Dragons and Trolls among them. Trolls aren't half as bad as Dragons, of course. Trolls cause mischief when they're on the loose, but Dragons really upset the applecart. They are a powerful force, Jack Andrew. Why, just their breath alone can foul the air for miles! And the imprint of a Dragon's paw will poison whole fields! Some Dragons are worse than others, of course. Desperado is one of them."

He paused, and his eyes twinkled as they found Jack's. "All Dragons are bothersome, but Desperado is the worst. Now and again he breaks free, and then there's the very Devil to pay. Fortunately, that doesn't happen too often. When it does, someone simply has to lock Desperado away again." He winked enigmatically. "And that takes a very special kind of magic."

Daniel lifted suddenly and bore them away, soaring out of the shadows and the gray mistiness, breaking free of the gloom. The sun caught Jack in the eyes with a burst of light that momentarily blinded him.

"Jackie!"

He thought he heard his mother calling. He blinked.

"Jackie, where are you?"

It was his mother. He blinked again and found himself sitting alone beneath the pine, one hand held out before him, palm up. The hand was empty. Pick had disappeared.

He hesitated, heard his mother call again, then climbed hurriedly to his feet and scurried for the bushes at the end of his yard. He was too late getting there to avoid being caught. His mother was alarmed at first when she saw the knot on his forehead, then angry when she realized how it had happened. She bandaged him up, then sent him to his room.

He told his parents about Pick during dinner. They listened

politely, glancing at each other from time to time, then told him everything was fine, it was a wonderful story, but that sometimes bumps on the head made us think things had happened that really hadn't. When he insisted that he had not made the story up, that it had really happened, they smiled some more and told him that they thought it was nice he had such a good imagination. Try as he might, he couldn't convince them that he was serious. Finally, after a week of listening patiently to him, his mother sat down in the kitchen with cookies and milk one morning and told him she had heard enough.

"All little boys have imaginary friends, Jackie," his mother told him. "That's part of growing up. An imaginary friend is someone whom little boys can talk to about their troubles when no one else will listen, someone they can tell their secrets to when they don't want to tell anyone else. Sometimes they can help a little boy get through some difficult times. Pick is your imaginary friend, Jackie. But you have to understand something. A friend like Pick belongs just to you, not to anyone else, and that is the way you should keep it."

He looked for Pick all that summer and into the fall, but he never found him. When his father took him into the park, he looked for Wartag under the old stone bridge. He never found him, either. He checked the skies for Daniel, but never saw anything bigger than a robin. When he finally persuaded his father to walk all the way back into the darkest part of the woods—an effort that had his father using words Jack had not often heard him use before—there was no sign of the tree that imprisoned Desperado.

Eventually, Jack gave up looking. School and his friends claimed his immediate attention, Thanksgiving rolled around, and then it was Christmas. He got a new bike that year—a two-wheeler without training wheels—and an electric train. He thought about Pick, Daniel, Wartag, and Desperado from time to time, but the memory of what they looked like began to grow hazy. He forgot many of the particulars of his adventure that summer afternoon in the park, and the adventure itself took on the trappings of one of those fairy tales Pick detested so.

Soon, Jack pretty much quit thinking about the matter altogether.

He had not thought about it for months until today.

HE WHEELED HIS bike up the driveway of his house, surprised that he could suddenly remember all the details he had forgotten. They were sharp in his mind again, as sharp as they had been on the afternoon they had happened. If they had happened. If they had really happened. He hadn't been sure for a long time now. After all, he was only a little kid then. His parents might have been right; he might have imagined it all.

But then why was he remembering it so clearly now?

He went up to his room to think, came down long enough to have dinner, and quickly went back up again. His parents had looked at him strangely all during the meal—checking, he felt, to see if he was showing any early signs of expiring. It made him feel weird.

He found he couldn't concentrate on his homework, and anyway it was Friday night. He turned off the music on his tape player, closed his books, and sat there. The clock on his nightstand ticked softly as he thought some more about what had happened almost seven years ago. What might have happened, he corrected—although the more he thought about it, the more he was beginning to believe it really had. His common sense told him that he was crazy, but when you're dying you don't have much time for common sense.

Finally he got up, went downstairs to the basement rec room, picked up the phone, and called Waddy. His friend answered on the second ring. They talked about this and that for five minutes or so, and then Jack said, "Waddy, do you believe in magic?"

Waddy laughed. "Like in the song?"

"No, like in conjuring. You know, spells and such."

"What kind of magic?"

"What kind?"

"Yeah, what kind? There's different kinds, right? Black magic and white magic. Wizard magic. Witches' brew. Horrible old New England curses. Fairies and Elves . . ."

"That kind. Fairies and Elves. Do you think there might be magic like that somewhere?"

"Are you asking me if I believe in Fairies and Elves?"

Jack hesitated. "Well, yeah."

"No."

"Not at all, huh?"

"Look, Jack, what's going on with you? You're not getting strange because of this dying business, are you? I told you not to worry about it."

"I'm not. I was just thinking . . ." He stopped, unable to tell Waddy exactly what he was thinking, because it sounded so bizarre. After all, he'd never told anyone other than his parents about Pick.

There was a thoughtful silence on the other end of the line. "If you're asking me whether I think there's some kind of magic out there that saves people from dying, then I say yes. There is."

That wasn't exactly what Jack was asking, but the answer made him feel good anyway. "Thanks, Waddy. Talk to you later."

He hung up and went back upstairs. His father intercepted him on the landing and called him down again. He told Jack he had been talking with Dr. Muller. The doctor wanted him to come into the hospital on Monday for additional tests. He might have to stay for a few days. Jack knew what that meant. He would end up like Uncle Frank. His hair would fall out. He would be sick all the time. He would waste away to nothing. He didn't want any part of it. He told his father so and without waiting for his response ran back up to his room, shut the door, undressed, turned off the lights, and lay shivering in his bed in the darkness.

*   *   *

HE FELL ASLEEP for a time, and it was after midnight when
he came awake again. He had been dreaming, but he couldn't
remember what the dreams were about. As he lay there, he
thought he heard someone calling for him. He propped himself
up on one arm and listened to the silence. He stayed that way
for a long time, thinking.

Then he rose; dressed in jeans, a pullover, and sneakers; and
crept downstairs, trying hard not to make any noise. He got as
far as the back porch. Sam was asleep on the threshold, and Jack
didn't see him. He tripped over the dog and went down hard,
striking his head on the edge of a table. He blacked out momentarily, then his eyes blinked open. Sam was cowering in one
corner, frightened half to death. Jack was surprised and grateful
that the old dog wasn't barking like crazy. That would have
brought his parents awake in a minute. He patted Sam's head
reassuringly, pulled on his windbreaker, and slipped out through
the screen door.

Silence enveloped him. Jack crossed the damp green carpet
of the backyard on cat's feet, pushed through the bushes at its
end, and went into the park. It was a warm, windless night, and
the moon shone full and white out of a cloudless sky, its silver
light streaming down through breaks in the leafy trees to chase
the shadows. Jack breathed the air and smelled pine needles and
lilacs. He didn't know what he would tell his parents if they
found him out there. He just knew he had to find Pick. Something inside whispered that he must.

He reached the old pine and peered beneath its spiky boughs.
There was no sign of Pick. He backed out and looked about the
park. Crickets chirped in the distance. The baseball diamonds
stretched away before him east to the wall of the trees where
the deep woods began. He could see the edge of the river bluff
south, a ragged tear across the night sky. The cemetery was invisible beyond the rise of the park west. Nothing moved anywhere.

Jack came forward to the edge of the nearest ball diamond, anxious now, vaguely uneasy. Maybe this was a mistake.

Then a screech shattered the silence, and Jack caught sight of a shadow wheeling across the moonlight overhead.

"Daniel!" he shouted.

Excitement coursed through him. He began to run. Daniel was circling ahead, somewhere over the edge of the bluff. Jack watched him dive and soar skyward again. Daniel was directly over the old stone bridge where Wartag lived.

As he came up to the bridge he slowed warily, remembering anew the Troll's mean-looking eyes. Then he heard his name called, and he charged recklessly ahead. He skidded down the dampened slope by the bridge's west support and peered into the shadows.

"Jack Andrew McCall, where have you been, Boy?" he heard Pick demand without so much as a perfunctory hello. "I have been waiting for you for hours!"

Jack couldn't see him at first and groped his way through the blackness.

"Over here, Boy!"

His eyes began to adjust, and he caught sight of something hanging from the underside of the bridge on a hook, close against the support. It was a cage made out of stone. He reached for it and tilted it slightly so he could look inside.

There was Pick. He looked exactly the same as he had those seven years past—a tiny man with a reddish beard, green trousers and shirt, black belt and boots, and the peculiar hat of woven pine needles. It was too dark to be certain whether or not his face was flushed, but he was so excited that Jack was certain that it must be. He was dancing about on first one foot and then the other, hopping up and down as if his boots were on fire.

"What are you doing in there?" Jack asked him.

"What does it look like I'm doing in here—taking a bath?" Pick's temper hadn't improved any. "Now listen to me, Jack Andrew, and listen carefully because I haven't the time to say this more than once!" Pick was animated, his tiny voice shrill. "Wartag set a snare for me and I blundered into it. He sets such snares constantly, but I am usually too clever to get trapped in them. This time he caught me napping. He locked me in this cage earlier tonight and abandoned me to my fate. He has gone into the deep woods to unbalance the magic. He intends to set Desperado free!" He jabbed at Jack with his finger. "You have to stop him!"

Jack started. "Me?"

"Yes, you! I don't have the means, locked away in here!"

"Well, I'll set you free then!"

Pick shook his head. "I'm afraid not. There're no locks or keys to a Troll cage. You just have to wait until it falls apart. Doesn't take long. Day or two at most. Wouldn't matter if you did free me, anyway. An Elf locked in a stone cage loses his magic for a moonrise. Everyone knows that!"

Jack gulped. "But, Pick, I can't—"

"Quit arguing with me!" the Elf stormed. "Take this!" He thrust something through the bars of the cage. It was a tiny silver pin. "Fasten it to your jacket. As long as you wear it, I can see what you see and tell you what to do. It will be the same as if I were with you. Now hurry! Get after that confounded Troll!"

"But what about you?" Jack asked anxiously.

"Don't bother yourself about me! I'll be fine!"

"But—"

"Confound it, Jack! Get going!"

Jack did as he was told, spurred on by the urgency he heard in the other's voice. He forgot momentarily what had brought him to the park in the first place. Hurriedly, he stuck the silver pin through the collar of his jacket and wheeled away. He scrambled out of the ravine beneath the bridge, darted through the fringe of trees screening the ball diamonds, and sprinted across the outfields toward the dark wall of the woods east. He looked skyward once or twice for Daniel, but the owl had disappeared. Jack could feel his heart pounding in his chest and hear the rasp of his breathing. Pick was chattering from somewhere inside his left ear, urging him on, warning that he must hurry. When he tried to ask something of the Elf, Pick cut him off with an admonition to concentrate on the task at hand.

He reached the woods at the east end of the park and disappeared into the trees. Moonlight fragmented into shards of light that scattered through the heavy canopy of limbs. Jack charged up and down hills, skittered through leaf-strewn gullies, and watched the timber begin to thicken steadily about him.

Finally, he tripped over a tree root and dropped wearily to his knees, gasping for breath. When he lifted his head again, he was aware of two things. First, the woods about him had gone completely silent. Second, there was a strange greenish light that swirled like mist in the darkness ahead.

"We are too late, Jack Andrew," he heard Pick say softly. "That bubbleheaded Troll has done his work! Desperado's free!"

Jack scrambled up quickly. "What do I do now, Pick?"

Pick's voice was calm. "Do, Jack? Why, you do what you must. You lock the Dragon away again!"

"Me?" Jack was aghast. "What am I supposed to do? I don't know anything about Dragons!"

"Stuff and nonsense! It's never too late to learn, and there's not much to learn in any case. Let's have a look, Boy. Go on! Now!"

Jack moved ahead, his feet operating independently of his brain, which was screaming at him to get the heck out of there. The misted green light began to close about him, enveloping him, filling the whole of the woods about him with a pungent smell like burning rubber. There was a deadness to the night air, and the whisper of something old and evil that echoed from far back in the woods. Jack swallowed hard against his fear.

Then he pushed through a mass of brush into a clearing ringed with pine and stopped. There was something moving aimlessly on the ground a dozen yards ahead, something small and black and hairy, something that steamed like breath exhaled on a winter's morning.

"Oh dear, oh dear," murmured an invisible Pick.

"What is it?" Jack demanded anxiously.

Pick clucked his tongue. "It would appear that Wartag has learned the hard way what happens when you fool around with Dragons."

"That's Wartag?"

"More or less. Keep moving, Jack. Don't worry about the Troll."

But Jack's brain had finally regained control of his feet. "Pick, I don't want anything more to do with this. I can't fight a Dragon! I only came because I . . . because I found out that . . ."

"You were dying."

Jack stared. "Yes, but how——"

"Did I know?" Pick finished. "Tut and posh, boy! Why do you think you're here? Now listen up. Time to face a rather unpleasant truth. You have to fight the Dragon whether you want to or not. He knows that you're here now, and he will come for you if you try to run. He needs to be locked away, Jack. You can do it. Believe me, you can."

Jack's heart was pounding. "How?"

"Oh, it's simple enough. You just push him from sight, back him into his cage, and that's that! Now, let's see. There! To your left!"

Jack moved over a few steps and reached down. It was a battered old metal garbage can lid. "A shield!" declared Pick's voice in his ear. "And there!" Jack moved to his right and reached down again. It was a heavy stick that some hiker had discarded. "A sword!" Pick announced.

Jack stared at the garbage can lid and the stick in turn and then shook his head hopelessly. "This is ridiculous! I'm supposed to fight a Dragon with these?"

"These and what's inside you," Pick replied softly.

"But I can't——"

"Yes, you can."

"But—"

"Jack! You have to! You must!" Pick's words were harsh and clipped, the tiny voice insistent. "Don't you understand? Haven't you been listening to me? This fight isn't simply to save me or this park! This fight is to save you!"

Jack was confused. Why was this a fight to save him? It didn't make any sense. But something deep inside him whispered that the Elf was telling him the truth. He swallowed his fear, choked down his self-doubt, hefted his makeshift sword and shield, and started forward. He went quickly, afraid that if he slowed he would give it up altogether. He knew somehow that he couldn't do that. He eased his way warily ahead through the trees, searching the greenish mist. Maybe the Dragon wasn't as scary as he imagined. Maybe it wasn't like the Dragons in the fairy tales. After all, would Pick send him into battle against something like that, something he wouldn't have a chance against?

There was movement ahead.

"Pick?" he whispered anxiously.

A shadow heaved upward suddenly out of the mist, huge and baleful, blocking out the light. Jack stumbled back.

There was Desperado. The Dragon rose against the night like a wall, weaving and swaying, a thing of scales and armor plates, a creature of limbs and claws, a being that was born of Jack's foulest nightmare. It had shape and no shape, formed of bits and pieces of fears and doubts that were drawn from a dozen memories best forgotten. It filled the pathway ahead with its bulk, as massive as the crooked, shaggy tree from which it had been freed.

Jack lurched to an unsteady halt, gasping. Eyes as hard as polished stone pinned him where he stood. He could feel the heat of the Dragon against his skin and at the same time an intense cold in the pit of his stomach. He was sweating and shivering all at once, and his breath threatened to seize up within his chest. He was no longer thinking; he was only reacting. Desperado's hiss sounded in the pit of his stomach. It told him he carried no shield, no sword. It told him he had no one to help him. It told him that he was going to die.

Fear spread quickly through Jack, filling him with its vile taste, leaving him momentarily helpless. He heard Pick's voice shriek wildly within his ear, "Quick, Jack, quick! Push the Dragon away!"

But Jack was already running. He bolted through the mist and trees as if catapulted, fleeing from Desperado. He was unable to help himself. He could no longer hear Pick; he could no longer reason. All he could think to do was to run as fast and as far from what confronted him as he could manage. He was only thirteen! He was only a boy! He didn't want to die!

He broke free of the dark woods and tore across the ball diamonds toward the bridge where Pick was caged. The sky was all funny, filled with swirling clouds and glints of greenish light. Everything was a mass of shadows and mist. He screamed for Pick to help him. But as he neared the bridge, its stone span seemed to yawn open like some giant's mouth, and the Dragon rose up before him, blocking his way. He turned and ran toward the Indian burial mounds, where the ghosts of the Sinnissippi danced through the shadows to a drumbeat only they could hear. But again the Dragon was waiting. It was waiting as well at the cemetery, slithering through the even rows of tombstones and markers like a snake. It was waiting amid the shrub-lined houses of Woodlawn, wherever Jack turned, wherever he fled. Jack ran from one end of the park to the other, and everywhere, the Dragon Desperado was waiting.

"Pick!" he screamed over and over, but there was no answer. When he finally thought to look down for the silver pin, he discovered that he had lost it.

"Oh, Pick!" he sobbed.

Finally he quit running, too exhausted to go on. He found himself back within the deep woods, right where he had started. He had been running, yet he hadn't moved at all. Desperado was before him still, a monstrous, shapeless terror that he could not escape. He could feel the Dragon all around him, above and below, and even within. The Dragon was inside his head, crushing him, blinding him, stealing away his life . . .

Like a sickness.

He gasped in sudden recognition.

Like the sickness that was killing him.

This fight is to save you, Pick had told him. The Elf's words came back to him, their purpose and meaning revealed with a clarity that was unmistakable.

Jack went a little bit crazy then. He cried out, overwhelmed by a rush of emotions he could not begin to define. He shed his fear as he would a burdensome coat and charged Desperado, heedless now of any danger to himself, blind to the Dragon's monstrous size. To his astonishment, the walking stick and the garbage can lid flared white with fire and turned into the sword and shield he had been promised. He could feel the fire spread from them into him, and it felt as if he had been turned to iron as well. He flung himself at Desperado, hammering into the Dragon with his weapons. *Push him back! Lock him away!*

The great gnarled shapes of the Dragon and tree seemed to join. Night and mist closed about. Jack was swimming through a fog of jagged images. He heard sounds that might have come from anywhere, and there was within him a sense of something yielding. He thrust out, feeling Desperado give way before his attack. The feeling of heat, the smell of burning rubber, the scrape of scales and armor plates intensified and filled his senses.

Then Desperado simply disappeared. The sword and shield turned back into the walking stick and garbage can lid, the greenish mist dissipated into the night, and Jack found himself clinging to the shaggy, bent trunk of the massive old tree that was the Dragon's prison.

He stumbled back, dumbstruck.

"Pick!" he shouted one final time, but there was no answer.

Then everything went black and he was falling.

* * *

JACK WAS IN the hospital when he came awake. His head was wrapped with bandages and throbbed painfully. When he asked, one of the nurses on duty told him it was Saturday. He had suffered a bad fall off his back porch in the middle of the night, she said, and his parents hadn't found him until early this morning when they had brought him in. She added rather cryptically that he was a lucky boy.

His parents appeared shortly after, both of them visibly upset, alternately hugging him and scolding him for being so stupid. He was still rather groggy, and not much of what they said registered. They left when the nurse interceded, and he went back to sleep.

The next day, Dr. Muller appeared. He examined Jack, grunted and muttered as he did so, drew blood, sent him down for X-rays, brought him back up, grunted and muttered some more, and left. Jack's parents came by to visit and told him they would be keeping him in the hospital for a few more days, just in case. Jack told them he didn't want any therapy while he was there, and they promised there wouldn't be.

On Monday morning, his parents and Dr. Muller came to see him together. His mother cried and called him "Jackie" and his father grinned like the Cheshire cat. Dr. Muller told him that the additional tests had been completed while he was asleep. The results were very encouraging. His blood disorder did not appear to be life threatening. They had caught it early enough that it could be treated.

"You understand, Jack, you'll have to undergo some mild therapy," Dr. Muller cautioned. "But we can take care of that right here. There's nothing to worry about."

Jack smiled. He wasn't worried. He knew he was okay. He'd known it from the moment he'd pushed Desperado back into that tree. That was what the fight to lock away the Dragon had been all about. It had been to lock away Jack's sickness. Jack wasn't sure whether or not Pick had really lost his magic that night or simply let Jack think so. But he was sure about one thing—Pick had deliberately brought him back into the park and made him face the Dragon on his own. That was the special magic that his friend had once told him would be needed. It was the magic that had allowed him to live.

He went home at the end of the week and returned to school the next. When he informed Waddy Wadsworth that he wasn't dying after all, his friend just shrugged and said he'd told him so. Dr. Muller advised him to take it easy and brought him in for the promised therapy throughout the summer months. But his hair didn't fall out, he didn't lose weight, and the headaches and vision loss disappeared. Eventually Dr. Muller declared him cured, and the treatments came to an end.

He never saw Pick again. Once or twice he thought he saw Daniel, but he wasn't certain. He looked for the tree that imprisoned Desperado, but he couldn't find it. He didn't look for Wartag at all. When he was a few years older, he went to work for the park service during the summers. It made him feel that he was giving something back to Pick. Sometimes when he was in the park, he could sense the other's presence. It didn't matter that he couldn't see his friend; it was enough just to know that he was there.

He never said anything to anyone about the Elf, of course. He wasn't going to make that mistake again.

It was like his mother had told him when he was little. A friend like Pick belonged only to him, and that was the way he should keep it.

Introduction to
"The Weapons Master's Choice"

HERE WE ARE, back to another Garet Jax story. I should probably just give in to the undeniable impulse and devote a whole book to him tramping about the countryside doing in bad men and evil creatures in the manner of Conan the Barbarian. But so far I have kept myself under control and written only a few. This one took some thinking. I wanted to show how even a man who had mastered weapons and the martial arts—and had such a strong belief in his skills and experience that he was afraid of nothing—was not immune to pain of another sort.

His character had been fully established in *The Wishsong of Shannara,* so those who had been clamoring for another story already knew who and what he was and needed to be shown something they hadn't already seen. Garet Jax was a solitary practitioner of weapons usage; he was essentially a blade for hire. But he was haunted, as well: by his life, by those he had killed, by what he had made of himself. He was the best at what he did, but he was always testing himself to see if there wasn't something or someone better. It was the challenge this sort of testing offered that gave him his purpose in life. Others that were skilled with weapons, demons like the Jachyra he would eventually come to face in *Wishsong,* predators relying on sheer numbers to drag him down and finish him—what was out there that would require even more of him than had ever been given challenge before?

A harsh truth faces that man or woman who is the best. What is left when no further challenges remain? What gives life purpose when you have achieved everything? Garet knows the possibilities and continues to seek them out. He has never lost a fight, never lost a struggle, and never faced defeat because he is so good at what he does and so well prepared for whatever he might come up against.

What happens, then, when he encounters something completely different in look and tone from all the dark things he has faced before—something that he cannot come to grips with using martial arts or blades or past experience? What if he cannot recognize it for what it is when he encounters it?

What does he turn to then?

THE WEAPONS
MASTER'S CHOICE

HE HEARD THE woman coming long before he saw her. She was making no attempt to hide her approach, which suggested she intended him no harm, and this allowed him to sit back to wait on her. It was early evening, the sun gone below the horizon, the darkness settled in, and the purple-hued twilight filled with the sounds of insects and night birds. He was camped several miles outside of Tombara, an Eastland Dwarf village at the western edge of the Wolfsktaag Mountains below the Rabb River. He was there because he was looking for a small measure of peace and quiet and believed this was a place he could find it.

Wrong again.

Of course, she could have simply wandered in from the wilderness, following the smells of his dinner on the evening breeze. She could have appeared solely by chance and with no premeditation. The chances of that, by his reckoning, were only about a thousand to one.

Still, stranger things had happened, and he had borne witness to many of them.

He shifted slightly on the fallen log he was occupying, taking a moment to glance down at the skillet where his dinner was sizzling. Fresh cutthroat, caught by his own hand that very day. Fishing was a skill others would assume he had no time for, but a lot of the assumptions people made about him were wrong. He didn't mind this. If anything, he encouraged it. Wrong assumptions were helpful in his line of work.

He rose as he heard her near the edge of his campsite. His black clothing hung loose and easy on his slender frame, and his gray eyes were a match for his prematurely silver hair and the narrow beard to which he had taken a fancy of late. He was young—less than thirty—and the smoothness of his face betrayed this. He stared at the shadowed space through which he judged the woman must pass if she kept to her current trajectory, and then he heard her stop where she was.

He said nothing. He gave her time.

"Are you Garet Jax?" she asked from the darkness.

"And if I am?" he called back.

"Then I would speak with you."

No hesitation, no equivocating. She had come looking for him, and she had a reason for doing so.

"Come sit with me then. You can share my dinner. Are you hungry?"

She stepped from the trees into the firelight, and while she was in many ways a woman of ordinary appearance, there was something striking about her. He saw it at once, and it gave him pause. Perhaps it was nothing more than the unusual auburn color of her short-cropped hair. Perhaps it was the way she carried herself, as if she was entirely comfortable in her own skin and unconcerned with what others thought. Perhaps it was something else—a resolve and acceptance reflected in her strange green eyes, a suggestion of having to come to terms with something that was hidden from him.

She was carrying nothing. No pack, no supplies, no weapons. It made him wonder if she was alone. No one traveled this country without at least a long knife and a blanket.

She crossed the clearing, her eyes locked on his. She wore a long travel cloak pulled tight about her shoulders and fastened at the neck. Perhaps she kept her weapons concealed beneath.

"I am alone, if you are wondering," she said without being asked. "They told me at the Blue Hen Tavern in Tombara that you were here."

"No one knows where I am," he said.

"They didn't say you were in this exact spot. But they knew you were somewhere nearby. I found you on my own. I have a gift for finding lost things."

"I'm not lost," he said.

"Aren't you?" she replied.

He gave no response, but wondered at the meaning behind her words. She moved over to the log he had been occupying earlier and sat down—although not too close to where he stood. He waited a moment and then joined her, respecting the distance she had chosen to keep.

"Who are you?" he asked.

"My name is Lyriana." She glanced down at the long leather case propped up against a smaller log off to one side. "Are those your weapons?"

"Yes." He studied her. "But you already knew that, didn't you?"

"I know what they call you. The Weapons Master. But you seem awfully young to be a master of anything."

"How do you know of me?"

She shrugged. "Stories told here and there. Word travels, even to places as remote as where I have come from. Most of the stories are good ones. People like to tell stories of disappointment and betrayal, of men and women who have suffered heartbreak and loss. But they don't tell those stories about you. And they say you are a man who makes a bargain and keeps it."

"My word is an important part of what I have to sell."

"It's said you don't fear long odds. That you once confronted as many as a dozen armed men and killed them all in the blink of an eye with nothing but your hands."

"Two blinks of an eye and a knife. Why have you come to find me? What need do you have of a man like me?"

She thought about it a moment, and then she smiled. "Can we eat first? Your trout is in danger of being overcooked."

He poured ale from a skin into tin cups and they sat together in silence while they ate their meal. All around them, the night sounds quickened as the darkness deepened and the quarter moon and stars came out. From out of a cloudless sky, clean white moonlight flooded the woods.

When they were finished, he scraped the plates and rubbed them clean with grasses before beginning on the skillet.

"You take good care of your equipment," she observed.

He smiled. "What do you wish of me, Lyriana?"

She smiled back, but it was quick and small. "Help. I want you to come with me to Tajarin, my home city. I want you to stop what's happening there. My people are being decimated. A warlock of enormous power is preying upon them. His name is Kronswiff. Do you know the name?"

He shook his head. "Nor do I know of Tajarin, and I thought there was no city in all of the Four Lands of which I had not heard. How did I miss this one?"

"It lies far outside the usual routes of travel, north and east on the shores of the Tiderace. It is very old. Once it was a seaport, hundreds of years ago, but those days are gone. Now it is home to my people and no longer known to the larger world. But what matters is that those who live there cannot protect themselves against what is being done to them. They stay because they have nowhere else to go. They need someone like you to help them."

"The Tiderace is a long way from here. I am awaiting word of a commission from Tyrsis. Agreeing to come with you would disrupt those plans."

"Are you refusing me?"

"I haven't heard enough yet to decide."

Her lips tightened. "I need someone who will not turn on my people once the warlock is defeated. They are vulnerable, and I want to be sure they will be left alone afterward. There are few whose reputations suggest they could be counted on to do the right thing."

She paused. "I am running out of time. I was sent because I was the strongest and most capable. Kronswiff bleeds my people as cattle are milked; many are already gone. If we do not hurry back, they will all be lost."

"He is only one man. Are there not enough of you to stand against him?"

"He is not simply one man; he is a warlock. And he has men who follow him and do his bidding. They have taken over the city, and those of us he has not imprisoned are in hiding. No one dares to challenge him. A handful did so early on and were quickly dispatched."

She paused. "This will not be an easy task. Not even for you. The warlock is powerful. His men are dangerous. But you are our best hope."

"Perhaps a unit of the Border Legion might be a better choice. They undertake rescues of this sort when the need is clear."

She shook her head. "Did you not hear what I said? We are speaking of a warlock. Ordinary men—even ones with courage and weapons and determination—will not be strong enough to stand against him. Will you come?"

"What am I to be paid for this?"

"Do you care?"

That stopped him. He stared at her. "Are you telling me you want me to do this for nothing? That there is to be no payment?"

She curled her lip. "I had judged you to be a better man than this. I had been told that money meant nothing to you. It was the challenge you cared about. Is this not so? Is money what matters? Because if it is, I will pledge you all the coin in the city, every last piece of gold and silver you can carry away."

"All of your coin; all of your silver and gold? All of it?" He laughed. "What does that mean? That you don't have any gold or silver? Or have you so much you can afford to give it away?"

"It means that our lives are more precious than our riches. That our peace of mind and security are worth more than whatever must be paid to protect them. I'll ask you once again. Will you come with me?"

Something about what she was telling him felt wrong, and his instincts warned him that she was keeping secrets. But they also told him that her need was genuine, and her plea for his assistance was heartfelt and desperate.

"How far is Tajarin?" he asked her.

"Perhaps seven or eight days," she said.

"On horseback?"

"Horses can't get to where we are going. So mostly we must go on foot. Does this matter?"

He shrugged.

"Will you come, then?"

He finished with the skillet, taking his time. "Let me sleep on it. Come back to me in the morning."

She shook her head. "I have nowhere to go. I will sleep here with you."

He studied her carefully. Then he rose, brought out his extra blanket, and handed it to her. "Find a place close to the fire. It gets cold at night."

Wordlessly, she accepted his offering, walked over to the other side of the fire, spread the blanket, and rolled herself into it so that her back was to him.

He remained awake awhile longer, thinking through what she had told him, trying to come to a decision. It should have been easy. She was asking him to risk his life to save her people; he deserved complete honesty. If she was not telling him the entire truth, he should send her on her way.

But there was something about her that intrigued him, something that drew him—an undeniable attraction. He felt it in the mix of determination and vulnerability she projected. The contrast was compelling in a visceral way. He couldn't quite explain it, although he felt a need to do so. He would have to think on it some more.

He lay down finally, having no reason to remain awake longer, and was almost asleep when he heard her say, "You should make up your mind as soon as possible."

He opened his eyes and stared into the darkness. "Why is that?"

"Because I might have been followed."

HE DIDN'T SLEEP much after that, but when he sat up suddenly sometime after midnight, the moon had moved across the sky northwest of the clearing and the stars had shifted their positions. He hadn't heard anything, but he was the Weapons Master and his highly developed instincts warned him even in his sleep. He sat up slowly and looked around.

Lyriana was sitting on the log once more, still wrapped in her blanket. She met his gaze and pointed into the trees. He couldn't imagine how she had heard what was out there before he did, but apparently she had, and he reassessed his view of her abilities immediately. She was definitely something more than she seemed.

He slipped from the blanket, rolled it into the shape of a sleeping man, and left it on the ground. Then he brought out a pair of throwing knives from beneath his loose garments. He made no sound doing so and none as he moved toward the trees, listening. For long seconds, he heard nothing. Then there came a slight rustle of clothing and the scrape of a boot against the earth.

He dropped into a crouch at the center of a deep pool of shadows. There were at least two of them. Possibly three.

He glanced over his shoulder at Lyriana, sitting on the log, and motioned for her to lie down. If she remained sitting up as she was, she presented an inviting target for a blade or an arrow. He waited for her to comply, but she just shook her head.

Then he realized what she was doing. She wasn't simply being stubborn. She was offering herself as a target to distract their attackers.

He quit breathing and went perfectly still.

They came out of the trees, three of them, wrapped head-to-toe in black, faces covered, hands gloved, no skin showing. Two carried knives, the third a crossbow. Because they were looking for him to be sleeping by the fire with Lyriana, they didn't see him in the shadows, even when they were right on top of him.

Then the one with the crossbow raised it to eye level and sent a bolt whizzing toward Lyriana.

He was fitting a second into place when Garet Jax killed him, piercing his heart with one of the throwing knives. The Weapons Master went straight at the other two. Agile and cat-quick, he killed the first before the man could defend himself and was on the second an instant later. Locked in combat, the pair rolled across the campsite and into the fire. Flames snatched at their clothing and began to burn, but neither relinquished his hold. In a silence punctuated only by gasps and grunts, each fought to break the other's grip.

Until, finally, Garet Jax employed a twist and pull that yanked his adversary's knife arm down and in, turning his own momentum against him. The man stumbled away, his own blade buried in his chest. He was still trying to figure out how it had happened when the Weapons Master finished him.

Everything went silent then, a hush settling over the campsite and its occupants, living and dead. Garet Jax rolled to his feet, snuffed out the last of the flames that burned his clothing, and did a quick search of the shadows. Nothing moved, and no one else appeared.

He turned back to Lyriana, remembering the crossbow. But she was still sitting on the log, the bolt lying at her feet. She watched him a moment, read the unasked question in his expression, and shrugged. "I was ready. He waited too long, so he missed me."

Garet Jax moved over to the dead men, pulled off their masks, and began to search them. All three had a triangle with a star at each corner tattooed on their right wrists. They were Het— mercenaries out of Varfleet, killers for hire and very good at their trade. He looked back at Lyriana. How a Het could have missed his target from no more than twenty feet, even at night and in shadow, was difficult to imagine.

But he left the matter alone.

"Come here," she said.

He complied, and she lifted away the remnants of his burned tunic, turned him about so she could examine his wounds, and then seated him on the log. Pulling a pouch from beneath her cloak, she began placing leaves against his burns. As soon as the leaves touched his skin, they began to dissolve, becoming a kind of paste that cooled and soothed. He sat quietly while she worked, surprised anew.

"I have never seen such medicine before," he said. "Where did you find it?"

"You can find many things you never thought you would if your need is desperate enough," she answered.

When she was finished, she ran her hands over his shoulders, her touch making him shiver. It had been a very long time since he had been touched so. In seconds the last remnants of pain from his burns disappeared.

"*Now* are you coming with me, Garet Jax?" she asked.

He nodded. "Now I am," he said.

But he suspected she already knew as much.

THEY SET OUT at sunrise, walking back into Tombara where he purchased a pair of horses and supplies for the trip ahead. She had said it would take them at least a week, so he spent his coins accordingly, allowing enough for a few days extra in case things did not go exactly as planned. He asked her what had happened to her supplies and weapons while traveling to find him, and she told him she had used up the first and had not bothered to bring the second. When he suggested she needed both for the journey back, she surprised him by saying weapons were of no use to her.

Even so, he provided her with a long knife and sheath and a backpack. Since she had nothing to put into the backpack, he stuffed the blanket he had given her inside, along with a few coins, and suggested she rethink her needs.

Then leaving her to make her own decision on the matter, he went down through the village and made a few discreet inquiries regarding the Het. Had anyone seen them? No. Had anyone talked to them? No. Apparently, they had tracked Lyriana all the way to where she had met with him and then decided he was the one she had come to find—and this was reason enough to put an end to both of them.

Still, it bothered him. They had clearly followed Lyriana, but if she suspected this—which apparently she had—then why hadn't she done more to hide her trail? She seemed capable enough about so many other things. Was she simply inexperienced at concealing her tracks?

As they rode out of the village and traveled north along the base of the Wolfsktaag Mountains, he thought more than once to ask her. But each time he was on the verge of bringing the matter up, he backed away from doing so. It was hard to say why. Perhaps it felt too intrusive, too accusatory, when he did not want to appear to be either. Perhaps it bordered too closely on assuming a confrontational posture with someone he did not feel deserved it.

Or perhaps it had something to do with the inexplicable need he felt to share her company, a compelling pull on him he could not begin to explain.

Whatever the case, he let the matter drop and concentrated on the task of guiding them north along the base of the Wolfsktaag to where they could cross the Rabb River and travel on into the forests of the Upper Anar. By nightfall of the first day, they were well on their way toward the Ravenshorn and the darker forests that layered those jagged peaks all the way to the Tiderace.

When it was nearing nightfall, he brought them to shelter provided by trees and a series of rock outcroppings. Once the horses were cared for and their camp set, he cooked them dinner. Afterward, they sat together in front of the fire and watched it turn slowly to embers.

"Will your people join me in my fight against Kronswiff and his Het? How many of you live in Tajarin?"

She gave him a look. "More than enough. But they are not warlike. They do not understand fighting. They are helpless in the face of aggression of the sort that Kronswiff represents. So, no, they will not help you."

He shook his head. It seemed hard to believe that any people could be so passive. Yet there were examples of this sort of domination throughout history, of a few intimidating many. He was being judgmental and he had no right to be so, especially when the leader of the enemy was a warlock. "Men do what they can, I guess."

"Men and women," she corrected, as if the distinction was important. "Perhaps you will inspire us."

"Have you family?"

"None. All of them have been gone a long time, save for my brother. He was one of those who stood up to the warlock."

He remembered something she had said earlier. "The warlock drains them, you said. He bleeds them out. Literally?"

Wrapped in her heavy cloak, she had the look of a shade. Everything but her face was covered, and the shadows cast by the folds of her hood had reduced her features to vague outlines. He watched her consider his question and took note of the sudden stillness that had settled over her.

"He bleeds them of their souls," she said at last. "He feeds on them as a dracul does. It is the source of his power."

"He nourishes his own life with theirs?"

Her eyes glittered. "He reduces them to husks. Then life

fades and they are gone. I have watched it happen. I have witnessed the results of his invasion. He would have taken my life, as well, if he had found me. But I escaped his notice for a long time. And finally, at the urging of others, I fled the city and came looking for you."

She paused. "But I am not a good and noble person, so do not try to make more of me than what I really am—a coward, fleeing what I fear to face. I am the representative of my people, but I do this as much for myself as for them. I do not pretend to any sort of elevated status, or to a courage I do not possess, or to anything but desperation."

"I think you underrate yourself," he said. "Coming to find me on your own, daring to risk capture and worse—that was brave."

"You risk more than I do."

"But I am better equipped to risk more. I have skills and experience."

And I have less to lose, he almost added. But he chose not to say that, because it would have required an explanation he did not want to give. He did not want to tell her his life held so little value that he barely cared if he lived or died. If he told her that, he would have to tell her, too, that the men he had killed and the risks he had taken were all he had to persuade him that his life had any meaning at all. When you began walking the path he had walked since he was twelve years of age, you found out quickly enough that it did not offer convenient escape routes. When you were so good that fears and doubts were almost nonexistent and challenges that heightened both were your sole pleasure in life, you kept walking because turning aside was a failure you could not tolerate.

She moved over to sit beside him—an act that surprised and pleased him—and he suddenly felt a need for her that was almost overpowering. He wanted to love her; he wanted her to love him back. What would it hurt, out here in the middle of nowhere? What harm could come of it, the two of them sharing a few fleeting moments of even the most temporal form of love?

But when he reached out to take her hand in his, she drew back at once. "Don't touch me," she whispered. He watched her shrink visibly. "Please, just sit with me. Just be with me. I cannot give you more than that."

So he settled for what she was willing to offer, and they sat together until the embers died and the night closed down.

But all the time he was thinking of what it would be like to share more.

THEY SET OUT again at daybreak, the first light a silvery blush against the eastern horizon, creeping skyward above the mountains and trees of the Ravenshorn and the Anar. He had slept soundly after they had gone to bed, their brief closeness ended, and the feelings he had experienced the previous night now seemed a lifetime away. He could not recapture them, though he sought to do so as they rode. He was troubled by this, but even more troubled that he had wanted her so badly. It was not his way to desire the company of others. He lived alone, he traveled alone; he existed as a solitary man. It could never be any other way, and he knew this as surely as he knew that his skills set him apart in a dozen different ways from normal men and women. Yet her failure to respond to him had left him strangely despondent.

Why did he feel this way? Why was Lyriana different from every other woman he had ever encountered? Because it was undeniable that she made him feel something others didn't; he could admit it if not embrace it. He was attracted to her—had been attracted to her from the first—in a way that was both visceral and emotional. It was a deep and painful longing, one that transcended anything he had ever felt.

Lyriana. What was it about her that compelled him so strongly? Try as he might, he could not identify it.

They rode through the day, traveling north and east to the shores of the Tiderace, where the Ravenshorn ended in huge cliffs that rose thousands of feet over the waters of the ocean. There was no passage offered along the shoreline and no trails into the mountains that would allow for horses. So after spending the night where they stopped to make their camp, they released their horses the following day to find their way home again and set out on foot. This was new country to him, a place to which he had never traveled and about which he knew nothing. They walked all that day and the next, climbing and descending along narrow footpaths, wending their way among massive rock walls and towering peaks, as tiny as ants against the landscape. The air turned colder the higher they went, and on the third night it was so frigid they rolled into their blankets and huddled together for warmth inside a shallow cave. But there was little warmth to be found, and they rose early. That day was the worst, so bitter that ice formed on the surface of the rocks and the wind cut with the sharpness of a knife blade.

But Lyriana never once asked to rest. He made her stop when he thought it necessary, but he never heard her complain and never saw her falter. She was amazingly strong and resilient, and she knew exactly where to go, leading him on with a determination and certainty that he did not once think to challenge.

They spoke little as they proceeded, in part because of the wind's howl and in part because she seemed to prefer it that way. His attraction to her did not diminish, but he sensed that she had moved away from him and might not come back again. He did not think it was anything he had said or done, but was instead based on something else altogether.

Even in the absence of conversation, he watched her. He watched her all the time, compulsively and unrepentantly. She walked ahead of him, and he studied the movement of her body, her gait steady and fluid. He tried to look away but found himself drawn back time and time again. Watching her was so pleasurable that he quickly found justification for doing so. She was in his care. She was vulnerable in ways he was not. She was right in front of him; where else was he supposed to look?

At least it passed the time. It made his travel more pleasant.

But it made his heart ache, as well. It made him think of things he had not thought about in years.

On the eighth day, having crossed through the Ravenshorn and begun their descent on the far side, they came in sight of Tajarin.

It was late in the afternoon, the skies heavily clouded and the smell of rain in the air. They were close enough to sea level by now that the chill was mostly gone, and a more temperate breeze warmed them sufficiently that Garet Jax had shed his travel cloak and strapped it over one shoulder. Lyriana still wore hers, however, seemingly indifferent to the rise and fall of the temperature. Ahead, through gaps in the peaks of the Ravenshorn, small swatches of dark water were visible where the Tiderace could be glimpsed. They were navigating a twisting path through deep clefts and narrow defiles when the way forward abruptly widened, and there was the city.

Garet Jax stopped where he was and stared. To say that Tajarin was bleak was a monumental understatement. It was a ragged jumble of walls and battlements and towers that looked to have been charred by a massive fire that—in some long-ago time—had swept the city. Everything visible was blackened; no hint of color showed. Low-slung clouds scraped the tallest buildings and cast a pall over the whole of the city, leaving it layered in shadows. There were no people visible on the walls. Within, no one could be seen moving about.

There were no lights anywhere, not even atop the watchtowers. The city looked dead.

Who comes to a place like this?

He could not imagine. It was certainly not a trade route; their journey in had confirmed that. There was nothing attractive or interesting about it, nothing that would bring people to visit for any but the most pressing of reasons.

Lyriana caught his attention. "My people—those who are not already prisoners of Kronswiff—are in hiding. But make no mistake. The Het are abroad and keep watch upon this road— and on the Tiderace, as well."

He pondered how they might escape notice when entering the city. Nightfall would help, if the moon and stars stayed hidden behind the clouds and no torchlight revealed their approach. He studied the bending of the narrow road that led up to the city gates, and then visually backtracked its route to see if another choice might present itself.

He found what he was looking for quickly enough. But while scaling the walls would prove easy enough for him, he wasn't so sure about Lyriana. And he would need her help once he was inside to find his way.

They descended farther, still sufficiently concealed against the dark backdrop of the mountains to escape being caught out. But once the way forward flattened and smoothed into a gentle slope leading up to the gates and the mountain walls fell away, he moved her back into the rocks.

"Sit here," he told her, after taking a quick look around to be certain they were well enough concealed.

She sat obediently, finding amid the boulders a resting place against a broad stone surface. Leaving her there momentarily, he stepped back outside their shelter to scan the scarred walls of the city, making sure there was no fresh activity, then rejoined her.

"We'll wait here for darkness," he said. "Then we'll go into the city and find Kronswiff and his Het."

"What will you do when you find them?"

His gray eyes found hers. "Whatever I think best."

"But you will set my people free?"

He nodded, saying nothing. He took some bread from his backpack, tore off a hunk, and handed it to her. Then he took some for himself.

"There are a great many for you to overcome," she said.

He shrugged. "There always are."

"I wish I could help you."

"Maybe you can. Do you know where Kronswiff can be found once we're inside the walls?" He waited for her nod. "Then that will be help enough."

They were silent for a long time after that, finishing their spare meal and washing it down with water from their skins. The darkness began to deepen as night settled in, and the wind died into a strange hushed silence.

"Why do your people stay in Tajarin?" he asked. "What keeps them here?"

She shrugged. "It is their home. For most, it is all they know. They seek quiet and seclusion; they desire privacy. They find it here."

"But doesn't it bother them to be so isolated? Surely no travelers come this way, or any traders. How do you manage to live? Have you livestock of any sort? Or crops? How do you find food?"

"We have gardens that in better weather yield crops. We have some livestock, a sufficient number that we don't starve. Sometimes we leave long enough to bring back supplies from other places. But no one comes to Tajarin. Not even ships, as in the old days. There are not enough of us to bother with. And the waters of the Tiderace are treacherous. The risk is not worth it. Only Kronswiff and his Het have come here in my lifetime. No one else."

He hesitated. "Have you thought about leaving? About going somewhere else? Before now, I mean? Before you came looking for me?"

She looked down at her feet. "Not before now."

The way she said it suggested that maybe she was considering the possibility. Perhaps because of him. But he said nothing of this, leaving the matter where it was. Another time, he would ask her, when this business with her people was over and done.

He kept them waiting another hour, remaining in the concealment of the rocks, biding their time. Her reticence was a clear indicator of her wishes, and they talked little. He let her be until the light was gone from the skies and the blackness complete, and then he brought her to her feet and took her back out onto the road.

The way forward was dark with shadows and gloom. His eyesight was good in the darkness—perhaps because he had spent so much time there—and after leaving the road, he found their path to the walls of the city without difficulty. Standing motionless, he listened for long moments but heard nothing. Producing a slender rope, he then fastened it to a collapsible grappling hook and heaved it over the wall. It caught on the first try, and after testing it with his weight he went up the wall like a spider. Once safely on top and having determined he was alone, he motioned for her to fasten the rope about her slender waist. Then he hauled her up, hand-over-hand, to join him.

Stashing the rope and grappling hook in his pack, he searched the maze of empty squares and city streets below. "Which way do we go?" he whispered.

She led him down a stone stairway to their left and from there into the heart of the city. Tajarin was built on a series of terraced levels that descended from high above the Tiderace—from where they had first stood upon the city walls—to the shores of a waterfront. Ships rocked at their berths against sagging wooden docks, and not one of them looked fit enough to set sail. Everywhere he cast about, he found dilapidation and ruin. The city appeared not to have been cared for in years. Decay and rot had weakened crossbeams and supports, and even the walls were beginning to crumble where wind and rain had scoured and eroded their surfaces.

The minutes crawled past as they made their way down one empty street after another, past gloom-filled alleyways and alcoves, past buildings dark and silent. No other person appeared, and not a single sound could be heard save the rush of the wind through the towers and parapets and the wash of the waves against the piers and shoreline.

Garet Jax glanced about, his gaze shifting. *Is there anybody here at all? Where are Lyriana's people?*

Only once did he detect another presence, and he backed them into a darkened entry and waited in silence as a pair of the Het passed by on their way to the back wall. A changing of the guard, he assumed, so at least he knew the city was not entirely abandoned and his purpose in coming was not in vain.

Finally, after descending through four of the terraced levels, they arrived at a complex of boxy, multistory buildings connected by adjoining walls so that they resembled a jumble of monstrous blocks. He had seen such buildings before in other cities, each designed to achieve the same purpose—to create something awe inspiring, something magnificent due solely to size and weight. But there was never any beauty or grace in such fat, squat structures no matter how large, and so it was here.

Ignoring his hesitation, Lyriana moved past him along the facing wall to where a single door was recessed into the stone. She produced a key from her pocket, and in moments they were inside, standing in the darkness.

He waited as he heard her rummaging about, and then abruptly a small light flared and he saw that its source was a crystal she was holding. "This way," she whispered.

They crept down countless corridors deep into the interior of the complex, edging their way forward with the help of the crystal's bright light. They passed dozens of doors and a handful of chambers open to the passageways they followed, but everything remained silent and empty. Once, they descended one set of stairs, and then shortly afterward climbed back up another. There were no lights anywhere. In a few of the corridors they passed down, windows closed over by heavy drapes and wooden shutters let in slivers of ambient light through cracks in the fabric and boards.

When they heard the first murmurs coming from somewhere still far ahead, Lyriana stopped him where he was and backed him against the wall.

"You must promise me," she said, "that if your efforts to save my people fail, you will not let me be taken alive."

He could barely see her face in the deep gloom—only the curve of one cheek, a burnished lock of auburn hair, a glint of bright eyes—so he could not read her intent in making this request.

"I won't fail," he said.

"I can't let Kronswiff do to me what he's done to the others," she continued, almost as if she hadn't heard him.

He was taken aback by the intensity in her voice. "No one will do anything to you. Don't even show yourself. Stay out of sight."

"You don't know. You haven't seen what happens yet. If you are killed, I don't want to be left in his hands. If I am to die, I wish it to be on my own terms. That will not happen if Kronswiff takes me alive. Promise me!"

He was stunned by the change in her behavior, as if simply the act of returning to Tajarin was enough to peel away the confidence she had displayed in coming to find him in the first place. There was real fear in her voice, and he was suddenly convinced there was something important she wasn't telling him.

He reached for her, intending to offer reassurance, but she shrank away instantly, just as she had at the start of their journey. "No, don't," she whispered so softly he could barely hear her. "Just promise me."

His hands dropped away. He felt a vague disappointment, but quickly brushed it aside with a small shrug. "All right. If it makes you feel better, I promise."

She started them down the corridor once more, still leading the way. As they progressed, the murmurs ahead grew louder and more distinct, containing recognizable words. Lyriana slowed, and he detected the beginnings of hesitation and uncertainty. He almost took her arm, but he remembered her earlier reticence and held back. Better to let her do this alone.

She did so, easing ahead through the darkness, tracking their way with the crystal's glow. In only moments a fresh brightness shone ahead, the flicker of torches burning through the dark. The voices rose and fell, interspersed with laughter and shouts. It sounded like a party, like men gathered in a tavern to share drinks and tales of the road. Garet Jax felt a surge of adrenaline as he anticipated what lay ahead.

But such was his conditioning that, for him, a sensation that would have made most men tense and even fearful instead had a strangely calming effect. He knew it well; it greeted him like an old, familiar friend.

When they reached a stairwell branching off the corridor and leading upward, Lyriana turned into it. They climbed twenty steps to an overlook encircling the chamber below, then moved forward to where they could peer downward through gaps in the stone balustrades.

The chamber floor was open and sprawling, and the torches generated more smoke than light, leaving the corners of the room layered in hazy darkness. A leather-wrapped settee sat atop a broad platform that dominated the center of the room, its brass-studded fastenings glimmering like cat's eyes. Upon it reclined a large, corpulent figure wrapped in dark robes and laden with silver chains and pendants. The Het were gathered all about—some acting as guards, others simply watching the proceedings. They joked and laughed freely and seemed unconcerned if they were heard or not. The figure on the settee ignored them, round face flushed and sweating as he drained a tankard of ale and gestured for more.

To one side, bodies lay piled in a wooden bin, collapsed like discarded dolls, arms and legs akimbo. Some seemed badly mutilated, and all had a strangely deflated look to them. Garet Jax counted at least ten, but there were likely others concealed by those he could see. As he watched, six of the Het shouldered the bin and carried it out of the chamber. They were gone for several long minutes, and when they returned they brought the bin back with them, empty and ready for further use.

Garet Jax studied the figure reclining on the settee. The warlock, he assumed, but he took nothing for granted. *Kronswiff?* He mouthed the name to Lyriana, gesturing. She nodded back, her face rigid with fear. *Watch,* she mouthed back.

While he waited, he counted the number of Het within the chamber below. He quit at twenty. There would be more beyond his sight lines, but hopefully not too many more. He would have to frighten off some of them. If they all came at him at once, he was finished.

Or he could wait for the group to disperse, track the warlock until he found him alone—or at least with fewer Het surrounding him—and dispatch him more easily.

A door opened to one side, eliciting shouts and cheers, and a clanking of chains announced the arrival of a prisoner. It was a woman, stooped and ragged, her head lowered as she was led into the chamber to stand before the warlock. The room settled into an uncomfortable silence as the corpulent figure rose slightly from his reclining position to study the woman, then gestured for the release. The chains fell away, but the woman never moved. She just stood there in a posture of hopeless acceptance.

Kronswiff gestured again, this time with both hands, and the woman's head snapped up so that their eyes met. She shivered violently, her body shaking as if from extreme cold, and she cried out in despair, her voice harsh against the sudden stillness. A strange line of darkness formed a link between the woman and the warlock, and the woman's arms lifted in supplication, the tattered sleeves falling away to reveal flesh that already seemed desiccated and scabrous. She thrashed, her back arching and whipsawing, her cries becoming screams of horror.

Lyriana had not lied about what was being done to her people. Kronswiff drained the woman's life through the link he had formed between them. He fed on her until her body folded in on itself, her flesh sagged, her bones collapsed, and she fell to the floor and did not move again.

Then two of the Het came forward, lifted the body by the arms and legs, and threw it into the empty wooden bin. Abruptly, conversation and laughter resumed, banishing the silence. Tankards of ale were hoisted and consumed. The woman was forgotten.

Lyriana was looking at him with those knowing eyes, dark and anguished. He leaned close, his words softer than a whisper as he mouthed them. *How long will this continue?*

She swallowed hard. *All night. At dawn, Kronswiff will sleep.*

Of course. Kronswiff was a dracul; he fed at night.

He is a monster, she mouthed.

And dawn was hours away. By then, dozens more of the city's populace might join the woman lying in the wooden bin. He would be forced to witness the draining process multiple times when just once was more than enough to turn his stomach.

He looked down on the assembled enemy once more. So many. But sometimes you did what you had to do despite the odds. Sometimes you acted because doing anything else was unthinkable.

Turning from the scene below, he backed from the railing to the balcony wall, beckoning for Lyriana to follow. When they were huddled in the shadows, he leaned close.

"Wait here until I call for you," he whispered. "If things go badly for me, go down the stairs and back out the way we came. Hide or flee, whichever seems best."

Her face hardened. Her voice was accusatory. "You promised you would kill me rather than let me be captured!"

He shook his head. "I cannot do what you ask. I cannot harm you. I need you to release me from that promise and save yourself. I will give you time enough to do so no matter how this goes."

"You are going down there right *now*?" She sounded shocked.

"Would you have me do anything else?"

She stared at him, and there were tears in her eyes. Then she reached up with her fingers to stroke his cheek. "Do what you have to. I release you from your promise."

He wanted to say something more. He wanted to tell her how she made him feel, how just her presence gave him pleasure, how much he wanted her to leave with him when this was over.

But the words would not come.

HE CREPT BACK down the balcony stairs on cat's paws, feeling his way through the darkness to the corridor below and then moving toward the torchlight burning in the central chamber. He went quickly and smoothly, without hesitation or regret. He still harbored doubts about the secrets he knew Lyriana was keeping from him, yet what difference did they make now? A man like himself made his choices and stood by them. He might die tonight—just as he might have died countless other times in countless other places—but he would not do so out of cowardice or lack of determination. He might be outnumbered, but he was more skilled and experienced than any adversary he would ever face. They were Het—but he was the Weapons Master.

He was at peace.

He brought out a brace of throwing knives from their sheaths, moved toward the door to the chamber ahead, and stepped inside.

They didn't see him right away. Another victim was being led in, another food source for the warlock. This one, too, was bedraggled and marked by lesions and bruising. All eyes were turned in that direction, and he was through the door and lost in the shadows along the wall before even the closest of those who kept watch saw him coming. As the raucous shouts filled the air, he eased along the wall to where the gloom was deepest, placing himself directly across from the settee and the creature that reclined upon it.

On the way, he passed two of the Het who were close enough

for him to reach. He killed them both before they could make a sound and left them where they had fallen.

But there were still too many for him to be able to overcome them all. He reaffirmed this, eyes sweeping the room, tallying up the numbers. He would have to kill the warlock first and hope the Het would lose heart when they saw that their leader was dead.

Except the Het were not usually inclined to back away.

When he was twenty feet from Kronswiff—the other's attention centered on the unfortunate man standing before him—Garet Jax hurled the first knife. It appeared as if by magic in the warlock's chest, the force of the blow knocking him backward. The warlock seemed confused, staring down at the handle protruding from his chest. One hand reached up tentatively to touch the knife, fingers exploring.

Abruptly, he was on his feet, seemingly unharmed, eyes sweeping the gloom as he roared in fury. Het scattered in response, searching for the source of his rage. Belatedly, the Weapons Master remembered that knives alone were not enough. This was a dracul as well as a warlock and would be killed only if he cut off the head.

Instantly he was moving, leaving the shadows and emerging into the smoky torchlight, racing for the platform and the monster.

It is a common belief among men that everything slows in battle in a way that allows you to see events more clearly and to react as if the struggle is unfolding in slow motion. Garet Jax knew better. Instead of slowing, everything speeds up, and there is neither time nor opportunity to consider what is happening or to determine what should be done about it. You don't stay alive because you make the right decisions; you stay alive because your reactions are quicker and your fighting skills better than your opponents'.

So it was here. The Het came at him from everywhere, and he countered them with agility and swiftness. He used throwing stars until his supply was exhausted and then turned to his knives. He killed or disabled his attackers faster than they could act to prevent it from happening. He reacted on instinct alone, going through them like a shadow, barely visible, hardly there, leaving them fallen in his wake. He used his skills, his experience, and his strength; he never paused. His purpose was clear; his goal was settled.

Reach the warlock before he could escape, then kill him.

Already Kronswiff was off the platform and lumbering toward the door through which his victims had been led, howling for the Het, his hands turning into claws that ripped the air. He might have more powers still, Garet Jax realized, and must not be given a chance to use them.

He was close now, the Het ranks thinning, some among them already falling back. He was cut and slashed in a dozen places and felt none of it. His mind blocked out the pain and the distraction of the wounds. His attention was focused solely on the attackers who came at him. His throwing stars were already gone; only two of his knives remained.

He pressed on, but the numbers were too great. He could feel the Het closing in on him. Yet miraculously, he stayed on his feet. Arrows and darts flew; none of them struck him. Blades whipped past but never touched him. Any number of blows the Het struck at him should have been enough to bring him down, but none did so.

He glanced upward to the balcony where he had left Lyriana and found her with her arms outstretched, her fingers weaving, her lips moving, her face intense with concentration.

Magic! Lyriana is skilled at using magic, and she is deflecting their blows!

He made the most of the opportunity she was giving him. Reaching for the short sword he wore strapped across his back, he whipped it out in a single fluid motion. Using it as a harvester of crops might use a scythe to cut wheat, he slashed at the men surrounding him. The room had descended into chaos, the

Het howling and screaming in pain and fury, the warlock struggling to reach the door and an imagined safety that lay beyond.

He caught up to Kronswiff there, hacking through the last of
the Het that sought to stop him. Wheeling back in desperation,
the warlock fixed his black eyes on his solitary attacker, employ-
ing his magic, attempting to form a link that would drain his
life. For an instant it was there, a dark ribbon hanging in the
air, joining them.

But Garet Jax was moving too quickly to allow the bond to
harden. Leaping onto the edge of the wooden bin and springing
into the air, he rose above the warlock, twisting his body so that
he led with his sword, descending like a bird of prey. He watched
as Kronswiff stiffened, arms extended in an effort to save himself. But the warlock was already too late. The short sword
whipped around with a strange whistling sound, severing both
of his upraised hands at the wrists and continuing on to his exposed neck. Kronswiff's head flew from his shoulders and disappeared into the shadows. His body remained upright for a
moment longer and then sagged to the floor.

Garet Jax landed on his feet, his sword streaked with blood.
In a crouch, he faced the remaining Het, sweeping his blade in
a slow arc from one adversary to the next in unspoken challenge. Then he howled like an animal—an impulsive earsplit-
ting cry born of bloodlust and rage, his black-cloaked form
spinning toward the Het as if heedless of the danger they offered.

He was too much for them. He broke the last of their resis-
tance, and they turned and fled into the gloom.

WHEN HE HAD recovered enough to call to Lyriana, she came
at once. Amid the dead, a solitary pair in the blood-soaked
chambers they had claimed, she would not let him move from
where they stood until she had examined his wounds and determined none was serious enough to require immediate treatment.

"You were a reaper's wind," she said to him, and he could read the wonder in her eyes. "You were death itself."

Her words made him uncomfortable. "And what of you? A magic wielder all along. Why didn't you tell me?"

"My magic is small and of limited use. Mostly, I use it for healing. It would never have been sufficient to overcome Kronswiff."

"It worked against his Het."

Her eyes lowered. "I was afraid for you. I had to act. I'm sorry for my deception. I should have said something."

Yet she hadn't. Again, that twinge of suspicion tugged at him. "We should see to your people," he reminded her.

She led him through the door to where dozens of them had been held prisoner, waiting to sate the dracul's thirst. They clustered in small groups, cringing when he appeared, afraid he was another demon to be faced, another threat. But Lyriana was quick to reassure them they were safe now, that this black-clad man was a friend and their rescuer.

As she said these things, chasing the fear from their eyes, he noticed something strange. All of those who occupied the antechamber were suffering from grievous wounds. Their flesh was blackened and raw. Pieces of their faces and bodies were missing. Some walked with the aid of crutches and staffs. Some were cloaked entirely, and he could smell the sickness that had claimed them.

"What's happened to these people?" he whispered when she turned back to him, unable to keep the anger and disgust from his voice. "What has the warlock done to them?"

He saw at once that he had said the wrong thing. Her face tightened, then collapsed. Tears came to her eyes.

"Kronswiff did not cause this," she said. "He took advantage of them because they were *already* this way."

He stared at her. "I don't understand. How could they already be like this?"

She took a deep breath and exhaled sharply. "They are lepers, Garet Jax. They suffer from a disease that ravages their bodies. They are people who have been shunned by the world and have come to Tajarin to be with their own kind. They take refuge in a place to which no others have any wish to come. Here they were left alone until Kronswiff found them and decided to feed on men and women who could not stop him from doing so."

Lepers. Just the word was enough to send a shiver through him. Victims of a flesh-eating disease out of the Old World that had disappeared for a time, but resurfaced as these things often do. He had heard of it—heard of colonies formed of those unfortunates who had contracted it and were forced to flee from the larger world to places like this one so they could live out their days in relative peace.

Though that had not happened here, because a creature who cared nothing for what they had become and only for the purposes they might serve had preyed upon them. Incapacitated by their illness, they could not fight back. They could only hide and hope they would not be found.

He looked around the room, his eyes shifting from face to face. Only a few managed to meet his gaze. Most turned away at once, hiding themselves as best they could, anxious that no one should ever look on them again. He understood this. His own revulsion was uncomfortably revealing. He could not help himself, even knowing it was wrong.

"I promised I would pay you for your services," she said, turning away. "Come with me."

She led him from the room into a maze of hallways beyond, producing the crystal once more to light their way. They proceeded through the darkness, following various corridors past closed doors and shuttered windows. They climbed a set of stairs until they were several stories higher and then walked from there until they arrived at a tiny bedroom. "This one is mine," she told him as they entered.

Still holding the crystal to provide them with light, she

crossed to an ancient cupboard and brought out a leather pouch. Then she came back again and handed it to him. When he opened it, he saw it was filled with gold coins.

"Is this payment enough?" she asked him.

"I don't want any money." He hesitated, searching for the words. "What I want is for you—"

"No!" she interrupted quickly. "Don't ask it of me. I can't do what you want." She took a deep breath. "It isn't only that I care for these people. I am one of them."

He felt all the air drain from him, her words leaving him emptied. Had he heard her right? One of them? A leper? No, he told himself quickly, he must be mistaken. There was nothing wrong with her. He could see there was nothing wrong just by looking at her.

But then he remembered how she had flinched when he reached for her that first night, how she had told him not to touch her. He remembered how she had been so careful to keep herself covered up while they traveled, always making sure to keep some distance between them.

He felt his heart sink.

"I came to Tajarin to help my parents and my brother, all of whom had the disease. While I lived among them, I contracted it, too. But I don't regret it. I did what I felt was right. When Kronswiff and his Het appeared, I went in search of you— a man whose reputation reached even so remote a place as Tajarin—because I was mostly sound still, mostly able, and the only one who had any use of magic. I was the one on whom the marks of sickness were least visible and who could use magic to help heal myself should I get worse. But it doesn't change the truth of my condition."

She pulled open her cloak and lifted her blouse. Large sections of her torso were blotchy and raw where the disease had settled in. Her eyes lifted to meet his. "I am too sick already to leave."

She dropped her blouse and closed her cloak. "I hid my condition from you so that you would come. I was afraid you wouldn't, if you knew. I kept my use of magic secret, as well. When the crossbow bolt was fired at me, I used magic to deflect the blow. I used it again to help you against Kronswiff. I had not intended to do so, but I felt I had to. No one else could have killed him, if you had failed."

Her voice gathered strength. "Kronswiff had learned of a leprous people living on the Tiderace, a population possessed of gold and silver kept concealed within the walls of their remote city. He came to rob us and to feed on us. It did not bother him that we were lepers. He was immune to our disease and hungry for our bodies and wealth. He took both. There was no one to stop him; no one cares about lepers. What did it matter what became of us? We were already the walking dead. We were at his mercy, and he had none to spare us."

"You could still come with me," he said. "Back down to the Southland. Your people are safe now. The Het won't return if there is no one to pay for their services. There are Healers at Storlock who could help you. There are medicines . . ."

He spoke the words in a rush, as much to convince himself as to persuade her. He couldn't leave her. He wouldn't. Not when there might be a chance, however slim, that she could be saved.

But she shook her head. "No, Weapons Master. I have to stay here. This is where I belong. Take the gold and go and know you did something important by helping us. We had no one, and we were being destroyed. Even lepers have a right to the life that is given them, no matter their condition, no matter their fate. Others would have passed us by. You were not one of those, and we will never forget you."

She paused. "*I* will never forget you."

Her eyes held him, and what he felt for her was so strong— even knowing how sick she was—that he could barely stand it. He had never felt like this about anyone before, and he was stricken at the thought of simply walking away.

She pointed to the doorway. "Go left down the hall, then take the stairs. From there, go straight through to the door at the end. It will lead you outside. You can find your way from there."

He nodded, knowing there was no other choice. He couldn't stay here. He didn't belong here. His life was outside these walls, but hers was not.

"Lyriana."

He spoke her name once and stepped close, bending his face to hers. This time she didn't move away, didn't flinch, didn't tell him not to touch her. Instead she lifted her mouth to accept his kiss and kissed him back.

He left her there and went down the hallway, out through the door into the streets of the city and over its walls to the world beyond. It had been a long time since he had cried, and he didn't cry now.

He understood better now why he had been drawn to her, what it was that had attracted him so. He had sensed the connection between them, but had not understood it. Now he did. He was as damaged as she was, and just as lost. He was fated to die of a cause not of his making as surely as she was; it was only a question of when. But while she had achieved peace of mind, his own remained a slippery and elusive thing. Lyriana had shown him how he must be if he were ever to find his way, and it had generated in him something that approached love.

Perhaps, in its own fashion, that's what it actually was.

The courage she evidenced in accepting what was to happen to her was the true measure of her strength. He would learn from that. He would find grace as she had. But he could not help wishing he had been able to do so with her beside him. He had wanted his kiss to express how much he wished it.

So much so that even the risk of contracting leprosy by placing his mouth on hers had not been enough to dissuade him from doing it.

For the first two days of travel back to Tombara, he was miserable. He could not stop thinking about her. He could not stop his aching. Then, on the third day, the pain began to ease as his thoughts drifted to other things. He was the Weapons Master first and always, and the time he had envisioned for himself and Lyriana—even in the best of circumstances—would never have lasted. It would have required him to change, and it was too late for that. His path in life was already determined, and he knew he was fated to follow it to its end.

In Tombara he found the commission waiting that would take him to Varfleet. And by then, Lyriana and Tajarin were already fading into the dark well of his past.

Introduction to

"An Unfortunate Influx of Fillipians"

A WHILE BACK, my Web Druid, Shawn Speakman—who manages almost all of my social media efforts along with carrying on a writing career of his own—asked me to contribute a short story to a new anthology he was putting together. Without getting into the particulars of how he managed to convince me I had time to write this short story (suffice to say it included equal measures of guilt, praise, and threats, coupled with my own realization that it was time to throw myself back into the short-fiction fray), I will simply tell you I agreed. Reluctantly.

For me, writing a short story is much harder than writing a novel. The effort required for a single short story seems much the same as walking to school during an Illinois winter snowstorm or trying to master Latin, so I don't go looking for reasons to engage. Better if I just stick to reading short fiction and let others do the grunt work of writing it.

At the time Shawn asked and I agreed, I was deep in Shannara and was uninspired by the idea of writing still more in that world, so I turned to Magic Kingdom. I had written exactly one book in that series in the past ten years—*A Princess of Landover*—so maybe it was time for a return visit. Two of the most popular characters in that series were the G'home Gnomes, Fillip and Sot. So I thought I would make them the centerpiece: a pair of cat-eating, hopelessly inept creatures who adored Ben

Holiday, the main protagonist—a predilection that almost always involved getting him and them into deep trouble.

I've always loved the *Star Trek* episode "The Trouble with Tribbles," and I thought it would be fun to riff on that. So I came up with the Fillipians. You can guess the origin of the name. But what could I do with Fillipians in the kingdom of Landover that would remind readers of Tribbles while taking the concept in a whole new direction?

Turns out, quite a lot.

AN UNFORTUNATE
INFLUX OF FILLIPIANS

ON THAT LATE-SPRING morning, it wasn't the weather that ended up ruining Ben Holiday's day, although the air was gray and coolish and uncomfortably slimy. It wasn't his teenage daughter, Mistaya, either, who of late had proved typically troublesome in that teenage sort of way. She was back in school in the Old World now, having talked her way into being reinstated after being booted out the year before for behavior unbecoming a student of Carrington Women's Preparatory. Nor was it the larger world of Landover, which sometimes seemed bent on disrupting Ben Holiday's peace of mind. It wasn't even Questor Thews making an ill-advised attempt at summoning yet another peculiar form of magic that was well beyond his somewhat limited abilities.

No, on this morning, it was a simple visit.

"High Lord?" a tinny voice called out from the other side of his closed bedroom door.

His eyes opened, and he lifted his head from the pillow. He had been awake earlier, up before the sun. But after deciding he had few demands on his time that day, he had allowed himself to fall back to sleep. Seldom did he get such an opportunity. As King of Landover, he ruled over an entire world of very strange creatures. And much of what he did involved protecting them—

frequently from one another. Or, rather sadly, protecting others—frequently himself—from them. And when momentarily freed from *this* effort, he had to keep the wheels and cogs of his makeshift government turning.

So a day of just lounging in bed would have been a glorious indulgence. But this was Landover, after all. There he was, sleeping undisturbed and without a care in the world—which maybe should have been a warning—when the voice called out a second time: "High Lord?"

The voice sounded familiar—and not in a good way. No, instead it rather aggressively nudged to life a clutch of dark memories that had been buried, if never quite eradicated, by the passage of time.

"Is he in there?" a second voice whispered, similar in tone but just different enough to be distinguishable.

"He must be. He sleeps in there, doesn't he?"

"He might have gone out."

"Where would he go?"

"Anywhere he chooses. He *is* High Lord."

Ah, Ben thought in dismay as recognition dawned. "Go away!" he shouted at the door. "*Far* away!"

Gasps sounded. Breath was exhaled in a mix of distress and awe. A jumbled muttering of indistinguishable words ensued. A shuffling of feet preceded the sound of bodies crowding up against the door in an effort to get closer.

"Great High Lord!" cried one voice.

"Mighty High Lord!" cried the other.

Fillip and Sot. If not his worst nightmare, then something close.

He squeezed his eyes tightly closed in disbelief. How had they gotten in here? Weren't there supposed to be guards protecting him from intruders? Wasn't he safe even in his own bed?

"Go away!" he repeated.

Fillip and Sot. Troublesome even for G'home Gnomes—a variety of Landoverian gnomes that were otherwise mostly innocuous. Most gnomes—the good kind—nested in the northern stretches of Landover, up around the Melchor Mountains. Where they behaved themselves. Where they didn't eat their neighbors' pets. Where they didn't steal everything that wasn't nailed down. Where they didn't start fires in people's living rooms just to see what would happen. All of which the G'home Gnomes did without a second thought. This was a tribe that had been told so often to "Go Home, Gnomes!" that the name had stuck. Unfortunately, no one—themselves included—could remember by now where that home was or how to get the gnomes to go back there.

Ben had tried everything. He had consigned them to parts of his kingdom—north, south, east, and west—at different times but with similar results. He had placed them in compounds in an effort to curtail their wandering ways. He had confined them behind chain-link fencing and, when that failed, barbed wire. He had assigned guards. He had cajoled and threatened and had finally given up. You could give a problem only so much of your time and energy before you were forced to pronounce it a hopeless endeavor.

Fillip and Sot were the worst of a bad bunch, and his annoyance was exacerbated by the fact that they inexplicably worshipped him.

"Great High Lord!" they called out through the door, chanting together. "Mighty High Lord!"

On and on.

Ben gritted his teeth. His thoughts were best left unvoiced, so he kept them that way. Instead, he climbed out of bed to meet his fate, already pretty much certain what it was. Not in the specific, of course, but generally. Every appearance by these two prefaced a disaster; only the nature of it varied.

He yanked open the door furiously. Two wizened, somewhat monkey-like faces looked up at him in adoration from three feet down. Eyes wide and adoring, beaming smiles revealing sharpened teeth, they bowed low.

"Great High Lord."

"Mighty High Lord."

"Stop saying that!" he snapped, causing them to flinch. "How did you get in here, anyway?"

"Oh, it was easy, High Lord," Fillip explained. "We just climbed the wall."

"You climbed the . . . Wait. That wall is a hundred feet high!"

"They wouldn't let us in through the gates, High Lord. They sent us away. They would not tell you we were here. So we climbed. It's very easy for gnomes to climb walls."

Note to self, Ben thought. *Find a way to better fortify Sterling Silver. Start by making the castle walls too slippery to climb. Maybe widen the moat and add a few hungry predator fish.* "What about the guards? I do still have guards, don't I? Didn't they see you?"

The gnomes looked at each other in confusion. "It was very dark. No one could see us."

Ben stared. "You climbed the wall *last night?*"

"It was necessary, High Lord!" Fillip said.

Sot nodded eagerly. "We have a problem, High Lord. We need you to solve it."

"We couldn't wait for morning," Fillip added.

"Well, not out *there,*" Sot amended, gesturing vaguely. "So we climbed the wall and waited outside your door."

Ben was appalled. But only for a second, because it was so typical of their behavior that it didn't bear dwelling on.

"We have a problem," Sot repeated.

"We do," Fillip agreed.

"Of course you do." Ben made a dismissive gesture. "When have you not had a problem? But you have to go through the gates and the front door and ask to see me! You do not get to see me by climbing walls and sneaking around to find my bedroom door and then waiting for morning to barge in uninvited! And waking me! I was sleeping!"

Both gnomes nodded sagely. "We slept a little, too," Fillip

announced, missing the point entirely. "Can we tell you about our problem now?"

Ben gave up. "Sure. Why not? Come on in. No need to stand on ceremony. Mi casa es su casa. Feel free to make yourselves at home."

He stomped back into his bedroom and threw himself down on the bed. The gnomes took this as an invitation and jumped up beside him. Ben was too worn down to do anything about it, but he did have enough presence of mind to wonder where Willow was. She had been there last night. Usually that meant she was there in the morning, but for some reason she wasn't today. She had probably heard the gnomes outside the door and was smart enough to get out while the getting was good. Still, it was strange he hadn't heard her go.

"We have a new pet," Fillip began, and Ben held up his hand.

"Tell me you didn't eat it!"

"No, it's *my* pet."

"When has that ever stopped you?"

"It is a special pet," Fillip announced.

"A special pet," Sot echoed.

"I found it," Fillip added.

"Sort of," Sot said.

They looked at him, waiting.

"So what's the problem?" Ben asked cautiously.

"My pet was stolen," Fillip announced, a frown adding further displacement to his wizened features.

"Sort of," Sot repeated.

There was a nuance to these last two words that Ben didn't miss. "Stolen or not?" he pressed, none too gently.

Fillip was looking daggers at Sot. "It *was* my pet!" he snapped.

"You both found it," Sot replied.

"It was mine!"

"It was his, too!"

"Wait a minute," Ben interrupted. "Someone else was with you when you found this pet?"

Fillip expressed his obvious disgust by clearing his throat loudly. "Shoopdiesel."

Another G'home Gnome that was always making unfortunate decisions and wreaking havoc as a result. Mistaya had encountered Shoopdiesel after her discharge from Carrington. But it was Ben, still in Landover, who was now stuck with him. Still, unlike Fillip and Sot, Shoopdiesel never spoke. As far as Ben was concerned, it was his sole virtue.

Ben rubbed his eyes wearily, wishing he were still asleep. "So you and Shoopdiesel found this pet together?"

"He is my pet!" Fillip declared vehemently. "I want him back!"

It was at this point that the bedroom door opened and Willow walked in. His wife took in the sight of her husband sitting in bed with a pair of G'home Gnomes and raised an eyebrow.

"A monarch's work is never done," Ben said with a rueful grin.

Willow, calm and steady as ever, nodded. "Indeed not. Is this about the pet?"

Ben stared. Well, who knew?

Once the guards had been summoned and the G'home Gnomes carted off to await Ben's summons (would he actually do something that foolish?), Willow sat him down to explain what she knew about this pet business. It was hard for Ben to avoid being distracted by his wife when they had these sorts of discussions, but she was an exotic creature and he was desperately in love with her, so his distraction was understandable. She had been born to a woodland nymph so wild she refused to remain behind to raise her daughter, and to a river sprite who had spent his life trying to persuade her to return. As a result of this unique genetic makeup, she could change into the tree for which she was named. And in order to survive, she was required to periodically take root in the soil of her birth world—something that seemed very odd, even in Landover.

On their very first meeting, Willow had told Ben that, in accordance with arcane fairy lore, he was meant to be hers—and she his. Needless to say, he was a tad skeptical if a bit intrigued. But Landover was not a world in which you dismissed such an unlikelihood easily. And sure enough, eventually it all came about, just as she had foretold.

All this had a tendency to stay with you—married or not, children or not, King of Landover or not—and it did so with Ben. His fascination with his wife was further enhanced by the fact that she was beautiful and smart and altogether too headstrong. You never wanted to take anything for granted where Willow was concerned, or assume that she would do what you expected.

So, in retrospect, he should not have been surprised that she was already aware of the mysterious pet, and had it covered.

"The pet belongs to Shoopdiesel, and I gave it back to him," she said. "He had it on a leash, it had his name on its collar, and he took it back from Fillip when Fillip stole it from him."

"Wait." Ben held up both hands. "How did you get involved in this in the first place? The last thing I remember was you falling asleep next to me in bed."

She gave her emerald hair a shake. "Caeris woke me early to tell me there was a gnome with a strange animal at the gate asking to see me. She thought I should speak with him right away. She wasn't wrong. I found him in a very distraught state."

Caeris was her new handmaiden from her home in the Lake Country, only recently arrived at court to provide her with a companion and helpmate. Ben had approved . . . until now. "She just came into our bedroom and woke you in the middle of the night?"

Willow shrugged. "She has my permission to do so, when she judges it important and it does not in any significant way disturb us. I trust her."

Ben hesitated, but there was nowhere reasonable to go with this. "So you spoke to Shoopdiesel? But he doesn't talk!"

"He signs in his own Gnomish language, which I can understand."

"But you still should have woken me. I would have gone with you."

She smiled and ran her fingers through his hair. Silken strands of moss (she was various attractive shades of green all over) trailed across his skin, tickling him. "What sense would that make? Do you really need yet another problem to add to those you already have?"

He had to admit he did not. Even though now, it appeared, he had one anyway. "Fillip seems to think the pet belongs to him. Are you sure about Shoopdiesel?"

She shook back her long green hair and leaned down to give him a meaningful kiss, making it last long enough that he was soon kissing her back.

"Does any of this really matter just now?" she whispered, pressing up against him.

He was pretty sure it didn't.

When he went down a bit later to announce his decision regarding the fate of the mysterious pet, he was in a considerably better mood. He noticed as he was giving his verdict that Sot was nodding along agreeably, even while Fillip was shaking his head in disgust. That pretty much confirmed what Willow had told him and what he already suspected—the pet was indeed not Fillip's. He emphasized that this was the end of the matter and that he fervently hoped never to hear another word about it.

Then he sent them packing.

It was only later in the day that he thought to ask Willow what sort of pet the gnomes were fighting over.

"I don't know," she admitted. "Some sort of lizard, I think. I've never seen anything like it before."

"Didn't they tell you what it was?"

"I'm not sure *they* knew."

For reasons he could not explain, this was vaguely troubling.

An entire week passed without further sight of the three G'home Gnomes. During that time, Ben tended to the business of the kingdom and gave little thought to the mysterious pet. Willow left for a visit with her father in the Lake Country, where she also planned a surreptitious rendezvous with her feral mother. Court Wizard Questor Thews announced plans for yet another attempt to change Court Scribe Abernathy back into a human, even though he was constantly making the same announcement without a clue as to how to go about it. (Abernathy was currently a dog.) Bunion, the kobold scout and Ben's personal bodyguard, caught a bog wump prowling outside the castle grounds and dispatched it. A delegation of Lords of the Greensward appeared to negotiate for higher rates on the farm crops their serfs grew in the rich black earth of the midlands, and a second delegation, this one from the River Master, came knocking to complain about the Greensward's ecologically damaging farming methods.

Things were back to normal.

Until two weeks later when the G'home Gnomes reappeared, all three at once, and none of them looking very happy. They managed not to climb the walls to Ben's bedroom, but simply showed up at the gates during business hours and were allowed into the throne room to present their latest . . . request, demand, complaint, announcement, or whatever it turned out to be this time.

Which, as it happened, was a little of each.

"Great High Lord," Fillip declared, bowing low.

"Mighty High Lord," Sot added, bowing even lower.

Shoopdiesel, as usual, said nothing.

Ben was sitting on his throne—something he did not much care for save when he wished to impart a certain impression, which he very much did with these three. *I am King; you are not. I am not to be trifled with; you are not to waste my time.* He sat tall and straight and tried hard to look stern, hoping his demeanor would suggest that they get on with it and depart as quickly as possible.

As if.

There was a momentary pause in the proceedings as Sot pre-pared to speak, and then suddenly Shoopdiesel threw himself on Fillip and began beating him. Fillip, who already looked like he might have gone a few rounds, fought back valiantly but sus-tained a number of fresh bruises and cuts before Sot could pull Shoopdiesel off.

Once separated, all three stood panting hard and looking at the floor.

"I thought you were friends," Ben said finally, still a little dazed by the sudden violence.

"Hah!" snapped Fillip.

Shoopdiesel stomped his foot.

Sot stepped forward. "Fillip ate Shoopdiesel's pet!"

At that moment, Willow—recently returned from visiting her father—walked into the room, heard Sot's pronouncement, shook her head in dismay, and—having clearly decided this was nothing she wanted to become involved in—turned around and walked out again. Ben wished he could do the same.

"Why did you do that, Fillip?" he asked the offender.

Fillip pouted and refused to speak. Ben looked at Sot.

"He was angry, High Lord. He thought the pet was his and should have been given to him. So he ate it." A small hesitation. "He wasn't thinking clearly."

Nothing new there. None of these three was given to clear thinking. In fact, they weren't much given to thinking at all. "All right," he said, after further thought. "What do you want me to do about it?"

None of them said anything, but after another few moments Shoopdiesel began gesturing wildly while the other two began making honking noises that could have indicated almost any-thing. Plus, their honking was long and loud and really annoy-ing.

"All right!" Ben shouted. "Someone just tell me what you think I can do about this!"

"Shoop wants another pet," Sot answered. "Of the same kind. We want you to help us find one."

"How am I supposed to do that?"

"You are High Lord Ben Holiday. You can do anything!"

Ben rolled his eyes. "Not in this case. All I can do here is send you back to where you came from and tell you this matter is over and done with! Find yourselves another pet. Or better yet, *don't* find another pet!"

As if in response to this pronouncement, Fillip began to choke and hack in the manner of a cat with a hairball. Sot started pounding him on the back to help him clear his throat, and then Shoopdiesel joined in, beating on him for the most part, it appeared, for the sheer pleasure of doing so.

Soon, all of them were beating on one another.

Ben jumped up, fighting his anger and frustration, and called for the guards to haul them out. But before that could happen, Fillip began to retch violently. He fell to his hands and knees, head lowered and drool running from his mouth. The hacking was bad enough that even his two companions stepped away, their wizened faces crinkling in distaste. Even the approaching guards hesitated, pulling back uncertainly.

Then Fillip began to vomit, regurgitating chunks of raw meat, one after another—a couple, a few, half a dozen, a dozen, more. The process went on long enough that it soon became clear that whatever was afflicting him was completely out of his control.

Willow ran back into the room, rushing toward the hapless gnome. But just then he stopped retching and sat up again, a dazed look on his face. As he did so, the chunks of meat scattered about the throne room floor began to move.

Willow sensibly turned around and departed once again.

The little meat bundles were growing legs and starting to walk around. Ben wasted no time waiting to see what else was going to happen.

"Send for Questor Thews!" he ordered. "Now!"

Shoopdiesel and Sot hauled the unfortunate Fillip back to his feet, and the three of them stood watching the meat bundles lurch back and forth.

"Babies!" Sot declared exuberantly. He clapped Fillip on the back. "You're a father!"

Ben could hardly believe what he was hearing. "He's not a father! You don't give birth to babies by puking! Males don't give birth at all!" He hesitated, examining this claim. "Wait a minute. G'home Gnomes don't, do they?"

But no one was paying attention to him, least of all the newborns, who were gaining speed and confidence the more they staggered about, bumping into one another and the curious gnomes, their blunted features slowly taking on definition and their meaty bodies developing a variety of different colors, none of them particularly appetizing. They were four-legged chunks with a tail and a head, their faces scrunched up and wrinkled, all of them looking not unlike smaller, uglier versions of the G'home Gnomes.

OMG, Ben thought. *Maybe they do!*

All of the gnomes, including Shoopdiesel, were looking decidedly pleased by the unexpected appearance of the regurgitated meat-lumps. Sot and Fillip were thumping each other on the back and talking excitedly about raising children and the joys of fatherhood, in what—to Ben—seemed a clear indication that they were losing touch with reality.

Finally, he shouted, "How can they be your children? They're just pieces of undigested pet!"

But the gnomes ignored him completely, now engaged in nudging the little creatures about with the toes of their boots. The baby meat-lumps seemed to like this, scrambling away and then racing back, frolicking about the throne room like puppies. At one point, the commander of his guards caught Ben's eye and silently beseeched him for directions, but he had no directions to give, so he simply motioned the guards away. Throwing out parents and their newborn children, no matter how odd the species or the circumstances, seemed heartless.

And at least the gnomes weren't fighting anymore.

Finally, Questor appeared, his multicolored robes and sashes flashing brightly, his white hair and beard looking windblown. The moment he saw the babies, he practically squealed and rushed over, dropping to his knees to join the G'home Gnomes in playing with the little creatures. Ben wanted to rush over and drag him away but settled for patience instead. Then, when it appeared that patience wasn't going to be enough, he shouted at Questor to tell him what he was dealing with.

"You're my Court Wizard, for cat's sake! What are these things?"

Questor smiled benignly. "I have no idea. But they are rather cute, aren't they?"

Having witnessed the manner of their birth, Ben was not inclined to agree. But that wasn't the point. Cute or not, it troubled him that no one knew what they were. So he filled in Questor on their backstory and asked if any of it raised red flags.

"Not a one," the other admitted. "But perhaps the squabble over pets has now ended. There are enough to go around. So perhaps they can all go home and stop bothering you, High Lord."

A fine idea. All for it.

"Clear everyone out," Ben ordered the guards, knowing a favorable opportunity when he saw one. "Parents and puppies outside, and then point one and all in any direction but this one! See that they have an escort for the first mile."

He took time to congratulate the G'home Gnomes and clap them on their backs while surreptitiously herding them toward the doors leading out.

"But mighty High Lord!" Fillip exclaimed at one point, turning back. "I want the chocolate one, and Shoopdiesel wants him, too! Make him give it to me!"

Ben patted him on the head and leaned down. "If you fail to settle this between yourselves, I will take the pets away from you and keep them for myself. And I will not let you keep even one of them, no matter how much you beg and plead! Do you understand?"

Fillip started to say something and then thought better of it. Instead, he nodded, tight-lipped and red-faced, and raced away, catching up to the others and trying to snatch the chocolate one (though burned toast was more like it) from the guards, practically knocking down Shoopdiesel in the process. The pushing, shoving, and arguing continued as they progressed along the hall and disappeared from view.

"I hope that's the end of this business," Ben muttered to himself.

Questor Thews came up beside him, stroking his white beard and nodding in satisfaction. "I think we can safely say that the matter is settled, High Lord. We shouldn't have to hear anything more about the gnomes or those little creatures—whatever they are—again."

Ben Holiday nodded. He was inclined to agree.

But they were both wrong.

ANOTHER WEEK PASSED. A week of relative peace and quiet. A week without a fresh appearance by Fillip, Sot, Shoopdiesel, or any of their new family. Word filtered back that, by agreement, Shoopdiesel had gotten to keep the chocolate pet while Fillip had been allowed to name the whole pet family. Not surprisingly, he decided to name them after himself. He called them Fillipians.

So for seven days the G'home Gnomes and the Fillipians hovered on the fringes of Ben's thoughts, but no word of further disturbances intruded.

On day eight, however, this changed.

Ben was finishing up with a delegation of farmers from the Greensward who had come to lodge a complaint about their unfair treatment at the hands of the Lords of the Greensward—a tricky proposition, since Landover still tolerated feudal laws in that part of the kingdom—when Questor Thews appeared at the rear of the assemblage making frantic gestures to catch Ben's attention. Excusing himself momentarily, Ben gestured Questor forward.

The Court Wizard leaned close, keeping his voice low. "There is a problem, High Lord, that requires your immediate attention."

"Tell me this doesn't have anything to do with the G'home Gnomes!"

Questor pursed his lips. "If I did so, I would be lying."

Ben sighed. "All right. What is it?"

"The baby Fillipians? They grew up. In the process, they seem to have found a way to multiply." He glanced over his shoulder at the farmers, all of whom were leaning forward, trying to hear what he was saying. "There are . . . rather a lot of them."

"Multiply," Ben repeated, an unpleasant picture entering his mind. "Sort of like before, perhaps?"

"Exactly like before."

Ben felt like screaming. "You're telling me Fillip began eating his own children?"

Questor pursed his lips so hard they disappeared into his beard—along with most of his mouth. "Not only Fillip, but Shoopdiesel and Sot as well. Apparently they thought this was a good way to cut down on the population. And, of course, they were hungry. The babies, I am told, did not protest. They seemed rather eager to be eaten—perhaps so they could reproduce. Perhaps this is simply an odd example of the circle of life. I don't know. But now we have an entire forest full of Fillipian babies, all of them running around without supervision and waiting for the inevitable, I imagine."

Inevitable, indeed. Ben felt like *inevitable* was the exact word when it came to G'home Gnomes. "What do you suggest?"

Questor's brows knitted like kissing caterpillars. "We must round them up and dispose of them in some way."

"Destroy them? We can't do that!"

"Really? Then let me provide you with fresh incentive. The babies have started eating the crops out of fields and vegetables out of gardens. Like locusts. They seem insatiable. If we don't do something, we will have a full-scale riot on our hands. These farmers you are speaking to? Once they find out what is happening to their livelihood, they will be back with pitchforks and torches."

Ben closed his eyes in dismay. Questor was right, of course. But there was still something inherently wrong with what he was suggesting. Nevertheless, they had to put a stop to this whole business before it got totally out of hand.

So he sent Questor off to make preparations and went back to his discussion with the Greensward farmers, listening to their litany of complaints and promising to do what he could to help improve their situation. It took some time to convince them he would be able to do anything, but in the end they agreed to let him try.

By midday, he was riding out with Questor Thews and a small band of soldiers, headed for Longthorn Woods, where the G'home Gnomes and the Fillipians were currently ensconced. It was a warmer, sunnier day than when Fillip and Sot had appeared in his bedroom, and Ben took some measure of satisfaction in this pleasant change of weather, ready to find reassurance and comfort anywhere he could. He had thought about bringing Willow along, but in the end had decided there was nothing she could do to help, and she might be better off not knowing what he intended.

Bunion led the way, scurrying ahead eagerly, traveling much faster than any of the rest of the company, making sure the way was cleared of obstacles and potential dangers. The kobold was so swift that, when he reappeared, it always seemed he came out of nowhere. So it was this morning, as they neared their destination and Bunion flashed into view with a Fillipian baby clutched in his teeth.

Ben did not assume the worst, although some who did not know kobolds might. Kobolds did not eat baby animals. They looked fierce and could be ferocious, but they were selective eaters. Mostly, they just flashed their teeth when angry or threatened, which was enough to ward off most attackers or enemies.

Bunion dropped the little creature on the ground where it began scurrying around playfully, trying to climb onto the kobold, possibly to get back into its mouth. Who knew? Bunion said something to Questor (Ben had not yet mastered the kobold tongue sufficiently either to carry on or even to understand a conversation) and went still.

Questor gave Ben a look. "He says there are hundreds more waiting up ahead, running about like little rodents. There might even be thousands. He saw no sign of the gnomes."

"Probably off looking for some other form of trouble." Ben made a face. "Why do we have so few men with us? Don't we need something closer to an army to get these Fillipians under control?"

Questor shook his head. "More men would just get in the way. Besides, trying to round up these creatures by hand would take days. There are far too many of them. No, magic will do the job more quickly and efficiently. I have something in mind."

Instantly, Ben was worried. But he could tell by the way his Court Wizard spoke and by the set of his jaw that there would be no arguing him out of it. There was nothing to do but hope that, whatever Questor Thews had planned, it would work out better than it usually did.

His concerns grew stronger when they reached Longthorn and saw how many Fillipians the over-hungry gnomes had produced. They were everywhere—running about through the trees, climbing over logs, grassy hummocks, deadwood, and themselves. They had not yet fully blanketed the ground, but they were getting frighteningly close. It appeared as if the entire forest was carpeted with romping Fillipians.

Ben climbed down off his horse and stood looking at what must have been thousands of small bodies. How many Fillipian pets had the gnomes had to eat for them to reproduce like this?

The answer was provided moments later by the reappearance of Bunion, who had disappeared back into the woods and now reemerged dragging a decidedly miserable Fillip behind him. Fillip wriggled and moaned, but it was probably more from overeating than mistreatment.

Bunion tossed him down at Ben Holiday's feet, and the unfortunate gnome cried out in a plaintive voice, "Mighty High Lord! I don't feel so good."

"No wonder," Ben said. "You appear to have eaten hundreds of your offspring."

Fillip nodded sadly. "They just taste so good, I can't seem to stop."

"So now you have created thousands more, and all because you can't control your appetite. Do you intend to eat yourself to death? Because right now, I would not object."

Shortly after, Shoopdiesel and Sot staggered out of the trees, equally bloated with Fillipian pets. Neither spoke, and both were moaning as they clutched their distended bellies.

Ben was beyond disgusted. No one had ever told him he would have problems of this sort. It was bad enough having to deal with the witch Nightshade and the dragon Strabo and the Lords of the Greensward and the once-fairy of the Lake Country and all the rest of Landover's odd denizens without having to be plagued by the G'home Gnomes and their Fillipians, too.

"Questor," he said quietly, "will you please use whatever magic you've prepared and put an end to this?"

"No, great High Lord!" Fillip exclaimed.

"No, mighty High Lord," Sot pleaded.

No! Shoopdiesel indicated wordlessly, using unmistakable gestures in place of words.

But Questor was already voicing the required spell. The air darkened to twilight and thickened with heavy mist; the temperature dropped precipitously, and the sky filled with black clouds. Lightning streaked from horizon to horizon in jagged bolts. It was an impressive display—and made all the more so by the fact that it was Questor Thews who was making it happen. Ben found himself stepping back in trepidation . . .

"Arrrazzz mantle bot!" shouted the wizard.

A whirlwind swept into the woods, scattering leaves and twigs and debris. Ben had to shield his eyes against its force, but he was able to discern large numbers of squirming, thrashing bodies flying through the air, picked up and swept away on the wind. One might have thought the world was coming to an end and the souls of the departed were being lifted Heavenward— save for the fact that the things flying about were clearly Fillipians.

The maelstrom of bodies and debris continued whirling as both King and attendants ducked frantically and in some cases fell to the ground, covering their heads in dismay—partly from the chaos, and partly because it was Questor Thews exercising the magic. But finally the wind died away, the skies cleared, and things went back to normal.

Save for one thing.

Thousands of Fillipians lay piled in mountainous heaps, limp and unmoving, seemingly lifeless.

"You've killed them!" Ben gasped, snatching at Questor's robes.

"What?" The Court Wizard stared at him. "Killed them? No, no, High Lord! What do you think I am? A barbarian?"

Ben didn't care to answer that and simply stared at the piles of Fillipians. "Okay, this is all well and good, but what are you going to do with them once they wake up again?"

Questor rubbed his hands gleefully, a troubling eagerness reflected in his sudden smile. "Just watch."

A second bout of magic-wielding ensued, with Questor gesturing and chanting. Only this time the air stayed calm and the sky clear, and there was no thunder and lightning. Instead, rainbows appeared at every quadrant of the horizon—huge and brilliant arcs spanning the color spectrum and suggestive of sugarplums and candy canes and the like. Slowly, the heaps of Fillipians began to encapsulate themselves in vast cocoons that took on the appearance of giant wasps' nests—a comparison Ben found unavoidable and decidedly unpleasant.

Questor finished and gave Ben a knowing look. "Patience, High Lord," he said with a wink.

So Ben waited. He had little choice. Long minutes passed and nothing happened. He began to grow uneasy—especially when he saw Questor frown in a way that suggested he was starting to grow uneasy, too.

More minutes passed. Endless minutes.

"Uh, Questor . . ." Ben said quietly.

Then, abruptly, the mounds of encapsulated Fillipians began to quiver and shake—a clear indication that something was about to happen. Everyone—Questor included—took a cautionary step backward, and more than a few blades and spear points were directed toward the mounds. Bunion, who was standing next to Ben, hissed loudly, showing all of his considerable teeth. There was no mistaking *his* feelings on the matter.

"Questor," Ben said again, a little more urgently this time.

Yet when the mounds split apart, neither demons nor monsters emerged, but thousands upon thousands of butterflies, in a colorful swarm of radiant wings. They were clustered in such droves as to turn the air about Ben and company into a dazzling kaleidoscope.

All too quickly, the patterns fragmented, and the butterflies fluttered into the nearby woods and disappeared.

"There you are, High Lord," Questor declared, clearly taking great delight in the shock and awe reflected on Ben's face. "Problem solved. No one hurt, no one killed, and the world made a slightly better place."

Ben had to agree. It certainly appeared that way.

But, then, where Questor was concerned, appearances were often deceiving.

TORSHAK THE TERRIBLE was prowling the woods just north of Castle Sterling Silver, searching for food or gold or trouble— all of which gave him great pleasure. Torshak was a troll from the Jorgen Swamp, not all that far from the Fire Springs where Strabo the dragon had made his home. Torshak liked to relate how, once upon a time, there had been an encounter between the two. It had not gone well for Torshak—although, if you considered the fate of so many others, apparently he had accomplished the impossible, for he had escaped with his life.

But not, however, without a few souvenirs of his troubles. He was always quick to point out the ridged scars from claws and teeth, and the rippled flesh from burns, that layered his mighty forearms and hands. He had been ill used by the dragon, and one day he would make the beast pay. It didn't matter that it was his fault—which it was, he freely admitted—for trespassing on forbidden ground and then attempting to remove healing stones from the fire ponds in which the dragon bathed. But he had been attacked and forced to defend himself against a much larger aggressor, which was patently unfair.

This was not, as it happened, even slightly true. He had received his burns as a result of his own carelessness in building a campfire while drunk and not because of Strabo at all. But that was how he liked to tell it: that he faced down the dragon, fought him to a standstill, and escaped with his life. It made a much better story, really.

So he blamed the dragon for what had happened and still, to this day, swore vengeance far and wide. At every opportunity, he would say to anyone who would listen, "One day, there will be an accounting. No one trifles with Torshak the Terrible and gets away with it!"

This was, not coincidentally, when he began calling himself Torshak the Terrible and not Torshak Pudwuddle, which was his real name. But the decision still seemed to him a valid one.

Torshak liked to reinvent his own history, so it made sense he would do so with his name as well.

On this morning, perhaps two weeks after the demise of the Fillipians, he was feeling particularly wrathful. His head hurt terribly from the aftereffects of consuming copious amounts of alcohol the previous night at a tavern in the village of Stink Whistle. That, and the blows struck him by the tavern owner when Torshak revealed that he could not afford to settle his bill.

So, hungry and hurting and hugely disgruntled, he was looking for something to make himself feel better. Hence the search for food, gold, or trouble. Not very imaginative, but well within his comfort zone.

What he found, however, was something else entirely.

The first creature landed right in front of him—an insect more than twelve feet tall, with a colorful wingspan that was larger still, claws each the size of Torshak's hands, and mandibles that looked exceedingly sharp. It shrieked and rumbled when it saw him, making an unpleasantly eager sound. Torshak had no idea what this creature was but he didn't think it necessary to find out. He began to back away, sensing that this was going to end badly if he stuck around.

But he got only as far as the wall behind him. Wheeling in dismay, he discovered another of these terrible creatures, no less terrifying than the first. He backed away in a different direction, seriously worried now. He was rapidly running out of space.

Then a third creature appeared, this one larger and more formidable in appearance than the previous two, descending from the sky and blocking his way once more. Now he was hemmed in on three sides, with no room left to maneuver. He did some quick thinking—well, quick for him, anyway—trying to discover a way out of his dilemma. It occurred to him that, if he were nimble and quick, he could duck under their wings or between their legs and flee to safety. But he possessed neither of these attributes, and in his present state—still hung over and aching from the blows he had received from the tavern owner—he was having trouble moving at all.

So he took the only course of action open to him. He drew himself up, faced them squarely, and roared, "I am Torshak the Terrible!"

Turned out the creatures didn't care.

They ate him anyway.

Then they began to follow his tracks back toward the unfortunate village he had come from.

IT WAS LATE the following day, and Ben was sitting with Willow on the balcony of their living quarters, watching a spectacular orange-and-purple sunset, when Abernathy appeared. Talking dogs were not unheard of within the Kingdom of Landover, but you never wanted to make mention of it to the King's Scribe. Abernathy viewed himself as a victim of an incredibly careless and unfeeling Questor Thews who—once upon a time—had deliberately changed him from a man into a dog. He had used magic to do this, but magic ill conceived and ill applied, even given the urgency of the moment and the circumstances that required such an act. It had accomplished its intended purpose—to save Abernathy's life from Questor's enraged older brother, the former Court Wizard (which is another story for another time)—but it was a drastic and arguably foolish act. Bad enough that he had done this much damage, but then Questor had found himself unable to change Abernathy back again. Although he had repeatedly tried, to date he had failed to make any real progress.

Abernathy still thought of himself as a man rather than a dog and struggled mightily to convince others to do the same.

After all, he had his human hands and brain and voice—even if the rest of him was a Soft-Coated Wheaten Terrier—and those were the parts that counted. His vocabulary, in point of fact, far exceeded that of most others at Sterling Silver and gave him a decided advantage in any conversation.

Not that he required much of an advantage on this occasion.

"High Lord, it appears we have a problem with the village of Stink Whistle," he announced. "A rather serious one."

Starting with the name, Ben thought. He had never heard of Stink Whistle and would have been perfectly happy if things had stayed that way. The one thing he knew he would never do was ask how the village got such an unfortunate name in the first place.

"What sort of problem?" he asked, trying to sound interested.

"People are being eaten by large insects."

"Have they tried bug spray?"

"These are not normal insects. They are gigantic, carnivorous creatures. Villagers are literally being snatched up and consumed."

Willow frowned. "What species are we talking about? I don't seem to remember insects like that anywhere in Landover."

"Precisely," Abernathy said.

Ben nodded slowly. "So, what you're saying is . . ."

"These insects are the direct result of ill-considered and ill-conceived magic," his scribe declared. "That's what I'm saying."

"Magic conjured by whom?"

"Questor Thews—once again practicing magic without a license, to the detriment and regret of all." A pause. "I've warned you about this before, have I not?"

"Repeatedly." Ben exchanged a look with Willow. "I don't seem to remember him saying anything about creating giant insects, however. Are you sure he's to blame for this?"

Abernathy drew himself up, a sneer tugging at his dog lips. "Quite sure. Our overconfident and marginally skilled Court

Wizard botched his attempt at transforming the Fillipians into butterflies, it seems. Some of those butterflies have become monsters with wingspans of twenty or thirty feet that prefer humans as sustenance. Now Stink Whistle is bearing the brunt of this failure."

He looked so self-satisfied that Ben could hardly stand it. Bad enough that he recognized the look by now without having to endure it. "Perhaps we should feel a little compassion for our friend?" he suggested.

"Compassion? Did you say *compassion*, High Lord?"

"Yes, you know. Sympathy. Empathy for his unsuccessful, though well-meaning, attempts to do the right thing. I'm sure you will agree that none of this was intentional."

Abernathy actually growled. "I'll agree to nothing of the sort! As for empathy, when he finds a way to turn me back into a man again, then I will extend him compassion and whatever else he requires. But not before!"

He actually barked involuntarily at the conclusion of his speech—something he almost never did—and Ben sighed. "So how, exactly, do we know these creatures are Fillipians? Or were Fillipians, anyway?"

"After eating a villager or two, they regurgitated the pieces. A characteristic that might remind you of something else?"

"So we now have more babies?"

"No, now we have body parts. The kind that simply lie about on the ground, waiting for someone to dispose of them. There are rather a lot of them at this point, since the creatures have eaten five villagers and seem eager to continue for as long as there is anyone in Stink Whistle to devour. The residents of the village have barricaded themselves in their homes, which for the most part are constructed of stone and therefore safe enough. For the moment, the beasts can't get at them."

Which might not be true for very long, Ben knew.

He got to his feet. "Assemble a company of soldiers. We'd better go see what we can do."

For the first time, Abernathy hesitated. "Perhaps it might be better to wait until morning? Haste does not benefit those who rush to—"

Ben shook his head, cutting Abernathy short.

"Right now!"

So off they went—a small army of the High Lord's finest soldiers, along with Bunion, Questor, Abernathy, and Ben himself. (Willow had given momentary thought to coming, but she had done this so many times before that she decided it would be better if she remained behind. Having a woman along on a rescue mission, she found, always seemed to upset everyone— possibly because men always worried they would end up having to save the woman when it usually ended up being the other way around, even if men didn't want to admit it.)

They rode horses north toward what had, of late, become known within the confines of Sterling Silver as the Fillipian Woods—just beyond which, Ben knew from consulting with Questor, they would find Stink Whistle and the marauding insects. They traveled quickly, anxious to cover as much ground as possible before sunset. They didn't get far, of course, because the sun had already been setting when Abernathy had brought the news. So they ended up riding most of the way in the dark, although two of Landover's moons were out that night and provided sufficient light to allow for safe passage.

It was well after midnight when the company finally arrived at the outskirts of Stink Whistle. Although Ben was expecting to hear sounds of mayhem and destruction, he heard nothing but the steady clop of their horses' hooves. No shrieks or screams; no grunts or roars. Only silence. When they rode down the main road leading into town, they saw no one. Apparently, they had arrived too late. It appeared the hunt for food was over, the beasts sated, and the villagers devoured.

Ben spurred his mount forward, fearing the worst. The rest of the company followed, weapons drawn. They proceeded cautiously, peering into shadows between buildings and encroaching groves of trees, watching for movement. There were glimmers of light in windows, but shutters everywhere were tightly closed. They came upon the remains of a horse and something that might once have been a man, but nothing like the carnage they had anticipated. There were no body parts scattered along the roadway. No villagers fled through the streets and alleyways, seeking shelter from their hunters.

More gratifying still, there were no signs of new baby Fillipians.

Huh, Ben thought as they reached the center of the village and came to a halt.

They were sitting atop their horses, looking around in puzzlement, when a nearby door creaked open and an old man stuck his head out. "They're gone!" he snapped.

Ben walked his horse closer. "Which way?"

"How would I know? I've been hiding in my house for two days! Are you the rescue party we've been waiting for?"

"I suppose so," Ben said.

"Took your sweet time, didn't you? Now, get after those things before they decide to come back . . . though you've got to figure out which way they've gone first. They fly, you know, so they could be anywhere!"

Ben looked at Questor, who shrugged. "Where is everyone?" he asked the old man.

"Hiding in their houses, you dang fool! You think they want to get eaten like Jens Whippet or that Forney kid? Who are you anyway?"

Ben didn't think he wanted to answer that question, so he smiled bravely and said, "You can come out now. The monsters are gone."

"Says you!" snapped the old man and slammed the door.

Ben shook his head. "Questor, Questor, Questor."

"I am terribly sorry about all this, High Lord," the other replied quickly. "But how was I to know those Fillipians could continue to change into other things once I magicked them?"

"It would have been a good idea if you had experimented on one of them first."

"Magic is unpredictable, High Lord. Never forget that."

As if this was a possibility where Questor was concerned. Ben searched the empty, darkened skies. "Do you happen to have any magic that might let us track these things? Anything that would tell us where they've gone? We have to find them before they attack anyone else."

Questor looked at him indignantly. "Of course I do!"

They rode all night, making their way to the northeast of the kingdom, crossing into the southern reaches of the Greensward. Although they searched for signs of the winged creatures, they saw nothing, and no one they came upon had seen anything, either. By the time they had reached the Eastern Wastelands and had still not caught even the smallest hint of their quarry, it was beginning to feel as if they were looking for a needle in a haystack.

It didn't help matters that Abernathy and Questor were bickering constantly. It got bad enough that Ben thought about sending them both home. Except he needed Questor (well, maybe) to help him search out the creatures they were hunting. And sending Abernathy back would require he also send an escort to protect him. That would embarrass his Court Scribe immensely. Better to weather the bickering, even if it was driving him crazy.

When they were nearing the Fire Springs, he called a halt. Going farther would mean entering Strabo's domain, and that was never a wise idea if you didn't have an invitation. Not that the dragon offered many, but at least you had to ask. So he sent Bunion ahead to inquire if the dragon had seen the winged creatures. It didn't pay to take anything for granted where Strabo was concerned. He tolerated Ben as Landover's King, but that attitude could change at any moment, given his mercurial nature. Strabo was nothing if not unpredictable, and Ben had experienced the repercussions of this more than once in the past.

With the arrival of dawn, Bunion returned. Always a difficult creature to read, let alone understand, he was particularly inscrutable this morning, his wizened face scrunched up with what appeared to be either tears or laughter or maybe both, his rough language so punctuated by odd mutterings that even Questor couldn't understand him clearly.

"It appears he found Strabo," the wizard said, "but I can't quite make out the result. It does appear the dragon is coming to us, however."

Not very helpful, Ben thought, resigned to talking to Strabo himself—not a very compelling prospect. He thought about sending Questor, but the dragon had less regard for Landover's Court Wizard than he did for Landover's King. He seemed to feel a kinship for Bunion, however, although Ben could not imagine why.

The problem soon resolved itself when a dark shadow fell over the entire company and Strabo sailed slowly out of the heavily misted horizon east. Everyone backed away immediately, save Ben. He was King, after all, so he couldn't very well show fear (even if he was experiencing it). Instead, he stepped forward to meet his fate.

Strabo landed, and the ground shook. The dragon surpassed huge in the way a mountain overshadows a flatlands. He was a massive beast, all black scales and horny protrusions, great wings carefully folding back against his armored body. Intimidation being a large part of his persona, he loomed over Ben as if he intended to crush him, forcing Ben to look skyward just to meet his baleful gaze.

"Holiday," Strabo hissed, his breath hot and raw enough to melt iron. "I had hoped never to see you again. How unpleasant to find out I was wrong."

Ben straightened. "Just once, I wish you would start a conversation with me that doesn't include an insult."

The dragon laughed, great jaws parting, revealing a hint of the fire that burned deep in his throat. "And what fun would that be? Tell me, does your neck hurt from having to look up so far? Do you regret that you are so small and puny? Others in your situation do—usually just before I eat them."

"I'm sure. But can we skip the threats and just talk?"

"Conversing with you is so boring. You have such trouble holding up your end of the interaction." His emerald eyes surveyed the rest of the company. "Is that Questor Thews? Is he still Court Wizard? How pathetic! You really ought to find someone even marginally competent. Isn't he the whole reason you're here?"

Ben was caught off guard. "You know why we're here?"

"Let's just say I have my suspicions. I must say, I keep wondering when you are going to get around to governing your kingdom in a reasonable fashion. Thus far, the whole concept of governing seems to have eluded you. You appear to believe that once you were named High Lord, you were no longer required to do anything but sit on your throne. Chaos reigns, your retinue of handlers wring their hands and engage in pointless attempts to stem the tide, and no one seems to understand that it's all your fault."

"What is it exactly that you think I should be doing that I'm not?" Ben demanded, now thoroughly put out. "Besides, who are you to sit in judgment of me? Who causes more trouble in this kingdom than you?"

"That is entirely beside the point. I cause trouble because that is what dragons *do*. This is not supposed to be the case with High Lords of Landover. High Lords are supposed to govern ably and keep things in balance. And this is where you have failed, time and again. I cannot help but feel we would all be better off without you. Maybe it's time for a new King."

"Fine!" Ben snapped. "So you want to overthrow the present regime and bring in someone more capable? Hasn't that been tried before? And hasn't it repeatedly failed? Miserably? You can wail about me all you want, but I am still better than the twenty-seven or so other kings who all fled for their lives in the first week of their rule." He paused, calming himself as best he could with a forty-ton dragon looming over him. "So what is it you are trying to say? What is your specific complaint?"

"*Specific* complaint? I have no *specific* complaint. I am *generally* dissatisfied with your efforts at ruling." The dragon sniffed. "But enough of that. I just wanted to voice my displeasure while I had your attention. Now, tell me what you're doing here, and we can all get on with our lives."

Strabo flexed his back muscles, and all of his considerable spikes stood on end. He yawned to emphasize his boredom and smacked his dragon lips lazily. "You know, I do like your queen, though—so much better than you. Dragons are like that: gracious and sentimental where ladies are concerned. We have a soft spot for such lovely creatures, especially when they are of the fairy persuasion. Such exquisite creatures." His nostrils flared. "But why am I wasting my time telling you all this? And why am I doing all the talking? Speak up, won't you? I don't have all day. What are you doing here?"

Ben took a deep breath. "Apparently, you already know the answer to that. Several winged creatures of considerable size are rampaging through the countryside, killing people and destroying property. I want to put an end to it. Have you seen them?"

"Of course I've seen them! They were trespassing on my domain, trying to steal cattle from my personal herd—cattle I had spent considerable time rounding up."

"Stealing, you mean," Ben interrupted.

"Semantics," Strabo countered.

"So where are they?"

Strabo regarded him with an expression that somehow managed to convey both scorn and disgust. "Why should I waste my time telling you? What do you think *you* can do about it?"

Ben shook his head in disbelief. "Oh, I don't know. Rid Landover of them, perhaps?"

"Really? Do you think you're up to it, you and this ragtag band of inept minions? Because I don't."

Ben gave up. "Just tell me where you saw them."

Strabo released a rush of smoky breath that engulfed Ben and left him feeling slightly singed and deeply violated.

"Look, Holiday. These are not the sorts of creatures that listen to reason. You will need to put an end to them. Termination with extreme prejudice. I would have eaten them and let them burn to crisps in my stomach, but as even you realize by now, no one in his right mind eats a Kringe."

"Wait a minute." Ben held up one hand. "You know what these things are?"

Strabo paused. "Don't you?"

"No. Why would I?"

"You are King of Landover. Read up on the history and cultural development of your domain and its inhabitants, why don't you? Certainly Questor Thews must know what the Kringe are."

"I've never heard of them, either!" Questor declared from somewhere in the deep background.

Strabo spat out several gouts of fire that sent everyone but Ben scurrying for safer ground. "I forget how very young and ill informed you all are compared with me," Strabo sneered. "Kringe are a form of changeling. Very dangerous, because they make themselves look harmless so you will take them in. Nasty little beasts. And sneaky mean. They've been around for a very long time, although most died out awhile back. I should know. I assisted in hastening their departure. But they are a persistent species. Sort of like humans. That's what you've been mucking around with, the two of you. I suppose I shouldn't be surprised at your stupidity."

"They started out as pets!" Ben snapped. "They didn't look dangerous."

"I'm sure they didn't. But perhaps you've heard that appearances can be deceiving?" Strabo shook his head as he looked past Ben at Questor. "You tried using magic on them, didn't you? But you can't get rid of them that way. Kringe are exceptionally hard to kill. And as you have discovered, even if you should eat it, it will come back to life. Not that I can imagine anyone doing such a loathsome thing. Even the dog." He nodded toward Abernathy.

Ben quickly brought the subject back to the matter at hand. "So how *do* you rid yourself of them?"

Strabo leaned close, lantern eyes glowing. "Brute force, Holiday. Like unpleasant bugs, you stamp on them. You squish them flat."

Ben swallowed. "With your foot?"

"What do you think?"

"I think my feet are sort of small for squishing something that big."

Strabo straightened, giving Ben space to breathe again. "You might want to give that some consideration. It's best to know your limitations, Holiday. Best to recognize them before you find out the hard way how big they are. *Un*like your feet."

"Just point me in the right direction," Ben snapped. "I'll find a way to deal with the Kringe."

"Oh, you will, will you? And just how do you plan to accomplish this? Will you make your feet bigger? Or the Kringe smaller? Maybe you can just keep stomping on them over and over until they are flattened; that should only take a week or two, if you are persistent. And if they agree to remain still and not simply eat you."

Ben held his ground. "Well, what do you suggest?"

"I suggest you turn around and go home until you find a better way of dealing with them. This task is beyond you."

There was a long pause as Ben and the dragon eyed each other. Ben felt his chances for accomplishing anything slipping away. Strabo was right. It was difficult to accept, but when you came right down to it, his reign as the King of Landover had been largely ineffectual. He should be better at what he did. He should be able to accomplish more. He was the ruler of an entire kingdom and responsible for its inhabitants and their welfare, yet so much of what happened seemed to simply overwhelm him, to overcome his best efforts and require others to fix it for him.

Now a talking dragon, no less, was taunting him with his failures. It was humiliating.

When he had left his old world behind after the death of his wife and daughter, and abandoned the practice of law in the wake of his discouragement over its inadequacies and failings, he had thought coming to Landover could provide him with a fresh start and a chance to accomplish something important as its King. Never mind that he knew rationally that Landover could not possibly exist. Never mind that he found that nothing was as he had thought it would be, and virtually everything occupying this strange world seemed to be set against him. What had mattered was that he had believed, in his heart of hearts, that it might be possible to start anew. Here was the chance he had been hoping for. This new life was what he had come searching for.

When it turned out that his faith might be rewarded, he had been both flustered and excited. But by now, almost twenty years into his reign, his hopes and expectations had taken a beating. He was weary of the struggle, and more and more frequently wondered if he had accomplished anything at all. That he had married Willow and fathered Mistaya were things he could point to with pride, but they were not exactly achievements. It didn't seem enough to say he had set out to be King and now he was. It didn't seem adequate that he had made the transition from lawyer in one world to King in another without being able to identify what exactly he had accomplished by doing so. And it didn't feel sufficient that he had spent the better part of his twenty-year rule just putting out fires.

Kings, he thought, were supposed to rule. But how much ruling had he actually done?

He wasn't a ruler. Not really. He was mostly a manager.

So how could he take any pride in that?

Yet Kings really *were* managers when you came right down to it, weren't they? Kings didn't rule their kingdoms, no matter what they might tell themselves; they just managed them. Just like leaders of countries everywhere, even back in his old world. All those leaders of nations seeking to make great changes and leave deep footprints? Mostly what they did was manage things as best they could while trying not to muck up the status quo. Those who ruled in any other way did so by domination and brute force, and he could never do that. He wasn't built for it. Maybe that was what Strabo expected of him, but it wasn't what he was prepared to give.

Besides, he knew he was better off as a manager than he would ever be as a ruler. It suited him perfectly, and gave him something he could feel confident about. It provided him with goals he could reasonably expect to attain.

And just like that, he had an idea.

"In spite of what you think," he said suddenly, breaking the silence, "I take my position as King of Landover seriously. I know my responsibilities, and I know what I must do to exercise them. But I know that I have my limitations, too. Obviously, this is one of them. Stamping out giant insects is not an integral part of my skill set. So I have a better idea. Why don't you do it for me? For me, as your King; for Landover, as your country—and for yourself, so you may receive Landover's Gold Medal for Exceptional Service."

Strabo glared at him. "What are you talking about? Aside from the fact that I have no intention of helping you, there is no such award."

"As a matter of fact, there is. It was conceived of and designed by Landover's Queen Willow. It's new, though—and no one has yet proved worthy enough to receive it. But you could be the first. I have reason to think I can persuade her to award it to you. I will certainly recommend it, since I have no desire to have any further dealings with the Kringe. If she agrees, she will bestow it on you personally."

"I have no need of medals or awards or . . ." He paused. "You said *Gold Medal for Exceptional Service*? Is that actually the metal of which it is made, Holiday? Gold?"

Ben nodded. "Featuring a fist-sized emerald set within the center of a graven image of your face, since you would be its first recipient. Also, there is something to be said about being the center of attention at an awards ceremony, featuring a Queen as lovely and kind and good as our own. Don't you think?"

Landover's histories recorded that dragons—even ones as large and ferocious and uncompromising as Strabo—had a soft spot for beautiful women and precious metals. Hopefully, offering both together would prove irresistible.

Strabo had gone silent, looking off into the distance. Ben waited, holding his breath. "Hmmm," the dragon mused. "An attractive offer, I admit. The pretty sylph, giving me an award. It does seem appropriate, even for so paltry a task as this one." He paused. "But I wonder. Could it be designated as more of a . . . Lifetime Achievement award?"

"Done!" Ben said at once. "Congratulations. Recipient of the first Gold Medal for Lifetime Achievement in Service to Landover! This is a proud moment for all of us."

The dragon drew himself up and nodded. "I suppose it is, isn't it?"

Ben smiled. "Now all you have to do is rid us of those flying insects, and an awards ceremony can be scheduled."

Strabo spread his wings wide. "Wait right here."

Lifting his great horned head, he breathed out a stream of fire that momentarily swept the sky and rained ash and smoke all over Ben. Then he spread his wings and lifted off with an earthshaking roar. The wind from his passing flattened grasses, scrub, and living creatures alike before he disappeared into the blue of the midday sky and was gone.

After a while, from not too far off, there came the sounds of stamping. The earth shook and the air was filled with further roaring; then there was silence.

Seconds later Questor appeared at Ben's elbow, his wizened face pinched with distaste. "Well, that was unnecessarily showy," he declared.

Ben nodded and turned away. Unsurprisingly, he was in a much better mood.

SEVERAL DAYS LATER, he received another unannounced visit from the G'home Gnomes. Fillip, Sot, and Shoopdiesel appeared on his castle doorstep in the company of a fourth gnome. This latest addition to the little band was another of those he had previously encountered and survived—an ingratiating fellow called Poggwydd. This time he didn't wait for the gnomes to be brought in, but went down himself to greet them at the gates. He ushered them inside and took them to the kitchen, then sat them down and had them fed. While they ate, he sat with them and waited patiently to learn what had brought them here this time.

Finally, when Poggwydd had finished his meal, he cleared his throat loudly and rose to his feet. The other three immediately rose with him, heads lowered. Only Poggwydd spoke.

"On behalf of my companions, I want to assure you, High Lord, they are very sorry for all the trouble they have caused. They regret they were so foolish and unthinking in their behavior regarding the . . ."

He paused and leaned close to Fillip. "Yes, the Fillipians. All of them wish to apologize for their actions. They have promised not to try to find any more of these . . . creatures. And further promised never to try to bring one home again. All they ask is that you forgive them and tell them you are still their friend."

He stopped talking. All of them waited—three with downcast looks, occasionally glancing up to reveal expressions that would have been downright heartbreaking on most creatures yet merely looked muddleheaded on them. But Ben had seen those looks before, and after similar promises, so he knew they were as genuine as G'home Gnomes could make them. It was just too bad they couldn't ever seem to follow through.

Manage, not rule. He said the words to himself and smiled.

He faced the gnomes squarely. "I do forgive you," he said to them aloud. "And I am still your friend."

Curiously enough, he meant it.

Introduction to

"Allanon's Quest"

THIS PARTICULAR SHORT story was one of three I wrote a few years back for reasons that escape me, though I think it was an effort to contribute to an ebook market I had pretty much avoided. In any case, I wrote them all at once, one right after the other—all original tales and all centered on familiar characters that had appeared in earlier Shannara books. They were published online as intended, available for sale there and there only. None of them ever appeared in print form.

But readers, being the voracious devourers of fantasy that they are, began making polite demands for a print run on all three. Since I don't control when, where, or how my books and stories are published, I promised that one day all three would appear in a collection of my short works. The immediate problem at that point was that I didn't have enough short material to make up a real collection. So I had to ask for patience.

Which brings us to the present. This particular story—in typical Brooks books fashion—is long and centered on a character readers have repeatedly wanted to know more about. Additionally, it deals with a period of time I have never written about. In *The Sword of Shannara,* the Druid Allanon comes searching for Shea Ohmsford, who is the last scion of the fabled Shannara line, because the Warlock Lord has returned to the

Four Lands and Shea is the last, best hope of the Races. But what happened just before the opening of *Sword*? I've never said. How did Allanon come to find Shea? What events transpired to lead up to that seeking?

"Allanon's Quest" answers those questions.

ALLANON'S

QUEST

THE STORM CLOUDS scudded across the night sky in roiling
clumps that blotted out the half-moon and stars and enveloped
the land beneath in heavy shadow. The woods surrounding the
village of Archer Trace, fifty miles north and east of the city of
Arborlon, stirred uneasily. The trees swayed, and their leaves
shivered with a metallic rustling as wind tore at the branches in
sharp gusts and rain pattered heavily against the leaves. A drop
in the temperature had already announced the storm's arrival,
and the air was damp, chilly, and raw. Intricate patterns of
lightning flashed, and bursts of thunder rumbled from across
the eastern edge of the Sarandanon.

Allanon pulled his black robes tighter and his hood closer as
he entered the Elven village, passing the first of the outlying
buildings and making his way along the empty pathways. Candlelight burned in the windows of a few cottages and huts, flickering behind glass panes or through open shutters, and this
small light was sufficient to guide him on his way. But most of
the buildings were entirely dark. The residents had gone either
to bed in anticipation of an early rising or down to the taverns
that provided the main source of entertainment for the village.

Had anyone been looking through windows or shutters, or
had he been careless enough not to disguise his coming, he
might have been observed. But Allanon was not the careless

sort, and he had used his Druid skills to change his appearance sufficiently that he seemed little more than another of the night's shadows. To anyone looking, he simply wasn't there. It was a Druid trick—one he had perfected during his early years, when he was just learning his craft. Bremen, who had taught it to him, was already gone by then, so he had mastered it on his own, expanding on his existing skills.

But while Archer Trace was the sort of miserable place where inhabitants and visitors alike made a point of watching one another closely, there was little vigilance on this night. The foul weather did not invite such monitoring, and the pleasures of the taverns provided a more attractive lure. So Allanon passed into the village relatively unseen, traveling along its single roadway to a cluster of ragged buildings that were illuminated by torches wedged down in iron brackets beneath their weather shields, fighting bravely to stay lit against the onslaught of wind and rain.

Slowing, he looked for the sign that would identify his destination and quickly found it: THE DRUNKEN FOOL. Big, bold letters—no doubt a reference to its patrons. But if it could provide him with the information he needed, what did the nature of the business or its patrons matter to him? He had come all the way from Arborlon on this slim hope of success because time and opportunity were growing short. And rumor alone was enough to send him on what others might have dismissed as a fool's errand. Lives were being snuffed out, and all that mattered might soon be gone—something that would prove disastrous to the Four Lands. If even one of those he sought could be saved, he had to do whatever it took to make that happen. There was more at stake here than his discomfort and risk.

He cast aside the magic that let him remain unseen as he pushed his way through the tavern's heavy door and into the smoky interior, then looked about. The room was crowded—more so than he would have expected, given the size and condition of the village. Most of the tavern's denizens were Elves—no surprise there; this was their homeland. But it appeared as if everyone who lived in Archer Trace or might even have been passing through had gathered. A few heads turned to look at him, but most turned quickly away. A man seven feet tall and possessed of rough features and a dark scowl did not draw many extended looks. He ignored the few looks he did receive and waited for the barkeep to acknowledge him. When the man gave him a nod of recognition, the Druid turned his attention to a small table in the back of the room and the two men who occupied it. A moment later, both men rose, having suddenly decided that it was time to leave—although neither could have said why.

He gave it a moment, then crossed to the table the men had vacated and sat down.

After a few minutes, the barkeep wandered over.

"Long trip?" He was a large, heavyset man with big features and a dour look. For an Elf, he looked downright sullen. "I know everyone in the village," he added. "You've come from somewhere else."

Allanon nodded. "A cold tankard of ale would ease my weariness."

The barkeep nodded and wandered off, and Allanon looked around at the room's patrons, his gaze moving from face to face, making sure that nothing seemed out of place and no one appeared to be a threat. By the time he had finished, the barkeep had returned.

"Anything else?" He set the tankard of ale down and waited. "Something to eat, maybe?"

The Druid shook his head. "Do you know where I can find a man called Derrivanian?"

"Might. What's your business?"

"My business is my own."

"Maybe so, but I don't like sending trouble to other people's doorsteps. Trouble finds them quick enough without my help."

"I intend no trouble." Allanon brushed the rain from his

shoulders and sat back. "He is an old friend. I knew him when he served as record keeper for the Elessedils."

"Oh, you know of that? So maybe you are a friend. But where's the proof? What's to say you aren't here to collect a bill or cause some other sort of mischief?"

Allanon gave him a look. "Derrivanian is an old man with an old wife and an old dog, and he hasn't got much of anything to give and no history of ever having done anyone harm. Why don't you just tell me where he lives?"

The barkeep shook his head. "I need something more than your word before I tell you anything. I don't much like the look of you—all in black, dark-faced, and grim. You're a big man used to getting his way. Well, I'm a big man, too, and I'm not afraid of you."

Allanon went very still. "It isn't me you should fear, barkeep." He locked eyes with the man. "Ask yourself this. Are you sure enough of yourself that you would risk a meeting with one who might not ask any questions but simply tear the information from you? Would you risk a meeting with those they call Skull Bearers?"

The barkeep paled. "Do not speak that name in here!"

"What name should I speak, then? I gave you Derrivanian. Should I give you another? The Warlock Lord's name, perhaps? Or is there another you would prefer me to speak?"

The barkeep backed away. "I want you out of here! Take your business elsewhere and seek your answers from another."

Allanon shook his head. "I have no time for asking others. I have chosen to ask you, and I will have my answers now. Look at me. Where will l find Eldra Derrivanian?"

The barkeep tried to back away, but suddenly his strength failed, and he found himself rooted in place. His face tightened with his efforts to free himself, and it was clear he saw something new in the Druid's eyes that made him realize what he was up against.

"Answer me," Allanon ordered.

"Take the road west out of the village." The barkeep was speaking in a different voice, one dredged up from the dark places you hide when you are very afraid. "Go about five hundred yards. Look for a fence and a wooden gate inset with the carved image of a rooster. He can be found there."

Allanon nodded. "My thanks. Now forget you ever saw me. Forget this conversation. Forget everything but your purpose in coming to my table with my tankard of ale." He paused. "What was it you wanted to ask me again?"

The barkeep's eyes, which had lost focus, suddenly seemed clear again. "Something to eat, maybe?"

When the barkeep had left the table, Allanon took a few minutes to finish the tankard of ale, relishing the cold liquid flowing down his throat and the fire it brought to his belly. He stopped examining the patrons and the room and delved deep into his own thoughts, musing on the Druid abilities he had developed since leaving Bremen to his fate at the Hadeshorn all those years ago. Sometimes, it seemed like a dream to him. He could still see the old man walking out onto the glistening black rock of the Valley of Shale to the edge of the lake's waters and into the arms of the Shade of Galaphile, then being carried beyond into the mists. He could still remember standing alone afterward and wondering how he could manage what he had been charged with doing.

He was only fifteen when Bremen had left him. Only a boy. But he had been strong, both physically and mentally, and he had grown only stronger with time. And he had used that strength in ways that now made his name a household legend.

He had restored Paranor to the world of Men, using the Black Elfstone entrusted to him by Bremen, and made the Druid's Keep his permanent residence. He had brought a fresh contingent of Elven Hunters—supplied at first by Jerle Shannara, then by those Elven Kings who had succeeded him—to act as protectors of the Druid's Keep and the Sword of Shannara, which had been set within a block of Tre-Stone and placed in a vault, there to await the day when Bremen had promised it would be needed again.

Then he had slept the Druid Sleep, deep and dark with magic that let time and aging pass him by.

But now the day that Bremen had promised had arrived—the day for which Allanon had been preparing himself all his life. A life that, because of his extensive use of the Druid Sleep, spanned almost five hundred years.

So fifteen years of age was a very long time ago, and that boy he had been was very far removed from who he had become.

He lifted his eyes from the tankard and looked out across those years to the many, many people he had left behind. He was in the prime of his life, while all those he had known as a boy and a young man were gone. It was a strange feeling to realize that so much had passed him by. It was a hard way to live your life, but he was the last Druid—the only Druid—and he wondered where he would find another to succeed him. He had looked, but no one seemed right for the weight of what he would have to ask of them. Who would willingly accept that burden? Worse, only someone who fully understood what it meant to shoulder such a load, and what responsibilities came with it, would be the right choice.

But that was another problem for another time, and this night was meant for other work.

He pushed back from the table and rose. The tavern seemed busier than ever, the bar crowded with laughing, shouting, jostling people. All the tables were occupied. He was barely on his feet before a pair of young men hurried over to claim his space, pausing only long enough to make certain he did not object. He nodded to them and walked away—ignoring the barkeep, who ignored him in turn—then moved back through the door and out into the night.

Wrapped in his cloak, he trudged up the muddy roadway, head bent but ears and eyes alert for sound and movement. The rain was a slow, steady downpour that had already soaked the ground and was now being channeled into low places to pool and settle. He kept to the drier parts of the sodden path as best he could, moving westward toward his destination, thinking about what he hoped to accomplish. So much depended on what Eldra Derrivanian remembered or what he had written down, or even what he might be able to divine. It had come to this: a sort of crazy guessing game as to who might still be out there that the winged servants of the Warlock Lord hadn't already found. Someone who hadn't already been revealed by traitors and sycophants eager to preserve the lives they were assured of losing. Someone who hadn't already been turned or killed.

Someone who might still have courage enough to do what was needed to save the Races.

But this was Eldra Derrivanian, and he might not care about saving anyone.

TWO WEEKS EARLIER, Allanon had thought his search a lost cause. He had known of the Warlock Lord's imminent return for months. All the signs were there for anyone who could read them. Winged fliers had been spotted in the north—Skull Bearers patrolling the night skies over the Knife Edge Mountains, bathing in the waters of the River Lethe to armor their skin by day. Bodies of travelers had been discovered in the surrounding regions, ripped to shreds and partially devoured. People and animals alike had gone missing, never to be seen again. Fire bloomed in the once-dead volcanoes that riddled the Charnal Mountains, and deep rumblings shook the earth at regular intervals.

The prophecy that Bremen had passed on to him all those years ago was coming to pass. Brona, the once-Druid who had fallen victim to his own pursuit of the dark magic and evolved as a consequence into the Warlock Lord, had not been destroyed as most believed. The Elven King Jerle Shannara had not successfully wielded the sword forged especially for this purpose, and though the Warlock Lord had been defeated and driven

from his mortal body and the Four Lands, still he was only diminished, not dead. One day, Bremen told the boy, the Dark
Lord would return. To that end, the Sword of Shannara must be
kept safe and made ready for an heir to the Elven house of Shannara. When the time came, whether during Allanon's lifetime
or the lifetimes of his Druid successors, a Shannara heir must
take up the Sword and stand against the Warlock Lord once
again.

It was easy enough to acknowledge this truth and set it aside
for another day, which is what Allanon had done. He had made
certain the Sword of Shannara was kept safe at Paranor and
gone on with his life. Years had passed, with no indications of
the expected return. Other matters had occupied his thoughts
and his time. Eventually, hundreds of years later, the prospect
of the Warlock Lord's return was all but forgotten.

Even so, he recognized it when it happened, and he understood what was needed to keep the people of the Four Lands
safe. But he had acted too slowly. He had failed to anticipate just
how the Warlock Lord would prevent the Sword from being
used against him a second time. The Sword itself was anathema
to both the Dark Lord and the Skull Bearers; they could barely
stand to be in its presence, let alone touch it for even an instant.
So lacking the means to take it for himself, Brona chose instead
to eliminate all those who might one day use it against him. He
decided to wipe out Jerle Shannara's line.

Systematically, he killed all those who were scions of the
Elven house. Since Jerle Shannara's direct descendants had all
died of natural causes within three generations of his own
death, the Warlock Lord needed only to search out those distant
relations who carried even a trace of his Elven blood. Allanon
did not realize at first what was happening. And by the time he
did and began his own search, he found himself arriving too
late to save any of the ones he sought. By then he was in steady
communication with the young Elven King Eventine Elessedil,
and the two of them were working together to glean any refer-

ences or scraps of information about Shannara descendants from the Elven genealogy records and histories that might help in their search.

It was Eventine's last message that had brought Allanon to Arborlon two weeks earlier and set him on his current hunt.

"You've had no luck finding an heir?" the young King had asked him after they had settled down in one of the private reception rooms. Eventine had only recently ascended to the Elven throne following the death of his father. Already, Allanon believed the Elf's potential was enormous. His charisma, his strength of character, his concern for his people—and his ability to act quickly and judge fairly—suggested he was a King in more than just name.

"No luck at all," he answered. "Every single source has yielded only the dead. We are running out of time."

"And out of names. I have exhausted my sources here. Are the Druid Histories and your personal records of no further help?"

Allanon was a historian of some note and a meticulous keeper of records. He had made a concerted effort to write down the names of the Shannara heirs over the years, recording deaths, births, and marriages. But even he had not been able to follow every thread in the line, and so the possibility existed that a man or woman possessing Shannara blood could still be found.

"I am out of ideas. I have nowhere else to turn."

"I thought as much. But there is one other possibility we have overlooked."

Allanon had been surprised. He had thought their search had ended with the deaths of the entire Waylandring family in Emberen a week earlier. He had thought there was no one left. "Who have we missed?"

"Not a descendant of Jerle Shannara, but a man who might know of one that we do not. His name is Eldra Derrivanian. He was the keeper of the genealogical records for the members of the royal families and the Elven High Council for many years.

He was there even before my father. His knowledge was phe-
nomenal, even for a keeper of records. He could trace almost
any branch of their lineage from memory. He kept his own set
of records in addition to ours, and he took those records with
him when he was dismissed from service just before my father
died."

"Dismissed? I sense a problem."

"You are not mistaken. Derrivanian left under very unfortunate circumstances. His son was killed while serving in the
Elven Home Guard. The killer was never found, and the reason
for his death remained a mystery. The circumstances surrounding the event were suspicious, and Derrivanian could not let the
matter drop. He demanded that my father do more. But my father was old and dying by that time, and failed in his efforts.
Derrivanian was so distraught, he began to ignore his work. In
some cases, he deliberately sabotaged it—in small ways at first,
and later in much more extensive ones. When my father found
out what was happening, he dismissed him. Derrivanian ap-
pealed to the High Council for help but was rebuffed. In the
end, he left Arborlon in disgrace."

"So he has no reason to want to help us."

"You will have to discover that for yourself."

"You know where he is now?"

"He was seen in the village of Archer Trace only a week ago,
discovered by a member of my Elven guard during our searches
for the descendants of Jerle Shannara. Finding him was a complete accident. He is living there with his wife. Both are quite
elderly. If he still hates the Elessedils as much as he did in the
time of my father and remains resentful of his dismissal, it may
be difficult to persuade him to help. But he might have his private records with him, or some memory of a member of the
Shannara family that could lead us to an heir."

"And you believe that if he understands the magnitude of the
danger to the Elven people—to his people—he might be persuaded to put aside his anger?"

Eventine had shrugged. "You are the best one to find this out, Allanon. You are, in all likelihood, the only one who can persuade him."

So here he was, off on another fool's errand, searching out an Elf who had no love for the Elessedils and a lasting bitterness toward his own people for their failure to support him in his complaints against the Elven throne. But it was the best chance left to him. Better yet, he might, for once, be one step ahead of his enemy. Derrivanian was not a member of the Shannara family, and so the Warlock Lord and his minions had no reason to seek him out. This time, Allanon believed, he might find the object of his search alive. This time, he might have a chance to discover information that was unknown to the Warlock Lord.

And if so, maybe all was not yet lost.

HE WAS ALMOST completely beyond the limits of Archer Trace when he passed the fence with the rooster carved into its gate. He paused to study the house it warded. Lights burned in the interior—enough to indicate that someone inside was still awake. He watched the windows for movement but saw none. He cast a net of seeking magic to spy out hidden dangers and found none of those, either.

Satisfied, he opened the gate, went up the path to the heavy wooden door, and knocked.

Immediately he heard movement within. "Who's there?" a man called out.

"A stranger to you," Allanon answered. "But I bring news from Arborlon that you will want to hear."

There was a long pause. "There is nothing I wish to hear from Arborlon and its Elves. Go away."

Allanon sighed, his dark face implacable. "The barkeep at The Drunken Fool seemed to think it was important enough to send me this way. Why not hear me out?"

Another pause. Then the locks released, the door swung open, and weak candlelight spilled out into the rain.

The man who stood there was bent with more than just the weight of years and the infirmities of age. Reflected in his eyes were anger and frustration, which spoke of injustices suffered and endured. Bitterness was there, and an expectation of further damage, waiting just around the corner and still out of sight but there nevertheless. There was weariness and a deep sense of resignation.

There was something else, too, but it took a moment for Allanon to sort it out from the rest of the burden this man bore.

There was fear.

"What do you want?" Eldra Derrivanian snapped at him. Then he paused. "Wait. I know you. You're the Druid Allanon."

"We've never met."

"No, but you were at the King's court and before the High Council often enough. I know you, even if you paid no attention to me. Now get out of here."

Allanon moved his foot swiftly to block the door. "First, you will hear me out. Once you've done that, I'll go my way. But not before."

Derrivanian stared at him balefully, then turned his back. "Do what you like. It means nothing to me."

Allanon entered the room and closed the door behind him. He glanced around quickly. The room was small, sparsely furnished, and unkempt. It even smelled unpleasant. Dishes were piled in a washbasin, and clothes were strewn about. He felt right away that something was wrong, but other than the obvious, he couldn't decide what.

"Where is Collice?" he asked.

Derrivanian's wife. The old man hesitated, then nodded toward a door at the back of the room. "Asleep. Sick. She tires easily these days. She goes to bed early. What is it that you want with me?"

Allanon moved over to the tiny kitchen table and sat, waiting. After a moment, Derrivanian sat down across from him. "I require your help," the Druid said, leaning forward, elbows propped on the table, chin resting atop his folded hands, eyes fixed on the old man. "And I hope you will agree to give it after you've heard what I have to say."

"My help to do what?"

"To think back in time and try to remember something for me. To use your exceptional mind to call up something that perhaps no one else can. And if that fails, to peruse your private records to jolt that memory."

The old man rubbed at his face. He was unshaven, and his cheeks and forehead were deeply lined. His ears drooped with age, and his slanted brows were shaggy and gray. His salt-and-pepper hair was wild and stiff as he ran his fingers through it. "Whom do you seek?"

"Anyone who is an heir to the Elven house of Shannara."

The other was silent for a long moment. "The Warlock Lord has returned, hasn't he? The rumors are true."

Allanon nodded. "He has returned, and he has brought his Skull Bearers with him. He is hunting down and killing all of the Shannara kin so that the Sword cannot be used against him again."

"How many are dead so far? Wait. Don't tell me. All of them, right? All that you can find, in any case. If you need my help, it must be as a last resort. How did you even find me?"

"An Elven Hunter searching for news of an heir saw you."

Derrivanian shook his head. "I was hidden here for three years. No one knew. I found some small measure of peace. And now this." He sighed. "I don't have any love for the Elessedils. I don't even have much love for the Elves, no matter if they're my own people. None of them did anything for me when I needed their help. They let my son's death go unpunished. They let his murderer go free. They tossed it all aside like it didn't matter."

Allanon held his gaze. "This involves more than just Arborlon and the Elessedils. The survival of an entire world is at stake. I need you to put your anger aside."

"Do you? Too bad. Why should I bother? Why should I care about the world or anything else?"

"Because you don't want it on your conscience if everything goes wrong and you could have done something to prevent it. Come, Derrivanian. You're been a good and faithful steward for too many years to throw it all aside when it could mean so much to so many if you could help. Stand up for those who can't stand up for themselves."

The old man rose and walked away, stopping to look out a window—perhaps contemplating what he saw, perhaps only gathering his thoughts. He was silent for a long time. Allanon let him be. Too many words of persuasion would have the wrong impact on this man. It would be better to let him come to the right decision on his own.

"You seem a strong man, Allanon," he said finally. "Is that so? Are you as strong as they say?"

Allanon kept quiet, waiting.

"Because I'm not a strong man. I am a weakling and a coward. I've lost a son, and I don't—" He stopped suddenly, shaking his head. "You don't know what you will do until you are faced with a situation that tests you. You think you know, but you don't."

Still, the Druid waited. But he couldn't help wondering as he did so what it was the man was trying to say.

Eldra Derrivanian turned back to him. "There is one last possibility, one last man who may have been overlooked by the Dark Lord. He is a distant relative, born to the son of a son of a cousin once removed from the direct line. His bloodline is true, though. He would have enough of the Shannara in him to serve your purpose. His name is Weir. Shall I tell you where he can be found?"

Allanon nodded slowly. "Tell me everything."

ALLANON DEPARTED THE cottage shortly afterward, pulling his hood over his head and his cloak tightly about his shoulders, hunching down against the onslaught of rain. He had what he needed to find the man Derrivanian had named, including the location of his home. Weir lived on a farm well outside any town or village, north of Emberen, close to the southwestern edge of the Kierlak Desert in country that was just barely Elven and in no way friendly. It was a day's journey in good weather and more in bad. It was better traveled by horse than afoot, and so the Druid went back into Emberen to find a room in which to spend the night before seeking a mount for the morrow's journey.

He was still troubled by his visit to Eldra Derrivanian. Something about it didn't feel right. The man himself, the words he spoke, his actions—none of it. He realized suddenly that there had been a mattress in one corner of the front room, shoved off in a corner. Why was Derrivanian sleeping there when his wife slept in the back room? Or was the bedding for someone else? His wife's sickness could account for the state of the cottage, but there was a furtiveness to him that was troubling.

On the other hand, this was a man whose life had been a shambles for many years, a man who had exiled himself from his people and his previous life and gone into the outback of Elven civilization. He had lost his son and his position and the respect of his King. He had become an object of scorn and pity and outright suspicion. Everything he had built his life around was gone. Perhaps it wasn't so strange that there seemed to be no substance to him.

Allanon spent the night at a rooming house set apart from the taverns, and in the morning he procured a horse and set out. He rode north at a steady pace through the forests, following a series of trails and paths toward the Streleheim. At midday, he passed onto the plains. The terrain changed abruptly, trees giving way to empty space and shade to heat. The rains had moved on, but the earth was left sodden and muddy, and the sun turned the standing pools to steam.

He let his horse meander across the uneven ground so that it could find decent footing, his thoughts straying to the task ahead. He was already thinking about what he would say to this man Weir to persuade him to take up the Sword in defense of his people. Over the past few weeks, he had composed dozens of arguments and hundreds of reasons for all those he had thought he would encounter in his long, fruitless search. In the end, he had needed none of them because there had been no one alive to persuade. If the same was true this time as well, he wasn't certain where he would go next. Back to Derrivanian, perhaps. He wasn't entirely satisfied that he had been given the truth.

But the hard fact remained that he still hadn't found the man or woman he needed, and the time left to do so was growing short. If Weir refused him, what would he do then? There was nothing to say the man wouldn't say no. Most would decline any sort of involvement in this business, no matter its importance and urgency. The danger was enormous, the risks terrifying. Jerle Shannara had been unable to kill the Warlock Lord, and he had been a King and a warrior. How could anyone expect an ordinary man to do better?

And yet that was what would be required. That was what would need to happen to end what had begun all those centuries ago.

He should have planned better, he chided himself. He should have known this time would come sooner rather than later, and he should have found the ones he needed and prepared them. He should have kept better records and spent more time sizing up the heirs who remained. He should have protected them all from what had happened.

He should have done so much more.

The day wore on, and the sun moved westward across the sky toward the horizon. As he neared his destination—a place called Rabbit Ridge—a man herding sheep passed into view. Allanon rode over and hailed him.

"Well met," he told the man.

The man just stared at him, saying nothing. Allanon could

read what was on his mind. He wanted nothing to do with this huge, black-cloaked rider with the grim countenance and imposing presence.

"I'm looking for a man named Weir. He lives on Rabbit Ridge. Do you know of him?"

The herder spit. He pointed left, made a warding sign, then turned away abruptly and hurried on, clucking to his sheep to move them along faster. Allanon watched him go, but he did not wonder at the man's reaction. In his place, he would have done the same.

He rode on, watching the shadows cast by his horse and himself lengthen in front of him, noting the twilight's approach. Not much farther, he thought. Then he would have his chance to persuade a man with no desire to place himself in harm's way that this was exactly what he must do. He wondered if he would find in this man the strength of character and courage and decency to invoke the magic of the Sword. He wondered how the man would react when he heard what the Druid had to say. He had rehearsed the moment so often without ever having come this close to experiencing it. He had prepared himself repeatedly, and all for nothing.

Would it be for nothing again?

He found Rabbit Ridge, a thickly wooded and rough piece of ground, and rode his horse up its slopes. Poor land for farming, he saw, mostly scrub and sparse stands of timber and rocky ground. Sheep might do well here. Was that what the man farmed? He hadn't asked Derrivanian. It hadn't seemed important then and probably wasn't now. Still . . . He was going to ask a farmer to come with him to stand against a monster. It was insane.

He reached the apex of the ridge and urged his horse along its length toward a broad stretch of grasslands that ran like a ragged carpet to the door of a house and barn. There were sheep in a fenced pasture, milling about, moving first in one direction, then in another, looking stupid and lost. He felt a sudden kinship. His eyes shifted to the buildings. There was smoke coming from a chimney attached to the house but no sign of occupants. The barn was big and empty-looking; the hinged doors facing him stood open to the darkness within.

The last of the daylight was fading as he walked his mount to the porch that fronted the house and climbed down.

"Hello the house!" he called out. "Anyone?"

No answer. He didn't care one bit for what that suggested. Draping the reins of his mount over the porch railing, he climbed the steps to the door and knocked.

Still no answer.

"Hello! Anyone?" he repeated.

He walked the length of the porch to peer through the windows. The house looked inhabited. It was well kept, with furniture intact, dishes set on a table, and ashes banked against a stack of wood burning in the hearth. It looked as if the owner had just momentarily stepped away.

Not that there was much of anywhere to step away to.

Except the barn.

Allanon left the horse where it was and walked toward the open doors, keeping a careful eye out for trouble. He had survived enough attempted ambushes and traps to be mindful, and he was not about to fall victim now. He glanced around the farmyard, but other than the sheep in the pasture, there didn't seem to be anyone or anything about. Even so, he fully expected to find Weir in the barn since he wasn't in the house and didn't appear to be anywhere else close at hand.

But when he got there, the building was empty. He walked far enough into the shadows for his eyes to adjust. The stalls were empty, the floor bare, and the interior of the barn silent. He glanced up at the hayloft, but there didn't seem to be a ladder at hand that would allow him to climb up.

He decided to make a more complete search of the level he was on. He walked into every stall, examined every corner, poked through the hay mound, and looked inside the tack room.

There was a toolshed attached to the barn, but the door that led into it was outside. So he exited the barn and walked around to where he could have a look. The shed was filled with hand tools, a workbench, and scrap metal. Nothing there, either.

He closed the door to the toolroom and walked back around to the front of the barn, glancing up momentarily to where the hayloft opened out on the yard.

"Up here!" a voice called suddenly from behind.

There was a man standing on the porch, waving. Allanon stared. Where had he been before? "Are you Weir?"

"I am," the other said. "Come closer, where we can talk."

Allanon started back toward the house. He was no more than ten feet from the man when he noticed the nervous shifting of his horse in the dusty yard, the stamping of hooves, and the sudden shaking of his head.

A warning . . .

Too late. The man on the porch moved first, one arm whipping up sharply, a throwing knife streaking toward the Druid and burying itself in his chest. Allanon tried to react but was a fraction of a second too slow. He staggered back, stricken.

Immediately a whole raft of armed men emerged, pouring out of the house, out of the barn, seemingly out of the ground, howling and brandishing weapons of every stripe. Allanon threw up a protective shield of magic, throwing back as many of his attackers as he could. He dropped to one knee to make himself a smaller target, then yanked out the knife as he tried to gather his strength. To remain where he was would mean his death. Once they sensed the extent of his weakness, they would be on him.

A handful broke through, but he was back on his feet to meet them and flung them away as if they were straw men. He moved quickly, rushing his attackers. They stumbled back from him, none of them eager to stand his ground against this angry giant. But one in their midst, a big man like himself, was shoved forward by the rest, perhaps to champion their failed efforts, perhaps out of desperation only. All dark fury and cold intent, Allanon was reaching for him when he caught sight of archers rushing forward and drawing back their bowstrings. The Druid barely had time to act. Snatching the tunic of the man in front of him, the Druid whipped him about and used him as a shield. A cluster of arrows struck the man, who jerked and went limp. Allanon threw him down in disgust and brought up his protective magic once again.

Those of his attackers still able to do so came at him, some throwing knives, some firing arrows, some using slings, all trying to bring him down. But he was warded by his magic and not so easily reached. His attackers were thrown back again. Even those remaining at what seemed a safe distance found that the Druid magic could reach them easily, and they were tossed aside as well. Bones snapped, and lives were extinguished. Twice more the attackers came at him, and twice more they failed to reach him.

Finally, their numbers reduced by more than half, they turned and fled into the fields and the surrounding countryside, the desire to fight gone out of them.

Allanon clung to one of the uprights supporting the porch roof, watching them flee. Derrivanian's help had been worth nothing. He would have to go back and start over. Once he healed, of course. Once he felt strong enough to do so.

Dizziness washed through him, and a glance down at his robes reinforced his suspicion that he was losing blood rapidly. He pressed gently against the knife wound, trying to stanch the bleeding, using a thin skein of healing magic to help close the ragged opening.

He was engaged in that effort when the Skull Bearer appeared.

He didn't see it at first, but he heard the slow beating of its wings. Then it was swinging around from behind the farmhouse, making no effort to disguise its coming, settling in slow, insolent fashion onto the corpse-strewn yard in front of the porch. Black-scaled from head to foot, and long-limbed in a way that made its crooked arms and legs seem all out of proportion, it was warded by the cape of its huge wings. Eyes, bright and expectant, glittered from beneath a heavy brow that shadowed its rough-hewn face.

"Druid," it hissed at him.

"You arranged all this," Allanon replied, making it a statement of fact.

"I did."

"Why go to such trouble?"

The other's breathing was deep and rough, as if its lungs could not manage to draw in enough air. "Because the Master wishes it. Because it pleases me. Do you know what you have done this day? You have put an end to your last chance at preventing our return."

Allanon stared, uncertain what the creature was saying.

"The man lying at your feet, the one you used to shield yourself? *He* is Weir, and he is the last of the Shannara. The last hope you had. We would have killed him ourselves, but you saved us the trouble."

Allanon felt despair fill him—what had he been manipulated into doing?—but his expression never changed. "Is this your hope, creature? I think a man who sold his services to the Warlock Lord was never the Shannara we needed, and killing him is of no importance." But doubt still nagged at him. What if the man had been an innocent, trapped, like himself, by the Warlock Lord's forces? What if his last hope truly *was* gone?

The great wings drew close about the dark body. "Think what you wish. It matters not the least to me. But your end draws near, Allanon. Like the man lying at your feet, you are the last of your kind. Time will not save you."

"Do you intend to finish what your assassins started?" Allanon asked the Skull Bearer. "Because your power lessens in daylight, does it not?"

The other hissed at him. "Why bother to kill you? I have

come to bear witness to your misery. You hide it well, but your despair is revealed nevertheless. You hoped this man would save your people, but now that cannot happen. Worse still is the way it was accomplished. You were betrayed, Druid. The one who sent you gave you over to me. Think on that. Then do with him what you will."

The Skull Bearer spread its wings and began to lift away, circling upward into the sky.

"My brothers and I will return for you soon, Allanon!" it called back to him. "Watch for us!"

Then the creature was gone, and the Druid was alone.

ALLANON CHOSE NOT to spend the night in the farmhouse even though his knife wound was serious enough that it would be wiser to stay where he was. But with dead men all around him and the prospect of the Skull Bearer changing its mind and returning—perhaps with others for company—the Druid decided it was better to put a little distance between himself and the day's events. Using his magic to strengthen himself as best he could and setting course for friendlier ground, he mounted his horse and rode south into the forests of the Elven Westland and found refuge with friends in a small outpost miles from anything.

There he allowed his wounds to be treated by the wife's practiced hands and took to bed, where he slept undisturbed for thirty hours. Then he rose to wash himself and eat and drink for the first time in two days, and went back to bed.

It took four days of rest, traditional healing skills, and Druid magic before he was fit enough to travel again. At the end of that time, as dawn broke and the day began, he reclaimed his horse, bid his friends farewell, and set out for Archer Trace.

His plans for Derrivanian were still unformed. He understood his options, and he knew that, when the time came, he would have to choose among them. But his thoughts were dark and tinged with anger, and he did not want to get too close to them until he understood for certain what had happened. It was too easy to conclude that he already understood everything. But he had believed that once before, when going in search of Weir, and it had almost been the death of him. This time he would be more circumspect—and less resolute about what he thought he knew.

He rode through the day at a steady pace, but he made frequent stops to rest and took time to eat and drink and replenish the magic that healed his wounds. He breathed in the spring air, feeling warmth in its breezes, the first hint of summer's approach. It was a time of rebirth in the world, the yearly beginnings of new life and fresh possibility. He wanted to feel just a little of that, wanted to hold it in his heart and draw from its strength.

Twilight approached as he came to the edge of Archer Trace and turned down the roadway that would lead to the cottage of Eldra Derrivanian. He no longer bothered to consider what he was going to do, even though it was not yet decided. He would know when he faced the man. His instincts and his intellect would show him the way. He was a Druid, after all, and a Druid always knew.

He reined in his horse at the gate bearing the rooster carving, left it tied to the fence, and walked to the door of the cottage. Derrivanian opened the door before Allanon reached it.

"You're alive," the old man said, and in the tone of his voice, Allanon detected an unexpected note of relief.

They stood on the porch staring at each other. "Why did you give me up to them like that?" Allanon asked finally.

Derrivanian shook his head. "I wasn't offered a choice. Come in. I will tell you everything."

They entered Derrivanian's home, which looked exactly the same as it had when the Druid had visited the last time— counters and dusty furniture cluttered with pieces of clothing and unwashed dishes, mattress and bedding shoved into one corner, and the bedroom door closed.

The old man beckoned the Druid to the kitchen table, asked if his guest would like a glass of ale, and, on receiving a negative answer, turned his back to pour one for himself. He studied the glass a moment, then returned to the table. Once again, the two men sat across from each other in the mix of fading daylight and approaching night.

"I did not want you to be killed," Derrivanian said.

"That's very reassuring." Allanon kept his voice steady even though he was seething. "But if you didn't want me killed, why did you put me in that situation? You aren't pretending you didn't know what they would do . . ."

The old man shook his head. "No, I knew exactly what they intended. The Skull Bearer told me when it came to find me several weeks ago. I don't know how it found me, but it did. It explained very carefully what I was to do and why I should do it. It told me that if I failed, Collice would die. If I did as I was told, she would be allowed to live. That was the choice I was given."

He rubbed at his eyes, and his knuckles came away wet. "It was plain enough. I was to let myself be seen by one of Eventine Elessedil's Elven Hunters. They come through here regularly, guarding against the Warlock Lord and his minions. Once I was identified, it was virtually assured that word would get back to the King. Because of my knowledge of Elven genealogy and your need to find a Shannara heir, you would be sent to speak with me. For something as important as this, no one else would do. When you came, I was to tell you of Weir. The Skull Bearers knew of him already, having tracked him down on their own. But he was an evil man and in no way likely to take up the Sword and become a champion for the Elves. He had already announced to the Skull Bearers that he wished to be an ally of the Dark Lord. What he didn't realize was that it had already been decided he would be used in another way."

"As a lure to attract me." Allanon saw it now.

"Yes. But not for the reason you think. Not to kill you. The

Warlock Lord had something more insidious in mind. Since Weir was the last of the Shannara, what Brona wanted was for his death to come at your hands. He wanted revenge against the Druids for the terrible harm Bremen had caused him all those years ago when he forged the Sword and placed it in the hands of Jerle Shannara."

Allanon's expression hardened, but still the knowledge served as a balm to his heart. He might have destroyed the world's last hope, but he had not killed an innocent man. "But if you knew it was a trap, why didn't you warn me? I could have helped you protect Collice."

Derrivanian was already shaking his head once again. "You couldn't have helped. No one could. And warning you wasn't possible. If I had told you anything other than what I did, Collice would be dead. The Skull Bearer was in the back room with her when you were out here talking with me."

Derrivanian's face was haggard, and his eyes were filled with despair. "Don't you see? I had to choose between you and Collice. I had already lost everything else that mattered in my life. I was not about to lose her, as well."

He leaned forward, the fingers of his hands knotted together. "The Skull Bearer cautioned against saying anything that would warn you. If Weir did not die by your hand, if anything happened to change that outcome, if you learned it was a trap— even by accident—it promised it would return for Collice."

"But you believed I might survive anyway?"

The old man could hardly bear to look at the Druid. "I hoped as much. Judge me as you wish. I deserve it. It was a roll of the dice with lives at stake. I knew the risks. I simply took the choice that seemed best at the time. I wagered your life against Collice's."

Allanon looked away. "You should know that the Skull Bearer still lives. I was too weakened from the struggle to destroy it."

Derrivanian shrugged. "It doesn't matter. It will gain nothing by killing me now. It's too late. I tricked it."

The Druid's eyes locked on him. "How did you do that?"

The old man had a strange look on his face. "It was surprisingly easy. I knew that no matter what happened, it would return for me eventually. It never intended to keep its word. Once I had done what it wanted and tricked you into going after Weir, it would have no further use for me. It would wait for a time, then it would come back to finish me."

He paused. "If I were in its place, I would do the same. But it waited too long. It made a mistake. It should have started by making very certain that Weir was indeed the last of the Shannara instead of wasting time playing games with you."

Allanon stared. "What are you saying?"

"When I told you that Weir was the last of the Shannara kin, I lied. Weir was not the last. There is another."

"Another heir? Are you lying this time, too?"

The old man shook his head. "It was necessary to tell you that Weir was the last. The Skull Bearer was listening. I was betraying you, but I was also using the betrayal to reinforce what the Skull Bearer wrongly believed. If you lived, I told myself, I would give the name to you. If you died, there was probably no hope for any of us. In any case, I would not allow my knowledge to fall into the wrong hands."

Allanon could hardly believe what he was hearing. "So you're sure? There really is another? Weir was not the last?"

Derrivanian shifted his gaze, first to the door, then to the windows, as if to reassure himself that no one else was listening. "There was a boy who was orphaned as a child, a boy whose father was an Elf and whose mother came west from the Borderlands."

He paused. "The boy approaches manhood now, but he is not yet fully grown. His parents were good people, intelligent and responsible, the right sorts. It may be so with this boy."

"His name?"

"Aren Shea."

Allanon shook his head in rebuke, his dark face intense. "I

recognize the name. But a fever took him while he was still very small, shortly after his parents died. That was years ago."

"Yes. Tragic. He was the last of his line. The burial service was poorly attended since there were no longer any living relatives among the Elves. He was buried and forgotten. Even by you, it seems. Though you can visit his grave site in Arborlon, if you wish."

The Druid paused. "Are you saying he didn't die?"

"Exactly—though I arranged for the circumstances surrounding his death to look as convincing as possible."

"Because you knew. Even then. You knew he would be hunted."

"His parents were killed under mysterious circumstances. Just before this happened, his mother brought the child to Collice and asked her to take him. She sensed the danger, I think. The women were close friends, and the boy's mother knew my wife could be trusted. She asked Collice to keep him until she was certain the danger was past, then she would take him back. But if anything happened to the parents, we were to fake the boy's death, then convey him to her brother's home in the Borderlands and tell no one what we had done. We were to hide the truth from everyone so that her son might have a chance to live."

"So you did as she asked? And the Warlock Lord and his Skull Bearers have not discovered the truth?"

"They have no reason to suspect the boy still lives. No one in the whole of the Westland knows the truth."

"You are certain of this?"

"As certain as I can be. You will have to determine if I am right or not for yourself. The boy's name is different now. He is called Shea Ohmsford. He was given his uncle's surname. He resides in the village of Shady Vale in the forests south of the Border Cities."

Derrivanian gave a weak smile and a shrug. "I have done what I promised myself I would do if you returned. It is the only thing I can offer as recompense for my behavior. I hope you can understand." Then he gestured toward the door. "You should go now. Find the boy. Save him."

Allanon rose. "You should take your own advice, then. Leave here immediately. Take your wife to Arborlon and ask the King for protection."

The old man shook his head. "I sent her away to stay with friends the moment the Skull Bearer left to follow you. I asked them to hide her until they heard from me. I don't know where she is."

"Then join her. Do so before the Skull Bearer comes for you."

The other man smiled, but there was no warmth. "No, it's too late for that. It was always too late." He took the glass of ale he had brought for himself and drained it. His eyes fixed on Allanon. "Do you really think we would be safe from the Warlock Lord and his Skull Bearers in Arborlon? Do you think we would be safe anywhere?"

"Eventine Elessedil is not his father. He harbors no bitterness toward you. He is dedicated and compassionate. He will do his best to protect you."

"I am the only one who can do what is necessary to protect Collice, and I have done it." He gestured toward the glass. "You see this? A permanent sleeping potion. The kind you hear about all the time. I am putting myself beyond the Warlock Lord's reach. I know myself. I am weak, and if pressure were brought to bear, I would give up everything I know. But if I can't talk, I can't tell."

Allanon stared. "You took poison?"

"I have betrayed you once. I would do so again. I would betray everyone. But I could not bear to let such a thing happen." He shrugged. "I have lived my life doing the best I could. I would like to think I died in the same way." He was already slurring his words. "Maybe, if you have the time, you could tell Collice . . ."

Then his eyes fixed, his head fell back, and he was gone.

Allanon rose, lifted him out of the chair, and laid him on the mattress in the corner. He placed a blanket over the body. It was the best he could do in the time he had. He couldn't stay longer. He would tell someone about Derrivanian on the way through town.

He stood for a moment, looking down at the body. The old man had ended things on his own terms. He was probably right about his wife. Once he was dead, the Skull Bearers would not bother hunting her. There was no longer a reason.

He went outside into the twilight, wondering if Eldra and Collice Derrivanian would have found sanctuary in Arborlon as he had advised, or if they were both better off now.

He was uncertain, but the choice had not been his to make.

Minutes later, he was riding east toward the Borderlands and the hamlet of Shady Vale.

Introduction to "Indomitable"

THERE IS ENDLESS interest in the fates of the major characters in all the books of the Shannara series, and Jair Ohmsford is no exception. First appearing in *The Wishsong of Shannara*, along with his sister, Brin—both the children of Wil Ohmsford of *Elfstones* fame—Jair was young even at the end of the book, and at the time nothing further had ever been written about him. This sort of open-ended conclusion to my books is a very deliberate choice. Someone once said that all good fiction opens and closes in the middle of a longer story; there is more to the story from before and more after. Readers are left to imagine what those stories are because this helps to engage them further in the characters' lives.

So it was with Jair. Mostly, when the story of a character is told, that's all I want to say about it. The rest is up to the readers. And my answer to all those questions dealing with what came before or after always elicits the same response: *What do* you *think?* But in all fairness, in Jair's case, I had always known what his future would be—in part, at least. But I wasn't moved to write an entire book about it, nor was there story enough. A shorter form, however, was another matter. So when an opportunity came along to write a novella set in the Shannara world, I didn't hesitate. Now I had a path to writing a story about what became of Jair and a few other characters from *Wishsong*. Now

I had the impetus needed to finally satisfy all those readers who had wanted to know.

But even more to the point, I had a chance to discover for myself how Jair found out something important about himself that he had never even suspected.

What is the old saying? The past is never dead; it isn't even past.

INDOMITABLE

THE PAST IS always with us.

Even though he had recently crossed into manhood, Jair Ohmsford had understood the meaning of the phrase since he was a boy. It meant that he would be shaped and reshaped by the events of his life, so that everything that happened would be in some way a consequence of what had gone before. It meant that the people he came to know would influence his conduct and his beliefs. It meant that his experiences of the past would impact his decisions of the future.

It meant that life was like a chain, and the links that forged it could not be severed.

For Jair, the strongest of those links was to Garet Jax. That link was a repository for memories he treasured so dearly that he protected them like glass ornaments, to be taken down from the shelf on which they were kept, polished, and then put away again with great care.

In the summer of the second year following his return from Graymark, he was still caught in the web of those memories. He often woke in the middle of the night from dreams of Garet Jax locked in battle with the Jachyra, heard echoes of the other's voice in conversations with his friends and neighbors, and caught sudden glimpses of the Weapons Master in the faces of strangers. He was not distressed by these occurrences; instead, he was thrilled by them. They were an affirmation that he was keeping the past he cared about so deeply alive.

ON THE DAY the girl rode into Shady Vale, he was working at the family inn, helping the innkeeper and his wife as a favor to his parents. He was standing on the porch, surveying the siding he had replaced after a windstorm had blown a branch through the wall. But something about the way the girl sat her horse caught his attention, drawing it from his handiwork. He shaded his eyes against the glare of the sun as it reflected off a metal roof when she turned out of the trees. She sat ramrod-straight astride a huge black stallion with a white blaze on its forehead, her dark hair falling, thick and shining, in a cascade of curls to her waist. She wasn't big, but she gave an immediate impression of confidence that went beyond the need for physical strength.

She caught sight of him at the same time as he saw her and turned the big black in his direction. She rode up to him and stopped, a mischievous smile appearing on her face as she brushed back loose strands of hair. "Cat got your tongue, Jair Ohmsford?"

"Kimber Boh," he said, not quite sure that it really was. "I don't believe it!"

She swung down, dropped the reins in a manner that suggested this was all the black required, and walked over to give him a long, sustained hug. "You look all grown up," she said, and ruffled his curly blond hair to show she wasn't impressed.

He might have said the same about her. The feel of her body against his as she hugged him was a clear indication that she had also moved beyond childhood. But it was difficult to accept. He still remembered the slender, tiny girl she had been two years ago, when he had met her for the first time in the ruins of the Croagh in the aftermath of his battle to save Brin.

He shook his head. "I almost didn't recognize you."

She stepped back. "I knew you right away." She looked around. "I always wanted to see where you lived. Is Brin here?"

She wasn't. Brin was living in the Highlands with Rone Leah, whom she had married in the spring. They were already expecting their first child. If it was a boy, they would name it Jair.

He shook his head. "No. She lives in Leah now. Why didn't you send word you were coming?"

"I didn't know myself until a little over a week ago." She glanced at the inn. "The ride has made me tired and thirsty. Why don't we go inside while we talk?"

They retreated to the cool interior of the inn and took a table at a window where the slant of the roof kept the sun off. The innkeeper brought over a pitcher of ale and two mugs, giving Jair a sly wink as he walked away.

"Does he give you a wink for every pretty girl you bring into this establishment?" Kimber asked when the innkeeper was out of earshot. "Are you a regular?"

He blushed. "My parents own the inn. Kimber, what are you doing here?"

She considered the question. "I'm not entirely sure. I came to find you and to persuade you to come with me. But now that I'm here, I don't know that I have the will to do it. In fact, I might not even try. I might just stay here and visit until you send me away. What would you say to that?"

He leaned back in his chair and smiled. "I would say you were welcome to stay as long as you like. Is that what you want?"

She sipped her ale and shook her head. "What I want doesn't matter. Maybe what you want doesn't matter, either." She looked out the window into the sunshine. "Grandfather sent me. He said to tell you that the task we thought we had finished two years ago isn't quite finished after all. There appears to be a loose thread that needs snipping."

"A loose thread?"

She looked back at him. "Remember when your sister burned the book of the Ildatch at Graymark?"

He nodded. "I'm not likely to forget."

"Grandfather says she missed a page."

THEY ATE DINNER at his home—a dinner that he prepared himself, including a soup made of fresh garden vegetables, bread, and a plate of cheeses and dried fruits stored for his use by his parents, who were currently traveling south to places where their special healing talents were needed. Jair and Kimber sat at the dinner table and watched the darkness descend in a slow curtain of shadows that draped the countryside like black silk. The sky stayed clear and the stars came out, brilliant and glittering against the firmament.

"Your grandfather wouldn't tell you why he needs me?" Jair asked for what must have been the fifth or sixth time.

She shook her head patiently. "He just said you were the one to bring—not your sister, nor your parents, nor Rone Leah. Just you."

"And he didn't say anything about the Elfstones, either? You're sure about that?"

She looked at him, a hint of irritation in her blue eyes. "Do you know that this is one of the best meals I have ever eaten? It really is. This soup is wonderful, and I want to know how to make it. But for now, I am content just to eat it. So why don't you stop asking questions and just enjoy it, too?"

He responded with a rueful grimace and sipped at the soup, staying quiet for a few mouthfuls while he mulled things over. He was having difficulty accepting what she was telling him, let alone agreeing to what she was asking. Two years earlier, the Ohmsford siblings had taken separate paths to reach the hiding place of the Ildatch: the book of dark magic that had spawned first the Warlock Lord and his Skull Bearers in the time of Shea and Flick Ohmsford, and then the Mord Wraiths in Jair's own time. The magic contained in its pages was so powerful that the book had taken on a life of its own. It had become a spirit able to subvert and ultimately re-form beings of flesh and blood into monstrous, undead creatures. It had done so repeatedly and would have kept on doing so had Brin and he not succeeded in destroying it.

Of course, it had almost destroyed Brin first. Possessed of the magic of the wishsong—of the power to create or destroy through the use of music and words—Brin was a formidable opponent, but an attractive ally as well. Perhaps she would have become the latter instead of the former had Jair not reached her in time to prevent it. But it was for that very purpose that the King of the Silver River had dispatched him to find her after she had left with Allanon, so he had known in advance what was expected of him. His own magic was of a lesser kind—an ability to appear to change things without actually being able to do so—but in this one instance it had proved sufficient to do what was needed.

Which was why he was somewhat confused by Cogline's insistence on summoning him now. Whatever the danger of an Ildatch reborn, he was the least well-equipped member of the family to deal with it. He was likewise doubtful of the man making the selection. He had seen enough of Kimber's wild-eyed and unpredictable grandfather to know that Cogline wasn't always rowing with all his oars in the water. Kimber might have confidence in him, but that didn't mean Jair should.

An even bigger concern was the old man's assertion that somehow the Ildatch hadn't been completely destroyed when Brin had gone to such lengths to make certain that it was. She had used her magic to burn it to ashes—the whole tome, each and every page. So how could it have survived in any form? How could Brin have been mistaken about something so crucial?

He knew that he wasn't going to find out unless he went with

Kimber, but it was a long journey to Hearthstone, which lay deep in the Eastland—a draining commitment of time and energy. Especially if it turned out that the old man was mistaken.

So he asked his questions, hoping to learn something helpful. But, before long, he had asked the old ones more times than was necessary and had run out of new ones.

"I know you think Grandfather is not altogether sane," Kimber said. "You know as much even from the short amount of time you spent with him two years ago, so I don't have to pretend. I know he can be difficult and unsteady. But I also know that he sees things other men don't, and that he has resources denied to them. I can read a trail and track it, but he can read signs on the air itself. He can make things out of compounds and powders that no one else has known how to make since the destruction of the Old World. He's far more competent than he seems."

"So you believe there's a chance he might be right about the Ildatch?" Jair leaned forward again, his meal forgotten. "Tell me the truth, Kimber."

"I think you would be wise to pay attention to what he has to say." Her face was calm, but her eyes were troubled. "I have my own doubts about Grandfather, but I saw his face when he told me to come find you. It wasn't something he said on a whim; he's given it a great deal of thought. He would have come himself, but I wouldn't let him; he is too old and frail. So I had to do it myself. And I guess that alone says something of how I view the matter."

She looked down at her food and pushed it away. "Let's clean up, then we can sit outside."

They collected the dishes, washed and put them away, then went out onto the porch and sat together on a wooden bench that looked off toward the southwest. The night was warm and filled with the smells of jasmine and evergreen, and somewhere off in the darkness a stream trickled. They sat without speaking for a while, listening to the silvery sound of the water. An owl flew by, its dark shape momentarily silhouetted by moonlight. From down in the village came the faint sound of laughter.

"It seems like a long time since we were at Graymark," Kimber said quietly. "A long time since everything that happened, though it was only two years ago."

Jair nodded, remembering. "I've thought often about you and your grandfather. I've wondered how you were. I don't know why I worried, though. You were fine before Brin and Rone found you, and you've probably been fine since. Do you still have the moor cat?"

"Whisper? Yes. He keeps us both safe from the things we can't fight on our own." She paused. "But maybe we aren't as fine as you think, Jair. Things change. Both Grandfather and I are older. He needs me more, and I need him less. Whisper goes away more often and comes back less frequently. The country is developing around us. It isn't as wild as it once was. There is a Dwarven village not five miles away, and Gnome tribes migrate from the Wolfsktaag to the Ravenshorn and back again all the time." She shrugged. "It isn't the same."

"What will you do when your grandfather is gone?"

She laughed softly. "That might never happen. He might live forever." She sighed, gesturing vaguely with one slender hand. "Sometimes, I think about moving away from Hearthstone, of living somewhere else. I want to see something of the larger world."

"Would you come down into the Borderlands, maybe?" He looked over at her. "Would you come to live here? You might like it."

She nodded. "I might."

She didn't say anything else, so he went back to looking into the darkness, thinking it over. He would like having her here. He liked talking to her. He guessed that, with time, they might turn out to be close friends.

"But I need you to come back with me," she said suddenly, looking at him with unexpected intensity. "And it has more to

do with me than with Grandfather. I am worn out by him. I
hate admitting it, because it makes me sound weak, but he
grates on me the older and more difficult he gets. I don't know
if this business about the Ildatch is real or not, but I don't think
I can get to the truth of it alone. Perhaps I'm being selfish by
asking you to come to Hearthstone with me, but Grandfather is
set on this happening, so just having you talk with him might
make a difference."

Jair shook his head doubtfully. "I barely know him. I don't
see what difference being there would make."

She hesitated, then exhaled sharply. "My grandfather was
there to help your sister when she needed it, Jair, so I am asking
you to return the favor. I think he needs you, whether the danger from the Ildatch is real or not. Because what's bothering
him is real. I want you to come back with me and help settle
things."

He thought about it a long time, even though he already
knew what he was going to say. He was thinking of what Garet
Jax would do.

"All right. I'll come," he said finally.

Because he knew that this was what the Weapons Master
would have done in his place.

HE LEFT A letter with the innkeeper for his parents, explaining where he was going, packed some clothes, and closed up the
house. He already knew he would be in trouble when he returned, but that wasn't enough to prevent him from going. The
innkeeper loaned him a horse—a steady, reliable bay that could
be depended on not to do anything unexpected or foolish. Jair
was not so fond of horses, but he understood the need for one
here, where there was so much distance to cover.

It took them a week to get to Hearthstone, riding north out
of Shady Vale and the Duln Forests, around the western end of
the Rainbow Lake, then up through Callahorn along the Mer-
midon River to the Rabb Plains. They crossed the Rabb, follow-

ing its river into the Upper Anar, then rode down through the gap between the Wolfsktaag Mountains and Darklin Reach, threading the needle of the corridor between, staying safely back from the edges of both. As they rode, Jair found himself pondering how different the circumstances were now from the last time he had come into the Eastland. Then, he had been hunted at every turn, threatened by more dangers than he cared to remember. It had been Garet Jax who had saved his life time and again. Now he traveled without fear of attack, without having to look over his shoulder, and Garet Jax was only a memory.

"Do you think we might have lived other lives before this one?" Kimber asked him on their last night before reaching Hearthstone. They were sitting in front of a fire in a grove of trees flanking the south branch of the Rabb, deep within the forests of Darklin Reach. The horses grazed contentedly a short distance off, and moonlight flooded the grassy flats that stretched away about them. There was a hint of a chill in the air, a warning of autumn's approach.

Jair smiled. "I don't think about it at all. I have enough trouble living the life I have without wondering if there were others."

"Or if there will be others after this one?" She brushed at her long hair, which she kept tied back as they rode but let down at night in a tumbled mass. "Grandfather thinks so. I guess I do, too. I think everything is connected. Lives, like moments in time, are all linked together like fish in a stream, swimming and swimming. The past coming forward to become the future."

He looked off into the dark. "I think we are connected to the past, but mostly to the events and the people that shaped it. I think we are always reaching back in some way, bringing forward what we remember—sometimes for information, sometimes just for comfort. I don't remember other lives, but I remember the past of this one. I remember the people who were in it."

She waited a moment, then moved over to sit beside him. "The way you said that . . . Are you thinking about what happened two years ago at Heaven's Well?"

He shrugged.

"About the one you called the Weapons Master?"

He stared at her. "How did you know that?"

"It isn't much of a mystery, Jair. You talked about no one else afterward. Only him, the one who saved you on the Croagh. The one who fought the Jachyra. Don't you remember?"

He nodded. "I guess."

"Maybe your connection with him goes further back than just this life." She lifted an eyebrow at him. "Have you thought about that? Maybe you were joined in another life as well, and that's why he made such an impression on you."

Jair laughed. "I think he made an impression on me because he was the best fighter I have ever seen. He was so . . ." He stopped himself, searching for the right word. "Indomitable." His smile faded. "Nothing could stand against him, not even a Jachyra. Not even something that was too much for Allanon."

"But I might still be right about past lives," she persisted. She put her hand on his shoulder and squeezed. "You can grant me that much, can't you, Valeman?"

He could—that and much more. He wanted to tell her so, but didn't know how without sounding foolish. He was attracted to her and it surprised him. Having thought of her for so long as a little girl, he was having trouble accepting that she was now fully grown. Such a transition didn't seem possible. It confused him, the past conflicting with the present. How did she feel about him, as changed in his own way as she was in hers? He wondered but could not make himself ask.

In late afternoon of the following day, they reached Hearthstone. He had never been here before, but he had heard Brin describe the chimney-shaped rock so often that he knew at once what it was. He caught sight of it as they rode through the trees—a dark pinnacle overlooking a shallow, wooded valley.

Its distinctive, rugged form seemed right for this country: a land of dark rumors and strange happenings. Yet that was in the past as well. Things were different now. They had arrived on a road, but two years before there had been no roads. They had passed the newly settled Dwarf village and seen the houses and heard the voices of children. The country was growing up, the wilderness being pushed back. Change was the one constant in an ever-evolving world.

They reached the cottage shortly afterward. It was constructed of timber with porches front and back, its walls grown thick with ivy and the grounds surrounding it planted with gardens and ringed with walkways and bushes. It had a well-cared-for look. Everything was neatly planted and trimmed, a mix of colors and forms that were pleasing to the eye. It didn't look so much like a wilderness cottage as a village home. Behind the house, a paddock housed a mare and a foal. A milk cow was grazing there as well. Neatly painted sheds lined the back of the paddock. Shade trees helped conceal the buildings from view; Jair hadn't caught even a glimpse of roofs on the ride in.

He glanced over at her. "Do you look after all this by yourself?"

"Mostly." She gave him a wry smile. "I like looking after a home. I always have, ever since I was old enough to do so."

They rode into the yard and dismounted, and instantly Cogline appeared through the doorway. He was ancient and stick-thin beneath his baggy clothing, and his white hair stuck out in all directions, as if he had just woken. He pulled at his beard as he approached them, his fingers raking the wiry hairs. His eyes were sharp and questioning, and he was already scanning Jair as if not quite sure what to make of him.

"So!" He approached with that single word, standing so close that the Valeman was forced to take a step back. He peered intently into Jair's blue eyes and took careful note of his Elven features. "Is this him?"

"Yes, Grandfather." Kimber sounded embarrassed.

"You're certain? No mistake?"

"Yes, Grandfather."

"Because he could be someone else, you know. He could be anybody else!" Cogline furrowed his already deeply lined brow. "Are you young Ohmsford? The boy, Jair?"

Jair nodded. "I am. Don't you remember me? We met two years ago in the ruins of Graymark."

The old man stared at him as if he hadn't heard the question. Jair could feel the other's hard gaze probing him in a way that was not altogether pleasant. "Is this necessary?" he asked at last. "Can't we go inside and sit down?"

"When I say so!" the other replied. "When I am finished! Don't interrupt my study!"

"Grandfather!" Kimber exclaimed.

The old man ignored her. "Let me see your hands," he ordered.

Jair held out his hands, palms up. Cogline studied them carefully for a moment, grunted as if he had found whatever it was he was looking for, and said, "Come inside, and I'll fix you something to eat."

They went into the cottage and seated themselves at the rough-hewn wooden dining table, but it was Kimber who ended up preparing a stew for them to eat. While she did so, directing admonitions at her grandfather when she thought them necessary, Cogline rambled on about the past and Jair's part in it—a bewildering hodgepodge of information and observation.

"I remember you," Cogline said. "Just a boy, coming out of Graymark's ruins with your sister, the two of you covered in dust and smelling of death! Hah! I know something of that smell, I can tell you! Fought many a monster come out of the netherworld, long before you were born—before any who live now were born and a good deal more who are long dead. Might have left the order, but didn't lose the skills. Not a one. Never listened to me, any of them, but that didn't make me give up.

The new mirrors the old. You can't disconnect science and magic. They're all of a piece, and the lessons of one are the lessons of the other. Allanon knew as much. Knew just enough to get himself killed."

Jair had no idea what he was talking about, but perked up on hearing the Druid's name. "You knew Allanon?"

"Not when he was alive. Know him now that he's dead, though. Your sister, she was a gift to him. She was the answer to what he needed when he saw the end coming. It's like that for some, the gift. Maybe for you, too, one day."

"What gift?"

"You know, I was a boy once. I was a Druid once, too."

Jair stared at him. It was hard to think of him as a boy, but thinking of him as a Druid was harder still. If the old man really was a Druid—not that Jair thought for a moment that he was—what was he doing here, out in the wilderness, living with Kimber? "I thought Allanon was the last of the Druids," he said.

The old man snorted. "You thought a lot of things that weren't so." He shoved back his plate of stew, having hardly touched it. "Do you want to know what you're doing here?"

Jair stopped eating in midbite. Kimber, sitting across from him, blinked once and said, "Maybe you should wait until he's finished dinner, Grandfather."

The old man ignored her. "Your sister thought the Ildatch was destroyed," he said. "She was wrong. Wasn't her fault, but she was wrong. She burned it to ash, and that should have been the end of it. But it wasn't. You want to sit outside while we have this discussion? The open air and the night sky make it easier to think things through sometimes."

They went outside onto the front porch, where the western sky was turning a brilliant mix of purple and rose above the treetops and the eastern sky already boasted a partial moon and a scattering of stars. The old man took possession of the only rocker, and Jair and Kimber sat together on a high-backed wooden bench. It occurred to the Valeman that he needed to rub down and feed his horse—a task he would have completed by now if he had been thinking straight.

The old man rocked in silence for a time, then gestured abruptly at Jair. "Last month, on a night when the moon was full and the sky a sea of stars—a beautiful night—I woke and walked down to the little pond that lies just south of here. I don't know why; I just did. Something made me. I lay in the grass and slept, and while I slept, I had a dream. Only it was more a vision than a dream. I used to have such visions often. I was closer to the shades of the dead then, and they would come to me because I was receptive to their needs. But that was long ago, and I had thought such things at an end."

He seemed to reflect on the idea for a moment, lost in thought. "I was a Druid then."

"Grandfather," Kimber prodded softly.

The old man looked back at Jair. "In my dream, the Shade of Allanon came to me out of the netherworld. It spoke to me. It told me that the Ildatch was not yet destroyed, that a piece of it still survived. One page only, seared at the edges, shaken loose and blown beneath the stones of Graymark before it was destroyed. Perhaps the book found a way to save that one page in its death throes. I don't know. The shade didn't tell me. Only that it had survived your sister's efforts and been found in the rubble by Mwellrets, who sought artifacts that would lend them the power that had belonged to the Mord Wraiths. Those rets knew what they had found, because the page told them— a whisper that promised great things. It had life, even as a fragment, so powerful was its magic!"

Jair glanced at Kimber, who nodded knowingly. "One page," he said to the old man. "That isn't enough to be dangerous, is it? Unless there is a spell the Mwellrets can make use of . . ."

Cogline ran his hand through his wiry thatch of white hair. "Not enough? Yes, that was my thought, too. One page, out of so many. What harm? I dismissed the vision upon waking, convinced it was a groundless fear given a momentary foothold by an old man's frailness. But it came again, a second time—this time while I slept in my own bed. It was stronger than before, more insistent. The shade chided me for my indecision, for my failings past and present. It told me to find you and bring you here. It gave me no peace, not that night or after."

He looked genuinely distressed now, as if the memory of the shade's visit was a haunting he wished he had never encountered. Jair understood better now why Kimber felt it so important to summon him. Cogline was an old man teetering on the brink of emotional collapse. He might be hallucinating or he might have connected with the shades of the dead, but whatever he had experienced, it had left him badly shaken.

"Now that I am here, what am I expected to do?" Jair asked.

The old man looked at him. There was a profound sadness mirrored in his ancient eyes. "I don't know," he said. "I wasn't told."

Then he looked off into the darkness and didn't speak again.

"I'M SORRY ABOUT this," Kimber declared later. There was a pronounced weariness in her voice. "I didn't think he was going to be this vague once he had the chance to speak with you. I should have known better. I shouldn't have brought you."

They were sitting together on the bench again, sipping at mugs of cold ale and listening to the night. They had put the old man to sleep a short while earlier, tucking him into his bed and sitting with him until he began to snore. Kimber had done her best to hasten the process with a cup of medicated tea.

He smiled at her. "Don't be sorry. I'm glad you brought me. I don't know if I can help, but I think you were right about not wanting to handle this business alone. I can see where he could become increasingly difficult if you tried to put him off."

"But it's all such a bunch of nonsense! He hasn't been out of his bed in months. He hasn't slept down by the pond. Whatever dreams he's been having are the result of his refusal to eat properly." She blew out a sharp breath in frustration. "All this business about the Ildatch surviving somehow in a page fragment! I used to believe everything he told me, when I was little and still thought him the wisest man in the world. But now I think that he's losing his mind."

Jair sipped at his ale. "I don't know. He seems pretty convinced."

She stared at him. "You don't believe him, do you?"

"Not entirely. But it might be he's discovered something worth paying attention to. Dreams have a way of revealing things we don't understand right away. They take time to decipher. But once we've thought about it . . ."

"Yet why would the Shade of Allanon come to Grandfather in a dream and ask him to bring you here rather than just appearing to you?" she interrupted heatedly. "What sense does it make to go through Grandfather? He would not be high on the list of people you might listen to."

"There must be a reason, if he's really had a vision from a shade. He must be involved in some important way."

He looked at her for confirmation but she had turned away, her mouth compressed in a tight, disapproving line. "Are you going to help him, Jair? Are you going to try to make him see that he is imagining things or are you going to feed this destructive behavior with pointless encouragement?"

He flushed at the rebuke but kept his temper. Kimber was looking to him to help her grandfather find a way out of the quicksand of his delusions, and instead of doing so, he was offering to jump in himself. But he couldn't dismiss the old man's words as easily as she could. He was not burdened by years and experiences shared; he did not see Cogline in the same way she did. Nor was he so quick to disbelieve the visions and dreams and shades. He had encountered more than a few himself—not the least of which was the visit from the King of the Silver River, two years earlier, under similar circumstances. If not for that visit—a visit he might have dismissed if he had been less open-minded—Brin would have been lost to him and the entire world changed. It was not something you forgot easily. Not wanting to believe was not always the best approach to things you didn't understand.

"Kimber," he said quietly, "I don't know yet what I am going to do. I don't know enough to make a decision. But if I dismiss your grandfather's words out of hand, it might be worse than if I try to see through them to what lies beneath."

He waited while she looked off into the distance, her eyes still hot and her mouth set. Then finally she turned back to him, nodding slowly. "I'm sorry. I didn't mean to attack you. You were good enough to come when I asked, and I am letting my frustration get in the way of my good sense. I know you mean to help."

"I do," he reassured her. "Let him sleep through the night, and then see if he's had the vision again. We can talk about it when he wakes and is fresher. We might be able to discover its source."

She shook her head quickly. "But what if it's real, Jair? What if it's true? What if I've brought you here for selfish reasons and placed you in real danger? I didn't mean for that to happen, but what if it does?"

She looked like a child again, waiflike and lost. He smiled and cocked one eyebrow at her. "A moment ago, you were telling me there wasn't a chance it was real. Are you ready to abandon that stance just because I said we shouldn't dismiss it out of hand? I didn't say I believed it, either. I just said there might be some truth to it."

"I don't want there to be any. I want it to be Grandfather's wild imagination at work and nothing more." She stared at him intently. "I want this all to go far away and not come back again. We've had enough of Mord Wraiths and books of dark magic."

He nodded slowly, then reached out and touched her lightly on the cheek, surprising himself with his boldness. When she closed her eyes, he felt his face grow hot and quickly took his hand away. He felt suddenly dizzy. "Let's wait and see, Kimber," he said. "Maybe the dream won't come to him again."

She opened her eyes. "Maybe," she whispered.

He turned back toward the darkness, took a long, cool swallow of his ale, and waited for his head to clear.

THE DREAM DIDN'T come to Cogline that night, after all. Instead, it came to Jair Ohmsford.

He was not expecting it when he crawled into his bed, weary from the long journey and slightly muddled from a few too many cups of ale. The horses were rubbed down and fed, his possessions were put away in the cupboard, and the cottage was dark. He didn't know how long he slept before it began, only that it happened all at once—and when it did, it was as if he were completely awake and alert.

He stood at the edge of a vast body of water that stretched away as far as the eye could see, its surface gray and smooth, reflecting a sky as flat and colorless as itself, so that there was no distinction between the one and the other. The shade was already there, hovering above its surface—a huge dark specter that dwarfed him in size and blotted out a whole section of the horizon behind it. Its hood concealed its features, and all that was visible were pinpricks of red light like eyes burning out of a black hole.

—Do you know me?—

He did, of course. He knew instinctively, without having to think about it. "You are Allanon."

—In life. In death, his shade. Do you remember me as I was?—

Jair saw the Druid once again, waiting for Brin, Rone Leah, and himself as they returned home late at night—a dark and imposing figure, too large somehow for their home. He heard the Druid speak to them of the Ildatch and the Mord Wraiths. The strong features and the determined voice mesmerized him.

He had never known anyone as dominating as Allanon—except, perhaps, for Garet Jax.

"I remember you," he said.

—Watch—

An image appeared in the air before him, gloomy and indistinct. It revealed the ruins of a vast fortress, mounds of rubble against a backdrop of forest and mountains. Graymark, destroyed. Shadowy figures moved through the rubble, poking amid the broken stones. A handful went deep inside, bearing torches—down tunnels in danger of collapse. They were cloaked and hooded, but the flicker of light on their hands and faces revealed patches of reptilian scales. Mwellrets. They wound their way deeper into the ruins—into fresh-made catacombs, into places where only darkness and death could be found. They proceeded slowly, taking their time, pausing often to search nooks and crannies—every hollow in the earth that might offer concealment.

Then one of the Mwellrets began to dig—an almost frantic effort, pulling aside stones and timbers, hissing like a snake. It labored for long minutes, all alone; the others had gone elsewhere. Dust and blood soon coated its scaly hide, and its breath came in gasps that suggested near exhaustion.

But in the end, it found what it sought, pulling free from the debris a seared, torn page of a book—a page with writing on it that pulsed like veins beneath skin . . .

—Watch—

A second image appeared, this one of another fortress—one he didn't recognize right away, even though it seemed familiar. It was as dark and brooding as Graymark had been, as thick with shadows and gloom, as hard-edged and rough-hewn. The image lingered only a moment on the outer walls, then took the Valeman deep inside, past gates and battlements and into the nether regions. In a room dimly lit by torches that smoked and steamed in damp, stale air, a cluster of Mwellrets hovered over the solitary book page retrieved from Graymark's ruins.

They were engaged in an arcane rite. Jair could not be certain, but he had the distinct feeling that they were not entirely aware of what was happening to them. They were moving in concert, like gears in a machine, each one in sync with the others. They kept their heads lowered and their eyes fixed, and there was a hypnotic sound to their voices and movements that suggested they were responding to something he couldn't see. In the gloom and smoke, they reminded him of the Spider Gnomes on Toffer Ridge, come to make sacrifice of themselves to the Werebeasts—come to give up the lives of a few in the mistaken belief that it was for the good of the many.

As one, they moved their palms across the surface of the paper, taking in the feel of the veined writing, murmuring furtive chants and small prayers. Beneath their reptilian fingers, the page glowed and the writing pulsed. It was responding to their efforts and Jair could feel the raw pull of it, like a leaching away of life.

The remnant of the Ildatch—in search of a way back from the edge of extinction, in need of nourishment that would enable it to recall and put to use the spells it had lost—was feeding.

Then the image faded and he was alone again with the Shade of Allanon, two solitary figures facing each other across an empty vista. The gloom had grown thicker and the sky darker. The lake no longer reflected light of any sort.

In the aftermath of the visions, he had realized why the second fortress had seemed so familiar. It was Dun Fee Aran, the Gnome prison where he had been taken by the Mwellret Stythys to be coerced into giving up his magic and eventually his life. He remembered his despair on being cast into the cell allotted to him, deep beneath the earth in the bowels of the keep, alone in the darkness and silence. He remembered his fear.

"I can't go back there," he whispered, already anticipating what the shade was going to ask of him.

But the shade asked nothing of him. Instead, it gestured, and for a third and final time the air before the Valeman began to shimmer.

—Watch—

"I KNEW IT!" Cogline exclaimed gleefully. "It's still alive! Didn't I tell you so? Wasn't that just what I said? You thought me a crazy old man, Granddaughter, but how crazy do I look to you now? Hallucinations? Wild imaginings? Hah! Am I still to be treated as if I were a delicate flower? Am I still to be humored and coddled?"

He began dancing about the room and cackling like a madman—an act that went a long way toward negating his previous words. The Valeman watched him patiently, trying not to look at Kimber, who was so angry and disgusted that he could feel the heat radiating from her glare. It was morning now, and they sat across from each other at the old wooden dining table, bathed in bright splashes of sunlight that streamed through the open windows and belied the darkness of the moment.

"You haven't told us yet what the shade expects of you," Kimber said quietly, though he could not mistake the edge to her words.

"What you have already guessed," he answered, meeting her gaze reluctantly. "What I knew even before the third image showed it to me. I have to go to Dun Fee Aran and put a stop to what's happening."

Cogline stopped dancing. "Well, you can do that, I expect," he said, shrugging aside the implications. "You did it once before, didn't you?"

"No, Grandfather, he did not," Kimber corrected him impatiently. "That was his sister, and I don't understand why she wasn't summoned, if the whole idea is to finish the job she started two years ago. It's her fault the Ildatch is still alive."

Jair shook his head. "It isn't anybody's fault. It just happened. In any case, Brin's married and pregnant and doesn't use the magic anymore."

Nor would she ever use it again, he suspected. It had taken her a long time to get over what happened to her at the Mael-mord. He had seen how long it had taken. He didn't know that she had ever been the same since. She had warned him that the magic was dangerous, that you couldn't trust it, that it could turn on you even when you thought it was your friend. He remembered the haunted look in her eyes.

He leaned forward, folding his hands in front of him. "The Shade of Allanon made it clear that she can't be exposed to the Ildatch a second time—not even to a fragment of a page. She is too vulnerable to its magic, too susceptible to what it can do to humans—even one as powerful as she is. Someone else has to go, someone who hasn't been exposed to the power of the book before."

Kimber reached out impulsively and took hold of his hands. "But why you, Jair? Others could do this."

"Maybe not. Dun Fee Aran is a Mwellret stronghold, and the page is concealed somewhere deep inside. Just finding it presents problems that would stop most from even getting close. But I have the magic of the wishsong, and I can use it to disguise myself. I can make it appear as if I'm not there. That way, I can gain sufficient time to find the page without being discovered."

"The boy is right!" Cogline exclaimed, animated anew by the idea. "He is the perfect choice!"

"Grandfather!" Kimber snapped at him.

The old man turned, running his gnarled fingers through his tangled beard. "Stop yelling at me!"

"Then stop jumping to ridiculous conclusions! Jair is not the perfect choice. He might be able to get past the rets and into the fortress, but then he has to destroy the page and get out again. How is he to do that when all his magic can do is create illusions? Smoke and mirrors! How is he to defend himself against a real attack, one he is almost sure to come up against at some point?"

"We'll go with him!" the old man declared. "We'll be his protectors! We'll take Whisper—just as soon as he comes back from wherever he's wandered off to. Dratted cat!"

Kimber ran a hand across her eyes as if trying to see things more clearly. "Jair, do you understand what I am saying? This is hopeless!"

The Valeman didn't answer right away. He was remembering the third vision shown him by the Shade of Allanon, the one he hadn't talked about. It had been a jumble of uncertain images clouded by shadowy movement and wildness, and it had frightened and confused him. Yet it had imbued him with a certainty of success, as well—a certainty so strong and unmistakable that he could not dismiss it.

"The shade said that I would find a way," he answered her. He hesitated. "If I just believed in myself."

She stared at him. "If you just believed in yourself?"

"I know. It sounds foolish. And I'm terrified of Dun Fee Aran; I have been since I was imprisoned there by Stythys two years ago, on my way to find Brin. I thought I was going to die in those cells—and that maybe death was going to be the easiest part of it. I have never been so afraid of anything. I swore, once I was out of there, that I would never go back. Not for any reason."

He took a deep breath and exhaled slowly. "But I think that I have to go back anyway—in part because it's necessary if the Ildatch is to be stopped, but also because Allanon made me feel that I shouldn't be afraid anymore. He gave me a sense of reassurance that this wouldn't be like the last time, that it would be different because I am older and stronger now, better able to face what's waiting there."

"Telling you this might just be a way to get you to do what he wants," Kimber said. "It might be a Druid trick, a deception of the sort that shades are famous for."

He nodded. "It might. But it doesn't feel that way. It feels true."

"Of course it would," she said quietly. She looked miserable. "I brought you here to help Grandfather find peace of mind, not to risk your life. Now everything I was afraid was going to happen *is* happening. I hate it!"

She was squeezing his hands so hard she was hurting him. "If I didn't come, Kimber," he said, "who would act on your grandfather's dreams? It isn't something we planned—either of us—but we can't ignore what's needed. I have to go. I have to."

She nodded slowly, her hands withdrawing from his. "I know." She looked at Cogline, who was standing very still now, looking distressed, as if suddenly aware of what he had brought about. She smiled gently at him. "I know, Grandfather."

The old man nodded slowly, but the joy had gone out of him.

IT WAS DECIDED they would set out the following day. It was a journey of some distance, even if they went on horseback. It would take them the better part of a week to get through the Ravenshorn Mountains and skirt the edges of Olden Moor to where Dun Fee Aran looked out over the Silver River in the shadow of the High Bens. This was rugged country, most of it still wilderness, beyond the spread of Dwarf settlements and Gnome camps. Much of it was swamp and jungle, and some of it was too dangerous to try to pass through. A direct line of approach was out of the question. At best, they would be able to find a path along the eastern edge of the Ravenshorn. They would have to carry their own supplies and water. They would have to go prepared for the worst.

Jair was not pleased with the thought that both Kimber and Cogline would be going with him, but there was nothing he could do about that, either. He was going back into country that had been unfamiliar to him two years earlier and was unfamiliar to him now. He wouldn't be able to find his way without help, and the only help at hand was the girl and her grandfather, both of whom knew the Anar much better than anyone else he might turn to. It would have been nice to leave them behind in safety, but he doubted that they would have permitted it even if he hadn't had need of them. For reasons that were abundantly apparent, they intended to see this matter through with him.

They spent the remainder of the day putting together supplies—a process that was tedious and somehow emotionally draining, as if the act of preparation was tantamount to climbing to a cliff ledge before jumping off. There wasn't much conversation, and most of what was said concerned the task itself. That the effort helped pass the time was the best that could be said for it.

More often than he cared to admit, Jair found himself wondering how far he was pressing his luck by going back into country he had been fortunate to escape from once already. He might argue that this time, like the last, he was going because he had no choice, but in fact he did. He could walk away from the dreams and their implications. He could argue that Kimber was right and that he was being used for reasons he did not appreciate. He could even argue that his sister's magic had destroyed the Ildatch so completely that trying to re-create the book from a single page was impossible. He could decide that he was going home to ask for help from his parents and sister. It would be wiser to involve them in any case, wouldn't it?

But he would not do that. He knew he wouldn't even as he was telling himself he could. He was new enough at being grown up that he did not want to ask for help unless he absolutely had to. It diminished him in his own mind, if not in fact, to seek assistance from his family. It was almost as if they expected it of him. After all, he was the youngest and the least experienced, the one they all had been helping for so long. There was an admission of failure written into such an act, one that he could not abide. No, he had gone into this country once, and dangerous or not he could go into it again.

His mood did not improve with the coming of nightfall and the realization that there was nothing else to be done but to wait for morning. They ate the dinner Kimber made them, the old man filling the silence with thoughts of the old days and the new world, of Druids past and a future without them. There would be a time when they would return, he insisted. The Druids would be needed again; you could depend on it. Jair kept his mouth shut. He did not want to say what he was thinking about Druids and the need for them.

HE DREAMED AGAIN that night, but not of the Shade of Allanon. In his dream, he was already down inside the fortress at Dun Fee Aran, working his way along corridors shrouded in damp and gloom, hopelessly lost and searching for a way out. A sibilant voice whose source he could not divine whispered in his ear: *Never leavess thiss plasse.* Terrifying creatures besieged him, but he could see nothing of them but their shadows. The longer he wandered, the greater his sense of foreboding, until finally it was all he could do to keep from screaming.

When a room opened before him, its interior as black as ink, he stopped at the threshold, afraid to go farther and knowing that if he did so, something terrible would happen. But he could not help himself, because the shadows were closing in from behind, pressing up against him, and soon they would smother him completely. So he stepped forward into the room—one step, two, three—feeling his way with a caution he prayed might save him and yet feared wouldn't.

Then a hand stretched toward him, slender and brown, and he knew it was Kimber's. He was reaching for it, so grateful he wanted to cry, when something shoved him hard from behind and he tumbled forward into a pit. Unable to save himself, he began to fall. The hand that had reached for him was gone; any chance of escape had vanished. He kept falling, waiting for the impact that would shatter his bones and leave him lifeless, knowing it was getting closer, closer . . .

Then a second hand reached out to catch hold of him, in a grip so powerful it defied belief, and the falling stopped . . .

He woke with a start, jerking upright in bed, gasping for breath and clutching at the blanket he had kicked aside in his thrashings. It took him a moment to shake free of the dream completely, to regain control of his emotions so that he no longer felt like he might begin to fall again. He swung his legs over the side of the bed and sat with his head between his knees, taking long, slow breaths. The dream had made him feel so frightened and alone.

Finally, he looked up. Outside, the first patch of dawn's brightness was visible above the trees. Sudden panic rushed through him.

What am I doing?

He knew in that moment that he wasn't equal to the task he had set himself. He wasn't strong or brave enough. He didn't possess the necessary skills or experience. He hadn't lived even two decades yet. He might be considered a man in some quarters, but in the place that counted—in his heart—he was still a boy. If he was smart, he would slip out the door now and ride back the way he had come. He would give up on this business and save his life.

He considered this for long moments, knowing he should act on his instincts, and knowing as well that he couldn't.

Outside, the sky continued to brighten slowly into day. He stood, finally, and began to dress.

THEY DEPARTED AT midmorning, riding their horses north out of Hearthstone toward the passes below Toffer Ridge that would take them through the Ravenshorn and into the deep Eastland. A voluble Cogline led the way, having mapped out a route that would allow them to travel on horseback all the way to Dun Fee Aran, barring unforeseen weather or circumstances—a fact that he insisted on repeating at every opportunity. Admittedly, the old man knew the country better than anyone save the nomadic Gnome tribes and a few local Trackers, but what worried Jair was how well he would remember what he knew when it counted. Yet there was nothing he could do about Cogline's un-predictability; he simply had to hope for the best. At present, the old man seemed fine, even eager to get on with things, which was as much as Jair could expect.

He was also upset that Whisper had failed to reappear before their departure, for the moor cat would have been a welcome addition to their company. Few living creatures, man or beast, would dare to challenge a full-grown moor cat. But there was no help for this, either. They would just have to get along without him.

The weather stayed fair for the first three days, and travel was uneventful. They rode north to the passes that crossed down over Toffer Ridge, staying well below Olden Moor where the Werebeasts lived, traveling by daylight to make certain of their path. Each night, they would camp in a spot carefully cho-sen by Cogline and approved by Kimber—a place where they could keep watch and be reasonably certain of their safety. Each night, Kimber would prepare a meal for them and then put her grandfather to bed. Each night, the old man went without com-plaint and fell instantly asleep.

"It's the tea," Kimber confided to Jair. "I put a little of his medication in it to quiet him down—the same medication I used at Hearthstone. Sometimes, it is the only way he can sleep."

They encountered few other travelers, and there was an ordi-nariness to their journey that belied its nature. At times, it felt to Jair as if he might be on nothing more than a wilderness out-ing, exploring unfamiliar country with no other purpose than to have a look around. At such times, it was difficult to think about what was waiting at the end. That end seemed far away and unrelated to the present, as if it might belong to another experience altogether.

But those moments of complacency never lasted, and when they vanished he reverted to a dark consideration of the partic-ulars of what would be required when he arrived at Dun Fee Aran. His conclusions were always the same. Getting inside would be easy enough. He knew how he would use his magic to disguise himself, how he would employ it to stay hidden. Unlike Brin, he had never stopped using it. He practiced constantly, testing its limits. So long as he remembered not to press himself beyond those limits, he would be all right.

It was being caught out and exposed once he was inside the fortress that concerned him. He did not intend for this to happen, but if it did, what would he do? He was older and stronger than he had been two years ago, and he had studied weapons and self-defense since his return to the Vale. But he was not a practiced fighter, and he would be deep in the center of an enemy stronghold. That his sole allies were a young woman and a half-crazed old man was not reassuring. Kimber carried those throwing knives with which she was so lethal, and the old man his bag of strange powders and chemicals, some of which could bring down entire walls, but Jair was not inclined to rely on those, either. When he wasn't thinking about turning around and going home—which he found himself doing at least once a day—he was thinking about how he could persuade Kimber and her grandfather not to go with him into Dun Fee Aran. Whatever his own fate, he did not want any harm to come to them. He was the one who had been summoned and dispatched by the Shade of Allanon. The task of destroying the Ildatch fragment had been given to him.

His doubts and fears haunted him. They clung to him like the dust of the road—tiny uncertainties that this business was not going to end well, that he was not equal to the task he had been given. He could not shake them or persuade himself that their insistent little voices were lies designed to erode his already paper-thin confidence. With every mile traveled, he felt more and more the boy he had been when he had come this way before. Dun Fee Aran was a fire pit of terror, and the Mwellrets were the monsters that stirred its coals. He found himself wishing he had his companions from before—Garet Jax, the Borderman Helt, the Elven Prince Edain Elessedil, and the Dwarf

Foraker. Even the taciturn, disgruntled Gnome Slanter would have been welcome. But except for the Gnome, whom he had not seen since their parting two years earlier, they had all died at Graymark. There was no possibility of replacing them, of finding allies of the same mettle. If he was determined not to involve Cogline and Kimber as more than guides and traveling companions, he would have to go it alone.

On the fourth day, the weather turned stormy. At dawn, a dark wall of clouds rolled in from the west, and by midmorning it was raining heavily. By now they were through the Ravenshorn and riding southeast in the shadow of the mountains. The terrain was rocky and brush-clogged, and they were forced to dismount and walk their horses through the increasingly heavy downpour. Cloaked and hooded, they were effectively shut away from one another, each a shadowy, faceless form hunched against the rain.

Locked away in the cold dampness of his water-soaked clothing, Jair incongruously found himself thinking that he had underestimated his chances of success, that he was better prepared than he had thought earlier, that his magic would see him through. All he had to do was get inside Dun Fee Aran, wait for his chance, and destroy the Ildatch remnant. It wasn't like the last time, when the book of magic was a sentient being, able to protect itself. There weren't any Mord Wraiths to avoid. The Mwellrets were dangerous, but not in the same way as the walkers. He could do this. He could manage it.

He believed as much for about two hours, and then the doubts and fears returned and his confidence evaporated. Slogging through the murk and mud, he saw himself walking a path to a cliff edge, taking a road that could end only one way.

His dark mood returned, and the weight of his inadequacies descended anew.

THAT NIGHT THEY made camp below Graymark on the banks of the Silver River, settled well back in the concealment of the hardwoods. They built a fire in the shelter of oaks grown so thick that their limbs blocked all but small patches of the sky. Deadwood was plentiful, and some of it was dry enough to burn even after the downpour. Closer to Dun Fee Aran and the Mwellrets, they might have chosen not to risk a blaze, but the most dangerous creatures abroad in these woods were of the four-legged variety. This far out in the wilderness, they were unlikely to encounter anything else.

Still, not long after they had cooked and eaten their dinner, they were startled by a clanking sound and the sharp bray of a pack animal. Then a voice called to them from the darkness, asking for permission to approach. Cogline gave it, grumbling under his breath as he did so, and their visitor walked into the firelight leading a mule on a rope halter. The man was tall and thin, cloaked head-to-foot in an old greatcoat that had seen hard use. The mule was a sturdy-looking animal bearing a wooden rack from which hung dozens of pots and pans and cooking implements. A peddler and his wares had stumbled on them.

The man tethered his mule and sat down at the fire, declining the cup of tea that was offered in favor of one filled with ale, which he gulped down gratefully. "Long, wet day," he declared in a weary voice. "This helps put it right."

They gave him what food was left over, still warm in the cooking pot, and watched him eat. "This is good," he announced, nodding in Kimber's direction. "First hot meal in a while and likely to be the last. Don't see many campfires out this way. Don't see many people, for that matter. But I'm more than ready to share company this night. Hope you don't mind."

"What are you doing way out here?" Jair asked him, taking advantage of the opening he had offered.

The peddler paused in midbite and gave him a wry smile. "I travel this way several times a year, servicing the places other peddlers won't. Might not look like it, but there are villages at the foot of the mountains that need what I sell. I pass through, do my business, and go home again; I'm from out by the Rabb.

It's a lot of traveling, but I like it. I've only got me and my mule to worry about."

He finished putting the suspended bite into his mouth, chewed it carefully, and then said, "What about you? What brings you to the east side of the Ravenshorn? Pardon me for saying so, but you don't look like you belong here."

Jair exchanged a quick glance with Kimber. "Traveling up to Dun Fee Aran," Cogline announced before they could stop him. "Got some business ourselves. With the rets."

The peddler made a face. "I'd think twice about doing business with them." His tone of voice made clear his disgust. "Dun Fee Aran's no place for you. Get someone else to do your business, someone a little less . . ."

He trailed off, looking from one face to the next, clearly unable to find the words that would express his concern that a boy, a girl, and an old man would even think of trying to do business with Mwellrets.

"It won't take long," Jair said, trying to put a better face on the idea. "We just have to pick something up."

The peddler nodded, his thin face drawn with more than the cold and the damp. "Well, you be careful. The Mwellrets aren't to be trusted. You know what they say: Look into their eyes, and you belong to them. They steal your soul. They aren't human; they aren't even of a human disposition. I never go there. Never."

He went back to eating his meal, and while he finished, no one spoke again. But when he put his plate aside and picked up his cup of ale, Kimber filled it anew and said, "You've never had any dealings with them?"

"Once," he answered softly. "An accident. They took everything I had and cast me out to die. But I knew the country, so I was able to make my way back home. I never went near them again—not at Dun Fee Aran, and not on the road. They're monsters."

He paused. "Let me tell you something about Dun Fee Aran, since you're going there. I haven't told this to anyone. I didn't have a reason and didn't think anyone would believe me, anyway, but you should know. I was inside those walls. They held me there while they decided what to do with me after taking my wares and mule. I saw things: shades, drifting through the walls as if the stone were nothing more than air. I saw my mother, dead fifteen years. She beckoned to me, tried to lead me out of there. But I couldn't go with her because I couldn't pass through the walls like she could. It's true, I swear it. There was others, too. Ones I don't want to talk about. They were there at Dun Fee Aran. The rets appeared to see them, but they didn't seem to care."

He shook his head. "You don't want to go inside those walls again once you've gotten out of them."

His voice trailed off and he stared out into the darkness as if searching for more substantial manifestations of the memories he couldn't quite escape. Fear brightened his eyes with a glitter that warned of the damage such memories could do. He did not seem a cowardly man, or a superstitious one, but in the night's liquid shadows he had clearly found demons other men would never even notice.

"Do you believe me?" he asked quietly.

Jair's mouth was dry and his throat tight in the momentary silence that followed. "I don't know," he said.

The man nodded. "It would be wise if you did."

AT DAWN, THE peddler took his leave. They watched him lead his mule through the trees and turn north along the Silver River. Like one of the shades he claimed to have seen in the dungeons at Dun Fee Aran, he walked into the wall of early-morning mist and faded away.

They traveled all that day through country grown thick with scrub and old growth and layered in gray blankets of brume. The world was empty and still, a place in which dampness and gloom smothered all life and left the landscape a tangled wilderness. If not for the Silver River's slender thread, they might easily have lost their way. Even Cogline paused more than once to consider their path. The sky had disappeared into the horizon and the horizon into the earth, so that the land took on the look and feel of a cocoon. Or a coffin. It closed about them, embracing them with the chilly promise of a constancy that came only with the end of life. The desolation was both depressing and scary, and did nothing to help Jair's already eroded confidence. Bad enough that the peddler had chilled what little fire remained in his determination to continue on. Now the land would suffocate those coals as well.

Cogline and Kimber said little to him as they walked, locked away with their own thoughts in the shadowy coverings of their cloaks and hoods, like wraiths in the mist. They led their horses like weary warriors come home from war, bent over by exhaustion and memories, lost in dark places. It was a long, slow journey that day, and at times Jair was so certain of the futility of its purpose that he wanted to stop his companions and tell them that they should turn back. It was only the shame he felt at his own weakness that kept him from doing so. He could not expose that weakness.

They slept by the river that night, finding a copse of fir that sheltered and concealed them, tethering the horses close by and setting a watch. There was no fire. They were too close to Dun Fee Aran for that. They ate a cold supper, sips of ale their only ward against the chill, and went to sleep sullen and conflicted.

They woke cold and stiff from the night and the steady drizzle. Within a mile of their camp they found clearer passage along the riverbank, remounted, and rode on into the afternoon. Then, with night descending and an icy wind beginning to blow down out of the mountains, they came in sight of their goal.

It was not a welcome vision. Dun Fee Aran rose before them in a mass of walls and towers, wreathed in mist and shrouded by rain. Torchlight flickered off the rough surfaces of ironbound gates and through the narrow slits of barred windows as if trapped souls were struggling to breathe. Smoke rose in tendrils from the sputtering flames, giving the keep the look of a smoldering ruin. There was no sign of life—not even shadows cast by moving figures—nor did any sounds emanate from within. It was as if the keep had been abandoned to the gloom and the peddler's ghosts.

The three travelers walked their horses back into the trees some distance away and dismounted. They stood close together as the night descended and the darkness deepened, watching and waiting for something to reveal itself. It was a futile effort.

Jair stared at the keep's forbidding bulk with certain knowledge of what waited within and felt his skin crawl.

"You can't go in there," Kimber said to him suddenly, her voice thin and strained.

"I have to."

"You don't have to do anything! Let this go. I can smell the evil from here. I can taste it on the air." She took hold of his arm. "That peddler was right. Only ghosts belong here. Grandfather, tell him he doesn't have to go any farther."

Jair looked at Cogline. The old man met his gaze, then turned away. It was the first time since they had met that he had taken a neutral stance on the matter of the Ildatch. It spoke volumes about his feelings, now that Dun Fee Aran lay before them.

Jair took a deep breath and looked back at Kimber. "I came a long way for nothing if I don't at least try."

She looked out into the rain and darkness to where the Mwellret castle hunkered down in the shadow of the mountains and shook her head. "I don't care. I didn't know it would be like this. This place feels much worse than I thought it would. I told you before, I don't want anything to happen to you. This"—she gestured toward the fortress—"looks too difficult."

"It looks abandoned."

She gave him a withering look. "Don't be stupid. You don't believe that. You know what's in there. Why are you even pretending it might be something else?" Her lips compressed in a tight line. "Let's go back. Right now. Let someone else deal with the Ildatch, someone better able. Jair, it's too much!"

There was a desperation in her voice that threatened to drain him of what small resolve he had left. Something of the peddler's fear was reflected in her eyes, a hint of dark places and darker feelings. She was reacting to the visceral feel of Dun Fee Aran, to its hardness and impenetrability, to its ponderous bulk and immutability. She wasn't a coward, but she was intimidated. He couldn't blame her. He could barely bring himself to consider going inside. It was easier to consider simply walking away.

He looked around, as if he might be doing exactly that. "It's too late to go any farther tonight. Let's make camp back in the trees where there's some shelter. Let's eat something and get some sleep. We'll think about what to do and decide in the morning."

She seemed to accept that. Without pursuing the matter further, she led the way into the woods, beyond sight and sound of the fortress and its hidden inhabitants, beyond whatever might choose to go abroad. The rain continued to fall and the wind to blow, the unpleasant mix chasing away any possibility of even the smallest of comforts. They found a windbreak within a stand of fir—the best they could expect—tethered and unsaddled their horses, and settled in.

Their stores were low, and Jair surprised the girl and her grandfather by bringing out an aleskin he told them he had been saving for this moment. They would drink it now— a small indulgence to celebrate their safe arrival and to ward against bad feelings and worse weather. He poured liberally into their cups and watched them drink, being careful to only pretend to drink from his own.

His duplicity troubled him. But he was serving what he perceived to be a greater good, and in his mind that justified far worse.

They were asleep within minutes, stretched out on the forest earth. The medication he had stolen from Kimber and added to the ale had done its job. He unrolled their blankets, tucked them in under the sheltering fir boughs, and left them to sleep. He had watched Kimber administer the drug to her grandfather each night since they had set out from Hearthstone, and if he had judged correctly the measure he had dropped into their ale, they would not wake before morning.

By then, he would either have returned or be dead.

He strapped on his short sword, stuck a dagger in his boot, wrapped himself in his greatcoat, and set off to find out which it would be.

He did not feel particularly brave or confident about what he had decided to do. Mostly, he felt resigned. Even if Kimber thought he had a choice in the matter, he did not. Jair was not the kind to walk away from his responsibilities, and it didn't matter whether he had asked for them or not. The Shade of Allanon had summoned him deliberately and with specific intent. He could not ignore what that meant. He had traveled this path before in his short life, and by doing so he had come to understand a basic truth that others might choose to ignore, but he could not. If he failed to act, it was all too likely that no one else would, either.

In his mind, the matter had been decided almost from the outset, and his doubts and fears were simply a test of his determination.

He took some comfort in the fact that he had managed to keep Kimber and her grandfather from accompanying him. They would have done so, of course, well meaning and perhaps even helpful. But he would have been worried for their safety as well as his own, and that would have rendered his efforts less effective. Besides, it would be all he could do to conceal himself from discovery. To conceal two others while still gaining entry into Dun Fee Aran was impossible.

Mist and rain obscured his vision and he was forced to make his way cautiously, unable to see more than a few yards in any direction. Ahead, the dull yellow glow of Dun Fee Aran's torches reflected through the gloom as through a gauzy veil. Beneath his boots, the ground was spongy and littered with deadwood and leaves knocked down by the wind. The air was cold and smelled of damp earth and wet bark. The sharp tang of burning pitch cut through both, a guide to his destination.

Then the trees opened before him, and the massive walls of the fortress came into view, black and shimmering in the rain and mist. He slowed to a walk, studying the parapets and windows carefully, searching for movement. He was already singing, calling up the magic of the wishsong. Unlike Brin, he welcomed it as he would an old friend. And perhaps that had something to do with why he was here and not his sister.

Ahead, the main gates to the keep loomed—thick oak timbers wrapped in iron and standing well over twenty feet high. A forbidding obstacle, but he had already seen the smaller door to one side, the one that would be used to admit a traveler on nights such as this when it was too dangerous to chance opening the larger gates. He walked toward that door, still singing, no longer cloaking himself in invisibility but in the pretense of being someone he wasn't.

Slowly, he began to take shape, to assume the form that would gain him entry.

When he reached the smaller door, he sent a whispered summons to the sentry standing watch inside. He never doubted that someone was there. Like Kimber, he could feel the evil in this place and knew that its source never slept. It took only moments for a response. A slot opened in the iron facing, and yellow-slitted eyes peered out. What they saw wasn't really there. Because what they saw was another Mwellret, drenched and angry and cloaked in an authority that was not to be challenged. The door swung outward with a groan of rusted hinges, and a reptilian face appeared in the opening.

"Sstate what bringss—"

Then the sentry choked hard on the rest of what he was going to ask, for the Mwellret he had expected was no longer there. What waited instead was a black-cloaked form that stood seven feet tall and had been dead for more than two years.

What the sentry found waiting was the Druid Allanon.

It was a bold gamble on Jair's part, but it had the desired effect. Hissing in fear and loathing, the sentry stumbled backward into the gatehouse, too traumatized even to think to resecure the doors. Jair stepped through at once, forcing the Mwellret to retreat even farther. Belatedly, the ret snatched at a pike, but a single threatening gesture was sufficient to cause him to drop it in terror and back away once more, this time all the way to the wall.

"You hide a fragment of the Ildatch!" The Druid's voice thundered out of Jair. "Give it to me!"

The Mwellret bolted through the back door of the gatehouse into the interior of Dun Fee Aran, crying out as he went, his sibilant voice hoarse before he reached the central tower and disappeared inside. He did not bother to look back to see if Allanon was following, too intent on escaping, on giving warning, on finding help from any quarter. Had he done so, he would have found that the Druid had vanished and the Mwellret he had thought to admit in the first place had reappeared. Cloaked in his new disguise, Jair pursued the fleeing sentry with an intensity that did not allow for distraction. When other rets scurried past him, bound for the gatehouse and the threat that no longer existed, he either stepped back into the shadows or gave way in deference as a lesser to superiors, of no interest or concern to them.

Then he was inside the main stronghold, working his way along hallways and down stairs, swimming upriver against a sudden flow of traffic. The entire fortress had come alive in a swarm of reptilian forms, a nest of vipers with cold, gimlet eyes. Don't look into those eyes! He knew the stories of how they stole away men's minds. He had been a victim of their hypnotic effect once and did not intend to be so ever again. He avoided the looks cast his way as the Mwellrets passed, advancing deeper into the keep, leaving behind the shouts and cries that now came mostly from the main courtyard.

He felt time and chance pressing in on him like collapsing walls.

Where was the sentry?

He found him not far ahead, gasping out his news to another Mwellret, one that looked to be a good deal more capable. This second ret listened without comment, then dispatched the frightened sentry back the way he had come and turned down a corridor that led still deeper into the keep. Jair, mustering his courage, followed.

His quarry moved with purpose along the corridor and then down a winding set of stairs. He glanced back once or twice, but by now Jair had changed his appearance again, no longer another Mwellret but a part of the fortress itself. He was the walls, the floor, the air, and nothing at all. The Mwellret might look over his shoulder as many times as he chose, but he would have to look carefully to realize that there was something wrong with what he was seeing.

But what concerned Jair was that the ret might not be leading him to the Ildatch fragment after all. He had assumed that the sentry would rush to give warning of the threat from Allanon, and by doing so would lead Jair to those who guarded the page fragment he had come to destroy. Yet there was nothing to indicate that the ret was taking him to where he wanted to go. If he had guessed wrong about this, he was going to have trouble of a sort he didn't care to contemplate. His ability to employ the magic was not inexhaustible. Sooner or later, he would tire. Then he would be left not only exposed, but also defenseless.

Torchlight flooded the corridor ahead. An ironbound door and guards holding massive pikes blocked the way forward. The Mwellret he followed signaled perfunctorily to the watch as he stepped out of the darkened corridor into the light, and the guards released the locks and stepped aside for him. Jair, still invisible to those around him, took advantage of the change of light, closed swiftly on his quarry at the entry, and slipped into the chamber behind him just as the door swung closed again.

Standing just inside, he glanced quickly at the cavernous, smoke-filled chamber and its occupants. Seven, no eight, Mwellrets clustered about a huge wooden table on which rested bottles, vials, and similar containers amid a scattering of old books and tablets. At their center, carefully placed on a lectern that kept it raised above everything, was a single piece of aged paper, its edges burned and curled. A strange glow emanated from that fragment, and the writing on its worn surface pulsed steadily. The aura it gave off was so viscerally repellent that Jair recoiled in spite of himself, a sudden wave of nausea flooding him.

There was no question in his mind about what he was seeing. Forcing his repulsion aside, he gathered up the fraying threads of his determination and threw the bolt that locked the door from the inside.

Nine heads turned as one, scaly faces lifting into the light from out of shadowy hoods. A moment of uncertainty rooted the Mwellrets in place, and then the one the Valeman had followed down from the upper halls started back for the door, a long knife appearing in his clawed hand. Jair—still invisible to their sight—was already moving sideways, skirting the edges of the chamber, heading for the table and its contents. The Mwellrets had begun to move forward, placing themselves between the door and their prize, their attention focused on what might be happening outside in the hallway. All the Valeman needed was a few moments to get behind them and seize the page. He could feed it into one of the torches before they could stop him. If he was quick enough, they would never even realize he was there.

Stay calm. Don't rush. Don't give yourself away.

The Mwellret at the entry released the lock and wrenched open the door. The startled sentries turned in surprise as he bolted past them into the corridor beyond, searching. Jair had reached the table and was sliding along its edge toward the page fragment, a clear path ahead of him. The Mwellrets were muttering now, glancing about uneasily, trying to decide if they were under threat. He had only a few seconds left.

He reached the lectern, snatched up the page fragment, and dropped it with a howl as it burned his fingers like a live coal.

Instantly the Mwellrets swung around, watching their precious relic flutter in the air before settling back on the table amid the debris, steaming and writhing like a living thing. Shouts rose from its protectors. Some snatched blades from beneath their cloaks and began to fan out across the chamber. Furious with himself, terrified by his failure, and having given away his presence if not his identity, Jair backed away, fighting to stay calm. Magic warded the Ildatch fragment as it had warded the book itself. Whether this was magic of the book's own making or of its keepers, it changed what was required. If he couldn't hold the page, how was he going to destroy it?

He backed against the wall, sliding away from the searching rets, who were still uncertain what they were looking for. They knew something was there, but they didn't know what. If he could keep them guessing long enough . . .

His mind raced, his fading possibilities skittering about like rats in a cage.

Then one of the Mwellrets, perhaps guessing at his subterfuge, snatched up a round wooden container from the table, reached into it, and began tossing out handfuls of white powder. Everything the powder settled on, it coated. Once the powder was flung in his direction, Jair would be outlined as clearly as a shadow cast in bright sunlight. The best he could hope for was to find a way to destroy the Ildatch fragment before that happened, and he was likely to get only one more chance.

He glanced over his shoulder to where a torch burned in its wall mount behind him. If he snatched it up and rushed forward, he could lay it against the paper. That should be enough to finish the matter.

Steady. Don't rush.

The Mwellrets were moving back around the table now, hands groping the empty air as they attempted to flush out their invisible intruder. The Mwellret with the powder continued to toss handfuls into the air, but he was still on the other side of the table and not yet close enough to threaten Jair. The Valeman kept the wishsong steady and his concentration focused as he edged closer to his goal. What he needed was another distraction, a small window of opportunity to act.

Then the ret with the powder turned abruptly and began throwing handfuls in his direction.

The immediacy of the threat proved too much for the Valeman to endure. He reacted instinctively, abandoning the magic that cloaked him in the appearance of invisibility for something stronger. A memory of the old peddler resurfaced, warning him of the shades of the dead that roamed these halls. He summoned the wishsong at once, and images of Garet Jax flooded the room, black cloaked forms wielding blades in both hands and moving like seasoned fighters. It was all Jair could come up with in his welter of panic and need, and he grasped at it as a drowning man would a lifeline.

At first, it appeared it would be enough. The Mwellrets fell back in terror, caught off guard, unprepared for so many adversaries appearing all at once. Even the sentries who now blocked the doorway retreated, pikes lifting defensively. Whatever magic was at work, it was beyond anything they were familiar with, and they did not know what to do about it.

It was the distraction Jair required, and he took immediate advantage of it. He reached for one of the torches set in the wall brackets behind him, grasped it by the handle, and wrenched at it. But his hands were coated in sweat and he could not pull it loose from its fitting. The Mwellrets hissed furiously, seeing him clearly now behind his wall of protectors, realizing at once what he intended. Under different circumstances, they might have hesitated longer before acting, but they were driven by an

irrational and overwhelming need to protect the Ildatch fragment. Whatever else they might countenance, they would not
stand by and lose their chance at immortality.

They came at the images of Garet Jax in a swarm, wielding
their knives and short swords in a glittering frenzy, slashing
and hacking without regard for their own safety. The fury and
suddenness of their onslaught caught Jair by surprise, and his
concentration faltered. One by one, his images disappeared and
the Mwellrets' attention turned back to him.

The Valeman gave up on his effort to free the recalcitrant
torch and turned to face the Mwellrets. They were all around
him and closing in, their blades forming a circle of sharp-edged
steel that he could not get past. He had been too slow, too hesitant. His chance was gone. Despairing, he drew his own sword
to defend himself. He thought fleetingly of Garet Jax, trying
to remember the way he had moved when surrounded by his enemies, trying to imagine what he might do now.

And as if in response, a fresh image formed—unbidden and
wholly unexpected. In a shimmer of dark air, the Weapons
Master reappeared—a replication of the images already destroyed, black-cloaked and wielding one of the deadly blades he
had carried in life. But this image did not separate itself from
Jair as the others had. Instead, it closed about him like a second
skin. It happened so fast that the Valeman did not have time to
try to stop it. Again, he recalled the old peddler, warning of the
shades of the dead. Panicked, he fought to dislodge the one
clinging to him.

But it was already covering him, infusing him with its presence.

In seconds, he had *become* the image.

Instantly this hybrid version of himself and the Weapons
Master vaulted into the Mwellrets with a single-mindedness of
purpose that was breathtaking. The rets, thinking it harmless,
barely brushed at it with their weapons, and two of them died

for their carelessness in a single pass. Another fell to a lunge that buried Jair's blade so deeply, he had to wrench it free.

Belatedly, the Mwellrets realized they were facing something new. They slashed and cut with their own blades in retaliation, but they might as well have been wielding wooden toys. Jair heard the sharp intakes of breath as his knives found their mark; he felt the shudder of bodies and the thrashing of limbs. Mwellrets stumbled, dying on their feet, stunned looks on their faces as he swept through them, killing with scythelike precision.

It was horrific and exhilarating, and the Valeman was immersed in it. For a few stunning moments, he was someone else entirely—someone whose thoughts and experiences were not his own. He wasn't just watching Garet Jax, he *was* Garet Jax. He was so lost to himself, so much a part of the Weapons Master, that even though what he was experiencing was dark and scary, it filled him with satisfaction and a deep longing for more.

Now the ret guards rushed to join the battle, pikes spearing at him. The guards were trained and not so easily dispatched. A hooked point sliced through his sword arm, sending a flash of jagged pain into his body. He feinted and sidestepped the next thrust. The guards cut at him, but he was ready now and eluded them easily. A phantom sliding smoothly beneath each sweep of their weapons, he was inside their killing arc and on top of them before they realized they had failed to stop him.

Seconds later, the last of the rets lay lifeless on the floor.

But when he wheeled back to survey the devastation he had left in his wake, he saw an image of himself, standing on the far side of the table. His eyes met those of his shadow, and he felt something shift inside. The phantom Jair was fading away even as he watched, turning slowly transparent.

Do something!

He snatched up a torch mounted on the wall behind him and threw it into the powders and potions on the table. Instantly, the volatile mix went up in flames, white-hot and spitting. The Ildatch fragment pulsed at its center, then rose from the table into the scorched air, riding the back of invisible currents generated by the heat.

Escaping...

He snatched the dagger from his boot and leapt forward, spearing the hapless scrap of paper in midair and pinning it to the wooden tabletop where the flames were fiercest. The paper curled against his skin in a clutching motion and his head snapped back in shock as razor-sharp pains raced up his arm and into his chest, but he refused to let go. Ignoring the pain, he held the paper pinned in place. When the inferno finally grew so intense that he was forced to release his death grip on the dagger and back away, the Ildatch fragment was just barely recognizable. He stood clutching his seared hand on the far side of the burning table, watching the scrap of paper slowly wither and turn to dust.

Then he walked back around the table and through the image of the Valeman, and he was inside his own body again. Feeling as if a weight had been lifted from his shoulders, he looked over to where the shadowy, black-cloaked figure he had been joined to was fading away, returning to the ether from which it had come. Returning to the land of the dead.

HE FLED THE chamber, skittering through the sprawl of Mwellret bodies and out the door, hugging the walls of the smoke-filled corridors and stairwells that led to safety. His mind spun with images of what he had just experienced, leaving him unsteady and riddled with doubt. Despite having the wishsong to disguise his passing, he felt completely exposed.

What happened back there?

Had Garet Jax found a way to come back from the dead on his own, choosing to be Jair's protector one final time? Had Allanon sent him through a trick of Druid magic that transcended the dictates of the grave?

Or had the peddler been right, that the shades of the dead really did haunt Dun Fee Aran? And somehow, through his use of the wishsong, Jair had given his physical body over to that shade, becoming Garet Jax incarnate and leaving but a shadow remnant of himself—his own spirit, perhaps—behind? A shadow that might have become a shade itself had he not rejoined with it at the end.

It seemed impossible, but yet he believed it was the truth.

He took deep, slow breaths to steady himself as he climbed out of Dun Fee Aran's prisons. It was madness to think that his magic could give life to the dead. It suggested possibilities that he could hardly bear to consider. Giving life to the dead violated all of nature's laws. It made his skin crawl.

But it had saved him, hadn't it? It had enabled him to destroy the Ildatch fragment, and that was what he had come to Dun Fee Aran to do. So what difference did it make how it had been accomplished?

Yet it did make a difference. He remembered how it had felt to be a part of Garet Jax. He remembered how it had felt to kill those Mwellrets, to hear their frantic cries, to see their stricken looks, to smell their blood and fear. He remembered the grating of his blade against their bones and the surprisingly soft yield of their scaly flesh. He hadn't hated it; he had enjoyed it—enough so that, for the brief moments he had been connected to the Weapons Master, he had craved it. Even now, in the terrible, blood-drenched aftermath when his thoughts and body were his own again, he hungered for more.

What if he had not looked back at the last moment and seen himself fading away? What if he had not sensed the unexpectedly dangerous position he had placed himself in, joined to a ghost out of time?

He found his way up from the prisons more easily than he had expected he would, moving swiftly and smoothly through the chaos. He did not encounter any more Mwellrets until he reached the upper halls, where they were clustered in angry bands, still looking for something that wasn't there, still unaware that the Druid they sought was an illusion. Perhaps the sounds had been muffled by the stone walls and iron doors, but they had not discovered yet what had happened belowground. They did not see him as he passed, cloaked in his magic, and in moments he was back at the gates. Distracting the already distracted guards long enough to open the door one last time, he melted into the night.

He walked from the fortress through the rain and mist, using the wishsong until he reached the trees. Then he stopped, the magic dying on his lips. His knees gave way, and he sat on the damp ground and stared into space. His burned hand throbbed and his wounded arm ached. He was alive, but he felt dead inside. It was all his own fault. Wasn't bringing Garet Jax back from the dead what he had wanted all along? Wasn't that the purpose of preserving all those memories of Graymark and the Croagh? To make the past he so greatly prized a part of the present?

He placed his hand against the cool earth and stared at it. Something wasn't right.

If it was the Weapons Master who had fought against the Mwellrets and destroyed the fragment of the Ildatch, why was his hand burned? Why was his arm wounded?

He stared harder, remembering. Garet Jax had carried only one blade in his battle with the Mwellrets, rather than the two all of the other images had carried.

Jair's blade.

His throat tightened in shock. He was looking at this all wrong. The wishsong hadn't brought Garet Jax back from the dead. It hadn't brought Garet Jax back at all. There was only one person in that charnel house tonight.

Himself.

He saw the truth now—all of it, what he had so completely misread. Brin had warned him not to trust the magic, had cautioned him that it was dangerous, but he had ignored her. He had assumed that because his use of it was different from her own, less potent and seemingly more harmless, it did not threaten him in the same way. She could actually change things, could create or destroy things, whereas he could only give the appearance of doing so. Where was the harm in that?

But his magic had evolved. Perhaps it had done so because he had grown up. Perhaps it was just the natural consequence of time's passage. Whatever the case, sometime in the past two years it had undergone a terrible transformation. And tonight, in the dungeons of Dun Fee Aran, responding to the unfamiliar urgency of his desperation and fear, it had revealed its new capabilities for the first time.

He hadn't conjured up the shade of Garet Jax. He hadn't given life to a dead man in some mysterious way. What he had done was to remake himself in the Weapons Master's image. That had been all him back there, cloaked in his once-protector's trappings, a replica of the killing machine the other had been. That was why he had felt everything so clearly, why it had all seemed so real. It was. The Garet Jax in the chambers of Dun Fee Aran was a reflection of himself, of his own dark nature, of what lay buried just beneath the surface.

A reflection, he recalled with a chill, into which he had almost disappeared completely.

Because risking that fate was necessary if he was to survive and the Ildatch be destroyed.

Then a further revelation came to him, one so terrible that he knew almost as soon as it occurred to him that it was true. Allanon had known what his magic would do when he had summoned him through Cogline's dreams. Allanon had known that it would surface to protect him against the Mwellrets.

Kimber Boh had been right: The Druid had used him. Even in death, Allanon could still manipulate the living. Circumstances required it, necessity dictated it, and Jair was sacrificed to both at the cost of a glimpse into the blackest part of his soul.

He closed his eyes against what he was feeling. He wanted to go home. He wanted to forget everything that had happened this night. He wanted to bury the knowledge of what his magic could do.

He ran his fingers through the damp leaves and rain-softened earth at his feet, stirring up the pungent smells of both, tracing idle patterns as he waited for his feelings to settle and his head to clear. Somewhere in the distance, he heard fresh cries from the fortress. They had discovered the chamber where the dead men lay. They would try to understand what had happened, but would not be able to do so.

Only he would ever know.

After long moments, he opened his eyes again and brushed the dirt and debris off his injured hand. He would return to Kimber and her grandfather and wake them. He would tell them some of what had happened, but not all. He might never tell anyone all of it.

He wondered if he would heed his sister's advice and never use the magic again. He wondered what would happen if he chose to ignore that advice again or if fate and circumstances made it impossible for him to do otherwise, as had happened tonight. He wondered what the consequences would be next time.

The past is always with us, but sometimes we don't recognize it right away for what it is.

He got to his feet and started walking toward Kimber and his future.

Introduction to
"Don't Tell Dad"

OVER THE YEARS, I have become friends with a number of my readers through one means or another. One such family is the Barstow Bunch. Don't look at me; that's what they always called themselves. They lived in Southern California and came to see me regularly to get autographs for new Shannara books. On the first occasion, mother and son flew up to attend a book signing north of Seattle. Dad had footed the bill. They informed me they were there on vacation, but coming to meet me and get the books signed was what really mattered. It was good visiting with them; they were funny and open about their love of books. Near the end of the event, I asked exactly where they lived in California. When they told me Barstow, I mentioned I would be in California two weeks later on a book signing tour. Where would I be signing? I named the city.

Mother and son looked at me in horror. It was twenty miles from their home.

Without missing a beat, Mom turned to her son and said, "Don't tell Dad!"

I have hung on to that line for a long time, waiting for a chance to use it. This story gave me a chance to do so. Mistaya is Ben Holiday's daughter in the Magic Kingdom series, and like any father he is deeply committed to protecting his daughter. And like any teenage daughter, she is deeply committed to never telling him everything. You know. You've been there. Except that Mistaya is not your average magic-endowed child, and what she is hiding is a little different from what you or I might have encountered as parents—especially since it involves a dragon and a mud puppy named Haltwhistle.

DON'T TELL DAD

STANDING ON A grassy hillock about a mile from Sterling Silver on a beautiful moonlit evening, Mistaya Holiday faced down
Strabo with a combination of rage and distaste that bolstered
her courage beyond what an ordinary person might have mus-
tered. But then, she was not ordinary in almost any sense of the
word. She had been born in a pod inside her mother, after Willow had changed into the tree that bore her name—a physio-
logical condition periodically demanded of sylphs over the
course of their lives. She was the daughter of the King of Landover, had by the age of eighteen acquired the maturity of someone easily ten years her senior, and was fluid in two dozen
languages—half of which were indigenous to her father's old
world and half to his new. More to the point, perhaps, she was a
Princess of Landover—and the fact that Strabo was a dragon of
uncertain temperament did not intimidate a young woman of
her upbringing and experience in the least.

"You sent a *conjulant* into my *bedroom*!"

The dragon made a movement of one scaly shoulder that
might have been a shrug. "It requires considerable deliberation
and thought to choose how to approach a princess in a castle,"
he explained. "The most direct approach would have been to
appear unexpectedly and call out for you to wake and emerge to
greet me. Even if a princess knows a dragon—which, in this

case, she does—there is still an unsettling aspect to actually being summoned in such an abrupt fashion, and at such an unlikely hour. Besides, a dragon standing outside your window at midnight is never a comforting sight, I have discovered. The less intrusive approach required sending a messenger, asking if you would agree to meet in a more private location. I chose the latter to spare you any undue shock, which I thought rather considerate of me."

Strabo paused, then a hint of disapproval crept into his growly voice. "Although I must admit it has been my experience that, where you are concerned, shock is hard to come by."

Mistaya glared. He was one to talk. Besides, all this talk about consideration for her level of distress and inconvenience was bunk. He was tweaking her nose and enjoying it.

"So, in an effort to prevent any unnecessary *distress,* you sent a conjulant. A *conjulant!* Did you seriously think I would not be at least a little startled to find such a creature standing right at my *bedside?"*

And she cocked her head up at the dragon defiantly, making it plain she was not intending to let him off the hook so easily.

An impartial observer would have found the confrontation absurd. The Princess had to look almost straight up to chastise the beast, which loomed over her with all the menace of an overhanging cliff on the verge of giving way. The nighttime stars and moon were bright, but his great horned head cast such a shadow over her small form that she all but disappeared within it. But she reminded herself she was now and forever a Princess of Landover, and was not about to show even a hint of weakness to anyone or anything—not even if the creature in question was twenty times her size and might crush her with a sneeze.

The dragon eyed her momentarily, and she could have sworn she caught a hint of a smile on those toothsome jaws.

"Did it harm you in any way?" Strabo asked reasonably.

"That is beside the point!"

"Surely you know that, had it even looked at you wrong, I would have terminated it on the spot? Surely you know I would have made that very plain before sending it?" Another shrug. "And I would have sent something else, but I had to use what was at hand. Also, it is an important part of the reason I am here to speak with you."

Mistaya sighed. Up until now, Strabo *had* always been respectful of her. He had even come to her aid a time or two, although she always retained a suspicion that his help was centered on some well-concealed, self-serving purpose.

She glanced at the conjulant. A wolf-sized, scaly bit of muscle and bone, it looked a little like an unfortunate melding of lizard and hyena. Its head was dominated by jaws that opened all the way back to its ears and had teeth sticking out everywhere. Calling it ugly would have been a kindness. She had encountered only one conjulant before now, and that experience had been distinctly unpleasant—mostly due to the fact that it had been determined to eat her. And had she not possessed magic, it might have succeeded.

Her father had tried to soothe her concerns (she was fifteen at the time) by explaining that the creature was just doing what it had been born to do—to eat, indiscriminately and omnivorously—and she should not take it personally. Conjulants, he continued (up until then she hadn't even known its name), were creatures from another world, and this one must have wandered over through the fairy mists by mistake. Although, from what she knew of the mists and their fairy origins—and after no small amount of reflection—she had to admit she found her father's explanation rather hard to believe.

"Where did you pick this one up?" she asked, gesturing at the latest intruder.

Strabo snapped his massive jaws at the creature and it dropped into a shivering crouch, hiding its head under its paws.

"Cute, isn't it? It climbs walls with an ease I find astonishing. A perfect messenger, I thought, to reach you unhindered and unseen. I'm sorry you found my decision unsatisfactory."

He uttered this without an ounce of conviction in his voice, then quickly continued. "But let's move on. We could stand out here all night debating proper etiquette, or we could employ this conversation more productively. Now that you have responded to my summons, Princess, would you like to discover why I brought you here?"

She wasn't sure she would. Still, it would be best to act like an adult and not give the dragon any further satisfaction at seeing her out of sorts. She brushed back the stray locks of her honey-blond hair, smoothed down the fabric of her lightweight jacket, and straightened her shoulders. "Very well. But let me ask you something first. Are you speaking with me in this clandestine fashion because you don't care to speak directly to my father?"

Strabo managed to look insulted. "I don't care to speak directly to your father under any circumstances; I am far more intelligent and capable than he is. If I wanted something from him, I would simply ask for it. Or if need be, just take it. No, I have come to you directly as a sign of respect. And it is your help I need, not his. Is that so hard to understand?"

Mistaya frowned suspiciously. Not really, if she were living anywhere else but in Landover. It seemed to her that almost everyone who resided in this magic kingdom had boatloads of hidden agendas and nefarious intents up their collective sleeves. But then, scheming and manipulation were national pastimes almost everywhere, including her father's old world. A summer of working as a congressional aide in his nation's capital city, Washington, DC, was enough to convince her of that. Talk about a cesspool of ambition, self-entitlement, moral corruption, and thievery! Those government people were loathsome. So there was no point in singling out Landover for bad behavior and pretending it was unique.

Anyway, what did she know? She'd been to just two worlds (that she would admit to), and she was only eighteen. She had finally graduated from Carrington Women's Preparatory (with honors—one of them being Most Representative of the Ideal Carrington Student; take *that*, Rhonda Masterson!) and was now awaiting assignment. Which was to say, awaiting a determination by her father on whether he would insist on further old world schooling and renewed involvement with people whose lives had nothing in common with her own, or if she would be allowed to study magic and protocol under Court Wizard Questor Thews and Court Scribe Abernathy.

But that was a discussion for another day. Perhaps it would be best to focus on the matter at hand, whatever it was.

"I gather this must be important to you," she said, reclaiming her equanimity. "To bring me here in the dead of night, and in secret? To cause you—mighty dragon that you are—to ask for help from a mere girl?"

The dragon's lip curled—a rather off-putting sight. "Listening to your ill-considered assessment does have me rethinking my plans."

"Nonsense. A dragon does not equivocate. It never rethinks anything."

"True. But in your case, I might make an exception. And most of your assumptions are correct—save one. I have never viewed you as a 'mere girl.' You are anything *but* a 'mere girl' and we both know it. You are a trained magic user. You were taught first by the witch Nightshade—who turned out to be less adept than I would have expected—and more recently by Questor Thews, whom I must admit surprised me with his capabilities, even if he is a bit erratic at times. Now can we—how do you say it—cut to the chase?"

She nodded slowly. She was indeed an experienced magic user. And she had indeed been trained by the Witch of the Deep Fell. Trained so that she would kill her own father. Even a mention of the Witch of the Deep Fell was enough to cause a shiver to go up her spine. Thank goodness Nightshade was somewhere else these days—somewhere unknown to Mistaya—dispatched from Landover through misuse of her own dark magic. And although one day she would be back, she was out of the picture for the moment at least—and good riddance.

She nodded at Strabo. "I am listening."

"Here it is, then. Something is disrupting the fabric of the fairy mists, causing a loosening of the threads and a weakening of the stays. As a result, things from that world are beginning to make their way into others—worlds in which they do not belong. It has been a slow and gradual immigration, but the end result is the same—a disruption in the natural order of things. And worlds unfamiliar with creatures from other worlds tend to . . . overreact to their presence. But even aside from that, the creatures encroaching on these foreign worlds are not doing well. Both physically and mentally, they are not equipped to deal with what they encounter. So there are casualties on both sides."

"How did you come to be involved in all this? And why do you even care? Dragons aren't well known for their sense of civic responsibility."

Strabo gave her a look. "And how many dragons have you known?"

"One is quite enough. Why? How many am I supposed to know? I thought you were the last."

"Indeed, I am."

"Then I freely admit to basing my conclusion solely on what I know about you. But am I mistaken?"

The dragon made yet another attempt at a shrug, but he really wasn't built to pull it off.

"To answer your questions, I became involved because I am a dragon, and dragons can travel between worlds where others cannot. Opportunities for enhancing knowledge and education should not be overlooked, so therefore, it is our obligation to do so. During my recent travels, I began to see this unnatural shifting of certain species from one world to the next, and I witnessed the results. Very disturbing."

"Has this been happening for long?"

"Long enough. Perhaps for the last three years."

"And the cause?"

"Is unknown. Mostly. Would you kindly let me finish before burying me in questions?"

He was sounding a bit testy, so Mistaya apologized. "I didn't mean to interrupt," she said. "Please continue."

"Thank you. The question that kept coming back to me as I observed these occurrences was this: How were all these species able to cross through the fairy mists when the laws of nature and magic clearly dictate the impossibility of it? No other species save my own is allowed to travel from world to world unhindered. Oh, well, and your father, who has his medallion, and perhaps one or two other magic wielders or talisman holders. But certainly not whole species, with no regard for who or what or how many. So how is this happening?"

She waited for him to answer, but he remained mute. "Well?" she said finally. "Don't keep me in suspense."

"Allow me a few moments to do exactly that," the dragon replied. "Tell me instead if you would be willing to help me put a stop to it, knowing what you do about the potential repercussions if this is allowed to go unchecked."

She stared at him in confusion. "First of all, you haven't provided very much detail, so asking such a question seems premature. Second, why would you choose *me* to help you? It is not as if we are close friends."

Strabo moved back a short distance and then knelt before her, almost in the manner of a supplicant. "Princess," he growled, softly enough that it was almost endearing. "You are my first choice—and exactly the *right* choice, believe it or not. You underestimate your value to both Landover and to its people." He paused. "How can I explain? Consider. Your father is an off-worlder. He lacks magic beyond what is given him by virtue of his office as King and from having the Paladin as his significant other. Your mother, on the other hand, is the daughter of the River Master, the King of Landover's fairy folk—those who have chosen not to live within the mists, anyway. Hers is an inherited magic—not manifested so much in herself, but decidedly manifested in you. Yours is the true, raw magic of your mother's species, mixed with the admirable character and resilience of your father—though I hate to admit it."

"There are some very pointed words from my father's old world for such effusive praise, dragon . . ."

"Wait!" Strabo said quickly, with a hint of fire flaring from his nostrils. "Allow me a further moment to finish. I am not only trying to explain my reasoning, but to put words to something less easily expressed than might seem possible. A dragon has difficulty with friendships—of any kind. You might not see me as a friend, but I see you as one. Friendships for dragons have less to do with casual attraction and momentary infatuation and more to do with depth of character. I see you as one possessing great character—in the manner of both of your parents, I should point out—and therefore view you as someone whom I could trust and depend upon, should the need arise. Which, I believe, it has now."

"Do you?" she asked quietly—not in a snarky way, but rather in genuine surprise.

The dragon nodded. "I do. And it is for that reason I have come to ask for your help. Dragons are not often inclined to deal with humans, but it is my suspicion that the agent behind what is happening is not to be easily ferreted out, nor stopped. The barriers between the fairy mists and the other worlds are ancient and permanent, yet something has breached those barriers. Something has disrupted the natural order of things, and has done so quite deliberately. To what end, I cannot tell, but I think perhaps the answer lies in the Fairy Circles."

Mistaya sat down on the grass and stared at him. "What are the Fairy Circles?"

"Passageways, Princess. You can find them on every world. They are bare spaces that have been cleared of all living things in order to serve as paths for the fairy folk to cross from world to world. The mists offer the fairy folk concealment, but they can use the circles to travel to and from their lands. The circles are created by magic, and serve only those with fairy blood. But it is my belief some of the circles have been compromised and are now being used by other creatures entirely."

"To what end?"

"That remains part of the mystery. Who is doing this and why? If I am to find this out, I must seek my answers in other worlds. And for that, I believe I will need your help."

"My help," she repeated. "Again, why choose me?"

"You are unique. You are the product of two species and two worlds. You have considerable use of magic, and you are able to see things through different eyes. And it is my feeling that just this sort of different sight will be needed. Neither your father nor your mother alone can offer exactly what you can. Besides, who else is there for me to ask who might consider giving aid to a dragon?"

She realized abruptly what he was trying to say. A dragon has no real friends. A dragon is a lone creature with such presence and power that no one really wants to get close to it—for obvious reasons. Strabo was the last dragon, and he was looking for help in a world where help would not easily be found. But even still, he was seeking help that would have value, and believed she could deliver that.

Because of her unique mix of blood and history and skills, of course.

But mostly through what he perceived as her strength of character.

Well, who knew?

"What do you propose to do?" she asked finally.

"We will travel into a handful of these other worlds and attempt to find the source of the problem. Once we find it, we will stop it."

She realized suddenly that, even without consciously deciding to help the dragon, she had done so anyway. "I will have to find an excuse to disappear for a time. I don't think telling my parents—and especially my dad—of our true intent is a good idea. How long do you think we'll be gone?"

The dragon made a face. "I could not say. A few days, perhaps? Maybe longer."

Mistaya gave a moment's thought to what sort of excuse she could offer. It would certainly require something better than going off to gather berries and visit a friend. No, it needed to be an excuse that would prevent either parent from ever discovering the truth.

She got to her feet. "I suppose I'd better get busy with this," she announced. "I just hope the effort is worth it. Do you really think my presence can make a difference?"

Strabo stood, rising to his full height. He stood an intimidating thirty feet tall as he loomed over her. "Princess, I would not ask if I did not think it so."

She nodded and sighed. "Then meet me back here two days from now at dawn, and we'll see if I've found a way to manage it."

MISTAYA RETURNED TO her castle bedroom in Sterling Silver and slept late into the new day. It was almost midday when she finished washing and dressing—already too late for breakfast but still a little too early for lunch. Nevertheless, she went down to the kitchen and sweet-talked the cook into a sandwich and a glass of milk. Parsnip—a kobold like his cousin Bunion, who was the King's designated messenger and sometime bodyguard—was a fearsome-looking creature under the best of circumstances. His temper was short and his patience severely limited, and her initial request for food and drink made him scowl at her as if she had asked for admittance into the Royal Treasury. But the Princess knew Parsnip. In spite of posturing and vocal disapproval, he was something of a push-over. By the time she was done with him, he had added a salad and a chocolate éclair.

Leaving the kitchen behind, she wandered out into the main rooms of the castle in search of her father and found him in the company of Questor Thews and Abernathy, sorting through a cluster of plans detailing improvements and upgrades to various pieces of land and buildings scattered throughout the kingdom. Offering a brief greeting, she stood by silently as the three continued to discuss the matters at hand.

Finally, her father turned to her. "Was there something you wanted, Mistaya?"

Smiling, she said, "I just wanted to ask you something and see if it was all right with you."

Her father was no fool. When it came to his daughter's efforts to persuade him to a cause or to extract a concession, both frequently came with an ulterior motive. Having a daughter who was half fairy creature and in command of substantial fairy magic was not without its challenges. Even though he showed nothing, she knew he would already be on guard. Without bothering to dismiss the other two, he smiled benignly. "Why don't you go ahead and ask. These other matters can wait."

Mistaya stepped closer. "I have given quite a lot of thought to my future, and I think I should take a closer look at those colleges you suggested I visit. Would it be all right with you if I did that?"

Her father stared at her. "This is sudden, isn't it? I thought you had made up your mind to stay in Landover."

"I mostly have, but it couldn't hurt to go back to the States and be certain I am not making a mistake. Perhaps I should spend a few days at each, to get to know the school and the students better."

Her father looked suspicious. "Aren't you supposed to contact the schools first?"

Mistaya hastily composed her face into a meek expression. "I'm afraid I already have. I probably should have told you, but I wasn't sure if they would agree on such short notice. But they said I could come to visit anytime. So now I am asking your permission."

"Well, I'm afraid I can't go with you right now. Maybe in the summer I can make—"

"But I don't need you to go with me. I can go on my own. I know how busy you are, and I am perfectly capable of managing this myself. It will be a good experience for me."

Her father looked at her uneasily. "I know you are mature enough to do this, Misty, but I don't like the idea of letting you go alone."

She hesitated, then pulled out her trump card. "What if I take Haltwhistle with me?"

Her mud puppy companion—a strange magical being given to her a few years before by the Earth Mother. Possessed of an elongated body with stubby legs, a lizard tail, long floppy ears, webbed feet, and a rodent face, Haltwhistle looked as if he had been assembled from bits and pieces—and not very successfully at that. His continued presence also required her to speak his name at least once each day. If she did not, he would vanish forever.

As much as she loved the mud puppy—which was a whole bunch—she knew taking him with her outside of Landover was an outrageous idea that her father would never agree to. But suggesting it would prove she was making an effort to satisfy his concerns while reaffirming her determination to go.

And she was not disappointed by his response. "Absolutely not!" he said at once. Behind him, Questor Thews winced and Abernathy rolled his eyes. "Taking a mud puppy outside Landover presents all sorts of problems! No, choose someone else as your companion."

She paused, looking around the room. "Not Questor or Abernathy; you need them here. Would Bunion be all right?"

Ben Holiday sighed. "You know he wouldn't. Nor would anyone else who lives in the castle." He studied her a moment. "What about your mother? She hasn't left the kingdom for a time. She might enjoy accompanying you."

Admittedly, Mistaya hadn't seen that coming. Other than her father, her mother was the last person she wanted to go with her. She had tried to make it clear that she wanted to go by herself, and had been hoping her father would come to that realization on his own. Apparently, he had not. Sometimes he was so dense!

"You know she doesn't like it in the States," she said hastily. "Or anywhere in your old world. She needs the soil of Landover in which to root when it is her time of the month. She has obligations of her own . . ."

"I'll speak to her tonight," her father interrupted, making a dismissive gesture. "Or you can go speak to her now. The choice is yours. But you are not going alone."

And he went back to his conversation with Questor Thews and Abernathy, leaving her standing there openmouthed.

SHE SERIOUSLY CONSIDERED storming out of the room in a pointed display of irritation, but then thought better of it. Instead, she simply turned away without a word and departed back the way she had come. She would take a run at her mother next. She was closer to Willow than she was to her father, and she might have better luck with her.

She found her mother sitting on a wooden bench in the gardens she had planted when she first moved into Sterling Silver, admiring the flowers she had worked so hard to nurture. The sun was shining down on her, illuminating her beautiful green skin as if she were herself an exotic plant. Mistaya stood quietly watching her mother for long moments, gathering her thoughts, then walked over and sat beside her. For long moments, the two said nothing to each other, content simply to share the space and time and silence, and admire the broad carpet of colorful petals.

Finally, Mistaya said, "I need a favor, Mother."

Willow looked over and smiled. "This is about your father?"

Now it was Mistaya's turn to look over. "How did you know?"

Her mother met her gaze, brushing back a swatch of her long, dark-green tresses. "You're my daughter. It is my business to know such things. Besides, your face gives you away. Your expression says you asked something of him and he refused. Now you want me to intervene."

Mistaya rolled her eyes. "Great. My mother can read my mind."

Willow laughed softly. "It might seem that way, but I think it has more to do with how you were born. Your birth was premature, unexpected, and under stressful circumstances. I almost died saving you. I think that might have formed a special link between us."

"So you really *can* read my mind?"

"I can sense things about you. I cannot explain how or why; it just happens. It comes unbidden, whether we are together or apart. I can occasionally see your thoughts or hear you speaking. I can sense your intentions. But there is no pattern to it. It just happens randomly but infrequently."

"So you can look into my head, in other words." Mistaya rolled her eyes. "Not what I would have hoped for in a mother."

Willow looked away. "It is not what I would have hoped for, either, but there it is. So do you want to tell me what the problem is?"

Seeing no other logical choice, Mistaya told her about the request she had put to her father, to be allowed to go alone to visit colleges back in the States, and how her father had refused her. She explained that she felt she was grown up enough to make the trip alone and her father was treating her like a child. She ended by saying her father had suggested asking her mother to go, but then quickly added that she knew how uncomfortable that would make her feel and why it was wrong to ask her when there really was no need for her to go anyway.

Willow listened attentively and, when her daughter was finished, said, "So you're trying to spare me the discomfort of returning to a place where I feel entirely out of place by not asking me to go with you?"

Mistaya shrugged. "Mostly, I'm just trying to find a way to make this trip alone."

Her mother grinned. "You are right in assuming I have no interest in going back to your father's old world. People with green skin and green hair tend to draw unwanted attention. And I know that you are capable of going alone. But I think you have approached this in the wrong way. You want your father to feel you are mature enough to go alone and you want him to trust you. But tell me this, Misty. Do you think he might have cause to wonder if you are telling him everything?"

Mistaya looked away quickly and then back again. "What do you mean?"

"You know what I mean," her mother said gently. "What is your real reason for going? And please do not keep insisting it has to do with college. Tell me what it really is you plan to do."

Her daughter huffed in frustration and tossed her thick mane of hair irritably. "You probably already know, Mother!"

"No, I don't. I only know that it doesn't involve colleges because I can see that much in your eyes. So what does it involve?"

With a sigh, Mistaya told her about Strabo's visit and his request that she accompany him to a series of worlds beyond Landover in an effort to discover what was causing the fairy mists to break down. She explained the dragon's reasons for asking her along—fully expecting Willow to dismiss such far-fetched thinking—and sat back to await an unfavorable decision.

But she had misjudged her mother and ignored the obvious. Willow was one of the fairy. So she simply nodded when Mistaya had finished and took her daughter's hands in her own, gripping them tightly.

"You must learn to have more faith in your father and me, Misty. We have at least as much experience with the instincts of fairy creatures as you do, and do not tend to dismiss their ability to measure and judge the value of those instincts. Tell me, did you find Strabo persuasive?"

"I did."

"Yes, or why else would you have accepted this quest and been persuaded to find a way to do so in spite of the opposition you expected to encounter from your father and me?"

"You think I should have been more open in asking permission, don't you?"

Her mother nodded. "Do you still believe this effort to be worth your time and whatever risk might be involved?"

Mistaya thought about it a moment, then nodded. "I think the dragon is to be trusted. Strabo thinks too much of you to ever deceive me."

Willow smiled. "Then you have my permission to go with him. You are already a grown woman and, even at eighteen, you have more magic at your command than either your father or I—or even Questor Thews. But you must convince your father of this. He is the King of all Landover. Go to him again and tell him everything. I believe you will find him much more willing to listen than you think, once you speak the truth."

Mistaya rose and stood looking down at her mother in wonder. "I want to be you one day," she said quietly. "I want to be able to see things the way you do."

She bent to kiss her mother on the cheek and was about to leave when Willow called after her. "Did you say your father told you not to take Haltwhistle with you?"

Mistaya nodded. "I understand why . . ."

"Take him anyway."

Mistaya stared in shock. Take Haltwhistle? How was she supposed to do that? She wasn't even allowed to touch him.

"Mother . . ."

"Take him."

Mistaya stared at Willow a moment longer before nodding reluctantly.

Great. Just great.

SURPRISE, SURPRISE, HER father agreed she could go. Once she had confessed all, trying her best to make it sound as normal as taking a walk in the woods—after assuring him she believed Strabo's intentions to be worthwhile and honorable (jeez!); after insisting she felt perfectly able to look after herself; and after promising she would be careful and do whatever it required to keep safe and not do anything foolish or reckless and brush her teeth and eat right (well, maybe not those last two, but it felt like they might be included by implication given the number of admonitions he had uttered)—he had given his consent. It was a measure of his confidence in her, and it brought tears to her eyes when he closed by telling her how much he loved her.

TWO DAWNS LATER, she woke while it was still dark, washed and dressed, slipped from her room, and went out of the castle. Just beyond the gates, she paused and reluctantly called for Haltwhistle. It was one thing to defy her father; it was another altogether to disobey her mother.

The mud puppy appeared out of nowhere, slouching to reach her side, ears hanging so low they dragged the ground, soulful brown eyes looking up at her expectantly, stubby legs propelling him to her side. She knelt to greet him, his odd misshapen body and weird old face strangely reassuring.

"Atta boy," she cooed. "Good old Haltwhistle." She resisted the urge to pet him. Petting a mud puppy was forbidden. "Want to go for a ride? Want to go on a trip?"

The lizard tail wagged hard, the elongated body squirmed, and a small whine escaped the mud puppy's throat.

Mistaya rose. "Well, I just hope you can manage it. Come on. Let's go look for the dragon."

They set out for the hill where she had met up with Strabo two days before. In the east, the sunrise was bright silver where it outlined the horizon. The early-morning air was crisp and cool and invigorating. She liked the idea of going off on an adventure with a dragon; how many other young women got to do something like that? But she knew she would have to be careful, too. Strabo was mercurial and self-centered, given to impulses that were not always in the best interests of others. This was mostly because he was a dragon, and dragons more closely resembled armored bears (yes, she had read Philip Pullman early) than human beings. When you are virtually indestructible and possessed formidable magic of an ancient kind, you did not give a whole lot of thought to rash acts.

She found him today where she had found him last, comfortably settled on a hillside off in a wooded section of the lands that surrounded Sterling Silver, not more than a mile off. He was sleeping, but one scaled eyelid slid open the moment she came into view. He took in her appearance, then the eye closed again.

But a moment later he was rising to his full height, stretching his massive body and giving a yawn that was all maw and teeth and which was so terrifyingly savage and raw that she could have lived happily without it for the remainder of her life.

"Princess," he growled softly. "Good morning."

"Good morning," she replied, craning her neck upward to meet his baleful stare. She knew he wasn't angry with her (or at least she hoped he wasn't); dragons just looked baleful all the time because it was their natural expression. "I'm going with you."

"I thought you might be." Strabo smacked his lips as he continued his wake-up routine. "What sort of story did it require for you to gain permission, if I might ask?"

"You might. I simply told the truth."

The dragon stared. "How is that possible? This is your father we are talking about. Ben Holiday, the righteous defender of the kingdom of Landover and his daughter's virtue. Telling him the truth would not result in permission to come adventuring with me."

"Well, it did this time. I told him exactly what you told me, and reminded him I was a grown woman. So he agreed I should come."

"Ah. A grown woman. Wonder what that makes me? You, a human of some eighteen years, and me, a dragon of some seven hundred? What aren't you telling me about this? I know there is something more to his willingness to acquiesce. It isn't as if we are going for a walk in the park—if walks in the park were even something I would consider doing."

"I asked my mother, and she was the one who told me I should tell the truth. Maybe she talked to him."

"The lovely Willow; she is a treasure." The dragon seemed to engage in a moment of reminiscence. "That might explain it. Still, whatever it was that persuaded Holiday to grant permission for our outing, I am inclined to think a little more highly of him. A *little*. He has exhibited a sense of sound judgment here that is unexpected, given his temperamental behavior."

Pot and the kettle, dragon, she thought. "Well, where do we start? Where shall we go first?"

Strabo did a weird thing with his dragon lips as he lowered his scaly head toward her. "We start right here with . . ." He trailed off, suddenly distracted. "Whatever in the world is that thing hiding behind your legs?"

She looked back and saw Haltwhistle looking suitably cowed. "That's Haltwhistle. He's a mud puppy. He's coming with us."

"A *mud puppy*? Aren't those creatures all in service to the Earth Mother? Is that where you got this . . . *thing*?"

She nodded. "He belongs to me now, as long as I wish him to stay with me. He is very loyal."

Strabo sighed gustily. "Good for him, but he is not coming with us. For many reasons, not the least of which is I don't want him along. He looks fairly useless for anything we might require of him. And isn't it true that you aren't even allowed to pet him? You have to leave him behind, Princess."

"If you insist on leaving him behind, you will be leaving me behind, too. Perhaps it might help to know that it was my mother who ordered me to bring him?"

"Your mother?" The dragon rolled its eyes. "The world conspires against me. She knows I would never refuse her anything. Very well, Haltwhipple—or whatever his name is—can come. But he is your responsibility, not mine. Now, where were we?"

"I asked where we started, and you said we started here."

"Yes, yes. Quite true. Climb aboard, then. Sit just at the base of my neck. Bring your little friend, if you must, but it will be up to you to hold on to him so he doesn't fall off."

Well, that wasn't going to happen, but there was no point in telling the dragon. She simply climbed up his extended foreleg to her perch and watched Haltwhistle scramble up after her, more nimble in his efforts that she would have believed possible.

"Tickles," growled the dragon as the mud puppy found a suitable perch. "By the way, stay clear of the sack and its contents."

Mistaya glanced over her shoulder and saw a heavy sack strapped to the dragon's spine, several feet back. "Is that what I think it is?"

"Assuming you think it is the conjulant, yes. We will be needing it to find our quarry."

"I hate those things," she muttered.

"Well, too bad. I'm not fond of creatures that serve the Earth Mother, either. Or of carrying passengers, of any kind."

She gave a disinterested shrug. "Guess we both have our burdens to bear, don't we?"

Strabo did not answer.

*   *   *

THEY FLEW THROUGH the morning, north over the Heart and
the king's lands to the Greensward, and from there to the Deep
Fell. Mistaya had more than a few misgivings about going anywhere near Nightshade's former home, but she also knew the
witch had disappeared a few years back and no one had seen or
heard of her since. She had been gone long enough that many
had forgotten all about her, but not Mistaya. She remembered
all too vividly how she had been seduced by the witch and almost turned against her father. The memories returned in a
rush as she looked down into the dark pit of the Fell and saw
again how easily she had been tricked when she was younger
and more impressionable.

And she knew in her heart—where young women always
know such things—that she hadn't seen the last of Nightshade
or faced her last challenge in recognizing and resisting the
witch's manipulations.

"Why are we going this way?" she asked Strabo impulsively.
"Isn't this the long way?"

"It is the right way," the dragon growled irritably, without
bothering to look back at her. "Yes, it would have been easier to
go into the mists just south of your home, but here is where the
conjulant surfaced and here is where we must begin retracing
its steps. That is how we will find where it came from and who
sent it."

Then they were descending toward what appeared to be endless miles of heavy mists and clouds, forming an extensive and
impenetrable blanket over the ground below. Strabo descended
quickly and without slowing, dropping into the brume and
straightening out when they were submerged within its covering. But now the ground below was faintly visible. This was not
new territory to Mistaya, who had spent time in the mists before, but it was no less uncomfortable. The vaguely visible earth
below was monochromatic and shapeless and devoid of anything resembling life. Everywhere you looked, it was the same.

"Not far now," Strabo shouted unhelpfully.

Mistaya rolled her eyes. Time and distance were measured differently when you were seven hundred years old. Was that really his age? He had never said how old he was before. And when it came to dragons (even though she only knew the one), you could never be sure how much of what they uttered was truth and how much exaggeration.

And after they had flown on for another two hours, she was inclined to believe the latter.

When they finally set down within the mist, it was nearing nightfall, and the brume seemed even denser than before. Undeterred, Strabo suggested that Mistaya and her pet dismount, and while they did so he reached back with his long neck to take the sack containing the conjulant and set it on the ground.

Mistaya surveyed her bleak surroundings and discovered that the flat patch of earth on which they stood was covered with a series of circular depressions of varying sizes. All were perfectly formed, and within their circumferences no plants or grasses grew. The enclosed sections of earth were bare and empty of life, as if the ground had become toxic.

"Are these the Fairy Circles?" she asked the dragon.

His monstrous head hove into view. "They are. On the surface, they appear to be no more than odd depressions mysteriously formed and inexplicably barren. But in truth, they are doorways into other worlds for those who are trained to recognize them. This is where we begin."

He reached for the sack, loosened the ties, and dumped the conjulant unceremoniously to the ground. The beast stood, shaken and confused, panting heavily as its huge jaws hung open and its crooked teeth stuck out in all directions. Mistaya grimaced in spite of herself. It saw her looking and began to snarl menacingly, but Strabo made a small sound deep in his throat and the conjulant went still instantly.

"This unfortunate creature will guide us back to wherever it came from. Once there, we will begin the process of uncovering how it found its way to Landover." The dragon managed to frown. "It is difficult to know how much it will help us to find out *where* the conjulant came from, but it is the best we can do. Unless you have a better idea?"

He glanced over and Mistaya shook her head. "I don't have any ideas at all."

"Then, here." He bent down to the sack and removed a leash, taking it in his jaws and handing it to her. "Place that about its neck. Keep hold of the lead; it might try to bolt. Although, given my warnings, I doubt it will give you much trouble. Go on, fasten the leash in place."

Easy for him to say at twenty thousand pounds. Harder for her at about 130. She eyed the conjulant warily, then slowly bent to fasten the leash. Its mean, piggy little eyes followed her movements, and a curl of its lip revealed its dislike. But it made no move as she placed the leash about its thick neck and fastened it in place.

Once she was done, she stepped back quickly, brushing away stray strands of her honey-blond hair, which of late she had let grow longer.

"Take firm hold of the leash," the dragon continued. "Feel that little button on the end?"

She did—a small rubber knob. "Give it a squeeze."

She squeezed and the conjulant jumped three feet into the air and fell to the ground, quivering.

"A small reminder of who is in charge." The dragon sneezed, belched a gout of fire, then spat a massive wad of mucus. Mistaya grimaced and the conjulant covered its head with its paws. "Dratted mist! Always affects my sinuses. Anyway, press that if the creature attempts any nonsense. It won't do so a second time, I promise you."

Mistaya frowned. "You make it sound like you won't be going with me. I hope I misheard you?"

Strabo sighed. "That fact that I *can* do something doesn't always mean that I *should*. Do you have any idea how hard it is for someone my size to fit down those tiny Fairy Circles? Believe me, you don't want to know what that requires. So it is up to you to do the hunting. I will follow when needed."

Mistaya stamped her foot angrily. "So that is why I am here? To save you from doing the legwork? You expect me to risk myself out there in the great unknown while you nap back here, safe and sound?"

"A gross exaggeration. Besides, you overlook the obvious. You have magic at your command, Princess—magic that will protect you as successfully as anything I could manage even with my size and strength. Oh, well, all right, my fire and flying abilities would be useful, of course. But you can get into and out of places I couldn't begin to. You are smart and you recognize things others never would. Trust me, this arrangement has not been formed without considerable thought on my part, and it does not favor me any more than it does you."

She was pretty sure this was a lie and was about to call him on it when she realized it must have cost him something to have come to her in the first place. Strabo was notorious for never asking for help, and prided himself on his ability to manage any and all situations. Yet, here, he had been forced to seek her out.

"So what am I supposed to do now?" she asked.

"What I brought you here to do. Have the conjulant retrace its steps to wherever it came from and see what you find. If you need me, whistle me up and I will be there instantly. I can fit through those wormholes well enough when the need is there, and I won't abandon you. Take Halfwhittle, or whatever his name is, for company. But don't blame me if something unfortunate happens. I warned you about bringing him."

"It's not *him* I'm worried about!" she snapped.

She glanced down at the mud puppy, who looked back at her with his soulful eyes, as if to say, *Do you have any idea at all what you are getting us into?*

She didn't, of course. "Come on, Haltwhistle. Let's go down the rabbit hole."

Alice's Adventures in Wonderland had been another favorite book. She just hoped she wasn't about to experience an adventure quite as crazy as that one.

She clucked at the conjulant and jiggled the leash encouragingly. The nasty little beast glared at her with evil intent. She glared back, snapped the leash a little more forcibly, and gave it a foot to its hind end. A moment's hesitation, and it was moving forward, nose to the ground as if searching. It took her left and then it took her right, scouring about the Fairy Circles until it found one it liked. At which point it began tugging on the leash and pulling her forward. She brought it up short at the edge of the circle that had caught its interest.

"Oh, yes," Strabo called out suddenly, "I almost forgot. Take a deep breath before going under and hold it until the spinning stops. You can do that, can't you? How long *can* you hold your breath?"

She was staring back at him in confusion when the conjulant gave a mighty lunge that dragged her forward until both of them, along with a placid Haltwhistle, were standing in the center of the chosen circle.

And then the ground gave way beneath her feet and she was falling.

THINGS MIGHT HAVE turned out decidedly worse if she hadn't instinctively reacted by taking a deep breath as she tumbled away. An instant later she was engulfed in blackness and spinning like a top. She gritted her teeth and shut her eyes and held her breath as if her life depended on it—which, she quickly decided, it might. She could not tell anything about what was happening to her—how quickly she was spinning, what direction she was going, or what it was she was tumbling through. The Fairy Circle might have been composed of air or earth or sand or mud—or anything else under the sun—but she did not dare open her eyes to find out. She couldn't tell what had happened to either of her companions. It was all she could do not to give

way to the panic that threatened to overwhelm her. The sensation of falling was bad enough, but when coupled with the
strange shushing noise that her spinning fall seemed to be causing, and her complete inability to be able to sense whether she
was right-side up or upside down, she thought briefly that she
might go mad. Her heart was pounding, her lungs were starting
to ache from holding her breath, and her sense of being caught
in limbo was terrifying.

At one point she made a promise to herself that, if she got out
of this in one piece, she would never go anywhere with the
dragon again. Then she further promised herself she would
strangle him for putting her in this situation . . . until she realized how foolish that sounded, a waifish girl strangling a beast
that size! Why not beat on it a bit while she was at it? Really
pummel it!

She *was* on the verge of passing out.

Then, abruptly, the spinning stopped and she was sitting on
hard ground again. Or, rather, on something that at first she
thought was ground but on reflection decided was probably
something else. She took the risk and opened her eyes. She
looked down. Sand? She looked up again. What light there was
in whatever place she'd been sent was dim and misty, but she
could make out the conjulant sitting on its haunches nearby,
engaged in a staring contest with Haltwhistle. She remembered
the leash and realized she was still holding it. But otherwise . . .
nothing.

The Fairy Circle had sent her to another world. But which
world?

She took inventory. Her body seemed unharmed from tumbling down the rabbit hole, and she was indeed sitting on a
patch of sand at the edge of a vast body of water, the shoreline
stretching away in both directions until it disappeared from
view. She blinked and got to her feet—mostly to see if she could
manage it. But she had no difficulty. The spinning did not re-

turn, her head remained clear, and the air was breathable. Still, there was something decidedly off about her situation.

A moment later, she realized there were two suns in the sky, both of them much smaller than those she was used to either in Landover or on Earth proper. Small enough, in fact, that they seemed to give off no more than a twilight's fading glow.

Was this where she was supposed to begin looking?

The conjulant shifted to its feet and started away, tugging once more at the leash that bound it. She started after it, letting it lead, with Haltwhistle at her side. She had only gone a short distance when her guide abruptly turned into the trees bordering the beach, pulling her along with a sense of urgency she could not mistake. They had only just made the sheltering canopies of a grove of palms when a huge black shadow passed overhead—a winged monstrosity that she could not make out clearly but did not care to get close enough to do so. She huddled in the shadow of the palms until it had passed and was safely away.

"Where are we going?" she snapped at the conjulant.

Its feral features tightened in a snarl, but it turned away without challenging her. And without saying anything helpful, either. Likely it possessed no vocabulary. So she was forced to follow along for a considerable distance. The look of whatever world she had been brought to never changed, and the conjulant never slowed its pace. Instead, the conjulant, the girl, and the mud puppy made their way onward for what seemed like miles.

Finally, the trio reached a cove nestled in a series of cliffs that overlooked a pool of turgid water that swirled in a cluster of circles. The conjulant moved to the edge of the nearest cliff and peered down, then looked over at her questioningly.

Of course it would be water this time. Fairy Circles could be formed of almost anything, couldn't they? The whole thought of jumping into the circle set her teeth on edge, but she knew there was no help for it. There were no paths leading down off the cliff edge and no indications of anywhere else she might enter the water. To say that she was disgusted and angry by now was an understatement. But she had committed already to seeing this through, and turning back now would be admitting defeat.

So she walked up and stood beside the conjulant, ignoring the vast array of teeth it displayed as it attempted a smile, and simply said, "Jump!"

Together, with Haltwhistle right behind them, they went over the cliff and into the water.

THINGS BEING WHAT they were when magic was involved, the hunt seemed as if it would go on endlessly as they passed from there through another five Fairy Circles, the wormholes linking each world to the next failing to provide either direct routes or shortcuts to their final destination. Assuming the conjulant was simply retracing its actual path and not merely messing with her, it seemed that it had been forced to take quite a circuitous route to get to Landover.

She wondered, after emerging from Fairy Circle number five, how the conjulant had come to Landover in the first place. Had it known where it was going? Or had it just stumbled onto it by chance? Somehow, she didn't think chance entered into this. Landover had been its destination all along—as well as the destination of the other creatures Strabo had observed emerging from the Fairy Circles. But how had a creature as primitive and ignorant as a conjulant managed to navigate such a journey?

Not without help, she reasoned. Not without a guiding hand from someone or something else. And it was likely that same someone or something else was orchestrating these unauthorized travels for reasons that did not promise anything good for her homeland.

Her reasoning tightened into certainty as she endured each increasingly less pleasant wormhole experience. Each leg of her journey was a fresh test of her fortitude and commitment. One Fairy Circle ended in a circular depression within a deep snowbank. One dropped her into a boiling-hot whirlpool that left her not only drenched but just short of scalded. Another terminated in an odd sunspot so bright she was left blinded for long minutes after fighting her way free. And still another dropped her midair into a tornado that was passing over acres of wild grasses and animals that looked a little like six-legged cows with deer heads.

All the while, the conjulant pressed on as if everything it was seeing was familiar and did not trouble it in the least. Halt-whistle kept up without any noticeable distress, which left Mistaya feeling like the proverbial odd man (or in this case, woman) out. By the time she had emerged from a further two Fairy Circles in a field of similar round hillocks, barren and flat-topped, but surrounded by a vast carpet of brilliant scarlet wildflowers, she was convinced that some malefactor or other was using the Fairy Circles for ill intent, and wondered why the fairies weren't doing anything about it.

And there, seated on a promontory not too distant from her place of exit, was her answer.

Whatever she was looking at came to its feet instantly when she appeared, looking for all the world as if delighted to find her there. Mistaya was pretty sure this was a fairy of some sort. Its appearance was decidedly ephemeral, its body a shimmering in a mix of half-light and full transparency. But it looked nothing like any of the fairy forms she was familiar with. In fact, something in its makeup suggested it might have begun life as a failed experiment. She tried to think what it most reminded her of. There were arms and legs (or maybe just one or the other), with a body mass that suggested a Raggedy Ann or Andy doll (hard to tell which), but mostly just suggested a poor attempt at mimicking a scarecrow.

The conjulant practically dragged Mistaya down off her perch and into the pasture of wildflowers in its eagerness to reach whatever it was that waited to greet them. They were next to it within moments, staring at it in confusion. By then the creature, having seen the look on Mistaya's face, had decided that maybe it wasn't so happy to see her after all, but found its retreat blocked by Haltwhistle's stubby body and raised hackles.

"Who *are* you?" Mistaya demanded.

"Who are *you*?" the other replied.

"Uh-uh, I asked you first. You're one of the fairy, aren't you? What kind? I haven't seen any like you."

The creature straightened marginally, wheezing a bit through several facial orifices. "That's because there aren't any others like me. I'm an original. My name is Colkin."

"Well, Colkin, what are you doing here?"

"Minding my own business—unlike *some*."

Mistaya took a threatening step forward. "You're hardly minding your own business when you send a conjulant into my home! You did send it, didn't you? You don't deny it?"

Colkin shook his shaggy head. "I don't. Why should I?"

"And you sent a lot of other creatures, too, didn't you? Right through the Fairy Circles from their own worlds into worlds where they do not belong. Playing around with creatures that were perfectly happy where they were before you interfered! Why would you do that?"

Colkin hesitated, then shrugged. "I wanted to have fun."

Irritated beyond words by now, Mistaya seized the front of the tattered garment Colkin wore and shook him as hard as she could. To her surprise, she was able to do this. Most fairy folk would have quickly turned entirely transparent and therefore become untouchable by a human.

"You sound like you don't have a brain in your head!" Mistaya snapped angrily. "What's wrong with you, anyway?"

"Nothing! I'm special."

"Why? Because you can make a mockery of the Fairy Circles by using them for your own purposes? Because you can disrupt people's lives? How can you think this is a good thing to do? Or don't you care?"

Colkin shook himself free of her grip. "I was just doing what

I was told. I was just playing the game. I didn't know anyone would get so angry with me! Don't you sometimes just do things for no better reason than to have fun?"

"Not if I think it might cause others harm . . ." She stopped short. "Wait a minute. Playing the *game?* What game?"

Colkin made a gurgling noise that seemed to signify a burst of laughter. "Quidditch!"

Mistaya stared. "Quidditch? Quidditch isn't real. It's a game in the Harry Potter books." Another of her favorites. She'd read them right after the Alice books. "What are you talking about?"

"Quidditch is *so* real! You take creatures from different worlds and you move them around through the Fairy Circles until eventually you get them all mixed up and someone magic appears and straightens it all out. Then the game ends and you start over. And here you are, so now the game's over." A pause. "You are magic, aren't you?"

Mistaya felt a shiver crawl up her spine as a fresh realization set in. "Who told you all this? Who taught you this game?"

Colkin pointed to something behind Mistaya. "She did."

Mistaya turned slowly, already knowing who was waiting.

"Well, well," said Nightshade, her black-cloaked form tall and forbidding, a slow smile spreading across her lovely, pale features. "We meet again."

BY NOW, MISTAYA had concluded several things. First, Colkin's brain was likely missing a few bulbs from its candelabra, and the unfortunate fairy creature had allowed itself to be used by the witch. Second, this entire business of sending creatures through the Fairy Circles from one world to the next had all been done in an effort to draw her attention and bring her back within Nightshade's grasp. She didn't care to speculate on what the witch intended; it was enough to know that whatever it was, she wouldn't like it.

"There are those who know where I am," she said quietly, tightening her resolve.

Nightshade's smile widened. "Possibly. But there is nothing they can do about it now, is there? You're all alone."

Nightshade was wrong; she wasn't alone. She still had Strabo to back her up. And Strabo could do a lot. But maybe the witch didn't know about Strabo. And she mustn't forget about Halt-whistle. Haltwhistle was there, too. So maybe there was still hope.

But when she looked for the mud puppy, she couldn't find him. Apparently, he had gone into hiding—or maybe he had just left her altogether. If she didn't speak his name every day, he would abandon her. Had she spoken it since yesterday? She couldn't remember. If she hadn't, he would have disappeared for good.

And how was she supposed to summon Strabo? The dragon had never told her.

Her heart sank, but she was determined not to be cowed. "How did you know I would come? It could as easily have been someone else."

"Oh, Misty, you are so quick to catch on. Indeed, it could have been someone else. It should have been, in fact. I am usually able to avoid doing things that won't turn out exactly as I want them to, but it appears I failed here. Colkin was persuaded to play the Quidditch game to catch the attention of the dragon, who sees everything. I was quite certain the dragon would never come into the fairy mists itself to find out what was happening; after all, it cares nothing for the people of Landover and would consider the entire effort a foolish quest. No, it would go to your father to suggest he do his kingly duty and go into the mists himself to find out who was responsible. That was the plan all along. It was your father I wanted to trap. But fortune favors the bold, and you will do just as well. Once he knows I have you, he will come to your rescue. And I will be waiting for him. Eagerly."

Mistaya took a moment to digest this. For all her boasting,

Nightshade hadn't foreseen that Strabo would go to her and not to her father to discuss the matter of the Fairy Circles. Nor had she foreseen that the dragon would have a genuine concern for the fate of the Four Lands. Her reasoning had been wrong on several counts, yet still things had worked out for her.

But knowing that did Mistaya no good at all.

"You hate my father because he has bested you for years in all your attempts to have him removed from the throne of Landover. You even used me as a pawn not that long ago. You're pathetic. I won't help you to trap my father. Nor will I let you make me your prisoner. In fact, I am leaving and going home. Right now."

This was something of an idle threat, given that the witch was ten times more experienced in the use of magic than she was. It was further complicated by the fact that Nightshade stood squarely between herself and the Fairy Circle she needed to reach to escape.

"You're not going anywhere," Nightshade insisted.

"You can't stop me."

The witch shook her head slowly, her curtain of black hair shimmering in the pale light. "If I am forced to kill you, Misty, it would serve my purpose just as well. Your father would still come to me. Not to save you, but to seek revenge."

She was right, of course, but Mistaya would not give in.

"You better worry about yourself!" she snapped in reply.

Atop a pair of barren hillocks, Princess and witch faced each other over a sea of crimson petals, eyes locked, expressions of determination reflected on both their faces. Mistaya had no idea what Nightshade was feeling about this confrontation, but for her own part she was well and truly terrified. Out of the corner of her eye, she saw the conjulant drop flat against the earth and put its front paws over its eyes.

Strabo, she begged silently. *Where are you? I need you!*

Suddenly Colkin bounded over to Nightshade in a clear display of exuberance. "Wait! Stop! What are you doing? Look! I brought someone magic to you, so I win the game! Can't we play the game again now?"

Nightshade didn't even bother to glance his way. "The game is over. Move out of the way."

"But I thought you said we could play the game some more! You said we were friends, and we could play the game anytime we wanted to. You said you thought I was wonderful because I knew all the passageways through the Fairy Circles and could bring all those creatures from one world to another. You said it didn't matter that the other fairies didn't like me because I was different, that you liked me anyway." The creature was right up in her face now, practically blocking her view of Mistaya. "You said you would—"

The witch seized Colkin by his tattered tunic and thrust him aside. "Never mind what I said! Go find someone else to play the game. I don't want to play it anymore. Understand?"

Colkin staggered away, a look of disbelief on his twisted face. Then, with a shriek of rage, he threw himself on her, biting and scratching and hammering at her. But Nightshade caught him firmly with one hand and held him away from her, a look of disgust on her bladed features.

"You've served your purpose, little Colkin." Bright-green magic began forming at her fingertips. "Time for you to disappear!"

Mistaya didn't wait to see what the witch intended. Her own magic had already been summoned as a defensive measure, so she cast a separation spell at Nightshade that forced her to release Colkin and then quickly cast a levitation spell that threw Nightshade twenty feet into the air.

But Nightshade recovered midair and dropped swiftly back down again, unharmed and enraged. And there Haltwhistle was, waiting for her, returned from wherever he had been hiding, his hackles raised and steaming with icy purpose as he hammered the witch backward with a tremendous blow that would have put an end to someone less powerful. Sadly, the witch again proved a match for her adversaries, blocking the strike from the mud puppy and shrieking unintelligibly as her hands lifted to cast a spell that would destroy both him and Mistaya.

But before she could do so, the ground behind her blew apart in a shower of earth and grasses and scarlet wildflowers that took the entire top off the Fairy Circle that had brought Mistaya and her companions to this place and time, and Strabo hove into view like a massive jack-in-the-box. Huge and forbidding, his jaws breathing fire, he turned on the witch.

"Greetings, Nightshade!" he bellowed through flames and smoke. "Can I join the party?"

The witch paled, assessed the odds in the blink of an eye, and broke off the spell she was about to cast. In another blink of an eye she went up in a cloud of black smoke and was gone. The dragon stared at the place she had vanished for long moments, hovering in midair, then settled down slowly in front of Mistaya.

"I wonder how she does that?" he muttered to no one in particular, giving the empty space a final look before turning again to Mistaya. "Apologies for being so late, but it took me longer than expected to navigate all those wormholes. I was doing rather well until the one with the sunspot. That one blinded me sufficiently that it took awhile for me to recover my sight. But you seem to have carried on well enough."

She saw it then. "You followed me! You were right behind me the whole way. No wonder you never bothered to tell me how to summon you."

"It seemed the best way to find out who was behind all this. Although I had my suspicions, I still needed to draw her out of hiding."

Mistaya strode forward and slapped him rather pointlessly on his scaly foreleg. "You used me as bait!"

Strabo had the grace to flinch. "Well, I wouldn't put it that way," he rumbled. "More like a guide dog."

"Oh, that makes it *so* much better!" She gave him a furious look before composing herself. "At least you got here in time to help."

Then, at his very polite and solicitous request, she told him everything that had happened.

SOON SHE WAS back in Landover, standing on the very spot from which she had departed a day or so earlier, if travel through the wormholes hadn't skewed her sense of time's passage. She had freed the conjulant from its leash so it could be sent back to wherever it had come from after receiving a stern warning from Strabo about what would happen if it showed up in Landover ever again.

Then she had taken the unfortunate Colkin aside for a private word. "Are you all right?"

Colkin nodded. "I'm sorry for what I did," he said to her, obviously fearing the worst after a glance or two at Strabo, looming close by.

"I know. It wasn't your fault."

"But I did bad things. You said so. I sent all those creatures away from their homes and into places they didn't belong."

"But you didn't understand that what you were doing was wrong," she said, patting him on the shoulder. "Nightshade deceived all of us, me included. She is a bad person, and you should just forget all about her."

"She didn't ever want to be my friend," the fairy creature whispered.

"Nightshade doesn't want to be anybody's friend. She doesn't know how. She doesn't even like herself very much."

"Now I don't have any friends," it whimpered. "I'm all alone again."

She gripped the miserable creature's arm gently. "I will be your friend, Colkin. But I can't stay here with you because I have my own home. And this is yours, so you can't come with me. You need to find someone else. Be a friend and you will make a friend. There is someone out there in the fairy mists just like you, looking for a friend it doesn't have. You have to go find whoever that is."

Colkin nodded. "I will try."

Which is all any of us can do, she thought as she rose and bid Colkin farewell.

So now she was safely home again and, for the moment at least, finished with the business of creatures coming over from their own worlds into Landover or other worlds where they didn't belong. But Nightshade was still out there, and it seemed certain she was not about to stop trying to harm Ben Holiday.

"I'm still not happy about being used as bait," Mistaya announced to Strabo as he prepared to depart. "It seems to me you could have found another way."

The dragon sniffed loudly, and steam leaked from his nostrils. "Given enough time, perhaps. I judged that time to be unavailable. Perhaps you would have preferred to let me handle matters by myself?"

"No, no. I needed to be there. I needed to see Nightshade. I kept hoping she was gone for good, but that was foolish. She still wants my father dead."

"I am not enamored of your father, I admit, but I don't wish him harm. He is doing the best he can as king, flawed as he is. Which matters not the least to the witch." He paused. "I would watch my back, if I were you. I would suggest the king do the same. This isn't finished."

Then he stepped back a few paces, spread his great wings, and lifted away into the morning sky.

Mistaya watched him go until he was out of sight. *He isn't such a bad dragon,* she thought. *Rather a good one, all in all.*

She looked down at Haltwhistle, who was waiting patiently at her feet. "Come on, little one. Let's go tell Dad what happened."

But after a dozen steps or so, she added. "Well, maybe not all of it."

After all, he didn't need to know the whole story. If he did, he would pitch a fit and she would probably be grounded for months. She slowed her pace. But how could she tell him about Nightshade and her threat to come after her father without telling him the rest?

She stared off into the distance where the spires of Sterling Silver had just come into view. Where her father was waiting for her.

She looked down at Haltwhistle, who was looking back at her questioningly, and gave a heavy sigh. Better stick to what had worked before when she told him why she was leaving and where she was going.

Better to tell him everything.

With Special Thanks to the Barstow Bunch

Introduction to

"The Black Irix"

ANOTHER OF THOSE recurrent requests for a further story about characters in the Shannara books centers on Shea and Flick Ohmsford: the brothers from the village of Shady Vale who went in search of the fabled Sword of Shannara in the first book of the Shannara series. Along the way they met a Rover thief named Panamon Creel and his enigmatic companion, the mute Rock Troll, Keltset. Keltset was the recipient of an award from his people called a Black Irix—a secret not revealed until near the end of the book. The Irix disappeared at the end of the book. I thought now would be a good time to find out what happened to it.

So we have a new quest for the brothers Ohmsford and their rather unpredictable and often suspect friend Panamon. The Rover has found the missing Black Irix and intends to get it back from those who took it. For that, he needs help only Shea can provide. It is a favorite setup of mine, a plot device I have used over and over. Something is missing and needs to be found. Someone has the means of finding it but is reluctant to go searching. A reason is found for going anyway. Trouble lies ahead. But doesn't it always?

We can convince ourselves of just about anything if the reason for doing so is strong enough. Friendship is one of those reasons, and it is almost always a good one. But trust is a necessary ingredient of friendship.

Or is it? The Ohmsford brothers are about to find out.

THE BLACK IRIX

MORE THAN A year had passed since his return from the Skull Kingdom, and Shea Ohmsford was finally beginning to sleep through the night. For a long time, that had been unthinkable. Nightmares of what had been—and what might have been—plagued him like demon-spawn, startling him awake and leaving him sleepless after. The hauntings drained him, and for a time he believed he was in danger of dying. He lost weight, color, and spirit. He lacked not only the energy to do his regular work at the inn, but the will to do much of anything else.

Then Flick, his always-brother and forever-best-friend, took the unusual step of visiting a woodswoman who specialized in potions and spells to cure maladies and who, it was said, could divine the future. Her name was Audrana Coos, and she was neither young nor old, but somewhere between, and she was a recluse and an object of constant derision by all but those who had gone to her for help. Flick, never given to anything that wasn't practical and solidly based in demonstrable fact—and who would never have gone to such a person before the quest for the Sword of Shannara—made a leap of faith. Or perhaps, more accurately, a leap of desperation. And he went to see her.

There, deep in the Duln, miles from his home, he sat at a table with this odd-looking woman with her hair braided in colored lengths, her face smooth as a child's and painted with bril-

liant rainbow stripes, and her arms encased in gold and silver
bracelets from which tiny bells dangled, watching closely as she
read the waters of a scrye bowl and determined the merit of his
cause.

"He is very ill," she announced solemnly, her voice unexpectedly deep and scratchy. "He agonizes over what he might
have done . . . and what he did. He is damaged by the closeness
he experienced to the Dark Lord, and the poisons generated by
his contact with the Skull Bearers fester inside him. Long has
this sickness waited for its chance, and now it breaks free of its
fastenings and seeps through him. His life slips away."

She paused, as if considering her own words, then began rif-
fling through shelves of tiny bottles, leather sacks laced tight
with drawstrings, and packets whose contents were hidden from
Flick, her slender hands closing at last on a small brown bottle
that she handed to him.

"You must give him this," she told him. "Do so in secret; do
not let him see you do it. If he sees you, he may resist. Give it all
to him in a single serving. Mix it with a drink he enjoys and
make certain he drinks it down. All of it. Do it immediately
upon your return."

Flick studied the bottle doubtfully. "Will it cure him of his
dreams and wasting sickness? Will he return to the way he used
to be?"

Audrana Coos put a finger to his lips. "Speak not of other
possibilities, Valeman. Do not even think of them. Do not doubt
what I tell you. Just do as I say."

Flick nodded and got to his feet. "I thank you for your help.
For trying to cure my brother."

He began searching for coins to pay her, but she waved him
away. "I will not accept pay for giving aid to one who stood
against the Warlock Lord. I will not profit from one who can be
said to have saved the Four Lands and all those who dwell
within."

She paused, cocking her head to one side and looking down

again into the scrye waters, which had suddenly begun to ripple anew. "A moment. There is something more."

Flick peered down into the waters but could see nothing.

"Be warned," the seer whispered. "Not long after today your brother will journey to a faraway place on a quest of great importance. You will not wish it. You will not approve. But you cannot stop him, nor should you."

"This can't be true," Flick declared, shaking his head for emphasis. "Shea has said repeatedly that he will never go on another quest."

"Even so."

"He has said he will never put himself in danger like that again, and he is staying in the Vale with me and Father!"

"Nevertheless."

Flick dismissed the reading out of hand. He rose, thanked Audrana Coos once more, and with the potion tucked into his pocket set out for home.

When he got there, late in the day, he considered his choices. Even though he had possession of the potion, he was not entirely convinced of its value. What was to say it would not prove harmful to his brother in spite of what he had been told? Maybe he had been deceived. Maybe the claims of effectiveness were exaggerated.

But he could not persuade himself that it was better to do nothing than to try something. There was about Audrana Coos a reassurance that he could not easily dismiss. There was a confidence and perhaps even a promise in her words that dispelled his doubts and persuaded him to proceed with his plan.

So he waited until a worn and ravaged Shea was finished with his afternoon nap, walked his brother downstairs from their rooms, an arm about his waist to steady him, and sat with him on the inn's covered porch, watching the sun sink slowly behind the trees. Flick was animated and engaging on that afternoon as he related an imaginary tale of things he had never done, covering up the truth about where he actually had been.

He worked hard to capture his brother's full attention while encouraging him to drink down the tankard of ale he had given him, remembering what Audrana Coos had told him—that all of the contents of the bottle must be consumed.

And in the end, they were. Shea, almost asleep by then, head drooping, eyes heavy, drank the last of his ale, and Flick caught the tankard just before it dropped from his brother's hand.

Then he carried Shea to his room, tucked him into his bed, and went down to dinner alone. He ate in the dining room at a corner table, keeping to himself—his father was working in the kitchen that night—as he considered what he had just done and prayed to whatever fates determined such things that he had not made a mistake.

In the morning, when Shea woke and came down to breakfast, he looked much better. He was smiling and lively; he appeared to have begun his recovery.

"So you don't feel sick anymore?" Flick asked happily.

His brother shook his head and grinned. "No. I can't understand it. I feel like I used to. Much, much better."

Flick said nothing then about what he had done. He watched his brother closely for almost two weeks, constantly looking for signs of a regression into the sickness, worrying that the potion's effectiveness might not last. But at the end of that time, when Shea was still healthy and in all respects back to himself, Flick had to admit that the medicine Audrana Coos had given him had indeed worked.

It was then that he admitted the truth to Shea about what he had done, not wanting to keep anything from the brother to whom he told everything. He did so hesitantly, not certain what Shea's reaction might be and anxious to be forgiven for his deception.

But Shea simply clapped him on the shoulder and said, "Well done, Flick. No wonder I love you so much."

Emboldened, Flick then told him what the seer had said

about Shea going on another quest—one that Flick would not countenance, but one his brother would undertake anyway.

Shea laughed. "I'm not going on any more quests, Flick. I'm all done with that sort of thing. I'm staying right here in the Vale with you."

And Flick smiled and hugged his brother, and put the matter out of his mind.

FOUR MONTHS LATER, with the summer mostly gone and the first signs of an approaching autumn reflected in chilly early mornings and leaves turning color, Shea Ohmsford was hauling wood for use in the big stone fireplace in the tavern's common room. He did it by hand rather than by cart because he was still proving to himself that he was healed, that it wasn't a temporary cure. His day stretched ahead of him, filled with upkeep tasks—patching the porch roof and repairing the hinges on the side kitchen door after he finished hauling in the wood—all of it providing him with a feeling of satisfaction at being able to do something that four months earlier he couldn't have. Every day he celebrated his recovery, still remembering how sick he had been.

Flick had driven the wagon out to the miller's to haul back sacks of grain and would not return before late afternoon. On the morrow, they would go fishing in the Rappahalladran River, the day their own to do with as they wished. The air was pungent with the smell of dying leaves and smoke from fires, the sun warm on his shoulders, and the birdsong bright and cheerful. It was a good day.

Then he saw the rider approaching. Not on the main road leading into the village and past the houses and businesses that formed the bulk of the community's buildings, but through the woods behind the inn. The rider was sitting casually astride his mount, letting the horse pick its way through the trees, but his eyes were on the boy. Shea thought afterward that he probably knew right away who it was, but couldn't bring himself to admit it. Instead, he simply stopped where he was, a stack of wood cradled in his arms, and stared in disbelief.

It was Panamon Creel.

When he had first met him, the thief and adventurer had been clad all in scarlet—a bold, open challenge to convention and expectation alike. Now he wore woodsman's garb, all browns and grays—with the exception of the scarves tied about his arms and waist, bloodred and sleek, a reminder of the old days. His mount was big and strong, a warhorse from the look of it, with long legs that suggested it could run fast as well as far. Weapons sheathed and belted dangled from the horse and the man, strapped here and there—some fully visible, others apparent only from their distinctive shapes beneath clothing and his saddle pack.

He rode up to Shea and stopped. "Well met, Shea Ohmsford," he said, swinging down to stand before him.

"Panamon Creel," Shea replied in a voice that didn't sound remotely like his own.

"I should have sent word I was coming. But it is always more fun to show up unexpectedly. I trust I am not unwelcome here?"

"Not you," the boy said. "Not ever."

"Well, then, don't stand there with your mouth open—show some enthusiasm!"

Shea dropped the wood with a clatter, rushed past the fallen logs, and hugged the other to him, pounding his back happily. "I can't believe you're here!"

It had been over a year and a half since the culmination of the events leading to Shea's discovery and use of the Sword of Shannara against the Warlock Lord—an effort that would never have been successful if not for Panamon Creel. In the aftermath of Shea's flight from the Skull Kingdom, he had been forced to leave his friend behind and thought him forever lost. But Panamon had turned up again weeks later in Shady Vale, alive and well, eager to recount the tales of those earlier days and to learn the truth about what had really happened, for much of it had been hidden from him.

Now he was back again—the bad penny returned, the clever trickster everyone so mistrusted, but who had saved Shea's life over and over and about whom he could never think badly.

"You wouldn't happen to have a drink for a thirsty traveler in that establishment of yours, would you?" the thief asked, grinning. "I've come far and ridden hard, and I've a very parched throat."

"Come along," Shea invited, picking up the scattered chunks of wood once more and starting for the inn. "You can tie up the horse out back and come inside for a glass of ale."

"Or two, perhaps?" the other pressed, one eyebrow cocked.

He hadn't changed, Shea thought. He never would. In point of fact, he looked exactly the same as the last time the Valeman had seen him—sun-browned face, unruly dark hair with touches of gray at the temples, piercing blue eyes, and a ready smile. A small, thin mustache gave him a rakish look. He was always charming and never predictable. With Panamon, there was always more than what appeared on the surface.

Shea remembered it all, fleeting thoughts that came and went as he walked the other inside and dumped his load of wood in the bin next to the fireplace. Then he walked over to the bar, drew down a couple of tankards of ale, and led his companion over to one of the tables in the mostly empty common room.

Panamon raised his tankard in a salute. "To surviving the bad and enjoying the good."

Shea clinked his tankard with Panamon's and drank. "You look as fit as ever."

"Oh, I am. I don't age, you know. I prefer to stay just as I was when you first met me. I've found that age to be a perfect fit and have decided to keep it."

"Nice trick."

"Magic, of a sort. You can do it, but it takes practice." He leaned forward. "Rather like using those blue Stones you were carrying around when I went with you into the Northland. Do you remember?"

Shea nodded. "How could I forget?"

"Do you still have those Stones?"

Right away, Shea knew he was asking for a reason that went beyond mere curiosity. But this was Panamon Creel, and it would have been out of character for him not to be hiding something. "I do."

"You can still use them?"

He shrugged. "I haven't had reason to try for a while."

The thief laughed. "Good point. I certainly hope you haven't. The good life of the Vale is founded on peace and prosperity, not engaging in life-and-death struggles. You've been well, I trust, in the last year or two?"

He hadn't, of course, and he told Panamon about his struggle to recover from what had happened to him in the Skull Kingdom. Panamon listened and nodded and drank his ale, his eyes bright and interested, his face impassive. When Shea had finished, he suggested another tankard—for himself, since Shea had barely touched his.

Shea refilled the other's drink from behind the bar and then returned. He glanced around as he did so—a necessary habit when you are an innkeeper's son—to see if anyone needed anything. He was surprised to find that the room was empty.

"How is Curzad?" Panamon asked as he took his seat. "Your father has always looked like he might live forever."

"Just so," Shea answered. "It was being of his blood, I think, that kept me safe when things looked worst."

"Yes, the sickness." Panamon looked about casually. "I confess I came here for a reason, young Shea, beyond the obvious desire to visit an old friend. I have a favor to ask."

Shea nodded. *Now we are getting to it.* "Ask it."

"This may take a few minutes. Bear with me. Are you sure

you don't want a refill before we start? Once I get going, I like to keep going."

"Just say what you have to say," the Valeman replied.

Panamon squared himself up and leaned forward. "You will remember that we lost a good friend when we tried to escape from the Warlock Lord. He gave his life for us. He was my companion for many years, but almost to the end of his life he was a mystery to me. We found out together, you and I, the secret he was hiding when we were taken by Rock Trolls. Do you remember all this?"

Shea did, of course. Keltset, the giant Rock Troll, had been with Panamon when they had rescued Shea from Gnome raiders. Then, subsequently, when they were found by members of his own kind, he was placed on trial as a traitor for being in the company of people from a Race with whom his own were at war.

"Keltset," he said.

"You will remember, as well, then," Panamon continued, "that you and I were saved from being handed over to the Warlock Lord, and he from being thrown off a cliff, when he revealed he was the holder of the highest honor that can be accorded by the Troll nation to one of their own. He stood there before them and displayed it boldly—a challenge to all to dispute his loyalty and his courage when it was being questioned. That was an unforgettable moment, wasn't it, Shea?"

The Valeman nodded. Keltset had produced from a leather belt strapped about his waist an iron medallion with a cross embedded in a circle, held it up for all to see, then hung it about his neck in a dramatic display that had stunned all assembled and thereby gained them their freedom.

"Do you remember what that medallion was called?"

"The Black Irix," Shea answered.

Panamon Creel leaned back in his seat. "It was lost with Keltset when the walls of that mountain passageway collapsed on him. I intend to find it and bring it out."

Shea stared. "From under a collapsed mountain?"

"No, from wherever Kestra Chule has hidden it."

The Valeman considered. "Back up a bit. Who is Kestra Chule?"

"A buyer and seller of stolen goods."

"He has the Black Irix?"

"He does."

"How did he manage that? And how do you even know about this?"

Panamon Creel shrugged. "As to the first, I don't know. I don't even know how he found out where it was, let alone how he managed to dig it out. As to the second, I am a thief, as you have pointed out to me a time or two in the past. It is my job to know about such things."

"So you intend to steal it back from him? Why go to all that trouble for a piece of iron, no matter what it represents?"

"Because," the other said slowly, drawing out the word, "the Black Irix is immensely valuable. There are perhaps a dozen known Irixes in existence, and most of those are in the hands of the Trolls. You cannot overestimate what a collector would pay to get his hands on one. But it is valuable, as well, because the materials used to make it are extremely rare. An Irix is hammered out from a mix of metals—some used for strength and some to provide special value. Auridium is the most precious of those metals. Do you know of it?"

Shea shook his head. He had never heard of auridium.

"It is so valuable that there is only one known source. It is deep in the Eastland and mined by Dwarves, who trade half of what they acquire to the Trolls in exchange for a wagonful of high-quality weapons. That exchange has been going on for a long time. In any case, half an ounce goes into the making of every Irix. That alone would buy you a small kingdom."

He exaggerated, but Shea got the point. "So you want to recover the Irix from Kestra Chule. Why don't you just do so? What do you want with me?"

"As I said," Panamon replied, "Chule has hidden it."

"So how does . . ." Shea began and then stopped. "Oh, I see. You want me to come with you and use the Elfstones to find it."

"Because of the conditions under which I will be exercising my particular skills, it would be helpful to know where *exactly* the Irix is hidden in advance of extracting it. You could tell me that. Or, more to the point, your special Stones could. I am asking this as a favor to someone who has done much for you in the past."

Shea gave him a look. "Someone whose life you saved on more than one occasion. You forgot that part."

The other man shrugged. "I was holding it in reserve, in case further persuasion proved necessary."

"The problem with this request is that I have sworn to one and all—myself included—that I would not take part in another quest, no matter what. I have promised not to leave the Vale again. And after recovering from my sickness, I reaffirmed that vow."

"Are you saying you will not go with me? Even knowing how much you owe me?"

"I am saying I have made a vow and now you are asking me to break it."

"For a very good reason."

"A very good reason for you. But not necessarily for me."

Panamon sighed. "Shea, consider. You told me you were so sick you almost died, and that you found yourself blessed by your recovery. Of what use is all that if you spend the rest of your life hunkered down in Shady Vale, never venturing farther than its borders, never taking another chance on anything, never risking even once the possibility you might do someone a great service?"

Panamon held up his hand quickly to forestall the Valeman's next response. "And I am not talking about myself. I am talking about those who loved and cared for Keltset, and who would be made glad beyond words if we were able to recover his Black Irix and return it to them. Does that count for nothing?"

Shea tightened his lips, thinking. "What do you get out of

this? Wait! You are planning on returning it, aren't you? You don't intend to sell it yourself?"

Panamon looked shocked. "No, I don't intend to sell it myself! What kind of creature do you think I am? This is Keltset we're talking about. He saved our lives, and mine more than once! I'm doing this for him. I don't want Kestra Chule to make his fortune on the death of my friend! I intend that he not make a single coin, and that the Irix go back to Keltset's people where it belongs!"

"You're telling me the truth? You're giving it back?"

"What would you do?"

"What I would do isn't necessarily what you would do."

"Don't play games with this." Panamon was flushed, angry. "Just answer the question! What would you do?"

They were shouting at each other now, and upon realizing it they went quiet at once. Panamon picked up his tankard and drained it. Then he passed it across the table to Shea who took it without a word, carried it back behind the serving counter one more time, refilled it, and returned.

As he sat down again, he found himself remembering what Flick had said about the woodswoman's prediction. He hadn't believed it possible that it would come true. He had thought it funny that it would cause Flick to be so concerned.

Well, he wasn't laughing now.

"I would do what you are doing," he said quietly. "How soon do we leave?"

IT WAS THE sort of decision you made quickly. There wasn't much to think about when you came right down to it. You could make all the promises or vows you wanted, but ultimately everything hinged on the answer to a single question: How much did you owe someone who stood by you when you needed it and by doing so saved your life? If it didn't matter to you, you turned them down when they asked for your help. If it counted for something, you didn't.

No matter the doubts or inconveniences attached to making this trip with Panamon Creel, Shea felt honor-bound to go. He tried to explain that to Flick later that same evening when his brother returned from the miller's, but his efforts were futile. Flick was having none of it. Shea was deliberately and foolishly placing himself in harm's way out of a misguided sense of loyalty to a man of questionable character—although admittedly one who had helped him in the past. Was Shea forgetting that Panamon had tried to steal the Elfstones from him? Was he forgetting that Panamon's mission—no matter its claimed virtues—was essentially another theft? Was he forgetting that the thief had a tendency not to be entirely forthcoming with what he knew and tended to shade the truth of whatever he did tell?

"What about the fact that you only just got your health back?" he demanded as a last resort. "You almost died, Shea! Now you are going on a trip that could very well finish the job. Shades, you don't even know where you're going!"

They were standing out back by the woodshed, shouting at each other, while inside the patrons of the inn drank and laughed and talked loud enough that they could not hear a word of the argument taking place out back.

"I know where we're going. Panamon told me. It's in the lower Northland, not far from the ruins of the Skull Kingdom. I know a little about the country. It's wild, but not so dangerous anymore. We'll be close to Paranor and the Westland. Flick, listen to me. I have to do this. But I promise to be careful, and if I get sick or it becomes too dangerous, I will come home at once. I won't take chances."

"How can you say that?" Flick exclaimed in disbelief. "What makes you think you will be allowed to come back? He needs the Elfstones! In fact, what if it's the Elfstones he's really after? Have you thought of that?"

Shea had thought of everything. Some of it made him ashamed of himself, but Flick was right about one thing. This was Panamon Creel, and Panamon was capable of anything. So he wasn't going into this blind.

When it was all said and done, Flick stood firm on his insistence that Shea not go, but Shea persisted and went anyway. He advised his father he would be traveling with Panamon for as long as two weeks and rode out the next day on a horse he had rented from the local stable master, his gear and clothing stowed in a bedroll tied to the back of the saddle, the Elfstones tucked down inside his tunic. Flick, to his surprise and disappointment, remained behind. He had almost believed that his brother would come with him, just as he had on the quest for the Sword of Shannara. But the times and the circumstances were different, and apparently Flick had done enough questing in his life. He loved Shea and feared for him, but he simply refused to support a cause in which he did not believe.

"Turns out Audrana Coos was right," he said in parting. "Try not to make me regret it. Come home safe."

So Shea and Panamon Creel rode north out of Shady Vale into the Duln Forests until they reached the banks of the Rainbow Lake. There they turned west to follow the lakeshore around to where they could begin their journey toward the Streleheim and into the Northland.

Shea spent his time on horseback thinking of how long ago the last quest now seemed. It was almost as if it had happened in another lifetime—one he had lived as a different person entirely. He had grown up on that quest, seasoned and matured under the pressure of constantly being hunted and placed at risk, of facing death almost every day, of watching friends and strangers die all around him, and of knowing how much depended on the success of his efforts.

This time the feelings were altogether different. He was not being chased, and the threat of death seemed remote. He was placing himself in some danger, but what was at stake was much smaller and less world changing.

What troubled him most was the absence of Flick, who had

stuck with him before for as long as he was physically able, and had been there to reassure him when his doubts and fears threatened to undo him. He missed his brother and wished mightily he were there again.

So when, on the third day out, Flick appeared, it was almost like a miracle. He had left the same afternoon, after telling their father what he was doing, unable to stand the idea of Shea going without him, surprising himself with the intensity of his feelings. Taking the trail he knew they would follow to go north, he had tracked them until he caught up.

"Changed my mind," he announced as he rode up. Noting the look of dismay on Panamon's face, he added, "I can't have my brother going off like this without someone reliable watching out for his best interests."

Shea laughed and clapped Flick on the back affectionately. Panamon Creel said nothing.

THEY WERE THREE now as the journey continued. Panamon regaled the other two with tales of his exploits, most of which caused Shea to smile and Flick to roll his eyes. The thief made so many outlandish claims and recounted so many improbable happenings, it was impossible to believe half of them. But it was entertaining, and it helped the time to pass more swiftly. To his credit, Flick did not say or do anything to deliberately irritate Panamon. He did not question the purpose of their journey or the details surrounding how the thief intended to fulfill it, and studiously avoided offering any sort of challenge to the other's authority.

But Panamon was clearly irritated by his presence nevertheless, which eventually persuaded Shea to confront him.

"You don't seem too happy having Flick along," he said. They were standing alone at their campsite on the fourth day out while Flick was off gathering firewood. By now they were above the Dragon's Teeth and only a day from their destination. "Why are you so upset?"

"Because, Shea," Panamon replied in a dismissive tone, "this effort doesn't need a third person. It just needs you and me. Flick will only be in the way. He might even cause problems for us when we go after the Irix, just by being here. I didn't plan on him coming, and I don't need him."

Shea held his temper. "But perhaps I do."

"That's nonsense. You were on your own when I found you two years ago. You didn't seem to need him so badly then."

"Well, appearances can be deceiving. I missed him terribly. I can't tell you how much being separated from him bothers me. So let's understand something. I am happy he came to find us, and it would be a good idea if you stopped acting as if he shouldn't be here. It makes me think I shouldn't be here, either."

Panamon seemed to take his words to heart. On the following day, he went out of his way to speak with Flick, telling him how much help he expected he would be to them and how pleased he was to have him along. Flick was clearly doubtful at first, but after a while he began to respond to the other's efforts, and the ride north immediately became more pleasant for everyone.

During their travels, they had seen almost no one. By the time they reached the banks of the River Lethe and the Knife Edge Mountains came into view through a screen of mist and gray, the country had turned so barren that it seemed impossible anyone or anything could possibly find a way to subsist. The landscape was composed of rock and dirt and grasses that were so dried out and prickly, they cut like knives if you brushed up against them.

That was all you could see in any direction.

There was nothing out there. Anywhere.

Except for the Harrgs.

At least Panamon knew what they were and was prepared for them when they appeared. The travelers were camped on the evening of the fifth day, their horses tethered, their fire built, and the night black and silent around them. But moon and stars lit the blasted terrain surrounding them so they could see the squat shapes when they began to close in.

"What's that?" Shea asked, the first to catch sight of the creatures moving at the edges of the firelight like vague and indistinct shadows.

"Harrgs," Panamon answered casually. "Don't move."

"Don't move?" Flick asked in disbelief, getting a good look at what they were facing as the creatures edged close enough to be seen clearly. They not only sounded like pigs, snuffling and grunting, but they looked like pigs—pigs with tusks and huge, hairy bodies and mean little eyes. There were at least a dozen of them, moving back and forth like phantoms.

"What are those?" Shea whispered.

"Feral pigs, of a sort. Boars, really. They live here; this is their country. They eat those sharp-edged grasses, mostly. But they're omnivores, so we don't want to take chances. Quiet, now."

He was fumbling beneath his cloak in the pouch he always wore strapped about his waist, digging in it.

The Harrgs were getting close. Very close. Shea and Flick edged nearer the fire, scooting like startled crabs. "Panamon," Shea hissed.

A second later the thief leapt to his feet and flung what appeared to be a handful of pebbles at the Harrgs. The creatures backed off a few steps, hesitant yet undeterred. Then one or two of them inched forward, sniffing loudly. A moment later Shea and Flick could hear the sound of chewing.

But only a heartbeat after that the night silence was filled with the sounds of agonized squealing and snorting as one or more of the Harrgs went wild, leaping and charging about, sending the others into a frenzy that ended with all of them racing away into the darkness.

Panamon brushed off his hands. "Pepper root. The Harrgs can't stand it. I disguised the smell so they would eat it, knowing they will eat just about anything. They won't be back. Not that we were in any real danger from them."

"Those tusks suggest otherwise," Flick pointed out.

"Well, yes, perhaps they do," the thief conceded. "But Harrgs are not hunters; they're opportunists. They were more curious about us than anything."

He came back to where they were still crouched by the fire and sat down again. The night air had turned chilly with the deepening of the darkness, and he rubbed his hands briskly.

"Cold," he said.

"How do you happen to know so much about Harrgs?" Shea asked.

Panamon shrugged. "I know a few things."

"It was fortunate you knew about this one, wasn't it?"

Panamon did not miss the implication. He shrugged. "I knew about the Harrgs because I've run into them before." He cleared his throat and spit. "Now if you don't mind, I would like to leave any further discussion of the subject until morning. I am tired, and I need my rest."

Shea and Flick exchanged a quick glance as the thief picked up his blanket, found a suitable piece of hard ground, lay down with his back to them, and went to sleep.

He needs his rest, Flick mouthed to Shea and rolled his eyes.

THE MORNING DAWNED gray and sullen, the weather typical for the Northland and the country of the Skull Kingdom. No matter that the Warlock Lord and his Skull Bearers were dead and gone; the weather never changed. After eating breakfast and packing their gear—and at Panamon's urging—Shea reached inside his tunic and brought out the Elfstones to attempt to locate the Black Irix. While he hadn't said anything about it to his brother or Panamon, he had experimented with the Stones about a year ago after returning home, just because he wanted to know if he could still command the magic. He had gone deep into the woods before using them, then chosen a simple task—finding out what his father was doing back in Shady Vale.

He had gone through the process of forming in his mind a clear image of his father's face, and the magic of the Elfstones had warmed within his hand and then rushed swiftly through his body, filling him with their presence and an awareness of their power. Moments later the familiar blue light had materialized and begun to weave its way through the trees, back to his home and to where his father sat eating his lunch within the inn's kitchen. It illuminated the scene for several long moments, then vanished once more.

Shea had his answer. He could still summon the magic if he needed to. He could still wield the Elfstones' power. Satisfied, he had pocketed the Stones, taken them back to Shady Vale, hidden them away again, and not employed them since.

So this morning marked only his second attempt at using them since the search for the Sword of Shannara ended, but he had every reason to believe there would be no difficulty. He felt a certain amount of pressure from having Panamon standing right next to him, though not enough to rattle him. He pictured the Irix as he remembered it, called up the magic, then watched as it exploded from the Stones and rocketed away across the flats in a brilliant streak of blue light. It found the Knife Edge first and then a huge, pitted stone fortress that was walled about and defended by armed guards. Then it slipped inside and passed down a series of corridors, through several doors, and ended inside a sleeping chamber.

Once there, it swept the floor to where a broad woven rug decorated the center of the room, burrowed through the rug to a stone slab and beneath the slab to an iron vault embedded in the mountain bedrock, and finally inside the vault.

There, amid collections of gemstones and small chests of gold, silver, and ivory, lay the Black Irix. He saw the image clearly—as did Flick and Panamon—and then it vanished, and the light from the Elfstones with it.

Shea closed his fist about the Stones and looked at Panamon for confirmation. "Now we know for certain," the thief said. "All we need to do is complete our journey."

This was too much for Flick. "That's all, is it? Just ride a little farther, find a way to get inside an impregnable fortress, avoid being seen by any of perhaps a hundred guards, slip down to what likely is Kestra Chule's own bedchamber, open that vault embedded in the floor, and help ourselves to the Irix? Really? That's all?"

"Yes, it doesn't look quite as easy as you make it sound," Shea agreed.

Panamon was already loading his gear on his horse, only half listening to them. "That's because you're making assumptions you shouldn't. For example, we don't have to find a way into Kestra Chule's stronghold and we don't have to avoid being seen." He looked back over his shoulder. "We are invited guests."

Shea stared at him, speechless. "What are you talking about?" Flick demanded.

"Kestra Chule and I are longtime acquaintances. I've been here many times before, so I simply told him we were coming. Now mount up."

He refused to say anything more about it, adding only that after they reached their destination they should just play along and keep their mouths shut. "He doesn't know the real purpose of our visit, so it might be wise not to give it away."

They rode all that morning and through the midday, and by early afternoon they had reached the River Lethe and found a worn wooden bridge that spanned a narrows between high bluffs that dropped off into a canyon hundreds of feet deep. The bridge—an ancient structure formed of rotting planks, fraying ropes, and rusted-out iron supports—looked as if it was about to collapse. But Panamon ignored that, urging his horse onto the rickety wooden planking—the entire bridge swaying and creaking as he did so—and crossed without incident. Shea went next, his heart in his throat when one of the struts snapped explosively. Flick went last, his eyes closed the whole way, letting his horse decide if this was worth it or not.

"What's the point of life without risk; doesn't risk serve to make life sweeter?" the thief asked them afterward. It was a question neither cared to answer, even if speech had been readily available to them.

The way forward from there to the base of the mountains took another two hours, and that was because gullies and sharp drops had riven the rocky, barren terrain and needed to be carefully navigated. Progress was slow, and even after Kestra Chule's stronghold came into view, it took considerable time to reach it.

Time the brothers spent pondering the full extent of what they had let themselves in for.

Because the closer they got to the fortress, the more formidable it looked. It was a huge complex to begin with, embedded in the mountainside between two cliffs. Its walls were high and deep, the buildings disappearing far back into the shadow of the cliffs, with each tier set atop a series of rocky elevations that left the stronghold hundreds of feet high. The outer walls were manned, and the ramparts throughout bristled with mounted crossbows and catapults of all shapes and sizes. Massive towers buttressed the ends of those walls, and provided slits cut into the stone for firing on unfortunate attackers.

The whole of the fortress was blackened by ash and soot and pitted by age and weather, yet even where there were signs of erosion the huge stone blocks were so deep and so broad that there was little impact. The gates were ironbound and twenty feet high, their tops spiked and ragged. The guards on the wall wore heavy armor and carried huge pikes.

Even an entire army would have trouble getting into this citadel, Shea thought.

Then it occurred to him that getting out might turn out to be every bit as hard as getting in.

"You're sure about this?" Shea asked Panamon Creel impulsively, but the thief just smiled.

They rode out of the badlands and up to the huge gates, Panamon leading the way and showing no particular concern for what lay ahead. When they arrived at the walls, he called up to the watch to let them enter, giving his name. To the surprise of the Ohmsford brothers, the gates opened almost at once, allowing them to pass through into a courtyard where they were met by other guards. They dismounted, and their horses were taken from them and led away. A member of the household staff, clearly identifiable by his more ornate garb, came out to meet them and led them inside.

The interior of the stronghold wasn't much to look at, consisting for the most part of stone-block walls lacking decoration or softness; hard, bare surfaces were clearly the preferred decor. They passed down countless hallways, climbed dozens of steps, and entered and departed numerous chambers before finally reaching a dining room where they were met by other members of the household staff and taken to seats at a long wooden table. Platters of food were brought, and they were urged by their guide to eat all they wanted. All three were hungry enough not to argue the matter or ask after their host, and they set about consuming everything in sight. Ale was poured and musicians appeared from behind curtains, and all at once it felt like a festive celebration.

"Why are they so happy to see us?" Shea asked Panamon at one point, leaning close so that the attendants wouldn't hear.

The thief shrugged. "I told you. Chule considers me a friend. He's trying to make an impression."

Shea let the matter drop and went back to eating the first good meal they'd enjoyed since leaving the Vale. But just as he was finishing, he noticed that a number of guards from the gates had entered the room and were standing watch at all the doors. A sickening feeling swept through him.

He was about to alert Flick when a small, ferret-faced man

with a thick mop of black hair and a heavy mustache entered the room and called out to Panamon in a surprisingly deep voice.

"Well met, old friend!" he boomed. "Welcome, welcome!"

Panamon rose at once and moved out to greet him with arms open wide. Hugs and backslapping followed, and Shea thought it all just a little overdone given what Panamon had come here to do. But he supposed the thief felt it was necessary or he wouldn't be doing it.

When they finally ended their embrace, Kestra Chule turned to Shea and Flick. "And these are your young friends." He made it a statement of fact. Smiling broadly, his hands extended, he walked over to greet them. "Welcome to my home. So good of you to come."

He shook their hands and then looked past them. "Guards," he called out.

Before they realized what was happening, Shea and Flick had been seized and their wrists bound. Without a word to either of them, Panamon stepped forward, reached into Shea's tunic, and withdrew the pouch containing the Elfstones.

"Sorry about this, Shea," he said, hefting the pouch as he smiled at the Valeman. "Some things can't be helped."

He turned away and presented the Elfstones to Chule. The other man eagerly loosened the drawstrings and dumped the contents into his hand. "Oh, my! Look at this. The only ones of their kind, and now they belong to me!"

Shea felt a surge of fury on watching the man fondle and caress the Elfstones. But even now he could not bring himself to believe that this had been Panamon's sole plan. They had been friends for too long, had gone through so much together. He knew Panamon Creel and he trusted him. For Panamon to betray him like this was unthinkable.

"You are the lowest sort of vermin!" Flick was screaming at the thief. "You are worse than any snake!"

"Now, now," Panamon soothed. "Name-calling is pointless. Best just to accept things for what they are, Flick."

Shea tried to think. "You know you can't use them," he said to Chule. "No one who isn't an Elf can. You've stolen them for nothing."

"You don't understand, Shea," Panamon said. "Kestra doesn't have any interest in using the Elfstones. He simply wants to add them to his collection of rare artifacts. The Stones are more valuable and unique than the Irix; anyone who is a serious collector would want them for his own."

"At our expense," Flick spat at him.

"Unfortunately."

Chule was dumping the Elfstones back in their pouch as the thief turned to him. "Better make sure you lock those away somewhere safe," he cautioned. "Others will hear of this and try to find a way to relieve you of them."

"Oh, I don't think I have to worry about that," the other said, grinning. "This is a difficult place to break into. Nevertheless, I will lock them away with my other treasures."

"You'll keep our bargain, I trust?" Panamon asked.

"You mean the gold I promised you? Of course."

"I mean keeping these young men as your guests overnight and then releasing them in the morning."

Kestra Chule frowned. "I don't imagine they can do anything to hurt me. But still, we'll see. I'll have to think on it. Guards!" He beckoned. "Escort our young friends to their quarters. Lock them in and keep them there until morning. I'll decide what to do with them then." He glanced at Panamon. "That's the best I can do, I'm afraid."

Panamon smiled and shrugged. "Then why don't we sit and celebrate the successful completion of our arrangement with a glass of ale?"

Guards grabbed Shea and Flick and steered them across the floor and out of the room. "Release their bonds once you have them safely inside their quarters and ready to be locked up for the night!" Chule called after them as they were led away. "Good night, young friends! Sleep well!"

And with that the brothers were hustled from the room and down a succession of passageways and through countless doors deep into the bowels of the stronghold. For a time, Shea tried to keep track of their progress, but he soon grew so confused that he gave it up. The one thing he was certain about was that they were not going to find their way out easily.

Finally, they passed down a hallway with cell doors on either side, stopped at one midway down, and were ushered through the doorway, where two guards held each Valeman in turn while a third cut the bonds that secured his wrists. Then they were shoved down on their knees while the guards backed out and the door was secured.

The brothers stood together in silence as the footfalls receded and finally disappeared.

"I'M GETTING THE Elfstones back," Shea declared, pacing the narrow confines of their prison cell. "I don't know how, but I'm going to."

Flick sat glumly on the thin pallet rolled out on his wooden slat bed, his head in his hands. "We should never have come here in the first place."

Shea stopped and looked at him. "What? And miss out on these fine accommodations?"

Flick returned his gaze. He was not smiling. "I told you this would happen. I warned you. This was Panamon's plan all along. He was always after the Elfstones."

Their cell was roughly ten feet by ten feet, the walls windowless and the floor bare. The iron door through which they had entered provided the only exit. Except for a pair of rudimentary beds and a single wooden table with a candle on it, the room was empty of everything but themselves.

Shea stood close by the door, fruitlessly wishing it would open again. Then he moved over to sit by Flick. "Don't worry. Things will work out. Panamon's got something else in mind."

"Why were we so stupid? Why did we let ourselves be tricked

like this?" Flick lifted his head, his brow furrowed, his face stricken. "What were we thinking?"

Yet Flick had been the one to argue against going. And Shea had to admit that, as much as he needed to believe his friend had not betrayed him, their current situation looked pretty bad. He could not blame Flick for feeling as he did, but still he marveled at how his brother took an equal share of the blame on himself when all along it had been Shea forcing the issue.

A surge of love for his brother filled him. If he had led him into danger . . .

But no. He knew Panamon Creel. He would not leave them like this.

"Panamon has always been straightforward and honest with me," Shea replied firmly. "There's something else at work here. I know there is!"

"Based on what evidence? He was never reliable. You just thought he was. You think the best of everyone—even those who are looking to stick a knife in your back!"

Shea shrugged. "Because I prefer it that way. I'd rather think well of people than ill. Besides, giving up the Elfstones for a mere bag of gold doesn't make sense. Panamon knows that's nothing compared with what the Stones are really worth."

"Not if you can't make use of them. Not if you can't sell them without losing your head. Don't you think that when Eventine hears of this, he will bring the entire Elven nation down on Kestra Chule and his stronghold? It's safer for Panamon to take the gold and disappear." Flick paused. "It's also safer if he lets Chule get rid of us so we can't tell anyone what's happened."

Shea rose, moved over to the second bed, and lay down, hands behind his head. "It doesn't matter what you say. I can't make myself believe Panamon lied to us about the Irix, tricked us into coming, and then robbed us. It doesn't feel right."

Flick grunted. "Well, the fact that it's happened ought to go a long way toward convincing you."

"I don't know . . ."

His brother lay back as well. "Go to sleep. Maybe you can dream up a way out of this. Maybe you'll be able to concoct a plan to get the Elfstones back from Chule."

Shea looked over and smiled at him. "I'm glad you came with me, Flick," he said. "I'm sorry things turned out like they have, but I'm very glad you're here to help me get through them. I wouldn't want to be here alone."

Flick grunted and rolled over, facing away from the candle-light. "You know well enough I wouldn't let that happen."

Shea closed his eyes, and after a while he could hear Flick's breathing deepen. He remained awake for a short time, trying to work out what Panamon was up to. But in the end his weariness dulled his thinking, and he fell asleep.

THE SOUND OF the cell door lock releasing brought him awake again. He sat up quickly, blinking away the lingering vestiges of his sleep, his eyes adjusting to the light.

Panamon Creel stood in the doorway. Before Shea could say anything, the thief put a finger to his lips, signaling for silence. Then he moved over to Flick, fastened his hand over the Vale-man's mouth, and woke him. Flick struggled momentarily, but Panamon made hushing noises, speaking to him in low tones, warning him to be silent.

"Time to be going," he whispered. "Don't talk. Follow my lead. Do what I do."

Shea didn't argue, but a surge of happiness filled him. He motioned to Flick, and the two of them tracked Panamon out into the hallway where a pair of Chule's guards lay slumped on the floor.

"They were very tired," the thief said, cocking one eyebrow.

Shea grinned, then looked over at Flick, but his brother was still scowling suspiciously.

Panamon led them down the hallway and back up through the various levels of the complex—a slow and torturous journey in which Shea barely allowed himself to breathe. Every so often,

Panamon would stop, glimpse something he didn't like, and turn them back another way. But no one saw them.

Then, finally, they were outside again, standing in an open courtyard but still inside the fortress walls.

Panamon turned back to them and pulled them close.

"Our horses are in a stable just on the other side of that wall." He pointed. "We have to saddle and mount them and ride through the gates to be safe. We still have a couple of hours before dawn to distance ourselves from Chule. But we don't want to drag our heels doing it. Come on."

"Wait." Shea grabbed his arm. "What about the Elfstones? I'm not leaving without them!"

Panamon nodded, his face expressionless. "Of course you're not." He reached into his tunic, pulled out the pouch with the Elfstones, and handed them over. "That was never the plan."

Shea felt a rush of joy. So he was right. Panamon hadn't betrayed them after all. "What was the plan?"

"Later. When we are well away."

They slipped through a door in the wall that housed the stable, found their horses, saddled them, and rode down a narrow corridor along the outer wall to the main gates.

Guards stepped forward and stopped them, their faces dark with suspicion and their pikes held ready. "Where do you think you're going?" one asked.

"Back to where we came from," Panamon answered. "Chule told us we could leave in the morning. Morning is here. We want to get an early start on the day. We have a long way to ride, and the hardest part is getting out of the Northland."

The guards exchanged an uneasy glance. "No one told us about this."

"No? Then maybe no one thought it was something you needed to be told. Maybe they thought you could figure things out on your own. But if that's not so, why doesn't one of you go back inside and wake Kestra Chule to ask him? Or you could just detain us for another four hours until he wakes up on his own. I will ask him then how you two happened to be chosen for this duty."

The guards shifted uneasily, hefting their pikes in a threatening way and still blocking the gates as they looked back and forth between Panamon and the Ohmsfords and each other. There was a long few moments as they silently debated their options. Finally, one stepped aside and signaled up to the walls to winch open the gates.

Minutes later, Panamon was leading the Ohmsfords back through the ravines of the terrain that bordered the keep, moving slowly but steadily away from its imprisoning walls. They rode in silence, concentrating on finding a safe path through the treacherous landscape using what dim light the cloud-obscured quarter moon and scattered stars could provide. Shea kept looking back over his shoulder at Flick, who was bringing up the rear. Flick kept looking back at Kestra Chule's black fortress.

But there was no sign of activity on the walls and no sign of any pursuit. It seemed they had gotten away cleanly.

And with the Elfstones safely back in hand! Shea kept reaching up to feel their bulk inside his tunic pocket, fingering their familiar outline, reassuring himself that they were really there.

By sunrise, they had reached the banks of the River Lethe and were crossing the old wooden bridge to the northern fringes of the Streleheim and the promise of safety, and the Valeman could stand it no longer.

He rode up next to Panamon and caught his eye. "What just happened back there? What was that all about?"

Panamon looked over. Flick had ridden up to hear, as well. "A little sleight of hand," the thief answered with a shrug. "I knew Kestra Chule from his time in Varfleet, in days now gone, when he was a buyer and seller of stolen goods. We were friendly enough; I was a thief, he was a buyer. Eventually, he became a collector. He found that fortress we just left—perhaps once occupied by Trolls or even Skull Bearers, but then abandoned— and he moved in.

"A while back, while doing a bit of business with me, he mentioned that he was looking for someone to build him a vault to house some very valuable artifacts and precious metals from his collection. After a few drinks, he bragged about how he had recovered a Black Irix. He wouldn't tell me how he came by it at first, but then he mentioned that he'd had to move half a mountain to reach it.

"So I told him I'd heard a story about a Troll who had worn the Black Irix who'd died in the collapse of a mountain. He cocked an eyebrow at me in a way that told me we were talking about the same thing. So I mentioned the name of a vault builder I knew. Chule went to him, was shown the vault he wanted, was told how to set the locks to his own satisfaction, and the sale was made. Chule hauled the vault back to his fortress and installed it. He set the locks with his own set of numbers and twists of the dial, and put the Irix inside along with the rest of his treasure."

Panamon laughed. "He even bragged of it afterward. How clever he was! How foolproof his protections! But I knew something he didn't. Vault makers always put in a backup set of numbers and twists in their locks so that if something goes awry with the code entered by the owner, there is another way of getting inside. I went to the vault maker who had sold his product to Chule and convinced him to give me that information. He was willing enough once I handed over a substantial sum of money. He was never going to attempt anything against a man like Chule. What did he care what my intentions were?

"So now I had the means to steal the Irix. What I didn't have was a means of finding out where inside the fortress Chule had installed his vault and whether or not the Irix was inside it. Before going in, I had to know both. And I couldn't very well ask Chule."

"That's why you came to Shady Vale," Shea said. "You knew I could find out by using the Elfstones."

"Well, that was part of it," Panamon acknowledged. "The other part involved persuading you to go with me into the keep. Because I needed something to convince Chule my intentions were good. He'd always kept me at arm's length before, and I needed to get much closer than that. So I told him I would bring him the only Elfstones in existence. Of course, I demanded a huge fortune for this, all of which is now safely tucked away in my gear." He patted the blanket and bags strapped across the rear of his horse. "Right inside there.

"I gave you up to Chule so he would think well enough of me to engage in a little celebration afterward. That allowed me to slip a sleeping potion into his drink. After that, it was simply a matter of relieving him of the Elfstones, leaving him asleep on the couches to ostensibly retire to my bedchamber, but instead going to his, finding and opening the safe the Elfstones had revealed earlier, and taking out the Irix.

"Once that was accomplished, I came to find you and get you out of there. My initial plan was to leave things as they were until this morning so we could simply ride out together and leave him none the wiser until he decided to have a look inside his safe. But I didn't like what he had to say earlier about letting you go. I think maybe he intended to make sure you never told anyone he had the Stones. And since I had put you in harm's way, I thought it my obligation to take you out again."

"You should have told me what you were intending," Shea said. "That was a terrible thing you did."

Panamon gave one of his maddening shrugs. "But it was done for the right reason—to recover the Irix and return it to Keltset's people. Exactly what I told you I intended from the first." He sighed deeply. "I'm sorry, Shea. And Flick, too. But I couldn't tell you ahead of time; you might have inadvertently given the game away if you had known. Worse, you might have refused me right out of hand. It was a huge gamble, but I had to take it."

His familiar grin reappeared. "Life is a gamble, isn't it?"

"It's certainly a gamble where you're concerned," Flick snapped.

"He'll come after you, won't he?" Shea asked suddenly. "He'll know you stole the Irix and took back the Elfstones, and he'll hunt you down."

Panamon nodded. "He'll try. But I'm not so easy to catch."

"That won't stop him. You know it won't."

"Maybe not. But I might have mentioned something to the Trolls about his illicit acquisition. They didn't seem too happy about it. I think they will be watching for him to emerge from behind his walls into the open. When he does . . ."

They were passing through the area where they had encountered the Harrgs two nights earlier, and the sun was just cresting the horizon, sending its muted light through the cloud banks and mist, when Panamon reined in his horse.

"I leave you here to continue on to the Vale. Ride straight through the rest of today and for as much of tonight as you can manage. Keep close watch. I don't think they will catch up to you, but you want to be careful anyway."

"Where will you go?" Flick asked. He almost sounded sorry about it.

The thief pointed west. "I have a delivery to make, and the sooner it's done, the better. Temptation is a terrible thing, and I would hate to give in to it here."

"If you do, we will come looking for you," Shea declared. "And we will find you, too."

Panamon Creel laughed. "I don't for a moment doubt it. Goodbye, Shea. Goodbye, Flick. I hope you will find a way to forgive me for what I did. I hope that what I am about to do will put paid to my debt to you both and persuade you my intentions were always the best."

Off he rode, galloping swiftly away. They watched him until he was only a speck on the distant horizon.

As he disappeared from view, Shea heaved a sigh. He had

never really believed that Panamon had decided to abandon them. He had never been convinced—even though the evidence suggested otherwise and Flick kept insisting he was wrong—that his friend intended to leave them in the hands of Kestra Chule. That wasn't the Panamon Creel he knew. In spite of his other faults, it wasn't the sort of man he was.

Looking back on it now, he had never been so happy to be proven right.

FLICK, ON THE other hand, was thinking of Audrana Coos, thinking of the very last words she had spoken to him after noticing the turbulence in the waters of the scrye bowl and advising him of his brother's fate: *He will go on a quest, and you cannot stop him from doing so. Nor should you.*

Indeed. Shea had needed to go. He needed to help Panamon retrieve the Black Irix, and he needed to know it would be returned to Keltset's people. Flick had doubted the woodswoman and he had doubted Panamon Creel, and he should have managed to muster the faith that had sustained his brother. What was it his brother had said when they were locked in that cell? That it was better to think well of people than ill.

Next time they encountered Panamon, he promised himself, he would do the same.

It would be almost three years before that happened, and when it did Flick would find himself struggling to keep this promise.

But that's a story for another time.

Introduction to
"Last Ride"

THIS IS A new story set in the Shannara world—my first in quite a while. After forty years of writing the books in the series, there are plenty of choices for expansion. As I have said, I pay close attention to which characters readers want to hear more about. I don't begin to fulfill all their wishes, given time constraints and my overall plan for the series, which consists of always moving forward. (Although I violated that by writing about the prehistory some years back with the Genesis of Shannara set.) Anyway, when the stars align on a new story, it is always exciting—even if it involves throwing myself off a cliff in writing another short story.

So what we have here is a story about the Wing Rider Elves and a character named Tiger Ty, who first appeared in the Heritage of Shannara series way back in the early 1990s. I've wanted to come back to the Wing Riders for a long time, but never really found the story I was looking for. Then I began to wonder what had happened to Tiger Ty after he had taken Wren Ohmsford to the volcanic island of Morrowindl, where she had found the missing Elven nation and with the Wing Rider's help had returned it to the Four Lands. What did happen to Wing Riders as they grew older? What happened if their birds died before them, if they died first, if they grew too infirm to ride any longer? I imagined it might mirror our own experience with growing old and the limitations it put on us. How well do we handle being told we are no longer able to work the jobs we have worked for most of our lives? What do we do when we are sidelined by age and infirmity? It is a real question for all of us—myself in particular as I stumble into my seventies with the larger part of my writing life behind me.

In this story, I offer a few possible answers and a tale that once again involves Tiger Ty—this time with his family closely involved in providing a resolution to his reluctance to admit what we all come to face: Old age will find us sooner or later.

LAST RIDE

TIGER TY WAS old. Sitting in his rocker on the porch of his cottage, staring out across the choppy gray surface of the Blue Divide, he was more acutely aware of it than ever. It preyed on him—a weight of certainty that his life was numbered no longer in years but in months. If he was lucky. He was not normally one to brood, and did not spend his days in regret or despondency over the inevitable ending of his life. He was far too practical and tough-minded for that.

But today was different. Today, he was feeling less accepting and more regretful than he had felt in some time.

On the western horizon, dark clouds were gathering. A storm was coming on. Such weather caused his joints to ache and his bones to grumble, so perhaps that was what was affecting his mood. Dark and gloomy skies were never as welcoming as blue and sunny ones.

Yet he was not one to manufacture excuses, and he was not about to change now. He rose from his chair to look about for Grey, but the boy was nowhere to be seen. Off somewhere in the company of that girl with whom he was so besotted, perhaps. Never saw a lad so in love, he mused. Sometimes he wondered why he had never felt such an attachment to Jessa when she was alive, but he hadn't. The nature of his calling, he supposed. A Wing Rider couldn't afford the luxury of attachments that might cloud his or her judgment. He had to add *her* to the assessment now, since women had become active members of the Wing Hove in the last few years, intent on doing more than bearing and raising men's children. Not that this was a bad thing, of course. Women were good with the Rocs—sometimes better at bonding and controlling the great birds than the men. It was a step in the right direction. But it was still a change, and sometimes he had to remind himself of it when his thinking strayed to the old days.

Grey troubled him, he admitted, the gloom returning. Had for a while now. His grandson was a rebel. Grey had his grandfather's and his father's stubbornness clear through, but had chosen another path entirely. Tiger Ty shook his head. He still hadn't come to terms with it. His son had, but Tahere had a milder nature. He was settled comfortably within himself and thought Grey should be the same. If Grey didn't want to be a Wing Rider, he shouldn't have to be. It didn't matter what he was. Or who his famous grandfather might be.

Maybe so, Tiger Ty mused, but it still hurt.

He gave himself space for a few moments to ruminate on his legacy. It was almost twenty-five years ago now that he had carried Wren Ohmsford from the Four Lands to the island of Morrowindl—and then brought her back again, along with the missing Land Elves whom she had rescued, restoring them to the Westland where once they had been presumed extinct. His part in making this possible was almost universally celebrated—especially since Wren Ohmsford had become a great queen.

Still fighting his unexpected despondency, he left the porch and began to walk toward the business section of the Wing Hove. Well, began to *hobble* might be more accurate; the hitch in his movements was the result of a leg injury he had suffered five years back that had taken him off the Rocs for good. If you can't steer, you can't ride. And you can't steer if you don't have the strength in your legs to make the bird respond. The injury put a decisive end to his career as a Wing Rider, and there was no way to get it back. He was forbidden from riding Rocs—and in particular, his beloved Spirit—which left him with nothing much that mattered.

Friends and neighbors greeted him as he made his way into the village, according him a certain deference because of his fame—a recognition he appreciated but thought old news. Always short but now stout as well, his head grizzled and white, his hair cut short and turned to a mix of bristle and bald— though his beard was still as bushy as ever—he looked to be something of a forbidding figure and he knew it. He didn't desire this look, but he didn't try to hide it, either.

Tiger Ty was who he was, and it was way too late to change it.

A tall, athletic figure came rushing up the path to meet him, and he slowed accordingly. It was Pharis, the Hove's headman and the ostensible leader of its council, his face flushed and his expression etched sharply with concern. "Ho, Tiger. A moment, if you please."

Tiger Ty came to a stop as the other reached him. "You look frazzled," he said, furrowing his brow. "Has something happened?"

The other Elf, flushed and out of breath, nodded quickly. "Spirit just flew in. Without Tahere. There's no sign of him, Ty. Nothing to indicate what might have happened."

Tiger Ty nodded, holding his fears in check. Once he had been grounded, he had passed Spirit to his son, as was frequently done between fathers and sons. The passing had come at Tahere's urging, since his own Roc, Feltsen, had developed an unfortunate stiffening of the wing joints. A new Roc was required, and Spirit was the logical choice. Grey had thought it a dubious pairing. But still. "A search, then?"

"One is already under way. Fromme is leading the party, riding Spirit. He thinks the bird might lead them to wherever he and your boy parted ways. But that Roc's been a handful ever since you quit riding her, so I'm not sure it will help. But I thought you should know."

Pharis turned away quickly and was gone; no point lingering after giving bad news, Tiger Ty thought. Well, nothing was sure yet. Tahere was skilled and capable. He would find a way to bring the search party to him. No point in worrying.

But he couldn't help himself. He would worry whether he wished to or not. This was his son.

He set out to find his grandson and share the news.

GREY WAS SITTING on the edge of a headland south of the Hove, facing out toward the wide expanse of the ocean, when he saw his grandfather approaching. It was hard for Gramps to walk these days—hard for him to move around much at all—but he was moving at what, for him, was an accelerated pace, and it brought his grandson to his feet at once.

"Got some bad news," Tiger Ty announced, the way he always did. Whenever he wanted to talk to Grey, he always began by opening with *good news* or *bad news*. It was kind of annoying, but Grey understood it was just his grandfather's way. So he nodded without thinking too much about what sort of bad news Gramps was bearing, or even if it really was bad news at all.

He was a tall, athletic boy, which he knew made it all the harder for his grandfather to accept his disinterest in being a Wing Rider. He was expected to follow in the family tradition, and when it became apparent he had no intention of doing so, a rift had developed between them. He understood the reasons. Both Gramps and his father had given their entire lives to becoming and then serving as Wing Riders. It was the highest achievement a member of the Wing Hove could attain, and no one—least of all those two—could fathom why someone so obviously born to it and so well situated to achieve it would choose any other way.

But sometimes your heart wouldn't embrace what others believed was right, and when that happened you had to make a choice. Certainly, his infatuation with Alethea had influenced that choice, but not as much as Gramps and his father believed.

No, what had decided him was something else entirely.

"Your father is missing," Tiger Ty now said, coming up to him and stopping a few feet away, breathing hard. "I just learned. Spirit came back without him, and they've sent a search party."

Without asking me to go with them, Grey thought, stung.

"I told him not to trust that Roc," Grey muttered. It was natural that the Roc should pass from father to son, but Spirit was an unusual bird. He was wedded to Tiger Ty. Hard and fast.

"No, Spirit's right enough. Tahere just needed to spend more time with him, keep after him until he settled down and accepted his place. It was already beginning to happen."

His grandfather was wrong, but there was nothing to be gained by pointing it out. Spirit had become contrary and unpredictable in the way of a willful child, and had refused to come around despite constant efforts by both his father and himself.

For all that he didn't care to embrace the life of a Wing Rider, Grey *was* interested in the care and training of the Rocs. Ever since childhood, he had been fascinated by the great birds and wanted to know more about their behavior. By the time he was ten, he was a regular at the pens, watching and listening to the older trainers as they worked with the birds and talked about the particulars of their work. After a time, they began noticing he was always around, so a few began showing him a little of what was necessary to turn the Rocs from wild creatures into obedient companions. He went from feeding and grooming and cleaning up to working directly with a couple of the younger mounts, learning how they were taught to respond to their rider's movements—everything from leg and hand pressure to tugging on and slapping with the bridle reins. He discovered how the birds could be persuaded to react in predictable ways to small touches and soft words. He saw the benefits of treats—distributed and withheld, as rewards or punishments.

At fifteen, he was training Rocs on his own, an accomplished flier and handler both, becoming a welcome and respected member of the support staff. His talents were extraordinary, and his career path seemed determined.

Although not to his grandfather, who would regularly re-mark, "Your skills as a trainer are useful, Grey. It is a good and necessary thing to be able to connect with your Roc on every level—to understand how it thinks and know how it will react. But remember your calling. You are meant to be a Wing Rider, and it is to this end that you must direct the use of your talents. Our family are Wing Riders, and you will be one, too."

Only he wouldn't, he had decided. Because it was not his call-ing. Because even though he was not yet fully grown, he did not think this was meant to be his life's work.

"Spirit is a trained Roc," his grandfather continued, with a stubborn insistence. Gramps, he had long since discovered, heard only what he wanted to hear and believed only what he wanted to believe. "He bonded with your father just as he bonded with me. He will lead the searchers to Tahere."

Grey frowned. "Even in training, Spirit showed a strong streak of independence where Father was concerned."

Too often, he had ignored what Tahere had commanded. Grey had watched their interactions and knew it to be so. His father had accepted Spirit as his own because Gramps had wanted it, but that hadn't changed how the bird responded. "I think something more should be done," Grey now added.

Tiger Ty gave him a look. "And what more would you do? What more can anyone do? Tahere's Roc is his lifeline to the Hove. This responsibility is instilled in every single Roc from day one. It was no different with Spirit. He's reliable and well trained. He will respond."

"He never demonstrated sufficient responsibility to me."

"But apparently he did to other, more seasoned, trainers. Do we ignore their assessment in favor of your own?" Tiger Ty made a dismissive gesture. "Besides, what difference does it make now? He's all we have to work with. What matters is that we find Tahere, and Spirit's our best chance for doing so."

Gramps was clearly trying to convince himself. Grey didn't say so, but he knew his grandfather was thinking about what would happen if they lost Tahere. He would have to live with the possibility that it was *his* fault for forcing Spirit on his son, trying to relive his own experiences as a rider by doing so. Grey understood, but he thought Gramps was being overly hopeful.

Nevertheless, he nodded in agreement. "You're right. They'll find him. Father is experienced enough to help them, and Spirit will respond to his training."

His grandfather nodded silently and turned away.

BUT THE SEARCH party didn't find Tahere. They returned that night having found nothing, disgruntled and discouraged by their failure. And Spirit had indeed proved to be unreliable. He had flown them first one way and then another, and no amount of urging or cajoling from Fromme had been enough to persuade him to settle on a course that would lead to his missing rider. A new search would begin in the morning, it was decided—this time without Spirit, so that a fresh approach might yield something more concrete.

No one said what everyone was thinking: that perhaps there was no possibility of finding Tahere alive. That perhaps he had suffered a catastrophic fall or injury in the course of his work and he was lost to them for good. That would explain why Spirit could not lead them to him. That would explain why he could not be found.

For the first time, Grey was worried. His father's death seemed an impossibility. They were not living in a time of war, so the chance that he had been brought down by an enemy was remote. Besides, his father was an experienced Wing Rider and a cautious scout. That he had fallen from Spirit seemed unlikely. That he had been knocked off was even more difficult to accept.

No, Tahere was alive, and he was in need of help. And Spirit was still their best chance for finding him. He just needed the right rider.

And the right rider, of course, was Tiger Ty. Rocs bonded tightly to their riders. However, it was true that when their riders were lost to age or death, most Rocs eventually created a new bond with another rider. But Spirit was not most Rocs. Gramps was the rider Spirit had bonded with all those years ago—and Spirit, it seemed, bonded for life. For all that he was well trained and skillful and had proven himself over and over, he was also high-strung and temperamental. He was very much a one-man bird. Tiger Ty was his rider, and his bond with Tahere had always been suspect. At least to Grey, if not to his grandfather. Had it been anyone else, the trainers would have refused his grandfather's request to have his Roc bequeathed to his son. But he was Tiger Ty, a legend and a hero among the Wing Hove, and who was going to say no to him?

Grey had thought to speak up at the time, but he was younger then, and still learning. What he knew was more from instinct than training, and adults did not often listen to the advice of boys. So he had kept his mouth shut, telling himself it would work out, that his father would find a way to make the bond strong enough.

He thought about that at length that night while cuddled with Alethea. They were not yet partnered, but for them it was only a formality to be settled by this time next year, and sleeping together seemed natural enough when you were young and so much in love.

Alethea was small and willowy, only seventeen but mature for her age, and absolutely the most beautiful girl Grey had ever met. He had known what real love felt like the moment he had first seen her. He had known she was meant to be with him even before they were formally introduced. Within days, it was clear she felt the same about him. Now they were together constantly, planning for their future, imagining life once they had

taken their vows, talking about a home and family and everything they would do for the rest of their lives.

Presently they were rolled up together in the blankets they
had carried down to the oceanside, stealing away from their
families as they so often did to be alone. In other circumstances,
this time would be theirs, their dreams and their love for each
other all that mattered, but not tonight. Grey was thinking instead about his father, and Alethea was watching him, knowing
his thoughts as well as she knew her own.

"Maybe you need to go with them," she said after a long silence. "It might make you feel better."

He nodded into her shoulder. "I was thinking that, too."

"It's better to do something than nothing."

"But they didn't invite me to go with them yesterday."

"Then you have to ask to be included. They won't say no."

"I am not one of them, Alethea. I am not a Wing Rider."

"It doesn't matter." She pressed herself against him, the heat
of her body warm and welcoming. "You must ask them anyway.
You must tell them, if necessary. No one will refuse you."

"I know they have to use Spirit to locate Father, but they
need to find a way to make him respond to their commands.
Another rider might have better luck."

She stroked his long hair. "Perhaps you? No one understands
Rocs better than you do, Grey."

He shook his head. "It's more than just understanding that is
needed. It's in the bonding. Without that, everything else is useless. Spirit was always Gramps's mount and never my father's.
The bond is still there, and pretending it isn't is part of the problem. Spirit just doesn't feel the same toward Father as he did
toward Gramps. And I don't think Fromme or any other Wing
Rider has the ability to make him do what's needed. I've been
thinking about it, and I don't see how that can be changed."

"But you think it has to." She made it a statement of fact.

"I do."

They were quiet for a time, and then she said, "Too bad your grandfather can't fly anymore. He could search with the others. He would have the necessary bond with Spirit."

He would, Grey knew. But his grandfather had steadfastly refused even to visit with his bird since his grounding. Stubborn to the extreme, his grandfather. Tiger Ty, the most famous Wing Rider of his generation, could bring Spirit to heel quickly enough. If he could just find a way to ride the big Roc, he might consider changing his mind about even seeing him . . .

"You are so smart," he whispered.

He wrapped his arms around Alethea and hugged her tightly against him, and for a brief time there was nothing to think about but how much they loved each other.

Afterward they slept, and when they woke, Grey rose and dressed at once. It was still dark out, the dawn not yet arrived, and the air was crisp and damp with the ocean's mist.

"He can't fly, Grey," Alethea said from within the warmth of the blankets. "It would kill him."

"Maybe not" was the boy's answer, and then he was gone.

TIGER TY WAS sleeping when the rustle of the heavy canvasbound door brought him awake. "Gramps?" a voice whispered.

Grey. Tiger Ty sat up, vaguely irritated. "It's the middle of the night!"

"No, it's less than an hour before dawn." His grandson sat down on the bed next to him. "I have an idea of how we might go about finding Father."

Not giving his grandfather a chance to respond, the boy launched into an explanation. At first, the old man was dismissive, but the more Grey explained his reasoning, the more Tiger Ty began to see the sense of it. He even began to get excited. It gave him a chance for fresh purpose in his life, a chance to escape the feeling of uselessness that had plagued him. Because time was fleeting and his best years were behind him. The leg injury had taken him off the Rocs, but he suffered as well from aching in the joints, a shortness of breath, and a tendency to drift in his thinking. Besides, anything was better than sitting around waiting to find out what had happened to Tahere, and what Grey was proposing would provide a cure for that.

"We have to do this right away," his grandson finished. "Before sunrise. We have to do it before someone comes to stop us. Are you with me?"

Tiger Ty rose. "All the way. Let me dress and we'll head down to the pens and get started."

Within minutes they were making their way through the sleeping village to the place where the Rocs were housed, the old man moving as fast as his bad leg would allow him, his heart racing with excitement and expectation, his face flushed with thoughts of what he would be doing. Flying again—riding Spirit after so long. Going back into the sky, as a Wing Rider, one final time. He might never do so again, but doing it even this once would help to heal the hurt he had been feeling for so long. For a Wing Rider, to be grounded was a death sentence, and of late he had felt more and more as if that sentence was being realized.

Now he could change that. He could fly Spirit and find Tahere. Fly without worry of falling or losing control, because Grey would be flying with him. Grandfather and grandson, off on a mission together. Perhaps such an outing could even serve to persuade Grey that becoming a Wing Rider was his real calling.

Tiger Ty was smiling.

When they reached the pens, they found the night watchman, Pannit Whey, standing at the gates. He peered into the darkness and startled. "Tiger Ty? Gracious Protector, what are you doing down here? Come to visit your old friend?"

Tiger Ty knew he meant himself, but in truth he had come for Spirit. "Come for one last flight into the wild blue," he announced. He found he was breathing hard, winded beyond what he expected. "Is he rested sufficiently since yesterday's hunt?"

Big and burly, a longtime bachelor with his entire life as a

Roc minder spread out behind him, Whey understood and gave a quick nod. "You know him. Never was a Roc so tough-minded and strong-bodied as that one. He's still the same. But you're grounded, old dog. You can't just jump back up on Spirit because you take a notion to do so."

"He's not going alone," Grey interjected quickly. "I'm going with him."

"Two of you? Well, Spirit is capable enough, but I . . ."

"Pannit." Tiger Ty spoke softly as he stepped close. "I'm calling in a favor. My son is out there and I have to try to find him. Grey will do all the guiding, all the leg and hand work; he'll handle all the supervision. I'll just be a passenger, but it matters that I'm there because Spirit knows me. Grey thinks the bird might respond to me better than to others, and take us to Tahere at last. I think he's right. I have to do this; I can't just sit at home and let others take responsibility. Please. Give me a chance."

Pannit thought a moment and then grinned. "Well, it will be a first—a grounded Wing Rider and his young pup—but there's nowhere it's written down as forbidden. Might be after today, but it isn't now. Hurry up, then. I'll see Spirit saddled and bridled and on the springboard within five minutes."

Tiger Ty clapped him on the shoulder. "I won't forget this."

His friend laughed. "I'll make sure of it!"

WITHIN THE TIME allotted, they were walking up the launching pad of the springboard, where Spirit was tethered, waiting impatiently. The Roc saw Tiger Ty the moment he appeared out of the shadows and immediately sounded his shrill call, straining at the ropes that restrained him.

"There's a welcome for you!" Whey shouted. "He still knows it's you, Double T!"

Tiger Ty was all smiles and laughter as he walked up to the huge bird, but the tears were streaming down his cheeks. "Hey, old fellow, it's me! But you know that already, don't you? Always have. Shades, I've missed you!"

He reached out and the great Roc lowered his head in response, allowing him an embrace. Grey stood to one side, watching their reunion. He was touched by the obvious pleasure each was experiencing at being together again. He knew his grandfather had not been to see his Roc since the grounding, always saying it would be too hard on Spirit if he did, but all the time knowing that it would be too hard on him. So he had kept his distance, and it was killing him as much as his advancing age. But Gramps was stubborn, and once his mind was made up it was hard to alter. Grey had known this when he came to offer his plan for finding Tahere, knowing that it gave his grandfather a chance to change his mind about seeing his Roc once more without seeming to do so.

Knowing, too, that his grandfather's age was catching up to him.

He glanced eastward. First light was only minutes away.

"We have to go, Gramps."

Tiger Ty released his grip on Spirit, gave him a final pat on his beak, then readied himself to mount. With Grey and Pannit helping, he scrambled aboard, seating himself in the deconstructed saddle forward of those great wings, which were already spread wide in preparation for their flight. When he was seated, Grey climbed up behind him and fitted himself so that his legs and hands could be used to guide the Roc, then secured both his grandfather and himself into place with the necessary safety straps. Now Spirit could dive or roll, or bank right or left, without throwing them off.

"Ready on the pad?" Pannit Whey shouted, and Grey's arm rose in response.

"Ready!"

A pause as Pannit waved back. "Safe flight!"

The tethers were released, and an instant later the springboard catapulted the Roc and its riders skyward—an assist to helping them gain the necessary lift. Wings already spread wide with anticipation, Spirit caught the wind and began to soar. With Grey using his knees to provide directional pressure and his grandfather leaning forward to reassure the big Roc of his presence, they rose quickly into the morning sky.

Safe flight, Grey echoed in the silence of his thoughts.

The rush of the wind as they accelerated caught Grey in the face like a blow, causing him to squint against its force. Seated ahead of him, Tiger Ty roared, arms thrust skyward in glee. *He's waited a long time for this,* Grey thought. His own arms tightened instinctively about his grandfather's frail body, but there was no real danger. The air was where Gramps had lived almost all his life. He knew its ways. Grey understood this and felt his grandfather's exhilaration become his own. High enough up to almost touch the clouds, sweeping over the country below as no one but a Wing Rider could, he wondered for those few moments if perhaps he should take another look at his decision not to make flying his life.

In a matter of seconds, they were a thousand feet above the coast of the Wing Hove, skirting along the Blue Divide and headed out toward the islands that chained their way northwest: tiny bits of land that spiraled in odd designs across the surface of the water. There were dozens of them, big and small, high and low, some so flat they were underwater half the time, some so high their mountains brushed the low-slung clouds.

Their ride was smooth. Grey expended no effort after their initial ascent and did not bother trying to direct Spirit. Gramps and he had agreed that it was best to trust to the Roc's instincts and tracking skills and let him find his own way. Even so, his grandfather could not resist providing shouts of encouragement—discernible to the Roc even though mostly lost to Grey in the rush of the wind—speaking of Tahere and of loss and responsibility.

Find Tahere, big fellow! Go to where you left him!
Remember your training and your bond!
Remember you are one with your rider!

Each new exhortation left Grey smiling. Each fresh burst of energy seemed to give his grandfather new life.

And each time the Roc screamed in response as the words were shouted, appearing to hear and understand as it quickly set its course.

Grey watched his grandfather turn to look at him, grinning broadly. A nod, and the old man mouthed silent words that made his grandson smile.

Do you see that? He knows!

Grey grinned and nodded back. His grandfather was so excited. Grey's idea of getting him back into the sky one more time was working. Now all they had to do was find his father.

THEY FLEW ON for more than five hours without deviation or hesitancy. Spirit never once attempted a landing or a reversal of course. He never seemed to need guidance or to be instilled with purpose beyond what he already possessed. Even so, Tiger Ty kept urging him on, cajoling and reminding, speaking of Tahere and Wing Riders and Rocs and bonding, eyes fixed directly ahead with a determination that told Grey there would be no turning back from this effort no matter the obstacles or their consequences. The way was bright and beautiful, and there was nothing to hinder their efforts. How a Roc could track a rider over open water after as much as a week had passed, with winds that would have blown away tracks and all chance of scent on land, was a true wonder. He did not begin to understand how the great birds could find lost riders with so little physical help. But there was something in their makeup—in their instincts or psyche or in their bonding—that tethered them indisputably to their riders.

So when midday arrived and it was necessary to land long

enough for all three to eat and drink, Tiger Ty was still ebullient, confident their efforts would succeed.

"Boy must have flown a long way when they got separated," he ventured, "but Spirit knows where to find him. Notice he didn't pause once for a sweep search, but just kept pressing ahead?"

Grey nodded, but by now had become increasingly worried that the bird's behavior was something other than what his grandfather believed. What if Spirit wasn't actually searching at all? What if he was just out for a ride with his old friend and intended nothing more than for the two of them to enjoy the day? But Grey kept his concerns to himself. The sinking feelings such thoughts generated were more than he could tolerate. Best to tamp them down and keep them to himself.

They flew on through the afternoon, again with no stops or deviations, and by nightfall found themselves landing on the mountainous island of Corson, about halfway up the chain, still well offshore from the northern end of the Rock Spur Mountains. It was a landing initiated not by Spirit, but by Grey determining that they had completed as much searching for one day as was reasonable and that both riders and the Roc required rest.

As he sat with Gramps in the growing darkness, the pair eating their dinner and drinking a ration of ale, Grey found himself staring off into the distance to where Spirit was perched on an outcropping atop a cliff face, his silhouette caught in the pale light of the setting sun. His great leathery wings were spread wide to capture the last of the sun's heat until at last he folded them against his feathered body. Grey thought the Rocs were wondrous creatures. They were constructed so perfectly to serve their Wing Hove riders. There was not an inch of wasted space on their sleek, solid, muscular bodies. And Spirit's strength in particular was astonishing; his endurance was legendary. Once, his grandfather had told him, they had flown for two straight days before resting. Another time, he had carried as many as four riders for more than a hundred miles.

His grandfather rose as he saw his mount preparing to sleep and walked to the great bird. Whispering, he placed his leathery hands against Spirit's neck and body, slowly stroking the great bird. Spirit dropped his head so he could be stroked there as well. It was telling, this act. Spirit still belonged to Gramps— even now, in spite of Tahere. Even though forced to wait all this time for another ride with the man to whom he had first bonded. It was clear that persuading Gramps to undertake this search had made him feel younger than he had for years. It had given him renewed purpose and a chance for that one last ride. It had provided him with an excitement and purpose he had been missing. This search to find his father, however fruitless it seemed now, would have been worth it just for what it had done for Gramps.

And they would find Tahere, Grey told himself once again. They would find him safe, and they would bring him home again.

THEY SLEPT WELL that night and were aloft once more just after sunrise, continuing to make their way along the chain of islands. Spirit was still choosing his way, and his riders still giving permission. They flew on this second day in very much the same fashion as on the first.

But then, sometime just after midday, Spirit decided to land.

The island he chose was a smaller member of the chain, its name not one Grey remembered at first (Del Roke, he recalled later)—a heavily forested, hilly bit of earth and rock no more than a half a mile wide and twice as long. There were no beaches and no indications of landing spaces amid the densely packed trees, but the great Roc never hesitated in its descent, taking them straight down into a clearing that was not visible until they were almost right on top of it.

Upon dismounting, Grey was startled to hear Spirit give a wild, piercing shriek that reverberated off the trees and rocks and hung in the midday air.

"He's calling for his rider," Tiger Ty announced at once. "I know that call. This is where they parted."

They began a search of the clearing, scanning the earth for any indication of what might have become of Tahere, and within a matter of minutes were rewarded with several discoveries. Grey made the first and called his grandfather over.

Kneeling, he pointed at the ground in front of him. "Tracks. Multiple boot prints and signs of a struggle. See?"

His grandfather nodded. "Six or eight of them. Smaller prints gathered around a set of larger ones. The larger ones are Tahere's. Someone took him here. He tried to get away and failed."

Grey was confused. "But why didn't Spirit stop them? Rocs are trained to defend their riders. These tracks say Tahere's captors weren't big men. Spirit should have been able to fight them off."

"Don't know." Tiger Ty rose and began searching again. "No tracks from the bird. Where was he when all this was happening?"

They renewed their search and soon found the answer to the old man's questions. "See this?" he announced from the far side of the clearing. Grey walked over for a look. "Spirit was waiting here when Tahere was taken. There's no sign of him moving about the clearing. He just took off." He paused. "And there's only one reason for that: Tahere sent him away."

"Why would Father do that?"

His grandfather glanced over at Spirit. "Because he was afraid for him. Enough so that he sent him away before he could be harmed. Or taken. He gave himself up in order to save his bird. That's your father for you."

"But would Spirit actually abandon him?" Grey was doubtful. "I thought they were trained not to do that."

Tiger Ty nodded. "Normally they are. But I taught Spirit myself, and one of the first things a Roc learns is obedience. Even if it meant leaving me, Spirit would do what he was told. If I ever sensed he was in real danger, I did not want harm coming to him on my account, so I taught him to fly off if ordered to. Tahere knew this. He felt as I did about Spirit. He must have given Spirit that signal in order to save his life."

Grey looked over at the Roc, taking in his size and fierce eyes. "What could have threatened him?" he murmured.

"Well," his grandfather said as he got back to his feet, "that's what we need to find out."

Just as they were leaving, Grey caught sight of something else, a strange design in the loose earth to one side of the clearing— a sort of side-to-side sweeping. "What's this?" he asked, calling Gramps back.

Tiger Ty peered down. "Looks like something was dragged away, doesn't it?"

The marks did not look like that to Grey. Instead, they seemed to suggest the crawling motion of a very big animal—an animal too big to be his father.

"Come on," his grandfather called, moving away. "We're wasting time."

THINKING BACK ON it later, after they returned to Spirit and climbed back aboard, Grey realized something. When Gramps had looked at the marks on the ground, he *had* recognized them. A change of expression had given him away—a momentary flash of fear in his eyes. Grey had not misread those tracks. He almost said something, but then thought better of it. It was not his place to ask. Gramps had his reasons for keeping what he knew to himself. Better to let the old man tell him when he was ready. Better to just concentrate on finding his father and bringing him home.

The supposition that both men were now operating under was that whoever was responsible for this had departed the island with Tahere as a captive. Grey would not let himself consider the alternative—that his father was dead, killed instead of captured. No, his father was alive, and Spirit would find him.

The big Roc certainly seemed to think so. He was aloft almost before they were settled in place, lifting off swiftly and winging northwest once more. He was still following the chain of islands, sensing in that way Rocs did where their rider had gone. There was nothing to tell the two men which way to go, no indication of any kind to determine the right direction, but Spirit seemed to know, and he was hot in pursuit.

They flew through the remainder of the afternoon, and when they tried to set down to rest for the night, Spirit obstinately refused to land. But the skies were quickly darkening, and they were overtaken by a thunderstorm of such proportions that even a bird of Spirit's size could not fly through it. Rain hammered them as they began their descent, fierce enough that it knocked Spirit sideways. All three were soaked through by the time they landed on the nearest island, the water running off them in streams. Grey and Gramps took cover under a rocky overhang near their landing site atop a bluff, leaving Spirit to manage for himself.

Sodden and cold, grandson and grandfather stripped off their clothing, wrung it out, and hung it over a cluster of brush to dry out beside a small fire the old man had managed to build. At least partially sheltered by the overhang and warmed by their sleeping blankets, which had been kept dry by the waterproof skins in which they were wrapped, they huddled in the firelight and ate a cold dinner.

"Do you still think he knows where he's going?" Grey asked as he chewed a chunk of dried beef.

Tiger Ty was already finished eating and cleaning off his plate. He glanced over. "Do you?"

The boy shrugged. "Well, he's tracking by instinct, if he does. He lost his rider back on that last island, so he can't know exactly where he is."

"No, not exactly. But he knows approximately."

"Is it far now, do you think?"

"Nope." His grandfather shook his head slowly. "Close."

They were silent then, sitting companionably as they waited

for their clothes to dry. It took almost two hours, the air chill and damp, the storm still raging. Rain fell, lightning flashed, and thunder rolled as darkness closed about. They could neither see nor hear anything save for the storm.

Finally, they were able to pull on their clothing and wrap up again in their blankets. After that, they sat staring into the little fire for a time, listening to the pounding of the rain and watching the lightning flash. Eventually, Tiger Ty stretched out and fell asleep. Within moments, he was snoring loud enough that even the sounds of the rainfall, wind, and thunder were not enough to drown him out.

Grey sat up, too wide-awake to sleep. It might have been the sound and fury of the storm, still howling in spite of the clear diminishment of its power. It might have been his concerns about whether what they were doing was of any real value. He had not admitted it to his grandfather—he had barely admitted it to himself—but he was growing steadily more afraid that something really bad had happened to his father. He tried to imagine life without him and could not manage it.

He then found himself examining the nature of his relationship with Alethea and pondering how strongly it was tied to the history of his family—a family plagued by tragedy. Always, in such ruminations, it was the women who dominated his thinking. It was the women, after all, who had suffered the most.

His grandmother, whom he barely remembered anymore, had been a stoic, patient sort. As the wife of a Wing Rider, Jessa had learned to wait patiently for Tiger Ty to return from his long sorties as a scout for the Wing Hove. Grey remembered her as kind and always sort of sad, doing what was expected of her but never really able to accept the life that Tiger Ty had chosen for himself.

He remembered what she had said to him once, when he was very little. "Life is hard enough without the waiting, little boy. The waiting is terrible. I wait for your gramps because I must, but each time I wait a little more of me is lost."

When her husband had finally returned home for the last time, no longer physically able to continue flying the big Rocs, no longer able to act as a scout for the Wing Hove, his grandmother had been happy. But it was as if all the waiting had marked the completion of her life's work, and within a matter of weeks afterward she was dead.

He had been only thirteen then, but he remembered what she had said to him and what he knew the waiting had done to her.

His mother was another matter.

Wild and exotic, she was a creature constantly in motion, her long black hair wild and free as she darted here and there. She never walked, but always ran—as if life might otherwise pass her by. Her eyes were a startling green that seemed to see right to the core of you. She could look at her son and know at once what he was thinking.

"You need time at the pools today," she would say after giving him a quick look—which was exactly right.

"You're in love, little cub," she would say—as if he had already told her of Alethea. "That girl from Tendon. Alethea. Am I right?" She would wait for him to smile and then toss her ebony locks. "I remember well enough how it was. She's stolen your heart—just as your father stole mine."

She did not wait for her Wing Rider husband to leave and return as Jessa had, but had instead embraced the life Tahere had chosen. Though from another settlement in the Wing Hove, she was the child of a Wing Rider, too, and his parents' love for each other had been sealed in no small part by their shared life. But they were a tempestuous pair. Whereas his grandparents had been cool and detached with each other, his mother and father had been fierce.

Then one day his mother had flown out and never returned. A search was mounted, but no trace of her was ever found. Father and son had been devastated. Grey supposed this was why, at least in part, he was drawn to Alethea. She was a girl who wanted to have children and build a life—a girl who wanted stability in home and family. Her family had suffered the loss of several members who were Wing Riders, a brother among them. She did not want to lose Grey. She did not want to risk what might happen if he became a Wing Rider, too.

Grey understood. His interest was in training Rocs but not in riding them. He did not want to visit on Alethea the grief he had endured when he had lost his mother. Although he never admitted as much, it had almost destroyed him—a factor in what he was feeling now as he hunted for his father. The prospect of losing both parents was too much even to consider.

So it was that before leaving with Gramps to find Tahere, he had resolved that no matter how this journey ended, he would never ride the big Rocs again and never serve as a Wing Hove Rider. His grandfather would have to accept this, whether he liked it or not.

Grey was resolved. His future was his own to decide.

At least, that had been his thinking before setting out. Before the search through clouds and mist and sunlit days. Before flying a thousand feet over waters so blue they hurt the eyes. Before feeling for the first time what it was like to fly so far and so fast and so long he was beginning to feel bound to it in a way he had never thought possible.

So perhaps his future was not yet settled and his mind not so entirely set as he might have believed.

THE NIGHT PASSED and the storm with it, and by daybreak they were back in the air again, winging north along the ribbon of the island chain, their search resumed. Tiger Ty hugged Spirit as he mounted, and the bird responded by turning his head to coo at him. Once more the big Roc chose their path, flying straight with a clear certainty of purpose that was beyond understanding and devoid of doubt. Tiger Ty felt the eagerness and determination in the Roc—in the smooth, steady beat of his wings and the measured strength and endurance of his body as he bore them. Tiger Ty's own weariness came upon him faster, and the aching of his body ran deeper, but he pushed it all out of his mind. He laughed and crowed and cajoled in spite of himself, the thrill of flying one last time a reminder of the youth he could never recapture. He was so pleased Grey had suggested this, so proud of the unexpected thoughtfulness of his grandson. He wanted to tell him this, but he was not a man given to voicing praise aloud. He found it easier to dispense it through smiles and nods than through stumbling words that felt strange when he spoke them.

And the boy was a natural Wing Rider, however he might see himself. He might want to be something else when fully grown, but Tiger Ty knew better. Grey was born to this life in the same way that his grandfather and father before had been born to it. It was in his blood, and he might try to leave it behind, but sooner or later he would discover his mistake. He would eventually realize he was meant to carry on the family tradition and would come to fully embrace the life he was destined to lead.

Tiger Ty smiled at the certainty of it, made happy all the way through. He could not remember when he had last felt like this. One day, he would be there to see Grey realize his mistake and change his mind about the direction of his life. One day, they would share a celebratory ride aboard Spirit. Aches and pains and age be damned—he would see that day or know the reason why!

They were less than three hours into their flight when Spirit initiated a steep, swift descent toward the island of Trokar— a broad and heavily forested mass of mountains and valleys. It was the third largest island in the chain, and it was very near the northernmost end. The suddenness and quickness of their landing was a clear indication that Spirit was trying not to be seen from the ground. Something here was threatening enough that he preferred to hide his approach to whatever extent possible.

As well he might, if it turned out to be what Tiger Ty already suspected.

Once on the ground, the two men found themselves in a small clearing barely large enough to permit a Roc to land, let alone to take off again. In fact, there was some cause to wonder if lifting off from such a confined space was even possible. Tiger Ty watched Grey slide off the Roc's back and make a quick sweep of the open space, searching for signs of another presence.

"Nothing," he reported, looking at his grandfather.

Tiger Ty climbed down to join him, moving gingerly with the effort. "Whatever caught his attention is somewhere in there," he said, pointing into the heavy forest.

His grandson looked at the mass of trunks, limbs, and shadows and shook his head. "What do you think it is?"

"A successful end to our search. A path to your father." Tiger Ty was already strapping on a pair of long knives and a wide shoulder sheath filled with throwing stars. "Let's have a look."

They were just entering the tangle of vegetation when Grey slowed. "Is it safe to leave Spirit behind?"

His grandfather shrugged. "Safer than trying to find a way to take him with us, I expect."

Then he slowed, considering. Abruptly he turned back to his grandson. "Something I didn't tell you. Those strange markings on the ground, back on the island your father was grabbed from? Those were made by a Strangle. You know what that is, don't you? It's a big snake—grows up to twenty feet long. Lean and quick. They're the only thing that Rocs fear, because they hunt the big birds. If a Strangle gets hold of a Roc, it can crush it. Strangles can also climb trees to get at the Rocs, and even worm their way into their pens. The only place it can't reach them is in the air."

"So whoever took Father has one of these things?"

"It certainly seems that way. Besides, something has Spirit spooked, and there's not much else that can do that."

Grey gave him a long look. "Maybe we should do a flyover to see if we can spot whoever it is we're hunting."

Tiger Ty gave him a smile. "And be seen in the process? No.

Spirit came down quick enough that I could tell he didn't want to be seen. Surprise is the key here. Besides, Spirit's already done our searching for us. That's why he landed where he did. Your father is close by."

They set off into the trees, working their way in a counter-clockwise sweep of the area, with the old man in the lead and his grandson following close behind. Every so often, they would pause to listen before continuing on. The woods were eerily silent—no sounds of any kind from birds or small ground animals—which was a clear indication that something was amiss. Tiger Ty took his time, not intending to stumble into a trap or an unexpected encounter. Caution was needed, so better to go slow. After all, there were only the two of them.

Funny, he thought, but he couldn't remember anyone who had ever tamed a Strangle. He couldn't even think of how anyone would go about doing so. Snakes that size were not the sort of creature just anyone could successfully train.

They pressed ahead for several hours without finding what they were looking for, and then they found it all at once.

THEY HAD BEEN hunting for several hours when Gramps froze. Abruptly he dropped to the ground, and Grey dropped with him. The trees had opened up before them and another clearing had appeared, this one broader and dominated by clusters of massive boulders overgrown with lichen and ringed with tall grasses that were parched and withered. Again, the silence was oppressive. It was as if everything living had fled or gone to ground. There was no one in sight, no one moving about; no tents or equipment or fires or any other indication that anyone had ever been there.

Still, Gramps held them fast within the cover of the trees, watching. Grey noticed that the old man was looking not only into the clearing, but also up into the canopy of the surrounding trees.

Where a snake might climb.

Grey began looking, too. Then a small sound caught his attention, something on the ground, and he looked in the direction from which it had come. It took him a moment to realize what he was seeing, but then he managed to discern a layering of shadows and a change of terrain that marked the sides of a barely visible pit. The sound had come from there.

Still, his grandfather did not move.

Grey started to say something, but Gramps quickly stopped him with a shake of his head and a finger to his lips. He pointed to a gap in the cluster of boulders and held up five fingers.

Five of Tahere's captors were hiding in those rocks.

Then Gramps pointed into the canopy of the trees across the way and off to the left. Grey looked where he was indicating. He saw nothing at first, but then abruptly spied the Strangle stretched out in a tree across several broad limbs, with its tail end wrapped around the trunk. Its skin was almost exactly the same color as the bark, and its position gave it such perfect camouflage that, at a casual glance, it appeared to be nothing more than another part of its perch.

Grey stared, tracking the snake's length through the branches. It was huge. No wonder Spirit was so wary.

His grandfather motioned for him to move backward into the trees, and together they retreated until they were well out of sight and sound of those they were pursuing.

Gramps bent close, his voice a whisper so soft Grey had trouble hearing. "They saw us fly in. They know we're coming. Your father is in that pit—bait to draw us in. They'll let us get close to the edge, then the Strangle will drop down and that will be that. We have to do this another way."

Grey was already nodding. "Flush out the men in hiding, get rid of them first?"

His grandfather smiled. "I've said all along you weren't as dumb as you look. Now, how do we do this?"

Grey thought about it a moment and then pursed his lips. "Maybe we make it too hot for them?"

Tiger Ty nodded. "Maybe we do."

THEY WAITED THROUGH the balance of the day, content to make those they were stalking wait, too. Content to keep them wondering what had kept them away. Grey would have loved it if his father's captors had decided to find out. It would have made things so much easier if they could have been split up and dealt with separately. But the men remained where they were in the rocks, and the Strangle stayed in the trees as the day slipped away.

He wondered suddenly about his grandfather's physical condition. Was he even capable of sustaining himself in a pitched battle? He had evidenced problems with his breathing all during their flight, and he always seemed to be so tired.

But there was no use thinking about it. They were committed to this rescue attempt, and Tiger Ty would never turn aside now.

When sunset arrived and twilight settled in, grandfather and grandson began their attack. They did not discuss again what they had already decided. They did not equivocate over whether there was a better plan. They knew themselves well enough to trust in their skills and capabilities. All that remained was the doing.

The clearing looked just the same as before—quiet and empty. The Strangle was still visible, stretched out across the branches of the ancient old growth, and Tahere's captors were still in hiding. There was nothing to indicate that anything was amiss, nothing to suggest that a rescue was under way.

Then Grey was atop the boulders, come in from the back side of the hidden men, staying downwind of the snake, creeping to where he could just spy the opening into their hiding place. Using a heat stone, he fired the thick clump of grasses he carried under his arm and threw it into the gap amid the large cluster of equally dry brush that was serving as cover for those concealed inside.

In seconds the brush went up in flames, spreading across the entrance to the gap in the rocks and generating clouds of heavy black smoke. Grey was already moving, one eye on the snake, the other on the gap. The Strangle had left its perch and was lowering itself by its tail to the forest floor. It had just completed the effort, its movements still slow and cautious, when Tiger Ty appeared directly in front of it.

"Demon snake!" the Wing Rider roared in challenge and hurled first one and then another of the throwing stars at the snake's head.

The first throw was true; the star buried itself in one gleaming eye and blinded it. The second was slightly off the mark, catching the huge reptile just above its second eye, but opening a wound savage enough that at once it began to bleed heavily. Though undamaged, the second eye was instantly coated in blood, as the snake writhed in agony and rage, struggling to see what was happening.

Tahere's captors chose that moment to make a break from their smoke-and-fire-choked hiding place. It was a huge mistake. In rushing from the rocks, coughing and gasping and fighting for air, they passed right in front of the Strangle. The giant snake, even though blinded and pain-racked, could hear their movements. It did not bother to try to distinguish between friend and foe; it simply reacted. It attacked with furious quickness, smashing them with its heavy girth, snatching them up and throwing them like rag dolls against the rocks and tree trunks. The sounds of cracking bones and death wails echoed through the forest as, one by one, they died.

Pirates, from the look of their clothing and jewelry, Grey thought, moving swiftly to stay clear. *And not very good ones. Not much use as snake handlers, either.*

He charged past their ruined bodies in an effort to reach the pit and his father, but the Strangle was still twisting all over the

clearing, slamming into rocks and trees alike, flattening grasses
and brush, its rage at being blinded and the pain of its wounds
driving it into a frenzy.

"Get back!" his grandfather shouted at him, circling around
on the far side of the reptile, trying to reach the pit from that
angle.

Grey backed off, but he knew he had to do something to reach
his father. Sooner or later, the snake's struggles would land it
atop the pit.

Grey felt his choices disappearing. It was impossible to anticipate where the Strangle's thrashing might land it from one
moment to the next; the frenzy of its movements suggested it
had lost all sense of direction. Its entire head was covered in
black ichor, its blood a thick layer on the gleaming scales of its
head and neck. How it was still functioning at all was a mystery. With all that blood and the severity of its wounds, it should
have been dead.

The snake's tail lashed out suddenly and caught his grandfather with a wicked blow that threw him backward into the
trees. The old man cried out in pain, and instantly his attacker
turned in response, wriggling excitedly in his direction. Grey
charged in, using his sword to try to distract the creature, chop-
ping repeatedly at its thick hide. But no matter how hard he
tried to turn it away, no matter how many wounds he inflicted,
he could not manage to slow the Strangle's advance.

And then he saw in horror that, in its agonized writhing, the
snake had managed to wipe its good eye clean of blood, and that
eye was now fixed on his grandfather.

"Gramps!" Grey screamed in warning. "Run!"

But his grandfather was lying prone on the forest earth just
within the fringe of the trees, unmoving.

"Gramps, get up!"

A familiar shriek filled the air—high and piercing, the
sound so sharp-edged the boy winced in shock. His gaze shifted
to find Spirit, diving from overhead with such reckless speed it

seemed inevitable he would be killed upon impact. Yet on he came, heedless, his determination to reach his rider clear evidence of the love he still bore. Down he plummeted, a blur against the blue sky, his shriek sounding once more.

The Strangle slowed and lifted its ruined head, then Spirit was on it, slamming into its face, tearing out its eyes and ripping off the top of its head, all in a single frantic rending of talons and hooked beak. The snake absorbed the full impact of the strike, shuddered under its force, and collapsed.

Grey was next to his grandfather immediately, kneeling and lifting the old man, finding a pulse and then a heartbeat, seeing the aged eyes open and a dazed look fix on him. "Grey?"

"Right here, Gramps. You're all right. We both are. We're safe now. The Strangle is dead. Spirit killed it."

Tiger Ty gave him a wan smile. "Always did like that bird. He's a keeper, isn't he?" He coughed, a rattle in his throat. "I feel so weak. Like everything is draining away. I need to sleep. Just a bit."

Then he lapsed into unconsciousness.

WHEN HE DETERMINED his grandfather could be left alone, Grey found a length of vine that he could tie to the trunk of a nearby tree and used it to lower himself into the pit. He found his father waiting, and they embraced warmly. Tahere, dehydrated and starving, was only partially aware of what was happening. He had been kept a prisoner for these past few days by the pirates, who had caught him unawares and brought him along, believing he could teach them to fly Rocs. A foolish dream, but the sort pirates liked to fixate on when an opportunity for gain came along.

Once out of the pit and given food and drink, Tahere regained sufficient presence of mind to explain it all. He had been drawn to the island of Del Roke by what appeared to be a man who had been shipwrecked there. But on landing Spirit and climbing down off his back, he had been set upon and seized by the others. When the Strangle had emerged—a creature he learned later one of the pirates had raised from a baby—Tahere had been quick to send his Roc to safety, thinking he would bring help.

Now Grey understood. Spirit, ever independent and still forever bonded to Tiger Ty, had not trusted others to use him to reach Tahere. How much more danger would he be visiting on Tahere by doing so? Spirit had always been a one-man bird, and Tahere had never been bonded with him in the way Gramps had. In the end, it was Tiger's decision to agree to ride Spirit and come hunting for his son that had saved Tahere.

Grey woke Tiger Ty to make sure he was not head-damaged in any serious fashion. There were no signs of a wound, but he knew that men who received hard blows sometimes went unconscious and never woke up. Gramps, however, was well enough to grumble about pirates and Rocs and careless grandsons sufficiently to convince the boy that he was all right. So hoisting his father and grandfather atop Spirit and securing them in place, he climbed in front to take control and gave the Roc the command to fly for home.

Though struggling at first with the extra weight, Spirit complied and, once airborne, settled into a steady pace, winging south for the Hove.

It was difficult to talk a thousand feet in the air with the wind rushing past his ears and both listeners behind him, so Grey settled for silence, thinking how lucky they were that things had turned out so well and how anxious he was to see Alethea once again. He was aware of his passengers falling asleep at regular intervals, coming awake only when stopping for food and drink or when jostling from air currents shook them out of their slumber.

The journey took three days with two overnights spent on the ground to allow for the men to sleep and for Spirit to regain his strength. On the third day, as they neared the Wing Hove,

Grey was aware that his grandfather had gone quiet once more, his head resting against his grandson's back, his body slack. His father was awake now and looking down at the ocean and off toward the shores of the Four Lands on their left. When Grey shot him a questioning look to make sure he was all right, Tahere smiled and gave him a familiar hand signal of reassurance.

Grey smiled back in response and looked out over the vast expanse of the Blue Divide. Perhaps this would this be the last ride for all of them. He was finished, Gramps was finished, and perhaps his father would choose to stay grounded as well. Maybe his family of Wing Riders would spend the remainder of their days working other jobs at the Wing Hove. Maybe all their lives would be changed.

Alethea, he whispered to himself, thinking how pleased she would be.

When they arrived at the Wing Hove, members of the community rushed to greet them, Pannit Whey in the lead. Hands reached up to help them down. Grey was surprised to discover how exhausted he was, how depleted of strength and focus. He allowed himself to be laid on the ground and wrapped in blankets as others did the same for his father and Gramps. All were amazed and awed by what he had accomplished, even though he protested it was Tiger Ty who had made it all possible. An aleskin was pressed against his lips to allow him to sip the strong liquid within, and the familiar burning sensation gave him renewed strength.

"It was Gramps," he kept saying, over and over. "He was the one. And then Spirit. He saved us all."

When they finally got Grey on his feet, he saw them helping his father up, too. They exchanged a quick glance, but there was a dark look on his father's face that was immediately troubling.

Then he saw Gramps still lying on the ground, wrapped in his blankets. "Gramps?" he called.

Heads turned, among them Pannit Whey's, and Grey saw the tears in the other's eyes. Abruptly, Alethea was there, throwing her arms around him and holding him fast.

"Gramps?" he whispered, still looking at his grandfather.

"Shhh, shhh," she whispered in his ear, pressing her lips against it. "You're safe now, Grey. I was so worried!"

"But, Gramps . . ."

His father put his arms around them both. "He's gone, Grey. His heart gave out. Nothing either of us could have done would have prevented it. It must have happened earlier today, while we were still flying."

"He wanted you safe, and you are," Alethea said, turning him to face her. "Be happy for him. You gave him this last chance to fly, his last time with Spirit. It was what he wanted, wasn't it? And you did that for him."

Amid the blur of his tears and the heartache of knowing his grandfather was gone, Grey knew the old man had done something for him, too. He had opened his grandson's eyes to what being a Wing Rider really meant. He had shared, for those days they traveled together, the life he believed Grey might find if he gave himself half a chance. He had given Grey a closer look at what waited for him in the clouds and left him less certain of what he might do next. Perhaps he would remain grounded, a caretaker and trainer of Rocs for others. But perhaps he would end up doing what his grandfather had always wanted.

He would just have to wait and see.

Tiger Ty had lived most of his life in the air. It was fitting it should end while he was doing what he loved best. Grey could be sad for him, but he should be happy, too. Gramps would have told him as much if he were there. Grey should honor this. All of them should.

"Goodbye, Gramps," he whispered, managing a brave smile. "Safe flight."

Introduction to
"Warrior"

WHEN I APPROACHED my editor, Anne Groell, about gathering up all my previously written short fiction to publish as a collection, she was enthusiastic about it—but with a caveat. If I was going to do this, I needed to write some entirely new stories to add to the old. In particular, I needed a centerpiece novella— something that would serve to draw readers of all the other books into the collection. I hadn't considered writing anything this ambitious, but I quickly decided from which set of books this novella needed to be drawn. I already had a handful of stories from Shannara and Magic Kingdom either written or planned, but I had written nothing more from The Word and the Void world since the 1990s. Time to take the plunge.

I have never wanted to write more about the characters or story line from The Word and the Void. It has always seemed better to leave that series alone. Those three books represent, for me, the best work I have ever done—especially *Running with the Demon*. So I went all the way back to its origin: the short story "Imaginary Friends," which appears earlier in this collection. On rereading the story, questions immediately surfaced. Whatever happened to Jack McCall after his brush with a life-threatening cancer and his battle in Sinnissippi Park with the dragon Desperado? Had anything more ever happened? Had he ever crossed paths with the Lady or Two Bears? Had he been asked to become a Knight of the Word?

I decided to find out—but I wanted to change the scenario and stakes. I wanted him to be a different sort than John Ross. I wanted the demon threat to be entirely different as well, something more personal. I wanted him tested in a fresh way— a more extreme way than Ross had been tested.

The results can be found below. Welcome back, readers, to the first tale from The Word and the Void in over twenty years.

WARRIOR

One

HE STANDS ON *a hillock overlooking the old Winston home and listens to the silence of the shrouding night. All around him, from Lincoln Park to the Vashon ferry docks, the only light comes from the hazy cones of the streetlamps and the gaps in the shade-drawn windows of nearby homes. Almost no porch lights intrude, dimmed deliberately to allow for deeper sleep or simply left unlit out of habit. No one walks the streets at this hour. A few cars arrive home late at random intervals, but most of those who occupy the residences are asleep. This is a working neighborhood—few retirees or stay-at-home workers, not even that many housewives. Rise and shine and off to work is almost universal here. If you were to conduct a census, you would find almost every home consists of two working parents and an average of 2.5 young children. Evidence of this can be found in the discarded toys littering the yards, well-used but still serviceable gym equipment, basketball hoops, and bikes. A car or two sits parked in the driveways of homes that lack garages, which most of them do. This neighborhood is old and has survived redevelopment. Garages were not common when the homes were being built; then, more than one vehicle was considered less of a necessity. Now both parents usually work, and children grow up as latchkey kids, signed up for and fully engaged in multiple after-school programs to keep them from going astray.*

Except they too often do go astray, in spite of the precautions their parents take.

He studies the Winston home a bit longer, feeling the oppressive weight of its darkness on his shoulders. That darkness eclipses the night, reaches out for him and draws him to it with an irresistible insistence.

I have her, Jack, *the voice on the phone told him.* I have her, and I intend to keep her until you come to me. So, come quickly. I cannot be responsible for what happens to her if you do not. Such a tempting little morsel; such a tasty little treat. I am sure she and I can find enjoyable ways to pass the time, should you delay. So many lovely things we can do while we wait. She is such a promising playmate.

He has tried so hard to protect her. He has been so careful to keep her safe. But he has failed, and now he has no choice but to do what he can to change this fate.

He stares at the darkened windows of the Winston house and tries to think what he can do to save her. To save countless others that will face the same fate if he fails again. Ineke has warned him. He will find her, and he will use her, she said, and you will have to answer for it if you do not act quickly enough. Ineke, a fairy creature of no more substance than a minute and gone just as quickly. He marvels at the foresight and courage she has shown, at her willingness to sacrifice herself, at her fierce commitment to the power of her belief.

But commitment to belief is nothing new to Jack McCall. His life has been marked by sacrifices—sacrifices made by himself and by those closest to him. His life has been full of miracles, too—of overcoming impossible odds at the age of thirteen when he still lived in Hopewell. It was Pick who counseled him then, and gave him a sword and shield in the forms of a stick and a garbage can lid and told him to stand and fight back against the dragon that was threatening to steal his life.

A dragon, but not the kind people might imagine. He shakes his head in recognition of an undeniable truth. Something really bad is never what you imagine. Something really bad is always much more insidious. You can prepare yourself all your life for the unexpected. You can imagine everything that might come for you and how you will react when it does, and still you cannot be prepared when the moment comes. You can tell yourself what you will do and how you will handle yourself, fortified by having given thought to it all. And still you will be unprepared for the reality. And you will have to face it with an inescapable recognition that you never once thought it would look and feel as it does.

It just isn't given to us to fully imagine and confront the worst of our fears, because until they happen they are only abstract possibilities.

Jack McCall is forty years old. He has a wife and a daughter and a son. He is the owner of a private company offering individually designed planning, advice, and resource conservation programs for public and private entities engaged in parks and recreation development and maintenance. (Or, at least, that is how he pitches it to his clients.) He is a longtime resident of his community and well liked, if considered a bit odd because of his insistence on remaining a very private person outside of work. And because of the black staff he always carries with him. But those who know him well, those few who know some of the details of his life and his family history, understand. His is an odd story, one of miracles and strange events—of near-death experiences and unexplainable truths.

Some of what makes him seem so peculiar to others he has kept to himself. The fact that he knows good and evil exist in substantive form. The fact that he has encountered both all too frequently since he was thirteen and fought the dragon in Sinnissippi Park as a boy. The fact that some of the odder creatures of the park became known to him, including the protector of the park, Pick, and the owl, Daniel, and the troll, Wartag. The fact that he once shrank down so far that he was able to fly the length and breadth of the

park aboard Daniel, with Pick as his companion and guide. The
fact that the reason he fought the dragon was that he had cancer,
and to defeat the cancer he had to defeat the dragon.

All that is in the past, along with much more that he would like
to forget but cannot. Now he lives near Lincoln Park in West Se-
attle. So much has happened in the years since his miracle recov-
ery. His life has changed in so many ways. He no longer lives in a
small town but in a large city and is married with children. He
has finished school and works for a living. He has been healthy all
these years since his cancer went into remission; there has never
been a recurrence.

But there is one thing more, one thing that defines the nature
and boundaries of his life above all others. One thing that no one
knows.

He is a Knight of the Word.

And everything he sees and thinks as he stares down at the
Winston home is happening in a dream.

Two

JACK MCCALL WAS twenty-two years old, standing in a campus
parking lot, graduation over, parents come and gone, packed up
and ready to leave for Hopewell, when the stranger approached.
A part of him thought it would be a good idea to turn and walk
the other way when he saw the man. Well over six feet and close
to three hundred pounds, he looked as if he could deconstruct
someone who was less than six feet by several inches and nowhere near two hundred, just by giving him a hard look. He
appeared to Jack to be Native American, with a face that might
have been carved from granite. With his massive body barely
concealed under patched-up camo and worn combat boots, both
of which suggested military experience, he was of indeterminate intentions and wholly intimidating.

But Jack stood his ground because he had stopped running

from the things that frightened him by the time he turned fourteen.

"Are you Jack McCall, *kem'sho?*" the other asked.

Jack nodded uncertainly. *Kem'sho?* He brushed back his mop of blond hair where it drooped down over his forehead. "Do I know you?"

"You do not. I am called Two Bears—O'olish Amaneh in the language of my people. Now we are acquainted. Where can we sit and talk?"

Jack did not feel like engaging in a conversation with this hulk, but he also suspected he could not avoid it. "What do we have to talk about?" he asked.

Two Bears gave him a look. "That is what I wish to discuss with you. Why don't we get on with it?"

Chastened by the rebuke and by now a bit curious, Jack led the other out of the parking lot and onto one of the campus quads where empty benches occupied shady patches of lawn under centuries-old oaks and elms. The campus was practically deserted, the bulk of students, parents, professors, and other graduation invitees departed. Jack would have been gone as well if he hadn't stopped to help his roommates carry down their gear and pack their cars. He now found himself regretting his Good Samaritan act.

Sitting side by side on the bench, each turned slightly to face the other, they spent a moment in silence before Two Bears spoke.

"You don't have a plan for the future," he said, making it a statement rather than a question.

Jack nodded. "And you know this how?"

Straight-faced, Two Bears tapped his temple. "Intuition. I have a proposition for you. One that would give you a direction in your life that you currently lack. One that would provide you with a worthy purpose and an assurance that you would be helping a world in great need of assistance."

Jack smiled. "You want me to become a politician?"

Two Bears shook his head. "You are not listening. I used the words 'help the world,' not 'feed at the expense of the world.' "

"Look," Jack said. The lack of direction or purpose in this conversation was making him impatient. "Why don't you just tell me what you want?"

"I want you to travel to Wales for a week and speak with the Lady." The other's hard face wore an impassive expression. "I have the tickets for your journey in my pocket. You would leave in three days."

Jack stared. "You're kidding, right?"

Two Bears stared back, his face impassive.

Jack blinked. "Who is the Lady?"

"That is what you are going to Wales to find out."

"But I don't want to go to Wales."

Two Bears gave a shrug of his massive shoulders. "You just think you don't want to go to Wales. You think there is no reason for it. But you are wrong. There is every reason for you to go. College is over, boyhood is finished, and what lies ahead is unknown. But you must embrace it. You must learn for yourself what it is. My explaining it to you would be insufficient. Take the tickets and fly to Wales. Speak with the Lady. Pick would tell you the same thing I am telling you. It is necessary for you to go."

"Pick? How do you know . . . ?"

"Once upon a time, the fairy creature Pick—who was then and is still caretaker and guardian of Sinnissippi Park in the town you grew up in—helped you to find a way to defeat a dragon. You, in turn, helped him to save the park. Yours has been a special life, Jack McCall. You have found the magic in the world and embraced it. You have fought against the worst of it and channeled your efforts to good purpose. Did you think this would be the end of it? Did you think your involvement with the magic would stop there?"

Jack shook his head, now fully flummoxed. "But how do you know all this? How is it you know about Pick and the dragon and Sinnissippi Park?"

"It is my business to know." Two Bears rocked back an inch or two and then leaned closer. "Sinnissippi Park and much of the land that surrounds it is my ancestral home. It was the homeland of my people, the Sinnissippi, for centuries. Now they are all gone, and I am all that is left. The magic that was once ours and that once protected our homelands is still there, but it is threatened. So it is given to me to protect what remains of the legacy of my people and of the other Native Americans throughout this part of the world. To do so, I serve the Lady."

"But who is the Lady?" Jack practically shouted, his frustration reaching a new level.

Two Bears did not react. "We've come full circle, *kem'sho*. The answer to your question is to be found in Wales. You must go there to find it."

Jack was about to walk away, wanting no part of any of this; he was not even sure it was true. There were all sorts of ways Two Bears could have learned of Pick and the dragon and the park and himself. To just blindly agree to fly off to Wales meant he would have to put all caution and good sense aside and throw himself on fate and blind trust.

And yet . . .

"What does *kem'sho* mean?" he asked.

Two Bears gave a small nod of approval. "In the language of my people, it means 'warrior.' It describes what I think you are."

Jack hesitated, suddenly uncertain. The big man's words were persuasive and did not feel like lies or dissembling. Although wild and impossible, they nevertheless spoke to a truth he was reluctant to embrace. Once, he had believed in fairy magic, back when he was a boy. Once, he had believed in dragons and elves and magic of any sort. All that seemed far away now, but had he really stopped believing in things that had once seemed so real? Had he really stopped believing that he had beaten back the cancer that had riddled every part of his body and had saved his life by doing so?

"One thing more," Two Bears said quietly. "The Lady knew of your destiny, back when you were thirteen and dying. She was responsible for keeping the dragon from you. She was the one who summoned Pick to act on her behalf. That was how he found you and became your friend."

He rose abruptly. Reaching into a pocket in his camo shirt, he pulled out an envelope. "There are your tickets. Use them if you choose. But only by using them will you know if what you've heard is true."

He began to walk away, but Jack was on his feet now, holding the envelope he didn't even realize he had accepted. "Wait."

"If you choose not to go, if you decide not to seek out the Lady, you will wonder for the rest of your life if you should have. Be at peace, *kem'sho.*"

He walked across the quad without looking back and disappeared between the campus buildings, leaving Jack staring after him.

Three

THREE DAYS LATER, Jack McCall was landing in Cardiff, Wales. He was still not sure why he was doing this, save for those final words from Two Bears: *If you choose not to go, you will wonder for the rest of your life if you should have.*

Fair enough, he supposed. Yet he could not help but wonder if the reverse might not turn out to be true: *If you choose to go, you may end up finding out it was a huge mistake.*

In any case, he had made his choice, and he was soon driving through the Welsh countryside toward Snowdonia in the north of the country. Wending his way along scenic A470 on the west side of the River Conwy, he was pointing toward the villages of Llandudno and Portmeirion without intending to reach either.

His destination would not require him to travel that far, but only to just below the village of Betws-y-Coed. There, according to the instructions handed to him by Two Bears in the same envelope as the airline tickets, he was to take shelter in a small farmhouse, which was only three miles from where the Lady awaited him in an out-of-the-way tourist destination called the Fairy Glen.

Jack had never heard of it, not surprisingly, because when you came right down to it he had never heard much of anything about Wales. Since directions had been provided and he had made the commitment to see this through, he would follow the path laid out for him and save any further questions or concerns about why he was doing this for another time.

He kept close watch on the road signs as he drove to be sure he was doing everything he had been told. But as time wore on and the towns and farms grew sparser, he began to wonder if perhaps he had missed a turning. It wasn't until he saw a sign indicating Betws-y-Coed was only twenty kilometers away that he decided he was on the right track and began to look for the side road that would take him to his lodgings.

Once arrived, he would have two nights to wait for the rise of the full moon, and then he would meet the Lady. He was to ask directions to the Fairy Glen, but give no explanation as to why he was going beyond saying that he had heard it was beautiful during the full moon and he wanted to see if it was true. There was to be no mention of the Lady or Two Bears. There was to be no mention of anything that seemed out of the ordinary. He was simply to show up as requested, drive to the Fairy Glen, and listen to what the Lady had to say.

He didn't even know how he was supposed to let the Lady know he was there. Two Bears was no longer around to advise him, and he had already been told it would be a mistake to ask his host for anything other than directions.

So, when he pulled his rental into a parking area next to a well-kept stone cottage just off a side road he had only barely avoided missing, he was resolved to keep everything about what he was doing in Wales secret. He would simply pretend he was on vacation, having just graduated college. He climbed out of the car and was standing there, having a slow look around, when the front door opened and a bearded oldster wearing jeans and a flannel shirt came out to greet him.

"Mr. McCall?" the other asked, advancing down the stone walkway.

Jack waved. "That would be me."

"Arthur Henry." He arrived with his hand extended and a pleased look on his face. "Found your way here all right?"

"I had directions."

"Good ones, too. Most manage to miss us on the first try. Have to call in or muck around a bit first. None of that for you. Come on in. Here, I'll help with the luggage."

There wasn't much luggage to begin with, since Jack had packed everything in a duffel, but Arthur Henry insisted on carrying it himself, refusing to let Jack do the work. "You just go through, leave the rest to me. Got tea and beer, whichever you prefer. College student, right? Got to get a good education these days, if you want to get ahead in the world. Go on, sit in the room with the fire. It gets cold here at night."

Arthur Henry, it turned out, was a talker. He asked about Jack's flight, then told a few stories about flights of his own. He asked about Jack's education, then gave a quick survey of his own. He asked about Jack's plans for his future, then talked about his own plans for the cottage and the surrounding land. He spent a good deal more time afterward weighing in on the Welsh economy, Welsh politics, and Wales's place in the British Commonwealth and how it related to the place of Great Britain in the larger world. He then went on to advise Jack how best to use these first several months out of college before entering the workforce.

"Plenty of time to be a vital cog in the business world, Jack.

But you need a bit of seasoning first, and this is the time to get that odd bit of experience you won't find in the nine-to-five workday. Travel is the answer. See the world. See how the other nine-tenths live. This will give you a larger frame of reference, meaning you'll have a significant advantage over almost everyone else. Because most folks never see even a little of what is out there."

By now, they were settled in a sitting room before a fire blazing in an old stone hearth, glasses of Welsh beer in their hands and a ruddy glow on their faces. Arthur Henry hadn't stopped talking since they sat down, although Jack had managed to squeeze one or two words in edgewise in a futile effort to hold up his end of the conversation. Mostly, he just smiled and nodded and let the old man say whatever he chose, content to let him do so for as long as it took to exhaust him.

Although, as the first hour passed and a sizable chunk of the second with it, he began to wonder if he was expecting too much.

Finally, Arthur seemed to realize what he was doing and sprang to his feet with a hearty laugh. "Well, I'm just going on and on, taking up all the air in the room. Come, Mr. McCall, and share some dinner with me. If you're good, I'll spare you a few moments of the evening to talk a bit about yourself!"

A stew had been prepared on an old iron stove, and it was delicious. After adding fresh-baked bread ("Make all my own bread," Arthur advised) and another glass or two of the beer, Jack McCall could honestly say he had never enjoyed a meal more. And he could say that because his host finally took a break from nonstop talking to concentrate on his food.

When that was finished, Arthur directed Jack to his quarters— a cozy bedroom at the rear of the cottage, complete with its own bathroom—to let him unpack before coming to sit once more by the fire. He did invite Jack to talk about himself, and Jack managed to give a sketchy account of his early life, education, and family situation before his time was at an end and Arthur was off and running once again. Wife and kids (three), the former dead now, the kids grown and living elsewhere, life spent working at a lumber mill, fond of cricket, fond of football (European), politics mostly an exercise in futility in his opinion, and the world in shambles mostly because this new generation (Jack's?) just didn't understand what it meant to work for a living.

Finally talk worked its way around to Jack's plans for the time he was spending in Wales. Jack gave a brief overview, consisting of trips into the Snowdonia area, visits to some of the castle ruins that had once been Edward's detested Iron Ring, built to subdue the wild savages he believed the Welsh people to be, and finally a journey up to Llandudno for a night.

Then he added, as casually as he could manage it, "A friend of mine who's been here before told me there was a place I needed to visit that's right around here. Said it was very beautiful, almost magical. He called it the Fairy Glen. Do you know it?"

The old man grunted. "I do. Right down the road a short distance from here."

"Have you been there?"

"Aye. Twice. Once to see it, once to be sure I was seeing it right. You should go. But in the daytime, not at night."

"Why is that? I thought it would be beautiful under the full moon."

The old man went quiet for a moment, lost in thought. "Odd things happen there at night. You can't be sure what you're seeing. Daytime, you see it all much better, can't be so easily fooled. You go when there's sunlight."

He didn't make it a suggestion; he made it a command. And Jack knew when to back off. "Sure, I'll go during the day, if that's what you think best."

His host's sharp old eyes fixed on him. "That *is* what I think best."

Jack smiled to show his agreement, but Two Bears's instructions trumped the old man's superstitions. He would go on the night of the full moon, as requested.

Four

TWO NIGHTS LATER—when the sun was down and the stars just beginning to come out, but the full moon still below the horizon—Jack went to the Fairy Glen to meet the Lady.

He had gone to the glen earlier in the day, making a point of telling Arthur, providing him with some reassurance that he was doing what the old man had suggested. He found the Fairy Glen charming. It was a shallow gorge with a deep stream running along its winding floor. A waterfall, perhaps thirty feet in height, spilled down from a precipice at one end to feed the stream, which then tumbled in a series of rapids among huge, ancient boulders and broken rocks for several hundred feet before taking a sharp left and disappearing into the trees at the other end. A trail led down into the glen—a twisty descent—through slopes overhung by heavy tree limbs and thick with brush and wildflowers. The sound of the stream was a constant burbling that was matched by birdsong and the soft rush of the wind through the leaves.

If it isn't magical, he found himself thinking as he looked around, *it should be.*

He had stood there, transfixed. He was lost in the moment, and the moment stretched away endlessly.

When he went back to the house, he told Arthur he was going up to Llandudno for the night and would be back sometime the following day. Arthur made a point of asking him what he thought of the Fairy Glen, but Jack just smiled and dissembled. He said it was a pretty place, but nothing special. He said nothing about feeling that he was being watched while he explored. He said nothing about the voices that seemed to rise from the rushing of the stream's waters. He said nothing of the small, sudden movements he caught out of the corner of his eye at least half a dozen times while he stood there, a willing captive.

But he couldn't be sure he wasn't mistaken. Not until he went back. Not until he was there at night. There was enough happening in the daytime to persuade him he must.

More than once, he questioned his motives. Mostly, he wondered at his own willingness to blindly follow the orders of a stranger. This was not like him. He was usually very pragmatic—thought things through carefully, considered and weighed his options before making decisions. Yet this decision he had made impulsively, and mostly based on the fact that Two Bears knew so much about his past—about Pick and the dragon and Sinnissippi Park. And about his cancer, which he never talked about with anyone.

He still had questions, and secretly wondered if he might not find his answers tonight. He had no reason to believe he would, but still he kept thinking he might.

On his return to the Fairy Glen, he found a fisherman occupying the near bank, clothed in woodsman garb and an old fishing hat. He wore boots, and his pole was ancient and handwrought, with a strange reel attached—the likes of which Jack had never seen before. The man stood on the bank and cast, then slowly reeled in his line, hitched up his rod, and cast again. Jack watched for a while, then walked over.

"Catch anything?" he asked.

The man glanced at him and smiled but made no response. His beard was thick and his hair long, his face seamed, and his skin brown from the sun. He was of indeterminate age—neither young nor old, but some of both. Jack waited for the fisherman to say something, but he just went back to fishing as if Jack weren't there.

Jack turned away at the sound of a high, fierce shriek, searching the woods as a spike of fear ran up his spine, then glanced up at the rising full moon. There was a fresh chill in the air, and suddenly Jack felt a deep-seated sense of unease.

He looked back at the fisherman, but the man was gone.

Standing alone now on the banks of the stream, Jack watched the moonlight skip and dance along the rims of the waves and through the ripples caused by the water's anxious rush. An owl hooted somewhere nearby—a haunting sound that lingered as an echo. Off to his right, a long dark shadow moved within the brush, staying just out of view.

And then the fairies appeared. There was no question about what they were, no doubt in his mind. An explosion of bright forms surfaced out of the waterfall—silvery, twinkling apparitions that soared above the stream and skipped along its surface with unrestrained abandon. Bells sounded from all around, and bright bursts of light emanated from within the stream's flow, as if something living in its depths was seeking to break free. Jack might have turned and run if he had felt threatened in any way, but he did not. Rather, he felt embraced, welcomed, brought home to a place he had never known existed but had always been searching for. The feeling was so unexpectedly wondrous that he suddenly burst into tears, yearning to wrap himself up in it forever.

Then the Lady appeared—a diaphanous gowned bit of shadow and light, and beautiful beyond anything Jack had ever imagined possible. She floated above the churning surface of the stream, the fairies circling all about her as she approached, borne on the night air and the crest of white-capped waves. A procession formed as the Lady neared, a retinue falling into place behind her—reaching down to lift the train of her gown and to smooth the waters of the stream so her slippers might remain dry. Jack felt her eyes on him, this spirit creature not wholly substantive and not completely there, and her gaze warmed him. He saw the kindness in her face and instantly felt the blood rush to his cheeks in response.

Then abruptly she was standing before him, changed
entirely—become as solid as he was and no longer so much a
creature of another world. Her retinue disappeared. The waters
of the stream lost their bright shimmer, the bells went silent,
and the Fairy Glen became as it had been when he first approached it, as if none of what he had just witnessed had ever
happened.

"Will you serve me?" the Lady asked in a voice so warm and
musical it brought him to his knees.

He could not speak for a moment. Her request was a naked
plea that demanded explanation and yet offered none. At the
same time, it was so compelling, so impossibly irresistible, that
he could not envision a world in which he would refuse. In those
four words, he found a promise of the moral commitment he
had always been seeking. He found, too, the answers to all his
questions about his childhood brush with death—about Sinnissippi Park and Pick and the dragon that would have brought
him down, had he not defeated it.

With an eager willingness that frightened him, he whispered, "I will serve you."

The voice did not seem his own, and the words appeared to
come from somewhere else. Yet the Lady reached down and
stroked his cheek, a gentle brushing of fingers that reached deep
into his heart.

"Let it be so, then, Jack McCall. As of this moment, you are a
Knight of the Word. You must never forget what you are. And
you must never forsake me."

Then she lifted him up to stand before her and touched his
face once more. This time images began to appear before his
eyes, a long, continuous stream of history that revealed in detail
all that had gone before and of which he would now become a
part. Knowledge flowed into him and took root. It swept before
his eyes swiftly and without slowing, and yet he knew instinctively he would never forget any of it. The images seemed to last
only a few moments, but when they were gone he glanced up-

ward and saw that the moon had moved all the way across the nighttime sky.

"Know, brave Knight, that your service is unique. It will be required once and once only. But you will need to be vigilant always, because they will come for you and seek to destroy you, and this must not be allowed. You must be preserved for that one high service you have been chosen to perform."

"What service . . . ?" he tried to ask, but her fingers silenced his lips with a touch.

"It is not yet time for you to know. Go now. Go to the life you will make for yourself. Go to the family that will become your own. We will not speak again until the need arrives."

Her fingers found his chin. "Know this, too, Jack McCall. All brave Knights who serve the Word must suffer the dreams of the damned. All must dream of the future that arises when they fail in the present. For most, those dreams are of a future that lies generations away. But you, and you alone, will dream of a future that will come to pass in your own lifetime—a future that will befall you and yours if you fail in your service. Be wary of your dreams, brave Knight, for they will be treacherous and misleading, and not all that you dream will be as it seems."

One last time, the fingers shifted across his face, this time coming to rest upon his eyes, closing them so that he felt himself drifting into such a deep inexorable slumber that he could do nothing but let it take him.

"Sleep now," he heard her whisper, and he slept.

When he woke again, it was dawn, and he was alone in the Fairy Glen. He blinked and rose from his bed of damp grasses, shivering and confused. His thoughts returned to the events of the night just passed, and there at their forefront was the memory of his meeting with the Lady.

No other proof of it remained to indicate that it had ever happened, yet he knew—as surely as he knew his life was changed forever—that it had.

He went back to the cottage and Arthur Henry and rested.

He stayed for another day, so it would not appear that his departure was too abrupt, and then he returned home to discover how much of what the Lady had told him would turn out to be true.

Five

THEY CAME FOR Jack McCall less than two months after his return. The Lady had not told him who it was that would come for him or why. She had not told him what he was supposed to do if they did come. Had he been left to his own devices, he probably wouldn't have survived the encounter. But the Lady had foreseen what would happen and had taken steps to prevent any harm from befalling him.

With college behind him, Jack was back in Hopewell and living with his parents as he began his search for a more far-reaching future. His time with them was temporary, a bridge to finding a residence and a career of his own. He had already decided against going further with his schooling, anxious to get on with his life. He wanted to begin exploring its possibilities—through trial and error, if needed—while still asserting his independence. He found a job immediately, albeit one that might not last beyond the summer. He was hired by the Hopewell Municipal District of Parks and Recreation, through the encouragement of an old middle school teacher who had always liked Jack and had made the recommendation to a few of his friends who had connections, providing a strong letter of reference. Jack was hired on the spot as a park ranger and, within a week of returning, was hard at work patrolling and caring for the entire three-hundred-acre expanse of Sinnissippi Park.

The assignment was perfect—a job that required a daily commute of not much more than a short walk to the maintenance shed to fetch the all-terrain vehicle he was assigned. It was also ironic. Here he was, working for the benefit of the very park that Pick had told him he was responsible for as Guardian of the Magic ten years earlier. Jack thought there was a possibility they might meet again now, working in such close proximity on a daily basis.

But after a month with no sign of the elf—let alone even the slightest suggestion of a possible encounter—Jack was forced to admit that his hopes were dimming. He still looked for his little friend, but in his heart of hearts, where hard truths were kept stowed away with bad memories, he found the inevitability of his disappointment impossible to ignore.

When thirty days had passed with not a single sighting of Pick, he abruptly found himself face-to-face with Two Bears.

It was late in the day, and he had pulled the ATV into the maintenance shed and was securing his equipment and tools when the big man appeared. He didn't materialize out of thin air exactly . . . but close.

"Welcome back, Jack McCall," he rumbled. He stood there, backlit by the fading sun, his large body casting its big shadow, holding a staff in one hand with just the hint of a smile on his granite face. "I have something for you."

He extended the staff, obviously offering it. Jack took a moment to consider the gift. It was a black, gnarled length of wood, worn and scarred and riven with markings he could not quite make out, but which looked to be symbols or writing. Jack took a deep breath, reached out, and took it.

Though he had expected it to be heavy, he was surprised to discover it was light. It was sturdy, but did not feel cumbersome or awkward in his hands. If anything, it felt to be exactly the right weight and thickness—an extension of himself that he could sense simply by how easily he was able to handle it.

"You are a Knight of the Word now, and such men and women, one and all, carry this staff as a symbol of their office and the power invested in them. It will seem a perfect fit for whoever bears it, but will serve you and only you while it remains yours. There is power in it that will keep you safe. Such power will reveal itself when it is needed. It will teach you what to expect of it, and what in turn it will expect of you."

Oddly, there seemed to be unexpected warmth to the staff. "You make it sound like a living thing," Jack remarked with a smile, hefting it experimentally.

Two Bears nodded. "Because it is."

The smile dropped from Jack's face. "It's *alive?*"

The big man ignored the question. "You are never to go anywhere without it. Ever. When you set it down, for whatever the reason, you are never to place it beyond your reach. When you sleep, when you eat, when you leave your home and when you are in it, the staff must always be close at hand. This will cause you some inconvenience, I admit. But a park ranger carrying a staff will not seem all that unusual. No one will question that you bear it everywhere."

Jack pictured himself in church or at a social function, black staff in hand. "If you say so."

"Treat it as an extension of yourself. Treat it with respect. It is your strongest protection against the things that will come after you. It is your link to the Word, and it is the Word you now serve—just as the Lady and I do. You are a Knight of the Word, *kem'sho,* and you must never forget what that means."

As if I ever knew, Jack thought, without speaking the words aloud. *As if I had any real idea of what is expected of me.*

"Who is it that you and the Lady keep talking about? Who do you think it is that will come for me?"

Two Bears leaned close. "Servants of the Void. It is the Void that seeks to destroy us all, Jack. Including—and perhaps especially—you."

The big man straightened and turned away. A smile creased his stern countenance. "I do not think I have ever seen such a beautiful sunset. Look, Jack. Have you ever seen such a vivid display of colors in the evening sky?"

He stepped out of the maintenance shed and pointed to where the sun was dropping below the horizon, the light already become diffuse and the sky brilliantly colored with reds and pinks. He pointed as Jack joined him, and together they stared as the colors deepened and spread, and the summer day closed with an explosion of color.

"Can't argue with you about how beautiful that was," Jack said quietly, smiling in spite of himself. "I don't know when . . ."

He turned to face Two Bears. ". . . I last saw one like . . ."

He trailed off into silence because the big man was gone, and he was alone.

Although the resultant feelings were still new to him, they were ones he would get used to in the months ahead.

HIS FIRST ENCOUNTER with the servants of the Void— humans themselves, but demon-driven—happened less than two weeks later. Thanks to the staff Two Bears had brought him, he was not as unprepared as they thought to find him.

He was working in the far southeast corner of the park— down toward the river amid a large grove of aged oaks and elms and a few unnamed species that were so gnarled and twisted that some called them witch trees—gathering up deadwood to dump in a trailer hitched behind his ATV. He had been working there all day, save for short pauses to drink cold coffee from his thermos and one half-hour lunch break. It was a Monday, the week new. The neighborhood kids were back to school and their parents hard at work either at home or their place of employ- ment. Traffic in the park had diminished to almost nothing— a few hikers; a mother with her very young children back near the entrance, where the big toys were located; and a fisherman who had passed by on his way down to the river.

He was alone and decidedly isolated when the three men ap- peared out of the trees, dressed in leathers and jackboots and bearing chains and lengths of pipe. Jack didn't see them at first, absorbed in his work, so they were almost on top of him before they finally managed to catch his attention.

"Looks like hard work," said one, a big fellow with a bushy beard and sleeves cut off to reveal arms the size of Jack's thighs. "Can't be much fun."

Jack shrugged. "It's what I'm hired to do." He gestured toward the piece of pipe the man was carrying. "You fellows come out here to help?"

Another man, small and lean and roped with muscle, almost every inch of his exposed body covered in ink, laughed. "Good one. 'Help him out,' he says." He turned to the third man. "Guess that's what we're here for, right, Albie?"

"Naw, we ain't here to help him out." The last man spit into the dirt and shifted the length of chain he was holding from one hand to the other. He gave Jack a hard look. "We're here to mess him up."

Jack already knew what this was about and who these three were. He'd been expecting someone, of course—but not these three, and not so soon. He was about to be tested and there would be no talking them out of it. Whatever had brought them here, whatever persuasion had been used, it was to accomplish one thing and one thing only.

To demonstrate, in no uncertain terms, that Jack needed to be taught a lesson.

Jack walked around to the side of the trailer, reached in, and withdrew the black staff. He didn't say anything as he did so. Nor did he say anything as he walked back around the end of the trailer and up to the big man with the bushy beard and swung the staff with such force that, when the other man raised the pipe to ward off the blow, the staff shattered the iron into pieces.

The big man stood staring at the six inches of pipe that remained clutched in his left hand, shock etched on his features.

"Get him!" Albie roared, charging forward, chain swinging.

They were on him instantly, all three, chains and pipe, and now the big man had dropped what remained of his shattered weapon and snatched a knife from beneath his leathers. Jack braced to meet them, knowing he was in trouble. But something strange happened. Turning to meet their rush, Jack found his staff alive with bits of fire, the markings that were carved into its length suddenly bright. Sparks and flames erupted all up and down its length, but Jack felt no heat on the exposed flesh of his hands,

The staff—seemingly of its own volition—took over the fight. Two quick strikes, short and sharply dealt, were delivered almost before Jack knew what he was going to do. Down went the big man with bushy beard, felled with a blow to the head, his knife skittering away. Down went the inked man, caught with a second blow that swept away the pipe he was carrying, hammering into his arm on the follow-through and breaking it; the crack was loud enough to be heard above the sounds of the struggle.

The last man, Albie, slowed, his features twisting into an animal-like snarl, words of hatred pouring from his mouth as he yanked out a gun. In Jack's hands, the staff dropped so that its blunt end was pointing at the man. A burst of fire exploded from its length, engulfed the gun and melted it instantly, then climbed Albie's arm in a hungry rush that sent him sprawling to the ground, where he rolled around in a desperate effort to smother the flames, howling as the fire licked hungrily at his clothing.

The struggle was over as quickly as it had begun. All three attackers lay prone, groaning and hugging themselves, eyes squeezed tight with pain, all the fight gone out of them. Jack walked over and looked down at them.

"Get out of this park and don't come back. Don't speak of this to anyone. Not one word of anything that's happened. If you do or if I see you here again—anywhere in this community— I promise you won't much like what happens."

He took a moment to look at each of them in turn, making sure they were looking back. "Do you know what I am?" he whispered in something approaching a hiss. "Do you have any idea?"

They cringed visibly. "You're the devil's spawn!" Albie cried, eyes wide with sudden realization.

Jack nodded. *Close enough.* "Get out of my sight."

He watched them scramble to their feet and make their way back the way they had come, muttering to themselves and one another, casting frightened looks back at him, beaten predators he did not think would return. He could not deny the keen sense of satisfaction he felt on having passed his first test as a Knight of the Word. Discovering what his staff could do and how well he could protect himself if it became necessary was a revelation.

But he still was unsure of what the Lady expected of him in return. His service was centered on a single event, and he still had no idea of its nature. His ignorance nagged at him, and he was stymied over what to do about it.

Those feelings would stay with him for years to come, and when they were finally resolved, it would not be a pleasant experience.

Six

THERE WERE NO further attempts at dissuading Jack from serving the Word following his encounter with the three thugs, and life went on pretty much as before.

He remained in his position as a park ranger for the municipality for several years, assigned to Sinnissippi Park and living in Hopewell. He moved out of his parents' home by the end of the summer and into an apartment of his own. His work was steady and satisfying, and he advanced to become assistant director and eventually director when the current officeholder decided to retire to Arizona.

From there, his situation advanced dramatically. Five years into his new job, he was appointed superintendent of parks and recreation for the entire county, and by the end of the following year had been asked to present at the National Convention of Parks and Recreation. He gave an impassioned speech about conservation in the face of rampant population growth, touching on the need for sustainable resources, which was well received and written up in several journals. Other administrators of parks and recreation facilities began coming to him for advice on issues of innovative development and nurturing of state and local parks, to the point where he became recognized as something of an expert.

He was soon in such demand that he opened a consulting business on the side and began supplying everything from advice to wide planning guides. By year's end, he was advising and consulting with members of his field in more than a dozen midwestern states.

His social life, however, did not fare as well. He had a number of women friends, but nothing approaching a serious relationship. There were choices and opportunities, but none of them really interested him. Some of this was due to a failure to find common ground with these women, as their connection was limited to social gatherings and small talk. Some of it was due to the demands of his job and his private advising work, which demanded long, frequently irregular hours. And some of it, he imagined, had a lot to do with his insistence on going everywhere with his black staff, no matter how inconvenient.

But mostly it was due to not finding anyone that excited him enough to want to pursue anything beyond a casual acquaintanceship.

Until he met Anne.

He first saw her at the annual National Convention of Parks and Recreation, two years following his first presentation, and it was an encounter that changed his life. He was there by invitation of the national board of administrators but was not presenting and had come only to hear what he hoped were new ideas and fresh approaches to management from others in the field.

She was partly there to meet him, but he didn't find that out until later.

The convention kicked off with a meet-and-greet cocktail party of invitees and guests, offering an opportunity to renew old acquaintances. But the opportunities to find the people he wanted to see were severely limited simply by the huge number of attendees and the obvious difficulties of being able to find anyone in a room packed with hundreds of bodies.

An hour into the event, his interest in remaining was winding down. He had failed to find more than two of the people with whom he had hoped to speak, and was actually on his way toward the exit when she stepped in front of him.

"Mr. McCall, do you have a minute?" she asked.

Her smile alone was enough to stop him in his tracks. He smiled back. "Sure, but call me Jack. Mr. McCall is my father."

She was tall and slender with curly blond hair cut short and startling blue eyes. He tried not to stare, but he was already lost.

"I'm Anne," she said and offered her hand. "I wanted to tell you how impressed I was with your speech on sustainable growth. I wasn't there, but I watched the video later when my boss gave me a copy. You were so impassioned, so clearly dedicated to doing what you believed to be the right thing. You don't see that often enough."

Jack smiled. "I think I got carried away, but thanks. So, what are you doing here this year? Have you started coming regularly?"

She laughed. "Hardly. My boss couldn't come and sent me in his place. I'm just a lowly assistant to the chief superintendent of the Seattle Park District, so I don't get many chances like this. I came to get my feet wet. But I was hoping to meet you as well, so we could talk a bit about your speech."

He smiled. "What are you doing right now?"

"What do you have in mind?"

"How about joining me for dinner?" He gave her a self-deprecating look. "In spite of my speaking prowess, I seem to find myself without a dinner partner, and I don't much care for eating alone. What do you say?"

Her smile was back, and he felt electrified in the glow it produced. "I would love to."

So off they went to dinner, and that was the beginning of everything that followed. While eating, they not only exchanged views on park management, but also ended up talking about themselves. Dinner courses came and went, and afterward—when Jack had time to reflect on it—he could not remember a single thing he had eaten. He had an instant connection with her on so many levels, it was astonishing. They shared a similar sense of humor, a larger worldview, a vision for park management, and even an agreement on movies and music.

By the end of the meal they were sharing much more personal parts of their history—he, for the first time in years, about his cancer; she, in a low, almost inaudible voice, about a violent attack she had suffered in college that had left her mute for almost a year. Their attraction for each other grew steadily stronger, and by the time Jack flew home again they had agreed they would like to see more of each other in the months ahead.

Within a month, he flew to Seattle to visit her, where she showed him around the city, visiting all the parks for which her department was responsible. He was so in love by then he could barely catch his breath, and was over the moon when it became clear she felt the same about him. The first night he spent at her apartment, Jack slept on the couch. By the second he was sharing her bed, and they were talking about a future together.

Within two months, he arranged for her to come visit him in Hopewell, where he introduced her to his parents and announced that they had decided to move in together. The sticking point was which city they would settle in, but it was resolved when she told him she could not leave her parents untended, as both were frail and in poor health. Jack never hesitated about moving, especially when she suggested that maybe it was time to let go of his municipal job and take up providing private management advice full-time. His parents, recognizing his strong attachment to this young woman whom they very much liked, urged him to go. They were older now, but still perfectly able to look after themselves. They would miss having him in Hopewell, but knew he had his own life to lead.

So he left his position as superintendent of parks, packed up his clothing and gear, and moved west, driving across the country. By the end of the year, he had begun advertising his availability as a parks management consultant to the Pacific Northwest public and become engaged. The wedding took place six months later, and for Jack McCall, a new life began.

He did not see Pick ever again. He would go back to Sinnissippi Park each time he returned to visit his parents and eventually to bury them, but neither of his fairy guardians ever showed themselves.

He did not hear again from the Lady in the years that followed, either. It was apparently not yet his time to serve. He did not come into contact with any other servants of the Void after that first encounter in the park, even though every day he kept expecting them to come for him once more.

He carried the black staff he had been given for protection everywhere he went but never told Anne the truth about it. He also never told her about the dreams the Lady had warned him to expect, in large part because the dreams hadn't yet appeared.

But when his marriage and his new life in Seattle were nearly ten years along, they suddenly did.

Seven

JACK HAD GONE to SeaTac Airport to pick up a client who was flying all the way from Texas to receive a management plan for the park district he worked for in Dallas–Fort Worth. It was a Saturday night in early April, and the airport was crowded with people flying in to their Seattle homes and flying out to other cities—a steady mix of arrivals and departures common to every weekend. Because of security regulations, Jack had to wait for his client in baggage claim. He was early, so he bought a *Seattle Times* and took a seat near one of the reader boards to wait for information on his client's flight to appear.

He had waited for perhaps fifteen minutes, glancing up every now and then, when a swarm of passengers from a Los Angeles flight poured off the escalators, making a beeline for their baggage carousel. He watched them as they descended, idly noting faces and their carry-on baggage, until finally he lost interest and went back to his newspaper.

It was not more than a minute or two when he became aware of a shadow falling over him, partially blocking the light he was using to read by.

"Is anybody sitting here?" a deep voice asked.

He glanced up at the thickset, rough-featured man in front of him, then at the empty seat beside him and gestured. "It's yours."

The man sat down. He was dressed in a suit, but it wasn't the kind of suit businessmen wore. In fact, it wasn't the kind of suit anyone wore these days, and it took Jack a minute to realize where he had last seen one like it. It was in a movie—a western although he couldn't remember the title—and a gunman had worn it. Then he remembered the cover to the original paperback of the novel *Shane,* an Old West tale about a gunslinger, and remembered he had seen it there, too. The suit was black and consisted of pegged pants, a frock coat with a white shirt beneath, a string tie, and leather boots. The man wearing these clothes was tall and rangy, and looked very athletic. He sat down next to Jack without looking at him for several long minutes, then he pulled out a hand-rolled cigarette and stuck it in the corner of his mouth, looking around the baggage area as if to assess the advisability of lighting up.

"You can't smoke in here," Jack told him mildly. "Rules."

The big man gave him a smile. "Rules. Always rules. They get in the way of everything. You ever think how much easier life would be if we didn't have rules?"

"Wouldn't things be a bit chaotic?"

"Exactly my point. Chaos would dominate every aspect of our lives, and only those strong enough to survive the chaos would be able to determine how our lives were shaped."

Jack stared. What was this about?

"I learned this awhile back—far enough back that I can hardly remember that period of time in my life," the man continued. "I've been who and what I am for longer than you've been alive, as a matter of fact. Much longer."

Jack was suddenly uneasy. "Funny. You don't look that old."

"I suppose I don't." The big man stretched, his face contorting momentarily with the effort, giving him a very unpleasant look. Then his features relaxed, and he was back to himself again. "I've aged pretty well, kept myself in good shape, made certain that I met the goals that were set for me and not allowed anything to stand in my way. Sounds rather self-serving, but at the end of the day, isn't that what we all do?"

Jack frowned. "I'm not sure I agree with that. Many of us believe it's in our nature to try to do things that serve the interests of others."

The other man laughed softly. "I know. But I also know that all those I have encountered who chose to follow that path are dead now." He paused. "Jack."

His name on the big man's lips caused Jack to reach for his black staff, which was cradled against his body. "How is it you know my name?"

He knew the answer already, of course—knew, as well, what this man was and why he was there. He just couldn't believe at first that it was finally happening. He had almost persuaded himself, with the passing of time, that it wouldn't. It had been almost twenty years since he had been challenged by the Void, but it appeared from this conversation that he was about to be challenged again.

"Relax," the other man said, making a dismissive gesture. "I'm not here to cause you any harm. I just wanted to introduce myself. I don't think we should remain strangers, given what I've come here to do. I think we should get to know each other, try to find out how we match up, see if we can decide who might win the confrontation we're eventually going to have. Maybe you'll decide it wouldn't be a good idea to risk that confrontation. Maybe you'll choose to back off and rid yourself of the burden of that black staff. Oh, I know what the staff is and what it can do. I've encountered it before a few times. It's not going to be enough, Jack."

"Is that so."

"Yep. I've been able to determine as much. Several times. Tells you something about me, doesn't it? See, there aren't many like me, Jack. Some others who called themselves Knights of the Word found that out the hard way. They made the mistake I spoke of earlier—the mistake of thinking that choosing the interests of others over their own was somehow correct. Those men are dead. And all of them died horribly. In a lot of pain. Saw their loved ones die, too. It would be a shame if you were to make the same mistake."

Jack nodded slowly. "Not very subtle, are you? Who are you, anyway? What's your name? You already know mine. I should know yours."

The man in the gunslinger clothes shook his head. "I don't have a name. I'm only a rumor. No one wants to know the name of someone like me. They just hope we never come face-to-face. When they see me, they turn around and walk the other way. Could be that's what you should do, Jack."

"Could be. How did you find me, anyway? How did you even learn where I was?"

"Oh, it's a gift. A sort of sixth sense. I can smell you. Smell out any and all Knights of the Word. I can track them, find where they have their hidey-holes and ferret them out. You, I came across by chance. I was staying in a hotel where you were attending a forestry conference or some such. Knew you for what you were immediately. Found out your name and address from the enrollment forms—with a little help of a young lady working the tables. She didn't want to let me see them, but I changed her mind. I've come all the way from Los Angeles to meet you."

"I imagine Los Angeles is missing you already."

The big man snickered. "Funny." He looked off into space a moment and then back at Jack. "Let me explain what is going to happen. I've come to Seattle, I've found you here, I will find where you live, I will get to know all about your family and friends, I will make myself a part of your life, and there is nothing you can do to stop me. You can, however, rid yourself of me by being smart enough to avoid the mistakes of those other Knights of the Word I've been forced to dispatch. You can throw down your staff and walk away from your commitment to the Word. Do that, and you will be safe."

Jack felt a shiver of fear in spite of himself. He thought of Anne and the children—his daughter ten, his son only a baby—placed at risk from this monster. His friends, as well. But he held his ground because to show doubt or fear now would be a mistake.

"Maybe I don't believe you are as powerful as you seem to think."

The big man nodded slowly and got to his feet. "Well, that's as it may be. Let's give it a little time, see how things shake out." He touched his nose with one finger. "Be seeing you."

Off he walked without looking back. Jack watched him pass down the line of carousels until he found the one he was looking for, reclaim a black satchel, and walk toward an exit. Just before he got there, he turned back and gave Jack a final look.

Then he was gone, taking with him any chance Jack might have had of being able to stop looking over his shoulder in the days ahead.

Eight

THE FIRST OF the dreams promised by the Lady almost twenty years earlier arrived that same night. It arrived as dreams do, uninvited and unannounced, and in this case unwelcome. By the time it showed itself, Jack was deep asleep, with Anne curled up beside him. Ten-year-old Mila was tucked away in her bedroom down the hall, and the baby, Jack, Jr.—at fourteen months no longer requiring nighttime feedings but still prone to the occasional unscheduled nighttime waking—was in his railing-enclosed bed in the adjoining alcove where they could hear him cry should he unexpectedly wake.

Farther down the hall, the family cat—an orange tabby named Scoot, who had been rescued from the streets by Mila—was asleep in the laundry.

The lights inside the house were all extinguished except for one nightlight in the bathroom and a second in the alcove wall. Outside the skies were heavily clouded, erasing any trace of moon or stars and leaving the surrounding neighborhood wrapped in a hazy, misty half-light generated by a combination of city streetlights reflecting off the low-hanging brume and a few neighborhood porch lights.

Jack had managed to spend most of the evening not thinking about the man at the airport, having dismissed him from his thoughts after meeting his client and driving him to his nearby hotel. The memory remained, however, and refused to be so easily banished; the man's thinly veiled threats were troubling.

But on crawling into bed that night, Jack's mind went back to their meeting, and the unpleasant realization of who and what the man was, and lingered until he fell asleep.

And so the dreams began.

HE HEARS WHAT he thinks are the furtive sounds of someone creeping about outside his house, and he sits up immediately, alert and ready. Rising from his bed, he picks up the black staff, goes to the front door, and steps outside. The night is hazy and his surroundings indistinct. While there is no explanation for it, he is fully dressed and wearing a coat against the chill. He looks around, decides that the sounds he was hearing were from someone who had slipped away, and decides to go after them. It is a foolish decision; he is leaving his family alone and unprotected, but he goes anyway because somehow, some way, he knows he must.

He crosses his yard to the front sidewalk and turns up the dark-ened street. The one he is tracking has gone this way. Again, he just knows, although he does not understand why. He moves quickly up the street, anxious to discover if what he searches for presents a threat to his family, anxious to put a stop to it. He spies movement in the darkness ahead, a glimpse of a momentary shadow sliding across the edges of a circle of light from a streetlamp, there and gone again in an instant.

Got you, *he thinks.*

Sprinting ahead, he reaches the spot where his prey had given itself away, but there is no one there. He casts about, then spies faintly glowing paw prints indented in the soft grass to one side. Paw prints signal that whatever he chases is not human. He notes the size of the prints. Huge, deep outlines indicate something big and heavy—something much larger than he is. A creature of the Void, in all likelihood. A demon.

An ordinary man would turn back at this point, but he is a Knight of the Word and possesses the power of his black staff, which can overcome anything. There will be no hesitation, no turning back, no second thoughts.

He continues on, proceeding more quickly than before, his eyes scanning the gloom. He is moving between a screen of residences now, crossing a series of backyards, turning down alleyways, still following the faintly glowing tracks; the paw prints leave a clear, unmistakable trail for him to follow. He finds himself thinking that perhaps he is moving too quickly, rushing to a confrontation he might not be ready for. But the freshness of the tracks compels him to continue.

Then, abruptly, he reaches a neighborhood of stately old houses, most of which have been here for more than sixty years. They speak of stature and money, and they straddle portions of the tangled old growth that comprises Schmitz Park.

He has no idea how he has gotten this far from home. He is miles away by now. Impossible.

He slows now. The tracks are visible as he crosses Admiral to the park entrance, an open invitation. Come in; see if you can catch me. *This time Jack hesitates. There are no lights in the park, and the shadows cast by the great old trees are deep and concealing. Mingled with the drifting trailers of mist, they create a heavy blanket of gloom over the entire park. There is a silence emanating from that fortress of trunks and limbs that is unsettling. No sounds are audible, and nothing moves in the darkness.*

He is momentarily undecided.

Then, his decision made, he proceeds across the car lanes and into the thicket of Schmitz Park's formidable undergrowth, keeping to the pathways. Behind him, the last of the streetlights disappear. He is alone now, wrapped in mist and darkness.

To his left, shadows move suddenly, as something attacks. His hands lift his staff to protect himself. He is struck a blow that sends him sprawling and everything goes dark.

HE WAS IN his bed when he woke again—only this time for real—shocked out of his sleep by what he had dreamed. He waited until his head had cleared itself of the lingering aftereffects from his nightmarish dream and went into the bathroom. Once he had relieved himself and drunk some water, he walked down to the kitchen to find Scoot pawing at the back door and meowing. Since the cat was a stray and spent large amounts of time outdoors anyway, Jack didn't hesitate to open the door and let him out. Scoot was gone in a flash of orange fur, leaving Jack peering blindly into the darkness as if he might somehow see something from his dream. But there was nothing there.

After a few minutes of staring, he closed and locked the door and went back to bed.

Immediately the dream returned.

HE IS PICKING himself up off the ground now, aware that a night bird—likely an owl—has flown into his head, striking him a glancing blow but causing no other damage. He stands where he is for a few minutes, regaining his composure, waiting for his eyes

*to adjust to the darkness. They do so quickly, allowing him to lo-
cate the vague outline of a pathway that runs deeper into the park.*

*He no longer sees the glowing paw prints on the ground before
him.*

Until, suddenly, they appear again.

*He sets off to track them to their source, angry now at this in-
trusion into his sleep, but worried as well, as it increasingly appears that magic is at work. And not the good kind. Whatever is
out there is making a point of toying with him, always staying a
step ahead and just out of reach. But this will end soon enough
because he will catch up to his elusive prey and put an end to this
hunt.*

*Deep into Schmitz Park he walks, following the tracks, which
are staying on the pathway. Nothing has changed, and increasingly nothing seems to make any sense. Several times he thinks to
turn back, to end this foolishness. Let this creature he hunts go its
own way. Go back to bed and get some sleep before the night is
over. He will have other chances to encounter whatever leads him
on, and better opportunities for settling matters. All he is doing
now is wasting time and energy.*

*Yet he hates to give up. He hates to admit defeat, however tem-
porary or questionable.*

*He continues on. He walks until he reaches the darkest part of
the park and slows. Something waits on the path ahead—
something huge and unidentifiable in the gloom. The glowing
tracks end where it stands, fading away even as he watches.*

*He hesitates and then moves forward. The nearer he goes, the
less he can tell of what awaits. But his instincts scream to him in
warning. This is something very dangerous. This may be too
much for him.* Turn back now!

*But he doesn't, and suddenly he realizes that whatever has been
waiting is coming toward him. It seems to grow larger as it ad-
vances while at the same time becoming even less distinct. It is a
shadow, a patch of gloom, a monstrous gathering of inky darkness
formed out of a combination of his fears and uncertainty.*

It is his own death.

He attacks furiously, charging to meet its advance, determined to banish it or kill it or do whatever else is needed, but still it comes for him.

And then he realizes in horror that the magic of his staff is not responding, and the thing on the trail is on top of him, bearing him down, swallowing him up. He has no defenses, nothing left to turn to . . .

THIS TIME, WHEN he woke, he was sweating and had wrapped himself in the sheets and blankets. All of them. Anne was asleep next to him, but her huddled form suggested she was probably more than a little chilled. So he untangled himself and draped the bedding over her, careful not to wake her. Then he got up again and went back into the bathroom for another drink of water.

When he emerged, he paused. Something was drawing him toward the kitchen. He went down the hallway in the darkness, aware suddenly that he had left his staff in the bedroom. The doors were locked, the house quiet, and his instincts would have warned him if there were an intruder.

Still, something did not feel right.

He entered the kitchen and looked around. Nothing. He listened to the night for several long moments and heard only silence. He almost went back to bed and then remembered Scoot. Walking over to the back door, he turned on the porch light and looked out.

And saw what was left of Mila's cat scattered in pieces all over the walkway.

Nine

JACK SLEPT POORLY for the rest of the night, the dreams gone, but still a fresh, raw memory. It was bad enough that the dream had left him feeling as if he had been a witness to his own death—caused in no small part by the failure of his black staff, his sole protection as a Knight of the Word, to ward him against a creature of the Void. The fear that the talisman on which he relied so heavily might somehow fail him was distressing. But finding poor old Scoot eviscerated on his back porch—a real-life horror and not a dream—was worse.

On discovering the remains of the cat, he had acted quickly to remove all traces. He did not want Mila to wake and find Scoot's remains when she walked out the door. So he had thrown on a coat and slipped on his work boots and gloves and gone out into the yard in the dead of night to remove the evidence. He gathered up the remains, placed them in an old shoebox, then retrieved a shovel from the garage to dig a hole. It was cold, and the ground was hard. It was miserable work, but it had to be done. It took him about an hour to complete, and when he had finished by hosing down the walkway, he came back into the house to find Anne waiting in bed with the light on and a book in her hands.

"What was that all about?" she asked, giving him a look that suggested he best not sugarcoat it.

But he did anyway, unwilling as yet to reveal everything he knew—especially about the agent of the Void who had approached him at the airport and threatened to harm not only himself but also Anne and the children. So he simply said he had heard something outside—a fight of some sort—and found Scoot dead in the yard. He had buried the cat and would tell Mila in the morning. Must have been a large predator, he suggested, so he would need to warn the neighbors to keep a close eye on their pets and children for the next week or so, just in case it returned.

"It was pretty brutal," he added. "Poor old Scoot."

Anne didn't question him on the details, but he thought she suspected there was more to the story. They could always sense that about each other—that feeling of something being held back or watered down. Their unspoken pact to always be truthful with each other allowed them to see beyond words and expressions to what was in the eyes and heart. But Jack had never told Anne about his encounter with Two Bears or the Lady, had never mentioned his trip to Wales and the Fairy Glen, and had never said a word about his commitment as a Knight of the Word and the real purpose of the black staff he always carried with him.

He did not think now was the time to do so, either—even though he knew in his heart that what had happened to Scoot was not a coincidence and had nothing to do with wild animals. The arrival of the man in black almost certainly signaled the start of the struggle the Lady had warned about, but he had to be absolutely sure before he even thought about confiding in his wife.

And he wasn't at all sure he could make himself do so even then.

So when morning arrived, he rose, showered and dressed, waited for Mila to come down to breakfast, and broke the news about Scoot. He did not go into any details, but she was bright enough and old enough that she understood what had happened. She cried a bit before announcing she would make a marker for Scoot and put it on his grave, so she would always remember him. Jack hugged her and told her he loved her and promised he would come take a look at the marker once she had it ready to place. He said Mommy would come look, too, and maybe each one of them would tell a story or two about Scoot so that they would always remember him.

It was still early when he walked from his home to the grocery store five blocks away for orange juice, milk, and a newspaper. Seattle was a series of neighborhood communities, each identified by a specific name. There was Queen Anne, Capitol Hill, Magnolia, Ballard, Green Lake, the U District, and several more, all clustered about the downtown core. Jack and Anne lived in West Seattle, which occupied a peninsula that lay on the other side of Elliott Bay and directly across from the city.

They were actually close to the southern border of their neighborhood, not far from Lincoln Park and the Vashon Island ferry terminal. It was a mixed residential and small-business community, which Jack liked, because everything from gas stations to grocery stores to Starbucks to cleaners and a few cafés and bistros were an easy walk from home. There was a sense of belonging that he hadn't found anywhere else since he had married Anne, and not since Hopewell from before.

He entered the grocery store, grabbed a basket, and began to move up and down the aisles, picking out not only the items he had come for but also a few others he decided he might need. He was lost in thought and not paying any attention to who was around him until a shadow blocked his path, and he knew even before he finished looking up who it was.

The man he had encountered at the airport, still wearing the same black ensemble, stood there smiling. "Fancy meeting you again so soon," he said.

"Does seem like an odd coincidence," Jack agreed.

"Not so odd. It's my neighborhood store now, too. At least for a while." He paused, as if assessing Jack. "Hope you don't mind my saying so, but you look a bit tired this morning. Bad night, was it?"

"What do you think?"

Another smile. "I think your family lost a cat."

Jack looked away for a moment. "Yep. Wild animals. Never know what they'll do or where you'll find them these days."

"True enough. Got to keep a sharp eye out." The man gave a shrug. "Well, best be on my way. I expect we'll see each other again before too long. Give my regards to your wife and kids."

"I don't think I'll be doing that. Don't think I'll be seeing you around for much longer, either."

"Oh, I wouldn't bet on that. And one thing more. You should start pretending you're talking on your cell because, at the moment, it looks like you're talking to yourself. All these other folks?" He gestured. "They can't see me. Only you can."

"My bad luck, I guess. Maybe that will change."

"Maybe. Maybe not." The man touched the brim of his black hat. "Sorry about your cat."

Jack stared at him expressionlessly. "No, you're not."

The big man laughed. "No, I guess I'm not. But it was sort of cute. I hated to mess it up like that."

He was starting to walk past when Jack grabbed his arm and held him fast, their faces only inches apart. "Sometimes, it's best to leave well enough alone. Otherwise, your luck can turn on you. And that can be a nasty."

The man studied him calmly, then gently but firmly extracted his arm. "Likely we'll find out, won't we?"

He walked away, turned a corner at the end of the aisle, and disappeared.

JACK WENT HOME, thinking about what he should do. The demon was making no pretense at being anything but what it was. It was also making no effort to conceal its intentions regarding what was in store for Jack and his family. The need to alert Anne had taken on new urgency. If the demon intended to get to Jack through Anne or the children, didn't they need to be aware enough of the danger so they could be on the lookout? Certainly Anne was entitled to a warning. The baby was too little to understand any of this, and Mila was too young to have to deal with it even knowing what it meant.

So shouldn't he at least tell Anne?

But if he did, what then? What would she be able to do to protect herself? If the demon could get as close to Jack as it had already demonstrated it could, what chance did Anne have of avoiding it? She could lock herself and the kids in their house and stay there until this was over, but somehow Jack knew that even doing that wouldn't be enough to protect them.

But mostly—and certainly selfishly—he did not want Anne to find out about his connection to the Word and the Lady. He was afraid of what it would do to their marriage and to their lives as a couple. Would she even believe him, or would she think him deranged? There was every reason for her to question his story and even insist he go in for therapy. If she were the one telling him what he was considering telling her, that would be his first response. He would feel sorry for her, want to help her through whatever was troubling her, and book her an appointment immediately.

None of which would help protect them from the demon.

No, he decided after he was within half a block of their home. He couldn't do it. It was too much to ask her to believe. No matter how sincere he sounded, no matter how hard he tried, she would never be able to do it. He wouldn't have believed it, either, if he hadn't witnessed it and hadn't been exposed to the Lady and the creatures of the Fairy Glen. Just talking about it wasn't enough. You had to be there.

He stopped just outside his doorway, thinking. Could he take Anne to the Fairy Glen and persuade the Lady to tell her it was all true? Would the Lady even meet with them if he tried? Was there time enough for him to do this? What about Mila and Jack, Jr.? What would they do with the children while this was happening?

No, Jack realized at once. Taking her to Wales was only avoiding the inevitable. Sooner or later, he was going to have to face the demon. He made up his mind almost instantly about what he would have to do. It was a compromise, but it was sensible and would remove his family from the danger they would otherwise be in. At the same time, it would leave him free to find a way to remove the threat.

He entered his home and walked back to where Anne was sitting on the living room couch, reading, the baby wrapped in his blanket and asleep on the cushion beside her. Mila must be upstairs, working on Scoot's grave marker.

His wife looked up as he joined her and recognized at once the determined look on his face. "What?"

"I'm going to ask you to do something. You're not going to want to agree, but you have to. I will try to explain what I'm asking for and why it is so important, although you probably won't be satisfied when I'm finished. But this is one of those times you're just going to have to trust me. Knowing me the way you do, you will have to accept that I would never ask it of you otherwise."

She grinned. "Okay. So, who is this other woman you're throwing me over for?"

He sighed. "I wish it were that simple; that would be easier to talk about. I better just tell you."

She quit smiling at once and sat back to listen.

Ten

TWO DAYS LATER, an hour or so after midday, Jack bundled his little family into their SUV, along with fully packed suitcases, and set off for a limo service located at the edge of town. Under normal circumstances, he would have ordered a pickup at home, but now he was taking no chances. He did not go directly to the service, but drove around a bit, watching for signs of anyone following. When he was convinced no one was, he went straight to the service and unloaded Anne and the children and luggage.

"I don't like this idea," his wife told him while he was driving. "I don't like the idea of taking Mila out of school like this, and I don't like leaving you."

He nodded. "And you don't like it that I won't tell you why I'm doing it."

"That, too. Although I imagine you have what you believe to be very good reasons. And you will tell me them once this is over. Whenever that is."

"My word of honor. Everything. But I cannot emphasize enough how much I need to put some distance between myself and you and the children until then. If I want this to end well,

I have to know that I won't be putting you in danger. I would never ask this of you if I didn't love you so much and know that you believe I am doing what I think is best to protect you."

She nodded without speaking. In the back, Mila was singing a pop song she had recently fallen in love with. Better a song than a boy, he thought. Although it wouldn't be all that long until things went the other way.

"This isn't anything illegal?" Anne pressed him. "You're sure about that?"

"Very sure. It has nothing to do with legal or illegal. It has to do with right and wrong, in the moral sense. Look, don't ask me to talk about it now. Please."

She was quiet after that, and the remainder of the drive was spent in a cone of silence, save for Mila's singing.

At the limo facility, she embraced him, kissed him hard, and hugged him to her. Mila was standing by, holding Jack, Jr., in her small, protective arms.

"Don't let anything happen to you," Anne whispered. "Don't get hurt." She hugged him harder. "Don't leave us."

He nodded into her shoulder, hugged her back, and broke away, moving quickly to the SUV. "Call me when you get there," he called back over his shoulder. "Love you. Love you all."

He climbed into his car and watched them walk inside. From here, they would go to Portland where they would stay with Anne's aunt and uncle until he drove down to bring them home. No airports, which he had briefly considered and dismissed. Maybe it was because the demon had appeared at the airport, and even the thought of choosing that form of transportation made him uncomfortable. Better to use something more private and less easily tracked. If his family was away from Seattle, the demon couldn't get to them as easily and Jack might worry a little less for their safety. Of course, it had meant telling Anne what to do without telling her why, but that was better than telling her nothing.

It was awkward, and sad. He knew he was betraying her. He

knew she loved and trusted him and would never think he was doing something that would hurt her or their children. She did point out that they had always agreed to trust each other and keep no secrets, and he acknowledged this had always been the case. But this one time, he needed her to grant him a dispensation. One time, and one time only.

It was a fresh betrayal. He was not telling her about the staff or the Lady or his agreement to serve her. He was not revealing the truth about the demon and the threat it presented. Maybe it was because keeping these secrets was by now so common a practice. Maybe it was because he genuinely believed it was safer for her not to know, especially now that she and the children needed his protection. Whatever the case, he had kept the truth to himself and told her something else entirely.

She had reluctantly agreed, though he could see the skepticism in her eyes. How much he would tell her later, he wasn't sure. He supposed he would worry about that when the time came. Or *if* it came. Because he couldn't ignore the possibility that he might not come out of this in one piece—or even alive. But this was the time the Lady had told him about all those years ago—the one time he would have to serve as her Knight of the Word. He had sworn to do so, and he would not break his word.

At least then his service would be ended, and his life with Anne and Mila and Jack, Jr., would return to the way it had been before. He had to believe that would happen. He had to believe he could make it happen.

He drove into his driveway and parked the car. Got out and went inside. The day was already growing hotter, and the air was still and sultry. Not a day for working in the yard. A day for a nap, he decided suddenly. The urge to rest was so strong he could not resist it, though he might have tried harder if he had not welcomed a chance to escape his thoughts. Within seconds he was curled up on the couch, fast asleep.

In his sleep, he dreamed. A dark, devastatingly real night-

mare in which either Anne or Mila had been taken by the
demon and imprisoned in the old Winston house, close by Lincoln Park. The dream was fragmented, bits and pieces revealing a future so horrific he could barely stand to watch it unfold.
A phone call to Jack from the demon—the details of which were
implied rather than elucidated—if Jack failed to come save
them. The voice, but little more, of Ineke, who remained a mystery, reminding him of who and what he was. The promise of a
confrontation that would strip him of everything he treasured
in his life.

When he woke, the details of the dream faded. Jack was left
confused and filled with doubt, and he kept his eyes closed as he
tried to recall everything he had been shown. But the specifics
eluded him. Who was Ineke? She had featured prominently in
the dream, yet he had never heard the name before. Were Anne
and Mila in danger—either of them—or was this an empty
threat?

He lay where he was, waiting for his heartbeat to slow and
his pulse to steady. He started to drift again, oddly weary. As he
did, a by now familiar voice spoke to him, small and light and
ethereal. No face showed itself, no surroundings framed the
speaker. There was only blackness, and words spoken in a whisper.

Come to Lincoln Park at sunset tonight.
Ineke.

WHEN HE WOKE again, no more than an hour had passed, but
it felt as if he had slept all day. A glance out the window and
then at the clock told him it was just past midafternoon. The
words spoken in his sleep had stayed with him, fresh and new.

Come to Lincoln Park at sunset tonight.

They were real, even if their source remained a mystery.
How could he be sure Ineke was not a minion of the demon? Or
even the demon, itself? There was every reason to believe this
was a trap. Hadn't the dream warned him of what was waiting?

Hadn't he been told the demon had his wife or daughter? Or both? How was he to know if the second speaker and summons were not the demon's work, too?

Yet instinct told him they weren't, and he knew already that he would do as he had been told.

The remainder of the day passed in a blur, a waking dream in which he found things to do and things to avoid without distinguishing between the two. He ate an early dinner to allow time enough to reach the park on foot, and by the end of the daily commute he had set out. It was not that far from his home, and he preferred to leave the car and allow himself the freedom to move as quickly as necessary, should circumstances make it advisable. On foot, you could always run in any direction you chose. That might be a reaction to his already overactive imagination but having met the demon and seen what had been done to Scoot, he was not inclined to take chances.

As the sun slipped behind the Olympics west, he reached the park and entered through the Beach Drive parking lot. A few cars still sat waiting for their owners, but mostly it was empty. Shadows cast by the great old conifers were already lengthening to overlap the paths that led into the park, eating up the last of the light cast by the vanishing sun. Somewhere distant, he could hear children's voices, although it was hard to pinpoint their direction. An elderly couple passed him on the trail, nodding silently, but otherwise he saw no one.

He came here often, usually to think, but sometimes to escape his life, too. Not in the sense that it was too depressing to face, but because the change of scenery always proved refreshing. It was calming in the park, and foreign enough that you could leave your life behind for a bit simply by immersing yourself in a magical country you could not find anywhere else. He had always felt that way about parks—that they were magical. He had always found them soothing, a balm for the troubles, worries, pains, and losses that saddled him in his other life, so it was always good to abandon those for a bit before stepping back into the fray. It was his legacy from his youth, the feeling with which he had been left after coming out of his bout with cancer—and his successful battle with the dragon Desperado—those long-ago childhood rites of passage. Parks were healing, and none more so than those with forests and hills and rivers and that precious, longed-for sense of otherworldliness.

He had no idea where he was supposed to go, how long to wait, or what to expect. So he went to his favorite bench, his resting place for when he needed to sit and think. No one was there, and he was able to claim the bench for himself as the last of the light was leached from the sky and the world about him turned dark.

He gripped his black staff tightly and waited.

Waited some more.

Come on, come on!

But nothing happened, and no one appeared. The darkness deepened, the park emptied of occupants, and his thoughts drifted.

He thought about Anne and the kids, wondering if they were at her aunt's yet, wondering if his wife might have called. But she would have called him on his cell, which he carried in his pocket; he could feel it pressing against his thigh. There was no reason he wouldn't have felt it vibrate, had she rung him. But he worried anyway. His family was everything, and he could not help thinking of what it would mean if anything happened to them.

"The demon counts on that, you know," a familiar voice said.

Soft, whispery, and feminine—the voice from his dream. He didn't look for the speaker. It was too dark to see much by now anyway. "I suppose it does," he replied. "Hard for me to pretend I don't care, though."

He caught a flicker of light out of the corner of his eye, and then a creature of small size and little substance was standing in front of him. She was no bigger than a human child, but was something else entirely. Her face was chalk white save for her rosebud mouth and eyes wreathed in dark circles. Her hair was wispy and oddly colorless, framing her haunted features and trailing from her bare limbs. She wore diaphanous clothing from which small bits of light emanated, floating through the fabric as if through water, living embodiments of something Jack could only guess at.

"You're Ineke, aren't you?" he asked. He took a further moment to study her. "Are you a fairy creature?"

"I am a tatterdemalion," she answered, moving closer. "The Lady has sent me to you as a gift. I am to be your guide and, for the time I am allotted, a voice of reason should your darker nature surface. Which I fully expect it will."

Ineke. The name in his dream. He glanced down again at her clothing, at the things moving within its rippling surface, fascinated. She seemed to be little more than an image projected on the night air.

Her eyes flicked down to where he was looking. "I am made of the memories and dreams of human children that have died young and been forgotten. Bits and scraps of their lives are all that are left behind of them, and magic shapes and binds them to me until I am no more. Then they will scatter to seek new forms in which to reside and provide nourishment. But I am them, and they me, until then."

She glanced down at herself. "You see what remains of them and how they have become me." She paused, looking up at him again. "Your own life is not so different, Jack McCall. You are in your heart and in your essence the sum of your memories and dreams. Do you not feel it is so?"

He did. "Where are you to guide me?" he asked.

"To the demon's lair, but more important, to yourself. To a better understanding of how you must prepare for the confrontation awaiting you—for the challenge you face, and the fears and doubts you harbor that will hinder your efforts to withstand the power of a creature of the Void. You will be tested, you know."

"Did you send me a dream this afternoon?" he asked, and quickly described it. He could not seem to help himself. "Did you tell me that the demon has my family?"

She regarded him solemnly. "I sent no dreams. I lack such power. Dreams are the province of the Lady."

"Would she have sent me such a dream?"

"You are a Knight of the Word. Your dreams tell you of the future you will face if you fail in the present. Perhaps you are testing yourself. Have you fears and doubts you cannot manage?"

He frowned. "None, if my family is safe." He hesitated. "Wait."

He pulled out his cell phone, checked it, and waited. It rang through to Anne's answering service, and he left a hurried message for her to call him back.

He put the cell away. "I can't be sure. If I knew, maybe . . ."

"What is true is that however well you prepare yourself, you can never be sure of anything where demons are concerned. You must know it will not let you escape so easily. It will find a way it believes it can break you, and you will not necessarily see it coming. The nature of your challenge requires that you be ready, which means you must be true to your oath as a Knight of the Word and not betray the trust of the Lady or the code by which you have lived."

He thought it over. "All right. I see what you mean. I will welcome whatever help you can provide. Starting now."

Her taut, parchment-white face brightened. "I am at your service, Jack McCall. But we don't have much time."

"Because?"

She gave him a troubled look. "Because it probably already knows what you've done with your family."

Jack felt his chest constrict. "How could it know something like that? I only made the decision yesterday evening."

"Well." Ineke looked perplexed. "It's a demon. Demons find things out whether you want them to or not."

"Then Anne is in danger? And Mila and Jack, Jr.?"

"It would be best if you acted quickly to help protect them."

"How do I do this?" He spat it out, suddenly frantic. "How do I help them?"

"Confront the demon. Put an end to it."

"Now? Right now?"

"Now would be best. Are you ready to do it?"

Jack felt as if his world were collapsing around him. This was not supposed to have happened. He was supposed to have made Anne and the children safe by sending them away. Apparently, he had guessed wrong. As a result, his choices of what to do about the demon, and how soon to act against it, were reduced to one.

"Where is it?" he asked wearily.

Ineke turned away. "I will show you."

THEY WALKED TOGETHER through Lincoln Park, traveling south under an umbrella of hardwood limbs and in the shadow of towering conifers. The park had turned dark, the sky bright with moon and stars. No clouds lingered to disturb the firmament's majesty, the air had gone warmer, and the winds had died away almost completely. There was a hush to the place, a quietness that left the faint sounds of cars and voices and doors slamming the only indicators of life beyond the park's boundaries. And even these seemed to belong to another time and place, momentary interruptions in the otherwise deep stillness.

"Where are we going?" Jack asked. He thought he already knew, but he didn't want to speak the words. He was aware of his hands clasping his staff too tightly, and he forced himself to loosen his grip and breathe deeply to relieve the pressure in his chest. If anything were to happen to Anne or the children, he didn't know what he would do. The possibility haunted him, as had the cancer he had been diagnosed with all those years ago. It left him emptied of every consideration but finding a way to protect them from the demon's threat.

Ineke's small face glanced up at him. "It's not far."

The demon was a monster. It possessed no moral center and no conscience. It served the Void, and by doing so had abandoned both long ago. It did what it was told to do and never questioned the reasons. It commanded tremendous power, magic that might have no recognizable boundaries, no limits, and no control. Jack had sensed all this in his conversation with the Lady, all without being told—a sort of understanding that went with his agreement to serve as a Knight of the Word.

But the reality was overwhelmingly different. It was one thing to sense a possibility in the abstract and another entirely to encounter it as reality. He had thought he could overcome any challenge he might face, having overcome a dragon and a cancer. But both seemed long ago now and far away, and the immediacy of the threat from this frock-coated demon was both devastating and inevitable in a way he had not anticipated.

Suddenly he was something he had not been since he was a boy.

He was afraid.

"How can I defeat this demon?" he asked Ineke after long moments of silence.

She pursed her lips. "It will lie and attempt to deceive you. It will use whatever you fear most against you. It will seek to break you down before it attacks you, and then it will use its magic to smash apart your defenses and destroy you." She paused. "You must not allow it. You must resist."

"With my staff?"

"The staff will help. It serves as sword and shield, and it can give you the means to destroy your demon enemy. But it is your courage and strength of will that will aid you most."

She slowed and stopped. They were just within the fringe of the trees at the south end of the park. Ahead, from beyond a rise they were approaching, he could see the roofs and lighted windows of the neighborhood homes bordering Beach Drive. He caught himself as he realized he was standing in front of the hill on which he had stood in his dream when he had viewed the demon's haven.

"The old Winston house," he murmured. Just as he had feared. Just as shown to him in his dream of earlier that afternoon. He wondered at once if Anne was inside.

"The demon waits for you," Ineke murmured back. *Did I speak the words aloud without realizing it?* "It may have friends who will aid it. Creatures of the Void come over from the darkness to give it an edge in its battle. They will try to distract you. They will try to turn you from your efforts to reach their leader. Do not let them do so; cast them away from you."

"Cast them away?" *What is the tatterdemalion talking about?*

"See them for what they are. Demons and demonkind disguise themselves to hide the truth of what they are and pretend at being what they are not. Remember this. Protect yourself from the lies and deceits that cloak them all."

He shook his head. "How can I do this? All by myself, how can I survive what's coming?"

She reached up and brushed his cheek with her small white fingers. "The Lady chose you because she saw in you something she has not seen in others. The demon you face is a killer of Knights of the Word. It is a hunter of our champions, and it has slain many. Did it not tell you this itself?"

It had, Jack remembered, there at SeaTac Airport, that first time it had appeared before him and revealed itself. He understood now. "This is what she was waiting for," he whispered. "For this assassin to come seeking me so that, where others had failed, I might succeed. She thinks I can do what all those other Knights of the Word could not. But what if she is wrong?"

Ineke shook her head slowly, her feathery white hair a whiff of smoke against the night. She paused for a long time, her eyes boring into him, her features composed. "Do not ask yourself that question, Jack McCall. Do not even think it, or you are lost."

Jack stared in hopeless understanding. Ask it, and you have already lost, the tatterdemalion was telling him. Ask it, and you are ceding ground you cannot afford to relinquish. Put aside your doubts and fears. Trust in who and what you are and in the magic you wield.

His cell vibrated against his thigh and he pulled it from his pocket, glancing at the ID. *Anne!* He triggered the talk button at once. "Anne?"

"She's right here with me, Jack," the demon said. "But she's not taking any calls. Care to leave a message?"

Jack went cold clear through.

Eleven

THE DEMON HAD known right away what Jack McCall would do, able to read his thinking as easily as if it were its own. McCall would attempt to spirit his family to safety—to put them beyond reach—while he fulfilled his obligations as a Knight of the Word. He had sworn an oath, and he was the sort of man who felt that such oaths should be kept. With his family out of the way and presumably hidden from his adversary, he would stand against the demon in battle.

A futile effort, of course. He would end up just as dead as the others. He would end his life begging for mercy. But it was the gesture that counted to such men as McCall. It was the carrying out of his duty—his adherence to the promise he had made, strengthened by the knowledge that he had acted with honor—that mattered above all else. With his family protected, he would not waver, though it cost him his life.

The logical course of action was to not give him the satisfaction of knowing his beloved family was safe, but to make sure they were not.

It was easy enough to take the steps necessary to make that happen. An intercept on his phones—cell and home—to monitor his calls. A late-night visit to the limousine service to arrange for a look at the assignments, followed by a further visit to the driver's home to arrange for him to be replaced. Then nothing more to do but to wait for McCall to deliver his wife and children to the limo service, where he would confidently place them in the hands of his enemy to be spirited away.

But even demons can misjudge.

Anne McCall was not some simpering, easily frightened victim who would fall apart at the first sign of trouble. Long before she had met Jack, she had been a strong, determined young woman who had excelled at all levels in both academics and sports.

In college, she had been attacked, beaten, and violated, and had spent two years afterward recovering from the trauma. Therapy and an intense determination to find a way back had allowed her to heal. Even the failure of the authorities to identify and catch the perpetrators had not stopped her. Even spending the entire first year of her recovery not speaking had not deterred her. She was unwilling to concede anything to her fear and loathing. She refused to allow one experience—no matter how traumatizing—to define the rest of her life.

She was young when she attained her PhD in park management and forestry. She was on a fast track to a leadership position when Jack had met her, and afterward when she'd been offered the job in Seattle as assistant director of parks and recreation for half the city.

She had overcome a series of difficulties with those who sought to stop her from reaching her goals, and a few that might have derailed her entirely had she allowed them to do so. She had dealt with men and women who disliked her—some intensely—just because she was successful and personable. Some viewed her as an obstacle or potential rival that needed to be eliminated or discredited.

Such was the world in which we all live, but she was never one to think of herself as a victim.

Now she was a wife who wondered what her husband was keeping from her, and what danger it was she faced because of it. Whatever the answer, she had gone into protective mode—

a mother hard bent on keeping her children safe. Because she understood that whatever risk Jack was running might well impact her own safety and that of her son and daughter, she quickly fell into a mindset that caused her to be both wary and suspicious of everything about her.

So when she had been sitting in the limousine office for almost five hours and the driver assigned to transport them to Portland had not arrived, she began to suspect that something was wrong.

"Excuse me?" she said to the man behind the dispatcher's desk. "What's happened to our driver?"

He glanced up from his computer and then down again. "Delayed. He'll be here soon."

She stared at him, decidedly uneasy. His abrupt manner, his failure to provide her with any real information about why she was still sitting there with her children when they should already be on the road, and his insistence on staring at the same three sheets of paper for the entire time she had been there, were all evidence enough of his intentions.

"Why was he delayed?" she pressed.

The man looked up again, held her gaze, and shrugged. "Something about a family problem. He shouldn't be long."

I don't believe that, she thought. *He hasn't taken a call for the last hour. This is a large service with several dozen cars. So no one is checking in? No other customers are looking for service?*

None of it felt right. She pulled out her cell phone and called Jack. No answer. *No, wait.* She glanced at the phone. *No service!* In this office, where communications were essential? She was suddenly certain that whatever Jack was protecting his family from was going to appear on this doorstep very soon, and it was not likely to take the shape of the driver they were expecting. It was a debatable, perhaps entirely irrational conclusion, but she was also quite certain that if she stayed around to find out more, she was going to regret it. Whatever else she did, she had to bundle up the children and get out of there, now.

But how could she manage any sort of flight with a small girl and a baby? If she could get her hands on a car . . . No, she hadn't the first idea of how to do that. A taxi? No, she would be stopped from leaving.

Wouldn't I?

"Excuse me," she said to the man behind the desk. "Can I use your phone to make a call?"

The man shook his head. "Business calls only."

"But I want to call my husband."

He pointed. "You have a cell phone in your hand. Use it."

"It doesn't work."

He rose and walked over to her. His expressionless, dead eyes were fixed on her. "Let me have a look."

She gave it to him, and he fiddled with it for a few minutes. "Hmmm." He walked back to his desk, sat down, fiddled some more, and then set it down in front of him. "Seems to be broken. What's your husband's number? I'll make the call for you. We can forget regulations just this once."

She nodded her acquiescence, thinking they should already have his number in their records, but not saying so. He punched in the number on his phone, listened for a few minutes, then spoke a few words she couldn't hear into the receiver and hung up. "It went straight to voicemail."

She hesitated, and then rose. "I think I'll take the children and walk down the block to that Shell station and call from there."

He was out of his chair like a shot, moving quickly to stand in front of her. "I can't let you do that, Mrs. McCall. It's getting dark already. There's a storm coming on. It's not safe out there for you and your children. Best to remain here. Just be patient."

This was enough to convince her. This man—whoever he was—wasn't the regular dispatcher, and there was no limousine coming. Not unless she was reading this all wrong, and she was pretty sure she wasn't.

There she sat, a woman with a ten-year-old daughter and a

year-old son, trapped. Who was this man sitting behind the desk? Who was it that was coming for her? She knew so little. Jack should have told her what this was about. He should have trusted her enough to give her more information. She was suddenly furious with him for putting her in this situation, and at the same time terrified of what was going to happen to all of them.

She took a deep breath and exhaled slowly. If she panicked now, she was lost. She had to remain calm. *What can I do? How can I get out of here?* Beside her, Mila was reading a book. Jack, Jr., was sleeping in his carrier. Occupied, both of them. There was no good way to warn them—no way to prepare them.

Tears leaked from her eyes. She could not hold them back.

She reached into her purse, fumbling for a tissue to stop the flow. Her fingers brushed against a small metal cylinder, and with a shock she remembered. She was carrying a container of pepper spray Jack had given her years ago for protection against a worst-case scenario. She'd never used it—never even looked at it once she'd stuffed it in there. Her fingers closed over its smooth metal length, and she flipped off the trigger guard and fitted her index finger in place.

A sharp wave of relief flooded through her. Maybe she would be able to get her family out of this mess after all.

She took a deep breath and exhaled slowly to calm herself. She would have only one chance. Then the so-called dispatcher would be all over her. Did the spray even work by now? Was there a "use by" date? She didn't know. But this was her only chance, and she would have to take it. She took a quick look at her target. He was back to studying his computer screen. Slowly, she bent down to her daughter.

"Mila," she whispered, and waited for her daughter to look up at her. "Listen carefully. I'm going to hand Jackie to you. I want you to hold tight to him, no matter what. When I walk over to the desk, stand up and move toward the door. Slowly."

Her daughter peered up at her in confusion.

She swallowed hard. "I need you to be very brave, Mila. The man behind the desk is a bad man. We have to leave here right now. We have to run down the block to the gas station and call Daddy. All of us—you, me, and Jackie—we have to run as fast as we can. We can't stop or look back. Okay?"

Her daughter was staring, but her face was composed. Brave little Mila. "Mom, what's wrong . . . ?"

"No questions!" The words were an admonishment that sounded harsher than she had intended. Anne reached down at once and stroked her daughter's cheek. "Honey, I need you to be a big girl. Can you do that for me?"

Mila nodded slowly. The look in her child's eyes broke Anne's heart, but she fought down her dismay and simply lifted Jackie out of his carrier and handed him to her daughter. Then she stood up, holding her purse in front of her with both hands, and walked over to the dispatcher desk.

The man behind it looked up. "Mrs. McCall, you need to sit down and wait for . . ."

"What I need," she interrupted him, leaning forward, one hand inside her purse, gripping her pepper spray, "is for you to sit right where you are while the children and I walk out that door. Am I clear?"

The man stared at her for a second and then started to get to his feet. There was no mistaking the angry look that crossed his features. "I've had enough of you," he hissed.

She yanked the pepper spray out of the purse, pointed the nozzle at his face and pulled the trigger. A burst of white liquid flew out, coating him from forehead to chin. Filling his exposed eyes. Flying into his mouth as it opened in shock. He howled with pain, stumbling away from her, hands coming up too late to protect him. Abruptly, he lost his balance, lurched into his chair, and went over backward.

By then, Anne was moving toward the door, shouting to her daughter. "Run, Mila. Fast as you can!"

She had time for one quick glance behind her. The man she

had sprayed was rolling around on the floor, thrashing wildly, his face all red and swollen—as if a thousand wasps had stung him—his eyes squeezed shut. She hoped she hadn't blinded him, but it was his own fault if she had. She caught her daughter at the door, took Jackie in her arms, and together they went out of the building and into the night.

FARTHER DOWN THE road, the lights of the Shell station blazed against the darkness. A single car was parked next to the building; no one was gassing up at the pumps. There was only one attendant inside the building to help them. He would have to be enough. Anne was running hard, aware of Mila running right next to her, small legs churning. In truth, within seconds it became apparent that her daughter was in much better shape to make this escape than she was. Even carrying Jackie, she would have thought herself better able to flee a madman. But already she was tiring, legs aching, muscles tightening. Perhaps the stress and the urgency had worked to compromise . . .

"Mrs. McCall!" a ragged voice called out to her from behind.

She glanced back. The fake dispatcher had emerged from the building and was lurching after her. His face was a reddish ruin, his body all twisted and alien. But his eyes gleamed a deep red, reflecting in the streetlights like an animal's as they caught the glare.

"I'm coming for you!" he shouted. "Oh, yes, Mrs. McCall. I'm coming for you and your children!"

"Keep running," she said to Mila, who was already scurrying ahead even faster than before.

They reached the gas station and burst through the door. The attendant, a skinny young man of maybe twenty, was sitting behind the counter reading a magazine. He looked up in bewilderment and pointed toward the bathrooms.

"No, no!" Anne shouted. "Lock the door!"

The attendant gave her a goofy look. "What? I can't do that. We're open."

She rushed up to him, Mila clinging to her legs. Jackie was awake now and starting to cry. "There's a madman out there," she gasped in frustration. "Chasing us. He's not someone you want in here. Lock the doors!"

But the attendant shook his head. "Can't do that. Why don't you just use the restroom and go on to wherever it is you're going—"

"Call the police! Let *me* call them!" She realized in horror that she had left her cell phone behind on the fake dispatcher's desk. "Please do *something*, don't just—"

The door burst open, and a nightmare apparition barely recognizable as the fake dispatcher stumbled into the room. The young attendant realized at once that he had made a mistake and compounded it by making another. He reached into a drawer and pulled out a gun, pointing it at the intruder.

"Get out of here!" he screamed in warning. "If you don't, I'll shoot! I mean it!"

Maybe he did, maybe not. Whatever the case, the creature he confronted did not give him a chance to do anything more than stand there—frozen in place by its terrible eyes as they fixed on him. Anne shrank back, clutching her son and pulling Mila behind her. Grinning, the creature lurched to the counter, reached across, snatched the attendant by the neck, and yanked him right over the counter and onto the floor. The gun fell from the attendant's hands and skidded away as his assailant fell on him. He screamed once as he thrashed in an unsuccessful effort to free himself, and there was a terrifying sound of something snapping.

Anne was already moving back to the gas station door, dragging Mila with her. The creature rose and made a futile attempt to stop her. But he was too slow, hampered by the effects of the pepper spray. In a flurry of arms and legs, she was out the door with her children and running once more.

The thing they were fleeing—she no longer thought of it as a man or even as human—came after them. But there was something else coming, too. A series of shadowy forms had appeared—faceless and amorphous—closing in from either side. She screamed as she saw them, and Mila screamed with her.

Behind her, the limo dispatcher howled like a wolf at hunt.

THE MAN IN the black frock coat arrived at the limousine station to pick up Jack McCall's wife and children as planned, but the office was empty. No sign of McCall's family or the dispatcher. The demon sniffed the air for clues; its sense of smell was exceptional. A quick survey revealed the presence of pepper spray. Used on its minion, no doubt, to facilitate an escape. The demon smiled. Mrs. McCall was resourceful. She had discovered the truth, and now a chase was under way. Not that it would change anything. Its demon servant would follow her to the ends of the earth if need be, and it would take a good deal more than a woman and two small children to stop it. In the end, it would run them down and secure them. Human still, if barely, it would do what it had been ordered to do. That was the nature of demonkind. Once gone over, there was no going back. Any return to even a semblance of humanity was not permitted.

The demon glanced down and noticed the cell phone lying on the desktop. It picked it up, turned it on, bypassed the security code, and opened it. Ah, look at that; it belonged to Mrs. McCall. She had left it behind, no doubt in the flurry of activity required for her to escape. She must be regretting losing it about now, the demon thought, amused. She must be on the verge of panicking.

Smiling to itself, it went to the contacts list and called her husband.

Twelve

SHE'S RIGHT HERE *with me.*

The demon's words were a knife through Jack's heart. They

were an affirmation of the worst possible outcome he could have envisioned.

He could not accept it. He could not bear for it to be true.

"You don't have her," he said at once. "You're lying."

"She's safe for the moment, Jack," the demon whispered. "She and your children are quite comfortable. I will make sure nothing happens to any of them if you agree to come to me."

Jack went cold clear through. How could this have happened? Anne, Mila, and Jack, Jr.—in the hands of this monster. Intercepted on their way to safety. He felt a shudder pass through him and knew instinctively that what the demon was saying was true.

"I want them released," he said tightly, his words tinged with barely controlled rage.

"You shall have them back, Knight of the Word. But not until you come to me and lay your staff at my feet and promise never to trouble me again. You will renounce the Word and its acolytes and the Word's power over you. You will renounce your pledge and swear never again to take up your black staff. Then, and only then, shall I grant you your wish. Then, you can walk away with your family."

Jack squeezed his eyes shut against the choice he was being asked to make and turned off the cell, jamming it into his pocket. "The demon has my family," he said to the tatterdemalion, unable to look her in the face. "It has them and . . ."

"Saying doesn't make it so." Ineke looked at him appraisingly. "What did I tell you about demons?"

He paused. "That they lie. That they will say anything to try to break you down." He shook his head slowly. "But I don't think it's lying. Not about this. I have to do something to save . . ."

"You know what *it* wants," the tatterdemalion hissed roughly, interrupting. "But what do *you* want?"

"My family back again, safe."

"What will you do to make that happen?"

"Go to them. Rescue them."

"And if you can't?

"Die trying."

"Very noble. And very admirable. But your dying will help no one but the Void. Stop a moment and think this through. What will happen if you do as the demon asks of you? Do you think he will release your family? Do you think he will let you go—let all of you just walk away and never bother with you again?

Jack hesitated and then shook his head slowly. "Probably not."

"Probably not?" Ineke scrunched up her young face, pale features growing even more translucent. *"Definitely not!* It will make you its creature, subvert you so that you will be obligated to obey its every wish. It will use your family as playthings for its personal amusement. It will use you however it wishes, but in the end it will destroy you. It will humiliate and degrade you until you are reduced to nothing. And then it will kill you, along with your wife and children. I am not positing this, Jack. I am telling you what will happen. Because that's what demons do. A bargain with a demon is a bargain for your soul."

He shook his head. "I want this never to have happened."

She moved close. "Too late for that. You came here to find the demon and destroy it. Either commit to doing so or flee now, while you still can. You will not survive this encounter otherwise—not in any form you would recognize. And I, for one, do not care to risk myself for a failed Knight of the Word."

"But you would otherwise?"

"It was why I was sent to you."

"But what can you do? You are hardly even there. I can see right through you. You seem as if you might disappear entirely at any moment. How can you help me?"

She stiffened at the rebuke. "What do you know of me? What do you know of tatterdemalions at all, for that matter? I can help you in more ways than you can imagine. Not in a battle with a demon, admittedly. But in other ways. What do you intend to do about the demon? Will you submit to it? Or will you see it destroyed?"

He shook his head. "I don't know. What you are saying about the demon is probably true. I know what it is. I know I can't trust it. But what about Anne and the children? What if I have to watch them die in front of me because of my insistence on keeping my word to the Lady? My life would be over, no matter if I destroyed the demon afterward or not."

"What if you destroy the demon and by doing so save them?"

"I can't know it will happen that way! I would be risking their lives as well as my own!"

"What life will you have if you submit to it and are betrayed? What life will you have knowing you lost everything—your dignity included—for no reason at all? What will your family think of you if you do not stand against this creature? They will never see you the same way again, even if you survive the encounter. They will see you as a coward and a failure. The demon will make sure of it."

The little tatterdemalion was right, of course. Everything she was telling him was right. He would be less than half a man if he faltered and submitted to the demon's demands. He would be stripped of everything that mattered to him, and he would have done it to himself.

She paused. "What will those of us who serve the Lady and have committed our lives to the Word think of you? What will be your legacy to us?"

He laughed, bitter and filled with self-loathing. "Better to have died trying than to live in shame for not having tried at all—is that what you're saying, Ineke?"

"If the shoe fits." She moved away from him, deliberately distancing herself. "Now what's it to be? Time is fleeting, Jack McCall."

He knew there really wasn't any choice unless he was prepared to abandon all of his principles and all of his moral strength because his fear for his family demanded it. He didn't think he could do that, no matter the consequences. His fear was one thing; that was a weakness with which he could live. But to give in to it completely—to surrender everything he had always believed to be true about himself and cast off any semblance of moral responsibility—that was another thing altogether.

"All right," he said quietly. "I'll face the demon and do what I must to put an end to it. Maybe I can rescue Anne and the children while I'm at it." He shook his head at the impossibility of it all. "Will you still help me?"

She turned away. "If I can, yes. Of course I will help you. Beginning right now. Our path into the Winston house is known to me. I have looked it over in the form of one of my familiars— a tiny flying creature—so that I would be ready for this. Come, now. Stay close to me."

They moved off the crest of the hill and walked down into the trees at the park's southern boundary where it bordered on the lawns of the houses. Among those was the old Winston house—a timeworn brick-and-board three-story that had once housed a shipping magnate and his family. There were lights in most of the other residences, although not as many as he would have liked. The Winston house, however, was a dark and silent specter in their midst.

He slowed, suddenly wary. Ineke seemed to know what he was thinking. "There will be Void creatures waiting for you. The demon itself would never come alone to kill a Knight of the Word. But its minions will try to stop you from ever reaching it. I will find you a way in, but some of them will be waiting for you. You must be ready."

He thought about what that might entail, but there was no way of being certain. How many would be waiting? What forms would they take? How dangerous would they be? The questions buzzed in his head, angry wasps searching for a way out. He gave them the moments it took to reach the edge of the back lawn of their destination and roughly shoved them aside.

Then he noticed the shadows moving. All across the yard, dark forms were sliding across the lawn—hundreds of them, formless and featureless, although vaguely human-shaped, prowling through the night. Jack froze, staring in shock. "Are those what you were talking about?" he asked Ineke in a hushed voice, pointing. "Those shadows?"

She shook her head. "Those are something else. Feeders. They belong to no one, and serve only themselves. They gather in response to the coming confrontation, drawn by the prospect of the magic that will be wielded. They are devourers of that magic and its leavings. Pay them no heed. They can only harm you if you let them."

Devourers? Jack wasn't pleased to discover that in addition to the demon and its minions there were these things out here, too, but he forced himself to look away. Ahead, a wall of bushes blocked their path. Beyond, he could make out a scattering of ornamental trees, a swing set, a patio, a screen porch, and a back door. "Do we enter there?" he asked Ineke, pointing to the latter.

"Perhaps. For the moment, we need to cross the lawn to where the house sits. Unseen. For that, you will require a dusting of powder. Close your eyes and don't breathe until I am finished."

He did as he was told and could feel her moving all around him in slow circles. Something feathery was brushing against his exposed skin and, by dint of proximity, his clothing. A dusting, a layer. He stood still and waited, and finally she told him to breathe again. When he did, the scent of the air rushing in through his nostrils was tinged with the smells of trees and grasses, of the park's flowers and its earth.

"Now you smell just like everything around you, and your human scent is muted. A necessity, since a demon's sense of smell is its best defense against enemies. Unless they detect your movements, you will essentially be invisible to those who would sniff you out. Now come ahead."

She led him through the bushes and out onto the lawn. He was instantly casting about for anything waiting for him, searching the shadows, peering into dark corners and layers of deep blackness, expecting with every step that something terrible would emerge. The anticipation was excruciating, threatening his sense of balance. But in the end, nothing happened.

By the time they had reached the sheltering back wall of the old house, Jack was sweating freely and breathing hard. For all that his fears and doubts were crowding in, this felt too easy, too simple. Something was wrong, but he had no idea what it was. He cast about the yard and the trees of the park beyond in an effort to uncover whatever it was that was troubling him.

"Where is the welcoming committee?" he whispered to Ineke.

For a moment, she didn't answer. Then she lifted one slender arm and pointed behind him. He turned to look and immediately froze.

What approached did so on four legs, those in back longer and thicker about than those in front. It was wolflike in its head and jaws, and bearlike in the girth of its body and shaggy appearance, but it was also something else Jack could not define. Its eyes had a human look, an intensity, color, and shape that were unpleasantly recognizable as something he had seen in men and women he had known. The creature was prowling as it advanced, taking its time, sniffing the ground one moment and the air the next.

"It cannot see us," Ineke whispered in his ear—but when he turned to find her, she wasn't there. "Don't bother looking. You cannot see me in my present form. I am a bird for now, too small to be easily detected but swift enough to flee should the need arise. I am on your shoulder, close to your neck."

He ducked his head, tracking the sound of her voice, and saw the tiny iridescent bluebird perched on his shoulder. "You're sure?" he whispered back. "It can't tell we're standing right in front of it?"

"Poor eyesight, but good hearing. Stand still. Say nothing more."

He did as she told him to, watching the creature advance until it had reached them. It stopped not six feet away, testing the wind, growling softly. Long, sharp fangs revealed themselves. Suddenly Jack realized that this creature was what had torn Scoot apart. This was the creature he had chased all the way to the park. He closed his eyes and held his breath. The beast sniffed some more and then moved on.

When it had passed around a corner of the house, Jack breathed out again and felt the tension drain away. A quick glance around revealed no other sentries.

"That was an ur'demon called a Mange," Ineke advised. "Very dangerous. It was a good thing it didn't detect us, or you would have had a hard time of it." She flew off his shoulder and reverted to her ghostly little-girl form. "Let's get inside."

She led him away from the Mange and toward the other side of the house, where she found a window she liked and pointed to it. "This one. Use your staff to release the lock. Just think what you want, and it will happen. At least, it will with locks."

Jack touched the window with the tip of his staff, willing it to unlock, and he heard the lock release. In moments they were inside, standing in a library with floor-to-ceiling shelves filled with books. Jack looked around in amazement. It was a private library the likes of which he had never seen. Furniture provided for reading occupied the open space, and a ladder for reaching the higher shelves was attached to rollers that allowed for it to be moved easily about the circumference of the room.

"This way," Ineke ordered, wasting no time on looking around, moving toward the entry door.

"Does no one live here?" Jack asked as they crossed the room.

She shrugged. "The demon and his companions."

"But no Winston family?"

"Apparently not. This house appears not to have been occupied for a long time."

They slipped through the library door into a hallway, where the tatterdemalion paused. She sniffed the air (an unpleasant reminder of what the demons did) before indicating that Jack should wait where he was. Changing form to the tiny bird, she flew off into the shadows.

She wasn't gone thirty seconds when a shadow appeared at the end of the hallway and moved toward Jack. He watched it come, wondering if he was visible yet. Or visible to whatever was coming, in any event. The creature that approached walked upright, so that eliminated the Mange. It had a human definition to its shadowy form, and as it drew closer Jack could see that it was a man. Not the demon, but someone else.

It was his father.

Except that his father was dead. Gone for almost two years now.

"Jack!" his father exclaimed in surprise. "You're not supposed to be here!"

"You, either," Jack replied. "You're dead."

"Really?" His father laughed, that deep chest-booming explosion that was so familiar. "I thought it was just a trick of the light." He wiped his eyes, just like he always used to after laughing hard. "So I really am dead? No wonder I have trouble meeting people."

Jack smiled in spite of himself. Just like his father to say something like that. "Why are you here? This place isn't for you."

His father's face suddenly turned serious. "Are you sure?"

Jack felt something drop away inside, a fear he hadn't realized he harbored until now surfacing. What if his father had become a creature of the Void? Or worse, had been one all along. He had never seen his father that way, never thought of him as anything but a good man. But demons specialized in deceit, didn't they, and how could Jack be certain of anything at this point?

His father gave a weary sigh. "I'm here to warn you. I had to do that much. You have to get away from here. They're waiting for you, down in the arena. Too many of them for you to face alone."

"My wife and children are here. I can't leave them."

"You have to." His father shook his head firmly. "They are lost to you, their fate sealed the moment the demon caught them and brought them here. They were a lure to bring you. And sure enough, here you are, just as planned. It's too late to save them, Jack. Too late for anything but saving yourself."

Jack felt a momentary rush of despair. Anne and the children gone forever? His life would be damaged beyond repair. He closed his eyes in an effort to make it not so, to banish it from his mind.

"Jack, Jack," his father soothed, his voice drawing closer—comforting and soft with compassion. It was the father he remembered so well, the man who was always there for him when needed. The memories resurfaced—times he had thought lost to him, moments he believed forever gone. His thoughts were suddenly jumbled, and he dropped his guard. This was his father, returned to him. "It will be all right, son," his father was saying. "Just know I am here for you. Everything will be all right . . ."

"Jack!" Ineke shrieked in horror.

His eyes snapped open in time to see his father's face disappear and his head split open to reveal a huge pair of jaws full of crocodile teeth, gleaming with hunger and expectation. He flung himself clear of the clawed fingers reaching for him and whipped his black staff about in a savage blow that sent the demon spinning away. A follow-up strike crushed the jaws and the head. Fire burst from one end of the staff as he thought it into being, and the creature collapsed to the floor, where the feeders fell upon him and devoured what remained.

Ineke fluttered down in front of him as he staggered away,

changing from a tiny bird back into her usual form. "You let yourself be hypnotized by it, didn't you? That's what demons do. They make you believe they are someone else—someone you want them to be—and then they take you." She shook her head in admonishment, her long hair shimmering. "Remember. You must remember! Nothing in this house, aside from me, can be trusted. No one you encounter will be a friend. You must concentrate to see the demons as they really are, not as they appear. If you do not, you will not survive this night." She glared furiously, and then just as suddenly her expression softened. "At least now there can be no doubt they know you are here."

"No, they knew I would come."

"Yet they don't know yet what you can do. Let's go show them."

He hesitated. *But what* can *I do? Does it make any difference to these creatures?*

Jack McCall glanced at the pile of ashes to one side, thinking of how he had been tricked into believing it was his father. A part of him was devastated by his own willingness to embrace the impossible. But a larger part was infuriated by the nature and extent of the deceit. What else might they attempt?

He blocked his rage away long enough to see Ineke halfway down the hall, waiting for him to follow. He set off to catch up to her, determined not to be fooled again.

Determined, as well, to put an end to this nightmare.

Thirteen

THEY PASSED DOWN the central corridor of the home, the Knight of the Word and his tatterdemalion, passing rooms in which shadows dominated and anything might be hiding. But nothing threatened, and whatever danger might be lurking remained in the shadows and in Jack's imagination. In short order they were nearing the back of the house, where a wicked orange glow was emanating from behind a partially open doorway. There was a flickering quality to the light that suggested fire, but Jack knew that wasn't possible. Fire in this ancient structure would catch in the blink of an eye and burn the house to the ground. Nevertheless, the possibility felt so real it practically screamed at him to flee.

Ineke reached the opening first and pulled back the door to reveal a set of stairs leading down. The orange light passed right through her frail form, leaving her tinged with Halloween color. Jack moved to the head of the stairs and took a quick look down. The glow was rising from below, but its source remained a mystery. The stairs, steep and narrow, seemed to go on forever—for far too long for them to be ordinary stairs leading to an ordinary basement. It was a descent to another world, another realm, and the harsh and deadly promise of a terrible unknown. That there was something down there was an unavoidable certainty—a snake's hiss in his mind that warned him to flee now and not look back.

They are waiting for you down in the arena, his false father had said. The arena. Images of gladiators and beasts rose to mind, unbidden. Images of blood and gore and death from combat too horrible to contemplate.

"Brave Knight," Ineke said quietly, bringing him back to himself. "Do not doubt yourself. Do not be afraid."

He wondered if Anne and the children were really there, as the demon had taunted. Or was this just another lie? He hoped they were not; he prayed for it. But it felt as if he were trying to capture the wind.

Suddenly he was terrified, certain that he could not prevail against whatever was waiting for him. Doubts crowded to the forefront of his thoughts, overpowering whatever confidence he had managed to cling to. What was he doing here? Why had he ever agreed to be a part of this madness? He knew what was going to happen to him. He knew what the demon would do to him—this creature so powerful that he was nothing but an insect beneath its feet.

"I don't think I can do this," he whispered.

Ineke stared up at him. "You can, Jack McCall. I will be with you. I will be a voice in your ear, cautioning you, guiding you, warning you whenever necessary. Listen for me. It is why I was sent to you. I am to share your fate; I am to be for you what you must be for the Lady—a sacrifice to the commitment the Word has made to hold the magic of the world in balance. Remember what you must do as a Knight of the Word, no matter what waits for you."

"All I want to do is save my family."

She cocked her head. "You are here to destroy a slayer of Knights of the Word."

"I understand that!" Abruptly, he was shouting. "I have to destroy the demon in order to save my family. Doing the one is necessary in order to achieve the other. I get it! I accept it!" He took a deep breath to steady himself, his voice lowering to a furious whisper. "I will do what I have to."

He straightened, resigned to his fate. His fears served no purpose; his doubts provided no help. His words echoed in his head. *I will do what I have to.* He pulled himself together, letting the words repeat themselves, over and over.

"You need not go with me, Ineke. You have done enough just by bringing me this far and helping me to see what is required of me. No more wishing for things to be different. I can manage alone; you can return home."

"Jack McCall." She spoke his name as if in admonishment, but without rancor or disappointment. "You must understand— I am home."

She turned away and started down the stairs, an ephemeral presence that seemed to float toward the source of the orange glow as if a moth drawn to a flame. Jack followed, one hand gripping the black staff that would give him whatever chance he had of surviving this night. His footfalls were almost silent on the wooden steps, the sound muffled in a way that made no sense. He could no longer even hear himself breathing, the air hot and thick in his lungs. A thirst rose within him, overpowering and demanding, but he had no way to sate it. Nor time or space, had there been a way. He was on a pilgrimage, a death march, a crusade, a fool's errand—all somehow bound together, compelling him forward.

He lost count of the steps in his descent, but there were too many for the number to be real. Nothing could be this deep within the earth other than its core, and there was no indication of his journey drawing to an end. Time passed at a snail's crawl—seconds, minutes, hours? He found himself wondering why all this was happening, then almost as quickly as he asked the question, he answered it. The demon was attempting to break him down before it ever needed to face him. But the demon had failed to take his measure. Its plan for him would not work. He would not allow it. He would not be broken; he would not succumb.

And then suddenly Ineke disappeared—there one second standing before him and gone entirely the next, faded away into the orange light. *I am here,* she whispered almost immediately, a voice in his ear. *I am with you.*

He took a deep breath, realizing the stairs had ended, and he was standing in a large room, octagonal in shape and empty of everything. No doors or windows or furniture. Walls, floor, and ceiling: That was all there was. The orange glow seemed to issue from those walls, but still there was nothing to indicate its source.

Yet the light had grown harsher and was now streaked with dark streamers that might have been formed of ash or smoke, but which wafted on the air as if released in a recent conflagration.

Three figures materialized in front of him, slowly taking shape. They stood on their hind legs like humans, but any resemblance ended there. Hunched, crooked-backed, with their bodies warped and their limbs twisted into knots, they were monsters out of a horror story. Their faces were empty and blasted—as if caught in a terrible explosion so they had melted and fused like plastic. There might have been eyes, noses, and mouths amid the ruin of their features, but it was impossible to tell.

Jack's hands fastened on his staff as he prepared to face them, for there was no other reason for these creatures to be here, waiting. No other reason but to put an end to him. Their intent was clear, their purpose undeniable. But he was ready for them.

He watched them divide to become six, and then again to become twelve. It was a trick, he realized—a charade to steal away whatever confidence he might have in himself. *See them as they are*, he heard Ineke whisper in his ear. He stood waiting on them, slowing his breathing, calming the urge to despair and abandon hope. To flee. And one by one, they began to disappear, fading back into the flickering light, until only the original three remained.

They came at him then, all of them at once, in a silent rush—gnarled, misshapen forms with mouths (had they been there all along?) opening hungrily, and clawed fingers reaching. He pointed one end of his staff at them and, with a single incisive thought, blew them back across the room and into its far walls with such force that they simply exploded and were gone.

To be replaced, almost instantly, by the Mange.

He knew at once that this was no mirage, no trick of the mind, but a substantive presence that possessed the power and the ability to kill him. It stood before him, its shaggy head lowered, its greenish eyes glittering, its sturdy legs planted as if to withstand any attempt to move it from where it stood. It stank of sewage and rot, its thick fur crawling with creatures he could not identify—tiny scurrying beasties that burrowed and surfaced by turns. A low growl escaped its throat, its muzzle drawing back to reveal its blackened teeth, the rictus of its features a nightmarish promise of the agony it would inflict.

Steady, Ineke whispered. *Find a weakness.*

Very helpful, Jack remembered thinking in something approaching panic, just before the Mange launched itself at him.

He brought up his staff, trying to ward it off, concentrating on throwing it back, just as he had the creatures before it. But the Mange overpowered his futile attempt, which did little more than deflect its rush just enough that Jack was struck only a glancing blow by the massive body as it catapulted past and slammed into the wall behind him. A glancing blow was enough, however; he was nearly flattened. Shaken and dizzy, he spun around to face his attacker once more, watching it struggle up and turn back to come at him again. Jack knew that another rush would smash his defenses for good, and he would be lost.

He needed to finish it now, or it would finish him. One chance was all he would get. *A weakness,* Ineke was whispering frantically. *Find a weakness.*

Jack lit his staff with a blue fire of confidence and inner willpower that was almost overwhelming. Sheathed in his strength as a Knight of the Word, he stood waiting on it, refusing to yield. The air around him crackled as if alive with a reflection of his determination, fiery electricity issuing from his body in a deadly web.

The Mange attacked at once, charging from across the room, its huge shaggy body descending on him like a great darkness that would swallow him whole. He waited on it—though the wait was only seconds—a solitary presence at the center of the room. As the Mange reached him, jaws opening wide to take him in, he jammed the length of his staff down the monster's throat and sent the magic's fire deep inside. The jaws closed, enveloping him, and he was swallowed whole.

He knew at once that he was a dead man; he felt the power of this beast overwhelming him, its teeth ripping him apart, shredding him like torn paper. He had no protection sufficient to stop it from doing so. He was a fragile bit of flesh and blood held fast in its terrible grip. Yet he did not perish. He held his staff firmly in both hands and kept its power surging into the dark interior of his attacker in a steady stream that never faltered. He refused to give way to the fear that ripped through him; he refused to be devoured. He found a way to hang on, to fortify himself with an unquenchable determination to live. His was the greater strength, he told himself. And the iron of his self-belief blossomed to feed the power of his black staff's magic, which surfaced in a rush to shield him against the creature's efforts to consume him.

Survive! The word ratcheted through him, an echo that would not be stilled. *Endure!*

Then, abruptly, he was back in the room—alone once more, the Mange gone as if it had never been, his body untouched as if never attacked, the battle a dream. He took a deep breath to be sure, exhaled sharply, and looked around. Everything was exactly as it had been.

Brave Knight, Ineke whispered in his ear. *You have prevailed.*

For a moment, he thought she meant that his nightmare was over, that the demon was defeated—that transforming into a Mange in an effort to overpower him had failed and now it was gone.

But then he saw the orange glow brighten and the walls of the room fall away, and he was transported instantly into a massive cavern with walls that rose so high he could not find where they ended. All around him, dark and twisted figures occupied rows of bleachers like spectators in anticipation of a sporting event. Upon his appearance, their screeches and howls filled the air with a cacophony that hammered at his ears like a thousand horns wailing at once. They stamped on their walkways and pounded on their benches and thrust their arms and fists into the air. They were everywhere about him, and he could see at once that he was completely encircled.

So it wasn't over. He was in the arena where he had been told the demon was waiting for him, and he was the main event. He had prevailed over the ghosts and the Mange, but the one that mattered most—the slayer of Knights of the Word—he must still face.

And as if he had summoned it, the demon materialized.

Still dressed in its familiar black ensemble—frock coat, string tie, pegged pants, leather boots, western hat, and now wearing gloves as well—it stood on the far side of the area. Its eyes glittered with expectation and savage promise, its look at once predatory and pitying. "Jack McCall!" it howled, and the creatures gathered for the battle echoed the name in a raw frenzy of barely recognizable sounds.

Jack did not wait on his adversary. He started forward, his black staff already alight with blue fire, wanting to close the space between them, determined to see this business ended. He heard Ineke calling to him, but he was too enflamed by his rage and dark intentions to listen to her. He wanted to get his hands on this monster and throw him down and force him either to return his family or admit it was all a lie. One or the other, but he would have the truth and have it now.

Yet something was wrong. No matter how hard he tried to reach the demon, he seemed to be going nowhere. He could not lessen the distance that separated them, could not close the gap.

The demon's laughter rang out across the cavern, rising above even the shrieks and howls of its minion audience. "What's keeping you, Jack? Am I really so far away you cannot manage to reach me? Are you so weakened that such an effort is beyond you?"

Jack! Ineke hissed frantically. *Look around you!*

He did so and saw feeders everywhere—hundreds of dark forms, writhing and leaping, shadows frantic with need, climbing over one another to reach him, yet not quite yet able to do so. He understood at once. These were the manifestations of his darker emotions, materialized as a result of his fear and fury and bloodlust. They were here at his behest and they would satisfy their cravings at his expense if they were able. They were drawn by the magic that he would expend in his battle with the demon. If he faltered, if he gave in, if he failed to control himself sufficiently, they would devour him.

Jack remembered again the warning that Ineke had given him, about the efforts that would be made to break him down. Those attacks by the ghost creatures and the Mange had never been about killing him—though that might have simplified things for the demon. No, it wasn't killing him that mattered. It was weakening him—stealing away his strength through a series of ordeals.

Leaving him shattered.

He stopped running, slowed, and finally stopped altogether. "You can come the rest of the way to me!" he shouted back. "Or are you afraid?"

The demon moved toward him, easily covering the distance separating them. It approached without effort and without any evidence of tiring or exertion. "Want to see your family, Jack?" it asked.

"You don't have my family," Jack replied quickly. "That's just another lie."

"Really?" The demon was within a dozen yards now and stopped. "Is that what you believe?" The insinuation was evident in its tone of voice. "Or is that just what you *want* to believe?"

He made a sweeping gesture with one arm and a dark object began to lower from the ceiling, slowly taking shape as it descended. A cage, Jack saw, when it was close enough, containing his family. His throat tightened with sudden anguish. Anne was holding Jack, Jr., in her arms, and Mila was pressed up against her mother, arms around her shoulders. All three were crying, and the stricken looks on their faces were heart wrenching.

Jack! Anne called plaintively. *Daddy!* Mila begged. *Help us, please, help us!*

"You have a choice!" the demon shouted, turning in a circle so that his words would reach all those watching. "Either lay down your staff and renounce your service as a Knight of the Word, or watch them die!"

It's a lie! Ineke was screaming to him. *It's all a trick! He hasn't...*

A sudden gesture from the demon struck a sharp blow, hammering into Jack's head, right up against the ear in which the tatterdemalion was speaking. The blow rocked Jack sideways, and for a moment he was left dizzied. And her voice instantly stilled.

As he struggled to regain his balance, he could hear his wife and daughter pleading with him to do as the demon asked, so they could all go home and be a family again. He could hear little Jackie howling in misery, unable to understand what was happening. *A trick,* Ineke had warned. And indeed, he was reminded of how he had been tricked before. But suddenly he knew this was different. He *knew.* The tatterdemalion was wrong this time. What he had seen as he looked into the cage as it lowered into view could not be mistaken. His family had been taken, and his precious Anne and their children were now in the hands of the demon.

He straightened, trying to clear his head. A wave of understanding swept through him. It was asking too much to do anything but what the demon had commanded of him. He was helpless before its power, foolish to risk the lives of his family, stupid beyond words to think that anything mattered more than protecting those you loved.

A deep weariness settled within him. All he had done to make a good life for his family was being threatened. All he cared about was in danger of being destroyed if he persisted in his efforts to do as the Lady had asked. Why destroy one demon when there were so many more out there? What difference did it make? Why should he sacrifice everything just to kill a single creature of the Void?

A sudden wash of hopelessness descended, sapping his already fading resolve. He lowered his staff, his prior sense of commitment slipping away, preparing to accede to the demon's demands, preparing to capitulate.

Yet a nagging sense of wrongness persisted, and a refusal to give way to the doubts assailing him brought him up short. Memories of all that had taken place in the past few days resurfaced in a rush of warning. How many times had the demon attempted to trick him? How many efforts had it made to subvert his thinking, to bring him down with lies and deceits? Over and over, it had attempted to use his fear as a weapon against him, a crowbar to pry him loose from his resolve.

Was not that happening again here? Was any of this as real as the demon would have him believe?

Then a tiny bird appeared from nowhere, rocketing through the gloom toward the cage. A single heartbeat later it was inside the cage with Anne and the children, rushing back and forth with such frightening speed that all of them took on the appearance of flickering images on an ancient, deteriorating piece of film.

Revealing them to be nothing more than a mirage.

The demon howled in fury, wheeling on the cage, hands thrusting toward its interior in a frenzied movement. The bird faltered, collapsed, and went still.

Jack realized at once what he had almost given in to. The curtain of glamour cast by the demon's magic fell from his eyes. Ineke had been right; it *was* all a lie.

He went straight at the demon then, and this time nothing slowed his advance. Without a word, he attacked, no longer crippled by uncertainty, no longer shackled by fear. He struck out with the power of his staff, his thoughts of what he wished for the monster clear and bright as daggers.

The blow he struck was powerful enough to stagger it, but not to take it down. It recovered quickly, hands going to its sides, where it yanked its weapons free from the frock coat, in the manner of the Old West gunslinger it was emulating. A pair of short iron wands appeared, tips glowing with crackling green flames. The demon pointed the wands at Jack, and fire exploded in two jagged lines. Although his staff caught and deflected the flames, he was thrown backward. He regained his feet almost immediately, but fresh strikes from the wands took him down a second time. Burns and lesions blossomed on his skin, visible through the rents in his clothing. Fiery pain rushed through his body, and he felt his strength dissipate.

But he did not give in. He refused. He would die first. Memories of his boyhood struggle with the dragon in Sinnissippi Park resurfaced. He could have died then—perhaps should have—but he had stood firm, refusing to give in to the overpowering fears and doubts the possibility of dying woke within him. But it wasn't only his life that was at stake now. This was not just about him; it was about Anne, too. Anne, whom he loved beyond measure. Anne and his children, for whom he would do anything. He must survive for them. He must justify the faith the Lady had placed in him all those years ago, when she had asked him to serve. What remained of him if he did not? He had been given the black staff and assigned this single obligation, this single moment in time, this one and only battle, because she believed him stronger than the evil he would face. He could not fail her now.

He would not.

He rose and came on once more, barely aware of the damage that had been done to him or the fresh blows from the iron wands that continued to hammer at him. The demon shrieked with more than fury now. A Knight of the Word could tell; a Knight of the Word could know. Fear was in the demon's voice, distinct and unmistakable.

Jack struck at it with the magic of his staff, still advancing, never hesitating. Images of his wife and children, caged and helpless, flickered in his mind, reminding him of what the demon had tried to do. The feeders had gone into a frenzy, advancing with him. Memories of the demon's insidious words haunted him, barbs that ripped and tore at him. He had been such a fool! He had been so weak! What had he almost done because of it? What had he almost given up? He was ashamed and embarrassed. He was diminished by what it made him feel.

But he was newly committed, too. He was iron forged in fire. He was the man Ineke had urged him to be.

Around him, the demon's creatures had gone suddenly quiet, their voices stilled by what they saw happening to their leader, their confidence eroded. Jack fed off their loss of faith, his determination further strengthened. By now, his efforts were those of a berserker. Heedless of the danger to his life and the pain that racked his body, wrapped in the armor of the magic that had been bequeathed to him, he bore down on the demon until he was on top of him and could see as clearly as his own foolishness the bright look of fear in his enemy's eyes.

Down came one end of the staff, bright with fire and sparking with bright shards of magic that mirrored its bearer's rage. The demon faltered. Down came the staff a second time, and the wands dropped from its hands. Once more it descended, the arc of its swing leaving a path of blue fire like a contrail to mark its passing, and Jack McCall—a Knight of the Word at last— brought down his enemy for good.

And the feeders fell upon what remained eagerly.

IN THE AFTERMATH of his victory, the arena and its audience and the cavern and the cage and the remains of the demon and even the feeders all faded away. Jack was left alone in the basement in the old Winston house with only a single lightbulb dangling from the ceiling to give confirmation to what he knew had happened. He stood in the center of what had only moments earlier seemed an arena, looking around with a mix of shock and disbelief.

Then he remembered Ineke.

She lay a few feet away, reverted to her original form, her small figure curled into a ball, but her transparency increased enough that he could see through her to the concrete floor. He knelt beside her and lifted her head. Her eyes, closed until then, opened.

"Brave Knight," she whispered.

"Don't die," he whispered back, his fear for her a palpable presence. "Please don't die."

Her smile was wan and brief. "Do not be afraid for me. My time is over. What I came to do is done. I have to leave you now."

"No! You can stay if you try. I know you can!"

There were tears in his eyes, and she reached up to wipe them away. "I will stay, Jack McCall. I will stay with you always. I will be there in your memory of this night forever."

Then she was gone in a slow fading away that left him holding only air. She had given herself for him, just as she had said she had been sent to do, and he should not have been sad for her. But such fortitude of emotion and stoic acceptance was for someone stronger than he was, and he felt his sadness flood through him.

Long minutes passed as he knelt. But when his grieving had lessened sufficiently, he forced himself to rise and walk from the basement of the old Winston house, his body aching from the blows he had weathered, but his conscience healed. Once outside again, he paused to breathe in the cool night air and look up at open sky.

I am free, he thought. *My service to the Word is over.*

Then he made his way back along the tree-lined edges of Lincoln Park and through the neighborhood residences surrounding it to reach his home and find his family.

Fourteen

WHEN HE REENTERED his house that night, Jack found it dark and empty. For a moment, he despaired. The demon hadn't been lying after all; it had stolen away his family. But almost immediately he knew he was wrong. Whatever had happened to Anne and the children, they had not been prisoners of the demon. It didn't matter that the demon had Anne's cell phone. It didn't matter that they weren't here at home and he didn't know where they had gone.

Wherever they were, they were all right.

He searched the house from top to bottom, just to be sure he hadn't missed something. He tried to make himself call her aunt and uncle in Portland but hesitated when he realized it would only frighten them if they knew his family was missing. But he had to do something, so he pulled out his cell to make the call anyway and saw the familiar blinking light indicating MESSAGES WAITING and punched in the retrieval code.

First message.

"Jack! Where are you?" Anne, sounding frantic. "Something's happened. I need you to call me! The children and I are staying downtown at the Sheraton. We took a room for the night. Call as soon as you get this message!"

The call ended. He went to the next. The second call was pretty much a repeat of the first. Then he listened to a third, this one made less than half an hour ago.

"Damn it, Jack! Call me right now! Use the hotel number. I lost my cell."

Well, that explains the demon having it. He called the Sheraton and asked to be connected to her room. She answered at once. "Jack?"

"I'm here. Are you all right?"

"I am now, but . . ."

"Stay right where you are. I'll explain everything when I get there. I'm on my way."

After a quick shower and a change of clothes—he couldn't let her see him this battered and bloody—he was out the door and into his SUV. On the drive downtown, he realized he could not, in fact, tell her what had happened. She would never bring herself to accept the truth, and he knew it would eat at her for the rest of their lives. The knowledge of what he had been given to do by the Lady, and what she had been forced to endure as a result, required a more believable explanation.

Which meant he must again break the rule they had made to always tell each other everything and have no secrets.

He knocked, and she was in his arms the moment she flung open the door, and they held each other wordlessly for a long time afterward. The children were in bed asleep, she whispered. Then she pulled him inside to sit with her on the couch, and she related in detail what she had gone through that night.

"If I hadn't been able to stop a taxi on its way back from the airport, I don't know what might have happened to us," she finished. "The fake limo guy wasn't chasing us anymore by then, but that didn't mean he had given up. I couldn't bring the children home; I didn't know if we would be safe there. So I came here instead and started calling you."

She looked into his eyes and gave a weary, exasperated sigh. "Now you tell me what is going on. All of it. Every last bit."

But he did not. He told her instead that he had run afoul of some very bad people and seen something by accident that he shouldn't have. It had happened by chance while he was on a job, and there was nothing he could do about it. When he realized they would come after him, he had sent her and the children to her aunt and uncle, so she would be safe. He had no idea how determined they were to get at him, but the matter was finished now. He had done the right thing and brought in the police and they were all in custody.

She listened without saying anything, but he could see the disappointment reflected in her eyes. She knew he was holding something back. But she reached up to stroke his face. "I love you, and I trust you. If that's the story you want to tell me, fine. I don't think that's all of it. What I want to know—all I want to be sure about—is that this is the end of it. I want your word that we are all safe. I don't want to spend my life looking over my shoulder because you held something back you shouldn't have."

He nodded. "This is the end of it."

But even as he spoke the words, he wondered. Would other demons come looking for him because of what had happened here tonight? Would the Lady ask something more of him later? He wasn't sure. He wondered if he could ever be sure, or if the burden he carried of agreeing to serve her would follow him for the rest of his life.

"You don't look so good," she said, her hand still stroking his cheek. "You look like you've been in a fight."

He shrugged. "You should see the other guy."

She smiled. "I'd rather just see this guy. My husband, in bed with me. It's late. Let's get some sleep, tough guy. Then let's go home and put all this—whatever all this really is—behind us."

He smiled back, knowing it was the best he could hope for.

THEY DID NOT speak of it again—not in a direct way—but Anne let him know every now and then that she knew he wasn't telling her everything and she was not about to forget it. He did his best to live with that, trying to lead a normal life—one that did not involve demons of the Void and Knights of the Word and the possibility of unwelcome visits from things born of dark magic.

Even so, he continued to carry the black staff, his reassurance that he could still defend himself and his family if the need should arise.

Months went by, and life resumed a normality that suggested the past actually *was* behind them. Both Jack and Anne resumed their careers and care of the children, and they seldom spoke to each other—and never in the presence of Mila—about that night. Mila talked about what she remembered for a while, commenting mostly on some of the more terrifying and gruesome aspects of her experience, but both parents discouraged further talk, and her friends mostly responded by rolling their eyes. Soon enough she lost interest as other, more immediately pressing matters captured her attention.

Five months later, on a crisp fall day in late November, the approach of Thanksgiving imminent and thoughts of family celebrations ripe in everyone's minds, Jack was reviewing plans for an expansion and rehabilitation site in Lincoln Park when Two Bears appeared. He came out of a cluster of giant hemlocks where Jack was certain there had been no one a moment ago. Tall, broad-chested, and stone-faced, wearing the combat fatigues of his Vietnam service, he had the look of a man on a mission, and Jack was immediately on guard.

"Jack McCall," he greeted. "It is good to see you again, *kem'sho.*"

We'll see about that, Jack thought. But instead of saying so, he said, "And you, O'olish Amaneh."

The big man nodded. "You remember my given name. I am honored."

"Are you here to check up on me? Or is it something else that brings you back?"

"Why don't we sit for a moment?" the other suggested, gesturing toward a nearby bench.

It was cold that day, the wind gusting now and then, the sky gray and heavily overcast. The promise of winter's coming was unmistakable. Jack did not much care to sit around talking. What he wanted was for this meeting to be over.

They seated themselves and studied each other a moment. "You did well against the demon and his creatures," Two Bears said. "You did what many others failed to do. What many gave their lives for in their failed efforts. I think that says much about your character."

Jack shook his head, brushing aside the compliment. "Does this mean you're here to ask me to undertake something more for the Lady?"

"If I was, how would you respond?"

Jack almost said he would tell him to go jump in a lake, but then he hesitated. Would he really refuse the Lady's request outright? His memories of his meeting with her in the Fairy

Glen resurfaced, bright and shining images from the past. He would never forget how wonderful it had been just to be in her presence. He would never be able to ignore how she had made him feel. As if he were special. As if he were born to be more than he had ever thought he could be.

"It would depend," he said finally.

Two Bears smiled. "Diplomacy. It suits you well. But I am not here to enlist your services a second time. You were told you would be called on once and once only. A promise is a vow when given by the Lady. She sends me to tell you so. To reassure you that she will keep that promise."

He paused, his dark face gone serious once more. "And to do one thing more. Something that will offer proof your service to her is truly finished. I am to take back your staff."

Jack felt a sudden rush of uncertainty. Take away his staff? Take from him the talisman he had carried for so many years, his sole defense against the demons? It felt as if Two Bears was asking for his right arm and he would be left diminished in a way he could never compensate for.

Two Bears nodded, as if understanding what he was feeling. "You will not have further need of it, Jack McCall, but another will. Another who has just agreed to serve the Lady as a Knight of the Word."

Jack said nothing, only shook his head doubtfully.

"If you choose to keep it, you will remain in her service, a Knight of the Word. The staff will continue to serve you well. But it will attract those who would take it from you. And they will try, no matter what they have to do, to make it theirs."

Jack took a deep breath to steady a sudden shaking inside. "You mean no matter what they have to do to me or my family."

Two Bears shrugged. "You have lived with the staff long enough. Better it should go to another who has earned the right to bear it. Whoever receives it will have much to live up to. Your service to the Lady has set a very high standard."

Jack nodded. Two Bears was right. His time of service was

over; his time to possess the black staff was done. No matter his attachment and his sense of loss, he should let it go. He should not forget what it felt like to believe that by agreeing to bear it he had lost his wife and children. He should not forget what it had almost cost him. He should not forget his promise to Anne.

And he should not forget his brave little tatterdemalion, Ineke.

"Do the right thing, *kem'sho*," the big man said quietly.

Jack McCall looked at the staff one last time. Then he handed it over. He felt a sense of loss immediately, but undeniable relief as well. The events of that terrible night when the demon had come for him were finally consigned to the past. Anne had asked him then to promise her that the danger to their family was ended for good.

Now he had the chance to assure her that it was. And the chance to rethink his refusal to tell her the truth and to remove the stain of having kept that truth a secret from her. They had never had secrets before; they should not have one now. If you loved someone as much as he loved her, you trusted them to accept any truth.

He must do so here. He must repair the breach he had opened between them, no matter his hesitancy and misgiving.

Leaving Two Bears standing with the black staff firmly gripped in his huge hands, Jack McCall went home to make things right.

ABOUT THE AUTHOR

TERRY BROOKS is the *New York Times* bestselling author of more than thirty books, including the Dark Legacy of Shannara adventures *Wards of Faerie, Bloodfire Quest,* and *Witch Wraith;* the Legends of Shannara novels *Bearers of the Black Staff* and *The Measure of the Magic;* the Genesis of Shannara trilogy: *Armageddon's Children, The Elves of Cintra,* and *The Gypsy Morph; The Sword of Shannara;* the Voyage of the Jerle Shannara trilogy: *Ilse Witch, Antrax,* and *Morgawr;* the High Druid of Shannara trilogy: *Jarka Ruus, Tanequil,* and *Straken;* the nonfiction book *Sometimes the Magic Works: Lessons from a Writing Life;* and the novel based upon the screenplay and story by George Lucas, *Star Wars:* Episode I *The Phantom Menace.* His novels *Running with the Demon* and *A Knight of the Word* were selected by the *Rocky Mountain News* as two of the best science-fiction/fantasy novels of the twentieth century. The author lives with his wife, Judine, in the Pacific Northwest.

shannara.com
terrybrooks.net
Facebook.com/authorterrybrooks
Twitter: @TerryBrooks
Instagram: @officialterrybrooks

ABOUT THE TYPE

This book was set in Walbaum, a typeface designed in 1810 by German punch cutter J. E. (Justus Erich) Walbaum (1768–1839). Walbaum's type is more French than German in appearance. Like Bodoni, it is a classical typeface, yet its openness and slight irregularities give it a human, romantic quality.